SILVER RAIN

A NOVEL BY PATRICK HARRIS

ISBN: 978-0-578-50990-7

Second Edition: 2019

www.authorpatrickharris.com

The clouds gather on the horizon. The air fills with moisture. Be warned:

THE STORM IS COMING.

Deep underground, a madman plots. His science is diabolical, his terms are genocide. With the touch of a button, he launches toxins into a storm cloud, toxins that will turn the rain silver. There is no escaping it. There is no hiding from it. Worst of all?

IT'S COMING FOR US.

Elsewhere, two friends prepare to leave for a destination wedding. A family awaits the return of their father. A mother works hard for her children. It's another day in America. But when the storm looms and the clouds threaten to break, every eye will turn to the sky. Everyone will feel fear.

From the Sierra Nevada Mountains to the Appalachians, from the skyscrapers of New York to the hills of L.A., the world will shake in terror. This is…

SILVER RAIN

ADVANCE REVIEWS

"*Silver Rain* ... is a science fiction tale of the storm to end all storms. [It] is one of the most original plots I have read for some time. Sadly, and very frighteningly, he has drawn attention to something that could very well happen in the world at some point in the future... This is a mystery story, a tale of technology and science, with an outcome that actually fits more with *The Dawn of the Dead* - a zombie-like result. I thought this was incredibly well written, a great storyline with lots of depth to it. There is plenty of action and the characters are very well developed, fitting the story aptly. An excellent book, one that will be enjoyed by fans of mysteries and science fiction alike. I look forward to more from Patrick Harris in the future."

— *Readers' Favorite (5-Star Review)*

"Harris proves himself as a talented author once again with his latest novel. *Silver Rain* approaches the apocalyptic narrative in a unique and refreshing way. The plot is full of action and adventure, making you flip page after page, wanting more. The real gems are the characters, who prove that no matter what cards we are dealt in life, we can overcome anything by facing our struggles head on. We all have strength in us that can be found through hard work, perseverance, and love."

— Genevieve

"A master of his craft, Harris puts a whole new twist on the phrase every cloud has a silver lining. Filled with action, mystery, and intrigue, *Silver Rain* is a dramatic thriller that keeps your adrenaline pumping and your heart racing. Above all else, Harris portrays the importance of loving one's family and friends no matter how far apart they may be. Despite the dark and twisted obstacles the characters had to face, I personally loved that it was always possible for his characters to choose hope instead of despair. *Silver Rain* is definitely a novel worthy of being at the top of my bookshelf."

— Stacey

*To Jon,
who created a revelatory resolution*

*To Melissa,
who heard the story first
deep in the corn maze*

SILVER RAIN

A NOVEL BY PATRICK HARRIS

PRELUDE

Maximum Security Prison Facility
Death Valley, California

In a dank, cool room, the Griffin stared fixatedly at the grated bars. It made for a disjointed view of the quiet prison walkway and reminded the Griffin of long ago, back when he was a free man waiting for her under the grated stairs.

He licked his lips, reveling in the memory.

He remembered how he had turned the blade of the knife in his hand while he had been waiting. The sweet anticipation had been intoxicating. He had soaked in every moment, from the croak of the frogs to the dry wind in the air.

There had been a clip-clop of footsteps and she had bounced down the stairs from the upper parking lot. The Griffin had watched her go, gripping the knife.

When she had reached the bottom of the stairs, she had stalled. Perhaps sensing someone looking at her, she had turned. Her eyes had searched for a moment before settling on him. In an instant, her eyes had grown wide. Goosebumps had flushed her skin.

Even now, he could only imagine what she had seen under the stairs: a dark silhouette, the glow of a predator's eyes, the look of bloodlust upon a lover's face.

He had moved quickly, efficiently, brandishing the knife. She had tried to run, but she had been no match for his speed and agility. He had thrown the knife, which had caught her in back and knocked her to the ground before she had made it halfway across the lawn. When she had tried to scream, he had silenced her with his fist.

"You knew this was coming," he had told her as he had pulled the knife from her back and drew it tauntingly across her calves.

She had tried to scream more, but he had punched her hard again, shattering her teeth and stunning her into silence. The Griffin had then dragged her into their condominium, where he had finally ended her.

Not with the knife. With his hands.

As it turned out, someone had heard the screams or seen the attack. An hour after he had taken her life, the police had broken down the door and surged into the condo. But that had not mattered to the Griffin. He had accomplished his goal.

Even now, the memory of her death filled him and excited him. He sat on the edge of his bed, staring at the grated bars, lost in reverie. He could still feel her writhe as she struggled to live, her blood-slicked flesh slippery under his grip. Her pleading eyes burrowed into his own, invigorating him. He smiled to himself, squeezing his fingers together as though her flushed flesh was still in his grips.

Truth be told, the Griffin loved being in prison for this reason. He was allowed to mill around all day, relishing in the moment and fondling the memory.

Dr. Griffith "The Griffin" Avazino had once heard that prison did not rehabilitate inmates, but regressed them. He disagreed. Prison led to progression. His bloodlust and licentiousness had only grown behind these bars. He was fed, watered, treated well, and allowed to relive his glory time and again.

The cell door opened and a guard stepped in. As was expected of inmates, the Griffin stood from his bed and faced the opposite wall with his hands high. It was early for night checks.

Another man stepped into the cell, his face shadowed. He held himself like a politician and wore a three-piece suit.

"Dr. Avazino. Your country is not impressed," said the man. His voice was rough, like a tire turning on gravel.

The Griffin did not give the newcomer much more than a sideways glance, wondering how far the man would step into the cell before worrying about dirtying his shiny shoes.

The man continued: "Your government on the other hand is fascinated. We require your services."

"Sizable requests," the Griffin grunted. He turned to face the newcomer.

The guard shifted uneasily, fully aware of what the Griffin could do if he was within arm's reach.

"You start tomorrow," said the man. "Your assistant is expecting you."

"He'll be choking on his blood by morning. I work alone," the Griffin said.

"Your ego will be put aside," the man replied curtly, voice deep and grim. "His work is pivotal to our success, as is your collaboration. The removal of your death sentence and your immediate release are contingent upon your willingness to exercise that indispensable skill of teamwork you have sorely lacked thus far."

"Lots of big words from a fancy tie," the Griffin replied. He advanced another step, finally seeing the man's face and recognizing him as a well-respected senator, and sneered. "You bleat like a mule. Not that many politicians can do much better."

The senator held his ground, letting the Griffin finish before speaking: "You will do to listen well or history will be rewritten without you."

"You do realize what my work will lead to?" asked the Griffin.

The cell was filled with an unnatural silence.

"We will kill them all," the senator finally said.

"I never said I would join," the Griffin replied. "Litigation will stall my death sentence. I will live a long, healthy life behind these comfortable bars."

"This is your last chance," replied the senator curtly. "Say no, and you will never be let out. But if you come with me now, you will have the opportunity to destroy those who stopped your prior efforts."

The bait had been set. The Griffin, intimidating and controlling as he was, could not resist.

For the first time since he had been imprisoned, the Griffin thought of something other than her death. The senator's requests made the Griffin think of his previous work and what he had once hoped to accomplish. He remembered his laboratory and felt a surge of focus and drive. Anticipation filled him as he thought of all the worthless lives he would once again have the chance to destroy.

He had been right: prison was all about progression. Being here fueled the burning passions of the inmates. Killers wanted to kill and racists wanted to hate, perhaps more so than when they had first been locked up. In the same way, prison had fed the Griffin's bloodlust. He was ready to finish his work.

With a nod, the Griffin was let out of the cage.

PHASE 1
STORM CLOUDS

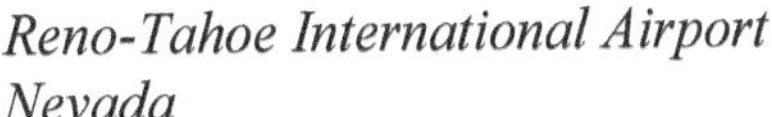

Reno-Tahoe International Airport
Nevada

"Thousands of years of human evolution and we still haven't managed to make a public restroom that doesn't smell like—"

"Roses left in a hot car all day?" Natalie Harper interjected, cutting off her fiancé.

Mark Hofland grunted, muttering under his breath as he crossed the airport concourse. His short, squat form dodged through the passersby as his oversized hands fiddled with his tie. He looked like a little kid playing dress-up in Dad's business suit. It was one of his endearing qualities that Natalie pretended to love.

Once beside her, Mark sighed heavily.

"Have you ever been in a restroom where you're cleaner going in than coming out?" he asked, motioning the restrooms from which he had come.

"Sounds like Mexico," Natalie replied. "You flushed the toilet with your shoe, didn't wash your hands, and opened the door with your tie."

He gave her a defeated look, suggesting he had just repeated this practice. "Close. But why would I open the door with my tie when my shoe was already sullied?"

"You opened the door with your shoe?" she asked, not amused. Mark lifted his foot, attempting to recreate the scene.

Natalie glanced over his shoulder as she said, "Don't look now, Mr. Sanitation, but you just attracted the attention of three TSA agents, and I doubt they'll care how you opened the bathroom door."

"I hope they stop me. I'll recommend Febreeze. Or heat-cooked roses."

He readjusted his tie again and pulled Natalie into his arms. She held him tightly in return, pretending she would miss him in the few days before their wedding.

As they held one another, a man walking through the airport paused, eyes catching on Natalie. The man left his luggage bag and approached her, withdrawing a notepad from his breast pocket.

"Ms. Harper, it's been a year!" he shouted, grabbing a pencil and putting it to the paper. "How are you coping?"

Mark sighed, letting go of Natalie. But before either Natalie or Mark could tell the journalist to scram, someone else had done just that. One of Mark and Natalie's close friends, Evan Silverman, appeared behind the journalist. Evan grabbed the journalist's collar and sent him stumbling back to his bag.

The journalist scowled at Natalie as he collected his bags and disappeared into the crowds.

"Thanks," Mark said to Evan as he gave Natalie another squeeze.

"Don't mention it. Are you two still saying goodbye?" said Evan, surveying his friends. He was tall and spindly with short, gelled hair brought to a point above his forehead. Natalie was confident Evan was more concerned with his appearance, down to the business suit he had probably been born in, than his morals or decency. She certainly knew his career mattered more than his conscience.

On the opposite side of the spectrum, however, was Evan's wife and one of Natalie's closest friends, Cori. She appeared beside Evan, a slightly plump lady no taller than five foot. Just as Evan wore business suits and a clean shave, Cori's face was perpetually stuck in a nervous smile. Even now, she was giggling at her husband.

"You're seeing each other again tomorrow," Evan continued to tell Natalie and Mark. "It's not like Mark is flying away forever. Say goodbye already."

"Not yet!" Mark shouted. "We're having toilet talk!"

"That sounds a bit dirtier than pillow talk," Cori commented. Natalie rolled her eyes at her best friend, feigning annoyance.

"Wrap it up, you two," Evan insisted. "Mark and I have to get out of here *before* the blizzard hits."

Mark gave Natalie another squeeze. She reciprocated to make him feel loved.

"Someday they'll stop caring," Mark muttered.

"You said that a few years ago," Natalie replied, knowing she would run into at least three more journalists before the day was done.

"Well…," Mark said. He paused and said happily, "Oh, oh, remember, don't go in my apartment while I'm gone. I have a surprise for you. And say hello to Toby for me."

"He won't even notice we're gone," Natalie said. "Just a few days and we'll be back."

"You make marriage sound like a chore," he chuckled.

"Only if I have to rowboat to you," she replied. She forced a smile. "I'll see you in a few days."

At long last they parted. Cori insisted on a prayer of safe travel over Mark and Evan before the two set off into airport security.

As Natalie watched Mark disappear into the crowds, she worked her face into a visage of wistfulness. Inside, however, she was ambivalent. What Evan had said was true: she would be seeing Mark the next evening, unless the impending blizzard delayed her flight. There was no need to be sad, anxious, excited, or feeling any other type of emotion. Everyone else seemed to be plenty excited anyhow. For now, Mark and Evan were joining their law firm, Harlem & Associates, for a company retreat in Hawaii. After the meetings were over, Natalie and Mark would meet on the shores and share their vows. Evan and Cori would be their witnesses, as neither Natalie nor Mark had any family left. The excitement among Evan, Cori, and Mark for the wedding was palpable, leaving Natalie calm and measured.

Natalie was still not completely sure how they had gotten to this stage, this thing called marriage, but she did not try to fight it. She needed this.

"It's strange, isn't it?" Cori said quietly. "We'll be seeing them tomorrow night, but I'm left with the feeling that this is the last time I'll see them."

"Aren't you supposed to be the eternal optimist?" When Cori frowned at her, Natalie forced a comforting smile and said, "We'll see them again."

No reply issued from Cori; Natalie assumed she was muttering a silent prayer.

Natalie did not pray. Talking to God seemed a sure way to crack her emotionally secure foundation that she was trying so diligently to keep standing. She was strong—an unbreakable fortress—and she did not need anyone glimpsing her innermost heart of hearts.

Yet Mark was an exception. He saw right through her fearlessness and pretending, and loved her for who she was. As he often told her, she needed him.

But now, when she needed him by her side, he was flying away.

Suddenly, that sadness she had pretended to have as Mark left began to trickle into her.

Natalie shook her head.

No, she thought. *Not now.*

"Amen," Cori murmured, and the two friends walked out of the Reno airport.

2

Natalie guided her vehicle fearlessly through the narrowest gaps of traffic. Cori gripped the passenger seat so tight that Natalie was sure fingerprints would be kneaded into the leather.

After parking, they headed into the hospital. In the foyer of the ground level, the receptionist named Yolanda greeted them with an enthusiastic, *"Hola!"*

Natalie mumbled in reply as they boarded the elevator.

Once on the long-term recovery unit, Natalie and Cori changed into smocks and went their separate ways to check on their patients.

Natalie first visited with Roger, who was bedridden from a sledding accident. He blinked infrequently and salivated often, still insisting he was suffering from mental psychosis. She took care to note how normal he said he felt when he was being medicated, though Natalie knew that Roger was being given sugar pills.

Next, Natalie visited Arlene, who was still recovering from surgery to mend her fibromyalgia. Natalie doubted Arlene would ever make it out of the hospital.

Last, Natalie met with Toby.

The young boy greeted her with a hearty smile. His bright green eyes were wide and excited. He looked far too spunky to be attached to a heart monitor and lying in a hospital bed. But underneath his smile and hospital gown were stitches concealing deep wounds. Toby was here for a reason—his father had seen to that.

"Less than two weeks," Natalie said to Toby as she entered the room. His face cracked into a telltale smile.

"Ten days actually," Toby corrected.

He sounded spry today, and Natalie was pleased to see steady vitals on the heart monitor.

"I bet you're happier than a flying penguin," he said. "I know penguins can't fly, but if they could, you'd be happier than them."

"I'll only fly as well as the plane carries me," Natalie replied. "How are we doing, Toby? Keeping your emotions under control?"

Toby nodded vigilantly, but his eyes betrayed him. She paused, waiting.

"I saw her again last night," he said after a beat of silence. "She told me it was okay to be afraid."

Natalie sat by Toby, taking his hand in hers.

"I know you miss her, Toby," she said, "but don't let your dreams get the best of you. You can't let your emotions get out of control. You are fearless and that is what makes you strong."

"Strong like you," he replied. "My new mom."

"Not yet," she said.

Toby's eyes sparkled with anticipation. In ten short days, Mark and Natalie would return from their honeymoon and, if luck was in their favor, adopt Toby.

Much like her impending nuptials, Natalie did not quite understand how she had come to this crossroads, ten days away from adopting Toby. Perhaps it had all started that night a little more than a year ago when Toby had been rushed into the emergency room. Natalie had been one of the nurses on the floor, just out of nursing school. Maybe a bond had been made with the scalpel—she had saved his life, sealing her fate as his future guardian.

Or perhaps it was a bond they had formed following his surgery. He had been in a medically-induced coma for several weeks. In the months since, Toby had been in and out of the emergency room and long-term recovery unit. All the while, Natalie had kept watch over him. Each day, they had talked a bit more, sharing stories and secrets. Natalie had come to discover the two of them shared many similarities in upbringing—absent and abusive parents, among other things.

Even Mark had seen the similarities when he had met Toby, saying that Natalie and Toby were kindred souls. A few months ago, Mark had mentioned adopting Toby, rather than letting the boy fall into the foster care system.

Perhaps that was how Natalie had fallen into the idea of adopting Toby. Maybe the idea of caring for him with Mark had convinced her to say yes.

But there was more, she knew it. There was another reason, a deep-seeded one that Natalie kept from Mark. While she felt little passion for anything else in the world, this secret was what truly motivated her to adopt Toby and be the best choice for the adoption agency.

To be "the best" required reams of paperwork for Natalie and Mark. Even now, after several weeks of working with the local adoption agency, there was still more papers to be signed. Natalie had yet to receive a sign-off on her psychological examination, a faux pas she had yet to share with anyone.

Combining this complication with the anxiety of impending matrimony, Natalie wished she could sail to a faraway island with Mark and Toby. There, they could simply declare themselves a family without anymore litigation or red tape.

It'll get fixed today, Natalie assured herself. One last visit to Dr. Cruze and the adoption troubles would be behind her.

"How many days until your Hawaii wedding?" Toby asked, bringing Natalie back to the present.

"Four days," Natalie replied. "On the beach, right as the tide is coming in. Forecast is calling for rain."

Toby's eyes lit with excitement. "Will the sun be out?"

Natalie shrugged noncommittally.

"It has to," Toby insisted. "So the rain will shine silver."

"Because of the sun?" Natalie asked.

Toby nodded vigorously. "I love the silver rain. Mom used to tell me it rained silver when God was calling someone home. She said she got it from a fortune cookie, but I've seen silver rain! It's beautiful. Have you seen it?"

"I can't say I have," Natalie replied. "But if it does rain silver at the wedding, I promise no one will be dying and we'll take pictures just for you. And then, after the honeymoon, we bring you home, assuming you don't pop another stitch."

"I'll be stitch-free," Toby said. "Are you nervous?"

Natalie slid closer and whispered, "To be honest, I'm more nervous that I'm not. We're one in the same, Toby. Not much can shake us."

"Fearless," said Toby, "and happier than flying penguins."

"Exactly," Natalie agreed, kissing him on his forehead.

"Sleep well, stay in bed, and we'll see you soon."

As she walked out, Natalie glanced back to see Toby waving. She knew that, although he could not feel it, his stomach must be full of butterflies and his nerves loaded with nervous energy in anticipation. She wished she felt the same.

3

Mark Hofland fumbled to retrieve his phone as he exited the plane. After listening to the prerecorded message of Natalie's voicemail, he said that he had landed safely in Los Angeles and would be taking off in a few hours for Hawaii.

"Love you lots," he said and hung up. He turned his attention to the airport's departure monitor above him, scanning the rows for their next flight and gate.

Evan Silverman walked up behind him, clapping him on the back.

"You leave enough voicemails to be a stalker," Evan said.

"A good-looking one, right?" Mark asked.

"Not if she's squeezing mucus out of you every night," was the sullen reply, but it was not Evan who said it. The voice had come from behind them.

Mark closed his eyes for a moment, already hating what was coming. He'd dealt with insults since he was six, but Danny Harlem's always cut him to the core.

Breathing slowly, Mark tried to think of what Natalie would do in this situation and smirked. Natalie would verbally emasculate the arrogant jerk in front of coworkers and strangers alike. Though it sounded fun, Mark couldn't bring himself to be that brash.

Danny clasped Mark on the shoulder like they were buddies.

"They offer treatment for that," Danny said, indicating to Mark's thick fingers.

"But not for your face," Mark responded curtly.

"My face, like the rest of me, is perfect as is," Danny replied. "Unlike you and your junkie girlfriend."

Mark clenched his fists.

"Mark," Evan said in a hushed, warring tone.

"No harm, no foul," Danny said. "Li'l ol' Thick Fingers knows she's the best he can get."

"Why, you—" Mark began, but cut his voice short as yet another hand clapped his back.

Seth Harlem, the big boss, founder of the law firm, and father of Danny, let out a cherry laugh as he joined their group. Unaware of the ongoing tension, Harlem looked up at the monitors. The far right screen showed a weather map of the nation.

"Lucky we got out of Reno when we did, boys," Harlem barked. "That blizzard missed us by an inch."

"It's just beginning now, sir," Mark said lightly. "I think we missed it by several hours."

Harlem said, "I sure hope your lovely fiancé makes it out safe."

"I have no doubt she will," Mark assured his boss. "Evan's wife, Cori, is travelling with her, and she can pray her way through any storm."

Evan nodded heartily. Danny rolled his eyes. Harlem let out another hearty chuckle.

"Good thing," he said. "We wouldn't want her to not hear the big news!"

Mark looked up at Harlem so fast, he thought he felt a bone in his neck crack. There was a stunned silence.

Even the coworkers behind Evan, Mark, and Danny paused.

Mark stared at Harlem, not believing his ears.

It was a poorly-kept secret that Harlem was planning on announcing the new associate lawyer during the Hawaii retreat. Evan was the current associate, but he would be stepping down to let someone else take the reins. Mark had applied for the position, as had Danny and many others. He had spent many a night hoping and praying for the job. But this statement from Harlem seemed to Mark as point-blank as a job offer for the role of associate.

Mark glanced over at Evan to see his friend smiling. That meant Evan knew too. Mark had been picked as the new associate.

The silence came to an abrupt end as the employees around Mark let out a cheer. Harlem looked confused for a moment, as though he did not think his words could have been as easily deciphered, and then joined in the cheers with another chuckle.

Hands slapped Mark's back. He shook Harlem's hand and gave Evan an enthusiastic hug.

"Dad," Danny whined, "I thought we talked about this."

Harlem looked over his thick glasses at Danny and swept him away from the group with a set jaw. Mark's fellow coworkers fell silent, eavesdropping. He wished they wouldn't. He had no need to hear what Danny had to say, but he heard it anyway.

"You said I had what it takes to be promoted over someone like him," Danny bemoaned.

A scowl broke Mark's face as he tried to block Danny's voice out.

"Son," Harlem said.

"That looks like a lovely father-son chat we should avoid," Evan commented, finally giving Mark something to focus on.

"I just can't believe it," Mark said. "He picked me?"

"He could hardly wait to tell you," Evan admitted. "I've been dying to tell you too! But Harlem said to wait until the trip."

"I can't believe it," Mark replied. He studied Evan's eyes. "You're sure you're ready to step down?"

Evan nodded confidently. "It's time."

Mark was still aghast.

"I'm just surprised you aren't being promoted to partner. All that work as associate and now back to paralegal?"

A weary look came across Evan's eyes. "It's where I belong," he said.

Before Mark could probe further, their coworkers stopped eavesdropping on Danny and Harlem and returned their attention to Mark. Hands were shaken and hugs were given. Congratulations came in from right and left, people celebrating in his success and reminding him of his upcoming wedding and fatherhood. The excitement started getting to him, and he started choking on mucus, so he took a few moments away from the group to take a lungful from his medicated inhaler.

Slowly but surely, the law firm walked toward their gate for their Hawaii-bound plane. Mark's happiness grew like a fire over a crimson ember. While he made sure to keep it in check to avoid aggravating his lungs, he could not help but smile like he was in elementary school getting his first school photo. Thinking of this reminded Mark that Natalie said she loved it when his kid-like spirit was showing. Impossibly, he felt himself beam even more. Not even seeing Danny's morose scowl as he walked by could perturb Mark.

His luck was unbelievable, Mark decided. Life had surely turned around from the old days. He was going to be associate attorney, he was getting married in four days, and he would be a father in a few days more. There was no end in sight to the bliss.

He took another breath from his inhaler, noting he was low and he needed to call the Pharmacy for a refill.

"Going to tell Nat the big news?" Evan asked as Mark fished out his phone.

"Nope, just telling her we're leaving," Mark replied. "I have to save a few surprises for after the wedding."

"She keeps secrets and you're the stalker with surprises," Evan said. "That sounds like a great mix."

"It must be. She agreed to marry me after all."

"Only after you promised to stop following her home every night."

"We lived in the same apartment complex, on the same floor."

"And the reason you knocked on her door, not yours, that one night?"

Mark deflated a bit. "The UPS guy dropped my medicine in her mail box."

"True love," Evan sighed sarcastically. "She held your life in her post office box."

"Don't even get me started on you and Cori," Mark said. When Evan digressed, Mark called Natalie. He left another voicemail to let her know they would be boarding soon and that he had big news. He hoped his voice didn't give away what had happened.

When the plane began to board, Mark glanced at a nearby television. The news station was broadcasting the incoming blizzard hitting the western states. It looked like a big one, big enough to stop a wedding.

Mark took a page out of Cori's book and said a silent prayer for his fiancé's flight as he boarded his plane to a new life.

4

"This is the Pharmacy, how may I help you?" the receptionist trilled.

"This is Cori Silverman, and I'm calling about the status of my shipment."

The receptionist asked for a plethora of identification from Cori to prove she existed and was indeed Cori Silverman. As she regurgitated numbers and letters, she felt a touch of nostalgia for the old days when her doctor simply gave her a medical prescription to be filled at the local supermarket without delay. Ever since the country had consolidated all pharmacies into one conglomerate, Cori's medical needs had gone from trifling to trying. Her medication was now two months overdue for delivery.

Cori tried not to get too angry about it. She understood that the nation as a whole was suffering economically. Everyone was cutting back wherever they could. The Pharmacy was fiscally logical and beneficial, but it was a shame it came at the expense of customer service and punctuality that Cori needed.

The line crackled as Cori was taken off hold.

"We have no prescriptions for you on file, Mrs. Silverman," the receptionist said.

"That's not possible," Cori said. "I've been calling for weeks to get my medicine."

"And whom were you speaking with?" asked the receptionist. Her sing-song voice was beginning to grate on Cori's nerves.

Cori gave the supervisor's name. Without so much as a breath or sign of remorse, the receptionist said that the supervisor had been fired.

Frustrated, Cori took a deep breath and tried a new tactic.

"I'm so sorry about all this confusion," Cori said, "but I'm desperate. My husband and I are running dangerously low on medicine, we're going to be in another state soon, and need to get this all fixed up before we go. Is there anything you can do?"

The receptionist did not take the bait. She briskly informed Cori to go to her doctor, request a prescription, and to not call back until she had. Before Cori could summon up the spunk to argue, the receptionist hung up. Cori was left holding the dead receiver, a trickle of fear running down her spine and settling in her knees. What if she never got her medication refilled? What about Evan? Would he have better luck if he called?

Cori hung up the phone and bowed her head in prayer. Evan would surely be fine without medication for a few months, but Cori was reliant on her medicine to keep under control. She was, as the economists said, one of the many degenerates sucking the pool dry with her money-wasting dependencies.

"If you dip your head a bit lower, it's an excellent stretch for your back," Natalie said.

Cori finished her prayer and gave her friend a cheery smile.

"I've never seen you pray at work," Natalie said. "What's going on?"

"The Pharmacy again," Cori said.

"Did you chew their hides this time?"

Cori shook her head.

"Maybe Evan will…"

Natalie frowned for a split second, so fast Cori almost missed it. Cori let her voice fade and cocked her head, staring Natalie down.

"Will you ever forgive Evan or will you always carry this grudge?"

Natalie stared back, her facial expression stoic. Cori held the glare for a moment longer before letting the moment pass. She couldn't stay mad too long anyway.

"It will all work out in the end," she concluded. "What about you?"

Natalie buried her nose in her charts and scribbled a few notes.

"All good here," she said. "Roger still thinks his psychosis is being kept at bay with those magic sugar pills. And Toby's great too. Now my only worry is getting to Hawaii in the middle of a blizzard with the paparazzi around every corner. When's it supposed to hit?"

"I think it's already here," Cori murmured, but then shook her head. "Natalie, don't change the subject. You know what I was asking you."

Natalie ignored her by stacking her charts together and stowing them on a shelf.

"Another day done. Time to go home and get packed," Natalie said.

Cori huffed and followed her to the changing room. One of their fellow nurses, Joaquin, was changing too and wished Natalie and Cori a safe vacation. After changing out of their smocks and saying goodbye to Yolanda, they headed for the car. As Cori had expected and Natalie had predicted, a few dedicated news reporters were waiting outside of the hospital. They shouted and hollered obnoxiously, demanding a few minutes of

Natalie's time. Natalie bowled through them, leading Cori to the car in the parking garage.

"There won't be any reporters waiting for you at your house, right?" Cori asked.

"If they are, I hope they're making snowmen instead of sitting around waiting for me," Natalie replied.

A row of snowmen in the front yard may have been possible, Cori realized as Natalie drove through Reno. Heavy flakes were accumulating on the streets. The steep mountains surrounding the city were shrouded in sheets of snow. As Natalie pulled to a stop outside of Cori's apartment complex, the car slid a few inches.

Before she got out, Cori gave Natalie a hug.

"I'm so happy for you," she said.

As she pulled away, Cori saw the muscles in Natalie's face working to force a smile.

"Thank you," Natalie replied in an earnest tone. "Pack light and I'll see you in the morning."

"Drive home safely," Cori requested. "Please avoid downtown until all the crazies get off the street."

"I'm headed straight home," Natalie promised, pointing down the street toward her apartment that was a few snowy blocks away.

"Home is where the heart is," Cori replied, pointing in the general direction of Hawaii, "and that's where we'll be tomorrow."

For the first time in years, Natalie's eyes lit up in what appeared to be genuine happiness, even if her cheeks quivered from the effort of trying to smile. But just as soon as it appeared, it was gone. Natalie's face settled into a forced smile, and the light in her eyes had disappeared.

Cori hesitated, wondering if it would happen again.

When Natalie just kept staring at her, Cori let it go, said goodbye again, and leapt out into the snow. It was about half an inch in places and starting to stick around the sewer grates. Cori lost herself in the moment and danced in the snow with delight, not noticing that Natalie had turned around and driven off in the complete opposite direction of her apartment.

5

Natalie journeyed back into the snow-skiffed downtown sector of Reno. Towering skyscrapers turned into moldering homes converted into offices for lawyers and backwoods doctors.

She scanned the sides of the road for the sign on the corner where she had to turn.

A few blocks away, she saw it: a vinyl sign that stretched around the corner of a law office's poorly landscaped yard. The sign read *Degenerate Lives Matter*. Since Natalie's last journey down this road, someone had spray-painted the word "All" over the word "Degenerate", and then someone else had spray painted over that with a rude statement against degenerates. Natalie read it, unperturbed.

She turned on the street with the sign, drove a few houses past the law office, and pulled into the cracked parking lot of a dilapidated building. Peeling paint hung from the corners of rotted wood siding. The porch sagged and the door squeaked in the cold weather. The rest of the street was just as run down, a sign of the rough times.

Natalie's eyes found the sign hanging from the porch, which read: *Dr. C. Cruze, MD, Psychiatrist*. It creaked in the light wind and snow. Watching the sign swing,

Natalie remembered the first time she had pulled into the parking lot. At that time, Mark had already passed his psychological examination. Natalie had been sent here by Dr. Hyatt to retake her preliminary exam.

"It'll be quick," Dr. Hyatt had said. "He's a bit shoddy, so he'll give you a pass in no time."

Their first meeting had lasted two hours and resulted in weekly visits with Dr. Cruze. Since, he had pushed Natalie to the breaking point and now, she'd had enough.

Gripping the steering wheel, Natalie set her mind. No more tests, no more experiments. No matter what Dr. Cruze told her, she would get the papers signed today. Then Toby would be hers.

The receptionist greeted Natalie as she entered the office and showed Natalie into the familiar back room. Natalie stood in the center of the room, glancing over the stools, cabinets, and counters. Finally, her eyes rested on the chair.

A fleeting rip of terror tore through her, but she fought to suppress the emotion. It was just a chair.

Even still, just glancing at it or seeing it in her peripherals caused her to become short of breath.

The chair had not filled her with such dread when she first saw it. In fact, her first appointment here had started quite casually. After waiting in this room for a few minutes, the doctor had arrived, introducing himself as Dr. Cruze. Then, he had explained that they were going to take a short mental status examination, or MSE for short. It was not the same test Natalie had experienced before. Rather, Dr. Cruze had asked her seven questions to analyze her demeanor, behavior, and cognition, ranging from ludicrous to intrusive. The prospect of being interrogated had not appealed to Natalie, and she had closed off instantly.

"Count backwards for me, starting from ninety-nine to seven," Dr. Cruze had requested, starting the MSE.

"Is this a joke?" she had asked.

When she had refused to take part in it, he had moved to the next question.

"When you walked in, how many fish tanks did you see?"

"Three," she had grumbled, rolling her eyes.

"Spell 'world' backwards."

Natalie had frowned and decided to go the sarcastic route.

"W-o-r-l-d b-a-c-k-w-a-r-d-s," she had spelled.

Dr. Cruze had grumbled, making several marks on his clipboard.

"Do you know why you're here?" he had asked.

"Because the adoption agency is a bureaucratic, overburdened system meant to make money, rather than help children."

More scratching on the clipboard.

"Tell me about your family," he had requested.

At this, Natalie had clammed up, letting Dr. Cruze stare at her, waiting until he had moved on.

"What are you afraid of, Natalie?"

"Nothing," she had replied quickly.

"And what do you love most?"

She had thought of the exam and its purpose: to prove she was fit to be a mother. She had smiled and said with as much endearment as she had been able to muster: "Toby."

Dr. Cruze had not been appeased. After taking more notes, Dr. Cruze had told her that she needed psychological counseling and therapy. The ensuing meetings had grated on Natalie's nerves and confidence. With each session, she had felt more broken. In defense, she had become more sarcastic, arguing that she did not need these treatments. Despite her disagreements, he had convinced her to return for regular visits and had subjected her to the chair.

Natalie was staring at it now, unable to look away from the chair. It haunted her, taunted her even.

The door creaked and Dr. Cruze walked in. Natalie tore her gaze from the chair and greeted the doctor, a toothpick of a man with sharp cheekbones and a widow's peak sharp as a mountaintop. They made small talk, dull conversation that tested Natalie's resolve to not get glassy-eyed.

At last, Dr. Cruze sighed, cleared his throat, and motioned to the chair.

"Have a seat, Ms. Harper," he said.

Natalie hesitated a moment, eyes surveying the ominous chair, before marching over and forcing herself to sit in it.

As he always did when their sessions began, Dr. Cruze sat across from her and pulled out the mental status exam. Without hesitation, he started asking her the same seven questions. Rolling her eyes, Natalie counted backward from ninety-nine to seven, recalled the three fish tanks in the lobby, and spelled world backwards. When asked if she knew why she was here, she said that Dr. Cruze enjoyed torturing her.

He made a tick-mark on the clipboard, and Natalie took a deep breath. She couldn't dig herself into a deeper hole. She had to cooperate if she wanted that form signed.

When asked what she feared, Natalie did not say she was terrified of the Easter Bunny's fluffy white tail, but said she was scared of being alone. When asked what she loved most, she resisted saying chocolate, and said that she loved Toby.

Dr. Cruze stared at her, pen hovering over the paper. He sighed and asked, "Have you yielded new emotions since the last session?"

"Yes," Natalie replied confidently, thinking of only a half hour ago outside of Cori's apartment. "So I'm good, right?"

He stared at her for a beat before asking, "What all have you experienced?"

Natalie sputtered, unsure what to share that would satisfy Dr. Cruze and end this appointment with a signature.

Before she could say anything, Dr. Cruze sighed again.

"Ms. Harper," he said wearily, setting the clipboard aside. "Dealing with post-traumatic stress disorder is not an exact science. I cannot meet with a war veteran, talk him through his fears, sit with him through our virtual reality training, and hope to wash away what four years of war has done. Likewise, I cannot subject you to a few of our little sessions and expect you to develop the emotions you have suppressed. You are laboring under the delusion that you have been cured completely in this short time, but you are a complicated layer of humanity that must be unwrapped slowly."

"I am unwrapped," Natalie insisted. "Now I want a signature, please."

"You want a mask," the doctor corrected. "You want to be an actor and fake your way through life. What good will that do? I am trying to help you find your true self again. I want you to be you."

"I was me," Natalie interrupted. "Years ago."

"But in the years since, you have all but forgotten yourself," he replied. "Do you even know who you are anymore?"

Natalie nodded stoically. "Of course—"

"How could you possible know?" Dr. Cruze interrupted. "You have closed yourself off completely! When was the last time you let yourself *feel* anything? Truly feel it and let if fill your very being?"

Natalie shifted uncomfortably in the chair.

"You have locked yourself away," Dr. Cruze continued. "You have altered your mind and removed yourself from your emotions. We need to remind you how it feels to *feel*. To love, to hate, to fear. *Then* you can find yourself."

"And I'm beginning to," she replied. She quickly explained the moment she'd had with Cori less than an hour ago, in which she had felt a surge of happiness. The moment had made her feel very uncomfortable and she had fought to suppress it right away.

Natalie watched the doctor, hoping that this instance would give Dr. Cruze the satisfaction he was looking for. But when she finished telling him what she had felt, his face was blank.

"One emotion is but a fraction of the iceberg of emotions you can experience," Dr. Cruze said when she finished.

"I don't need an iceberg," Natalie replied. "I need a signature."

Dr. Cruze narrowed his eyes. "I will not sign off on your psychological examination until I believe that you have dealt with the trauma in your past and begun to function as a normal person again. If I were to sign it now, I would be allowing adoption by an unfit parent."

Natalie began to argue, but the doctor cut her off.

"Your brain needs to be retrained," he said. "One step at a time. And we are getting closer. Last week, before you fled my office, I believe you felt a glimmer of something."

That she had, and it was an emotion she never intended to feel in full force again. She felt a speck of it every time she walked in this office and saw the chair, but she was able to push it away. There was no point in being terrified, no benefits of fear. She knew its power all too well.

"I was terrified," Natalie said defiantly.

"Exactly," he replied. "The emotion filled you completely. You felt it, but didn't know how to cope, so you ended the session and ran away. What happens when your son breaks his arm? Will you run for the hills to avoid panic? What if your husband leaves you? Will you bury yourself in emotionlessness and apathy until you have escaped your embarrassment?"

Natalie avoided Dr. Cruze's eyes, considering for a heartbeat if she could beat him into a stupor and get a signature.

"You can't bear to feel anything," Dr. Cruze continued. "That is exactly what I want to fix, Ms. Harper. From the moment you stepped into my office, I saw a soul in need. Even now, I see one who does not yet know she needs help, but I am here to help you nonetheless. I want you to be the best you that you can be. By facing the emotions you seek to avoid, we will find the old Natalie."

He paused to survey her facial expression, trying to read if he was getting anywhere with her.

"Will you let me?" he asked. "Will you let me help you, Natalie?"

She nodded stiffly and he nodded back curtly.

"Good," said Dr. Cruze. "I will make you a promise. One more session and I will give you the signature."

Natalie kept her face blank, but her heart began to beat quickly. She tried to breathe slowly and lower her heart rate, but it kept getting stronger. She wondered if she was trying to become happy.

"One more?" she asked.

"One last simulation," the doctor replied.

Natalie grit her jaw and breathed slowly. Her heart seemed to pound harder in retaliation, but she knew this was the only way.

"What are you looking for?" she asked. "Which emotion?"

"Fear," he said bluntly. "I want you to get lost in it. Through our sessions, we've discovered that the trauma of your past is rooted directly in fear, terror, panic, and ultimately loss. Grief is too potent an emotion to unravel just yet. However, if we exploit the emotion of fear, we will be able to break open a whole new world of feelings."

He stood and began adjusting the chair's machinery. Natalie resisted running out. She stayed stock-still as the machinery encased her into the chair.

"I will remind you again," Dr. Cruze said, "that what we are doing is unprecedented. Post-traumatic stress disorder virtual reality training is rare and only tested by the military. This machine is state-of-the-art. I wish you to respect my direction and do as I say. Do not try to beat the simulation; do not try to outthink it. Doing so could have irreversible ramifications on your mental and physical health. When you feel the intended emotion of fear, exit the simulation. Are we clear?"

Natalie nodded and translated: "When I get scared, press the red button."

"Good girl."

Dr. Cruze swiveled the armrest in front of her. She placed her hand atop the semi-circular red button installed on the armrest.

"Sit back, Natalie," he commanded her.

She did so, preserving her contact with the button. He moved one last piece of machinery, swiveling the headgear in front of her face. Her vision was filled with dark lenses. Knowing the next command to come, she closed her eyes and took deep breaths. She lost herself in the darkness, letting her stiff muscles relax.

"Take your mind back to where it began," said Dr. Cruze. His voice sounded distant, as though he were on the other side of a canyon.

Natalie let color flood the darkness of her eyes, taking her back to the red road that the journalists and reporters would not let her forget.

"Remember," the doctor requested and his voice was further away than expected, less than a whisper, "when you feel fear, press the red button."

6

Natalie sat in the passenger seat of the old car, watching the road flash by. The effect was mesmerizing and lulled her into a trance. Her mother, Rose, was driving them home from a tour of the doctor's offices.

Only fifteen, Natalie had told her mother she had wanted to be a nurse.

"I'm a nurse of types," Rose had said. "My boss is a doctor."

Because Natalie was bursting with excitement to know more, Rose had taken her to work for the day. Natalie had loved every minute of it, from meeting her mother's boss to watching her mom work. She had not really understood any of it—lots of computer work, coding, and playing with metals fine as sand that Natalie had not been allowed to touch. When Natalie had tried to open the container with the metals, Rose had leapt at her and pulled her hands back.

"Do as I tell you, Natalie Olivia Harper," Rose had said, as she always had.

Natalie had done as instructed the rest of the day, watching and not touching.

Now, the day was done. Natalie sat in the passenger seat, watching the road and pondering her future. She knew she should be watching her mother, but the way the world whizzed by, the details all blurring together, was transfixing and made her forget.

She felt the car start to veer and checked on her mother.

Her mother smiled at her from the driver's seat, her eyes sparkling.

"Just checking, sweetheart," she said.

Natalie chuckled and thought of a snappy response about her mother's narcolepsy, but did not have time.

It happened in the blink of an eye. Natalie watched as her mother's eyes slid back into her head and she slumped against the wheel, instantly asleep. Her foot relaxed, depressing the accelerator.

"Mom!" Natalie shouted.

She reached for the steering wheel, but she wasn't fast enough. The vehicle veered sharply, headed right for the concrete barriers lining the freeway.

Natalie braced herself, screaming for her mother to wake up. The car hit the wall at breakneck speed. Natalie jerked forward, her seatbelt cutting into her skin and snapping her collar bone. Her neck snapped back. She felt the seat shudder and her knees connected with the front console. The front of the car collapsed in on her, cutting into her legs. The air bag punched her in the face as cubes of glass showered her.

All at once, it was over. Though her head was spinning, Natalie knew that the car had stopped.

She moved slowly, careful to inspect her arms. One arm didn't work quite properly, probably thanks to the broken collarbone. Otherwise, they seemed uninjured, so she pushed the deflated airbag away from her. When she did, she saw the twisted metal and plastic of the front console jammed into her legs. Blood was trickling out of her.

"Mom?" Natalie whispered tremulously.

When her mother didn't answer, Natalie dared to look at her.

Her mother was still asleep in the driver's seat, but she was cut up. Blood ran from her nose, mouth, and a wound on her head. Something had pierced her side, perhaps part of the door that was missing. Natalie could hear the steady dribble of her mother's blood running out of the car and pooling on the black asphalt.

Natalie tried to wake her mother, but she did not stir.

Inside, Natalie felt her stomach curdle. Fear began to set in, terrible awful fear, and she wanted nothing more than to hit the reset button, escape that moment, and start over.

7

Natalie arrived at her apartment complex as the thickest flakes yet began to fall. The incoming blizzard must have run the journalists off, as no one was waiting on the doorstep or front yard of the apartments.

Not caring either way, Natalie trudged through the snow to the door and slid her keycard over the electronic lock several times before it let her in. By the time she got inside, her hair was coated in white.

She strode past Mark's apartment, nonchalantly remembering that she wasn't allowed inside. He had no doubt planned something special that she would have to pretend to care about.

Still unperturbed, Natalie arrived at her door. Once inside, she checked her phone to see that it had six messages, all from Mark.

"Through security," one said. "On the plane," said another.

Natalie deleted them one-by-one.

"In Hawaii," Mark's last message chirped. "Rough landing. The weather here is something else. Our local tour guide says it's been unnatural for months. Must be the mad scientists!" At this point, Natalie zoned out, waiting for Mark to finish. He kept talking as though carrying on a live conversation with Natalie until mercifully finishing with, "Hopefully I'll hear from you tonight or tomorrow morning. Love you."

As she deleted the final message, Natalie realized she was grinding her teeth. She stopped, wondering why she had been doing so. As she contemplated her reaction, a queer sensation wrested on her mind. It took her a heartbeat to realize she was feeling one of the many emotions she had long ago trained herself to ignore.

The instant she realized this—that she could be feeling something—she sought to shut it off. Dr. Cruze may have wanted her to encounter these feelings and learn to cope with them, but she was Natalie Harper. She lived without emotion.

On the counter, her phone vibrated. She glanced at it, focusing on feeling nothing. Mark had sent her a text with three words she hated hearing him say: *I love you.*

All at once, the emotion she had tried to suppress came pulsing through her, burning in her chest like a bomb that had imploded.

Irritation, raw and prickly, burst out of her. She grabbed the cell phone and hurled it across the apartment. Through gritted teeth, she screamed her frustration.

Lost in the moment, she thought of every person that had irked her. Of course there were the journalists who wouldn't leave her alone. Then there was Mark, the chief offender, who always needed to keep Natalie abreast of every situation. He continually had to end a conversation with, "Love you," which was just another reminder of how perfect he was compared to her. And last but not least, there was Cori, the eternal optimist and golden ray of sunshine, and Evan, egotistical but loyal. They were well-rounded, logical, and perfect. Just what the doctor ordered. Nothing went wrong in their happy little lives. Their flawlessness was a slap in Natalie's face, forcing her to acknowledge how broken she was. How inhuman. How abnormal.

Control, Natalie thought, fighting against the emotions pulsing through her.

She clenched the countertop, turning her knuckles white. She fought against the upsurge of emotions, detesting herself for allowing emotions in the first place. Had she not learned her lesson on the red road? There was no room for emotion. Feeling anything inevitably broke her down more than she already was.

Natalie blamed Dr. Cruze for this. Before wanting to adopt Toby, she had been an impervious shell, free from harm. But since these meetings and virtual reality trainings, she had lost her balance. There was a fissure in her shell, a crack in the wall. Emotions were seeping in like a trickle of rain through a tin roof. It dared to break through, but Natalie was fighting it. She wanted—needed—Toby, but would not have him at the expense of her own sanity. She refused to be broken.

Soon, she wouldn't be.

As she stood there, swimming in irritation and anger, she focused her attention on why she was marrying Mark and adopting Toby. It was not for love, because of similarities, or product of a bond they had formed. Her intentions were purely selfish.

Being married to Mark and having Toby as a child would send a sign to all the journalists and the concerned world at large that she was doing well. No one would ever again have to ask her if she was doing okay. Gone would be the days of journalists interrogating the woman whose life had been changed on the red road. Forgotten would be the days of the girl in the brown room, fighting a losing battle. They would only see this new woman, healed by a new family, whole, and for all intents and purposes, happy.

Truthfully, Toby would be the most powerful symbol that she was healing and moving forward. His enthusiasm for life would shine onto Natalie, and the journalists and reporters wouldn't have anything else to write about.

That was why she wanted Toby, she tried to convince herself. No other reason.

None.

Except, perhaps, that having him would be sweet, sweet vengeance.

Somehow, this deep-seeded thought quenched the emotions running through Natalie. Prickles of irritation and the boil of anger subsided.

At long last, Natalie felt empty again. Just the way she liked it. She retrieved her phone, turned on the television, and set about packing her suitcase. In an unattached, disinterested fashion, she listened to the evening news, which dramatized the latest shootings and sadistic hate crimes, rehashed political rhetoric against degenerates, and ended with a recap of the latest and greatest Halloween costumes from the previous weekend. Not caring in the slightest about politicians or the creepiest ghoul on the Trick-or-Treat block, Natalie finished packing and retired to bed. There, she watched the snow flurries gather on her tiny apartment windowsill until she had fallen asleep.

On her bedside stand, the alarm clock blinked to midnight. Had Natalie been awake or in a caring mood, she may have noticed that she was one day closer to Hawaii, to Mark, and to a new life.

8

Bonnie Matician exited the boardroom quietly and hid in the alcove between the lady's room and drinking fountain. Her cell phone buzzed in her hand, demanding attention.

"I've called four times," her husband said when she answered the phone.

"I was in a meeting," she explained. "You know I only take emergency calls."

"This constitutes," Brian replied, his tone hushed and hurried.

The airwaves rang with silence. Bonnie's nerves danced with anxiety and she felt lightheaded. The late night heat of L.A. was not helping.

"It's coming," he said.

Bonnie choked on her words. Her hand fished into her pocket, wrapping around the scrap piece of paper from a fortune cookie that Brian had given her.

"When?" she asked.

"Tomorrow," he answered. "They have a target."

"Us?"

Her husband answered in the affirmative and she thought desperately of her children. At least Bethany would be safe.

In a way, she wished Brian had never told her. What she would not give to be one of her coworkers in the boardroom, oblivious to the impending doom.

"I need you to listen to me," he requested. "You know who I'm working with. I'm as good as dead, so I have to set this right."

"This isn't your—"

"Yes, it is. I helped make this thing," he said, "and I'll be darned if I don't try to fix it."

"Isn't there a way to shut it off?"

"It's been compromised," Brian replied. He paused as though wanting to say more, but sighed before saying, "I have to work with the coding. I'm going to negate the algorithm or reverse it at the very least, try and destroy it completely, but you need to act like it's going to happen anyway. Get the kids to the safe zone as soon as you can."

"We won't make it," she said.

"Bonnie," he whispered, "there's no time for won't's and can't's. How soon can you get the kids?"

Panic choked her voice again. A coworker gave her an alarmed look as he strolled by.

"Where are the kids?" Brian asked, dread finally seeping into his voice.

"At Mom's," she finally replied.

"Call her right now and get them to the airport," he insisted. "Call your sister too, if you can reach her. You need to get here now."

"I'll try," she said, but knew she must do better than try. There was no room for mistakes.

"You are the bravest woman I know," he replied. "If anyone can do this, it's you."

"Don't talk like that," she said.

"Like what?"

"Like you'll never see me again."

His voice lost all urgency and was filled with remorse: "I won't, Bonnie."

Tears threatened to flow, but she batted her eyes until they left.

The time for tears was past. She had a mission now.

"Can you fix it?" she asked.

"There's so little time, I can only try."

She forced herself to stay strong for him. "I know you can. You've raised three beautiful kids and put up with me for ten years. You can fix this."

"I'd fix the whole world if it meant one more moment with you," he responded. "Kiss the kids for me and send your Mom my love."

"Don't go, not yet," she implored. There was still so much to say.

"I will love you until the end," he said with a note of finality.

"Until—"

The line went dead before she could finish. In her pocket, she let go of the paper fortune and clenched the Leatherman. It would not protect her from what was coming, but holding it tightly gave her a sense of defiance that she could at least try to defend herself against even the most unstoppable of forces.

PHASE 2
SILVER FALLS

1

Brian Matician studied the computer screen feverishly. Green characters blurred in his tired eyes. The floor beneath his feet hummed with the power of a nuclear generator. Dawn crept ever closer and he knew deep down that he wasn't even close to atoning his sins and mending his errors.

In this control room was where it had all started. A wonderful idea had turned terribly wrong. Now, against all hope, he was determined to set things right.

The control room itself was circular. Brian sat at the computer bank against a rounded wall adorned with a dozen televisions. Muted news broadcasts showed countries all over the world reporting the day's events, upcoming or ongoing. Hopefully, if Brian had anything to say about it, this would continue the next day and the next: reporters covering one boring story after another with no catastrophe to proclaim.

To the right of Brian's computer was a bell jar. The glass canister was filled with silver that sloshed from side to side and appeared to be liquid. Brian knew better. They were nanobytes: extremely tiny, programmable computers as miniscule as a human pore. The canister withheld billions of them, so compact and tiny that they moved like liquid metal.

The canister of silver was connected to a customized platform that fed to the computer. Every calculation and algorithm put into the computer would program the nanobytes.

Behind him, in the center of the control room, was a clear, hollow tube that ascended into the ceiling, leading to the surface several stories above. Surrounding the base of the tube was a control panel with a multitude of buttons. There was also a loading dock where Brian could load the canister of nanobytes into the hollow tube, but it was the last place Brian wanted to place the canister of silver right now. That red button though, a bulbous button on the control panel, could have solved everything if it hadn't been deactivated.

Beyond the control panel and hollow tube, standing at the door, was a guard. There were only three people in the facility; everyone else had left hours ago. When the yearlong trials on the silver nanobytes had finally been successful, the staff had been relieved. Only Brian, Dr. Avazino, and the guard remained.

Armed with an M16, the guard was watching Matician with the persistence of a dog waiting for its bowl of food to be filled. If the guard had been gone, Matician could have just destroyed the canister of silver or maybe infected himself with it. Perhaps he could have deleted all of the mathematical directives. At the very least, he could have reactivated that red button, which would have set off an electromagnetic pulse that would have destroyed the nanobytes. Unfortunately, the EMP had been disengaged hours ago by technicians. Reactivating it would be laborious and alert the suspicions of the guard. In fact, all of these solutions, from the EMP to destroying the canister, would have been extremely obvious to the guard and resulted in

Brian's death. Instead, he had to be coy, painstakingly hovering over the computer screen, undoing everything he had spent a year creating. He wrote out each algorithm and negated it, making the directive obsolete. Algorithm by algorithm he went, calculating and corrupting. It was his only chance and the country's only hope.

This need to save the day had fallen onto Brian's consciousness a few hours ago. As the staff of the facility had left, Dr. Avazino and Brian had been given small vials filled with silver nanobytes. It was meant as a gift for their service, a memento of what they had created. By that point, Brian had realized what the silver could do, and had thrown the vial down the drain once he was alone. In that moment, he had called Bonnie, realizing that he must find a way to mend his mistakes. He had been a fool to work on this for so long, not realizing what he was doing, not taking the time to comprehend his work and settling for the paycheck and confidentiality. If he had tried to understand it, he would have realized their work with the nanobytes would saturate the world in spilled blood. He cursed himself now, wishing he had realized it sooner, wishing for more time.

So here he sat, indiscreetly working on complex mathematics to reprogram the nanobytes. It was maddening work that wore on his stamina and mental power.

Glancing over the dozens of algorithms that could still execute their original directive, Brian picked one to fix. He wrote it down on one of the pieces of scratch paper not covered in the chicken scratch of reworked calculations. He computed this new algorithm recklessly, not stopping to double-check his work. The franticness of this moment made him melancholy for his Oxford days, when making an error in computations would culminate in a pitiful test score. Here, any mistake could be catastrophic. He could make this disaster even worse. Lives could be affected forever. His wife, his children…

The clock on the screen chimed three hours from dawn. He had three hours left before the launch.

Suddenly, there was a muted yelp behind Matician, followed by a sharp snap like dry branches cracking. Startled, Matician dropped the pencil and spun around.

Dr. Griffith Avazino stood in the threshold of the control room. The behemoth of a man was holding up the guard, whose head was pointed the wrong way. Avazino was hardly even breathing, as though snapping the guard's neck had been as easy as unscrewing the lid of a jelly jar.

Struck with fear, Matician leapt from his seat. He had enough sense to gather up the scratch paper of reworked equations and stuff it into his pocket. Was Avazino here to launch the silver?

Dr. Avazino stepped calmly over the guard's body, popping his fingers. He was an imposing man with dark eyes, a barrel chest, and scarred hands. His eyes swept over Matician and the computer station.

"Mr. Matician," Dr. Avazino said, his voice jovial and relieved. "We share the same intentions!"

Matician's mind scrambled for answers as to what was happening. Had Avazino come to the control room early to destroy the nanobytes too?

Convincing himself this was true, Brian sighed in relief. Avazino continued to walk slowly around the hollow tube in the room's center.

"I was starting to feel like a fool," Brian said, motioning to the canister on the computer dock. "Help me stop this."

Avazino paused for a moment before giving Brain a disturbing smile.

"I'm afraid, Mr. Matician," Avazino said, "that the only fool here is you."

Brian paused, his eyes growing. He had been wrong, and his first instincts had been correct. Avazino was not here to destroy the nanobytes, but to launch them.

"You can't possibly want this," Brian said. "There is no telling how many lives will be taken."

"Hopefully all of them," Avazino replied, walking ever closer. "Including yours."

"Why are you doing this?" Brian shouted. "You can't want this! Don't let our benefactor—"

Avazino withdrew his vial of silver from his pocket and shook it.

"Our benefactor?" he said plainly. "This is not his doing. It is mine. This is my masterpiece."

Suddenly, Brian understood. The nanobytes weren't the pet project of their mysterious political benefactor. They were Dr. Avazino's creation.

"You're a monster," Brian said, hating how cliché it sounded.

"No," Avazino growled, placing the vial back in his pocket. "I'm a griffin."

Avazino made it around the hollow tube, now only a few feet from Brian, the computer, and the canister of silver.

Too close, Brian thought. He spun and grabbed the canister, about the size of a flour container, and wielded it threateningly at Avazino.

"Everything you worked for will be destroyed," Brian proclaimed, holding it high over his head. The silver sloshed back and forth, buzzing as the billions of nanobytes bounced off the glass.

Avazino did not even reply to Brian's threats. He charged, shockingly fast. With the strength of a grizzly bear, Avazino collided with Brian, pushing him up against a bank of computer servers. Air knocked out of him, Brian slid down the tower of servers, a sharp pain throbbing in his chest. He felt Avazino grab the canister and fought to hold on, but Avazino was stronger, rending the canister from his hands.

Spluttering in pain, Brian tried to get to his feet, weaving blindly with stars in his vision.

A knee slammed into Brian's stomach, forcing vomit into his mouth. He collapsed to the floor again, heaving for air and choking on his puke. His chest throbbed like a rib had been snapped.

Finally, Brian's vision cleared. Avazino stood by the circular loading dock for the hollow tube in the center of the room. The silver canister had been placed on the loading dock.

"No," Brian muttered, but he could hardly stand.

Avazino's hands danced across several buttons at the loading dock, initiating the launch sequence. Below them came the groan of the nuclear reactor powering the entire facility. It hummed with intensity.

With a whir of mechanics, the hollow tube opened. Avazino pushed the canister of silver and its dock into the bottom. The tube sealed with a pop of air, encapsulating the canister and cutting out the buzz of nanobytes.

Brian tried to get to his feet again, but severe pain raked his innards.

"My masterpiece," Avazino crooned, eyes traveling the length of the tube. "Let it begin."

Brian shouted, but no amount of words could stop Avazino from pressing the button.

The canister full of silver burst open. The silver nanobytes swarmed through the tube like angry gnats. The nuclear reactor groaned several levels below them. There was a belch of pressurized air and the silver particles shot up and out of sight.

Brian's heart sank in despair. Within seconds, the nanobytes would propel into an elevation of six kilometers. There, the nanobytes would coalesce with cirrostratus clouds for a few hours before activating and reorganizing weather patterns. It would cascade to the east, far from Hawaii, and fall. A few hours more and blood would redden the rivers and streets.

The silver rain was coming and there was nothing Brain could do to stop it anymore.

2

Mark Hofland awoke a few hours before dawn with phlegm coating his throat and a banging at the hotel room door. He coughed up a lungful of mucus, took a breath with his inhaler, and made for the door. Another knock came—it had to be Evan.

"Evan," Mark shouted, "if you're getting me up early after partying all night on the one day I get to sleep in…"

He threw open the door. Evan was leaning on the door jam, yellow fabric tucked under his crossed arms. Surprisingly, Evan had shed his business suit and was dressed head-to-toe in a yellow jumpsuit.

"You'll do what?" Evan asked. "Hold me in contempt?"

"Hold you by your big toe until you cry," Mark threatened.

"You wouldn't hurt a fly, let alone my big toe," Evan said and thrust a yellow jumpsuit into Mark's hands.

"Is this the new business uniform?"

"Only for today, sunshine," Evan replied. "Harlem sleeps like a vampire and won't be up for a century, which gives us more than enough time for an adventure. Come on! Haleakalā calls!"

Mark distantly recalled glancing out the window the previous evening to see the silhouette of a tall mountain in the distance. Someone had called it Haleakalā.

"The three-thousand meter tall volcano, you mean?" Mark asked. "Let me go pack a new set of lungs."

"We're not *climbing* to the top, Hofland, we're biking. Well, actually riding in a van to the top and bike-riding down. Come on! It's Haleakalā!"

"And the urine-colored suit?"

"To disguise any loss of bladder control during the descent. Our tour guide says it's a bit of a rush. Personally I'm hoping Danny turns his suit brown."

Mark couldn't stop his groan. "Danny Boy is coming?"

"I don't want to hear it," Evan replied. "You're the new associate lawyer, which means you will have to put up with him more, and if you can bike together—"

"If you say, 'We can work together,' I'm riding my bike off the cliff."

"You can work together," Evan finished. "Now suit up, grab your medicine, and meet me downstairs in ten."

"I'm right behind you," Mark said, checking his pockets for his hotel room card.

Evan paused, looking at him warily.

"What about your medicine?" he asked.

"I have my inhaler," Mark assured his friend.

"Don't you need extra?" Evan asked. "Just in case?"

"Evan," Mark said lightly, "this is Hawaii. It's only the cold that gets me."

"And humidity," Evan interjected. "And moisture. And physical exertion. Which Hawaii has plenty of, if you haven't noticed."

"You said it's *downhill*," Mark shot back. "Besides, I have an extra cartridge and emergency injections in my suitcase. You can cart my sorry self back here if you need to."

Evan looked concerned, but Mark was confident. He had an inhaler in his pocket and wouldn't need any extra medication.

"Everything is going to be fine," Mark assured his friend, closing the door to his hotel room.

"That's not what you said earlier when you threatened to ride off a cliff," Evan replied with a smirk.

Mark's joke became a tempting offer the longer they were in the van. The entire forty-five minute drive up the winding road of the extinct volcano, Mark, Evan, and three other coworkers had to listen to Danny complain about how early it was, how foreign countries were so bizarre, and how he was going to have to be in front of the bike line to guarantee no one got hurt.

Trying to stop himself from punching Danny out of the car, Mark looked out the windows. The island outside was still shaded in darkness, twilight only a few minutes away. High above, Mark couldn't see the stars. They must have been covered by clouds. Curiously though, he kept seeing twinkling high above as though the occasional star were popping through.

"I didn't know clouds sparkled," Evan said, looking out the window too.

"It has to be the stars," Mark replied, squinting at the darkness. "Or the aliens. Looks like they come in pieces."

As Mark watched, the sparkling specks in the sky began to move, flying east. He could only tell this because the sparkles began to streak, leaving tails of light behind like a shooting star.

"Do UFOs move that fast?" Mark asked.

"Clouds definitely don't," Evan replied.

Danny spoke up now, clearly wanting to be the foremost voice in this topic.

"These foreign countries always have affiliation with aliens," he said. "It explains their bizarre customs."

Mark, Evan, and the rest of their coworkers groaned.

They finally reached the summit of Haleakalā after another grinding twenty minutes that tested Mark's patience and mettle. As he got out of the van, Mark smiled sympathetically at the Hawaiian driver, hoping the driver did not think all American mainlanders were like Danny.

When Mark stepped out of the van, he gasped. He was one of many, including his coworkers and perhaps twenty people from other vans, staring in every direction. The view, now coming to life with the twilight, was a stunning vista of greens, maroons, and blues. The island of Maui was startlingly small but rich with texture. Navy blue ocean washed up on shores from every direction. Dark grey and indigo storm clouds moved across the brightening sky from the west, clouds to the east beginning to burn yellow with the sun. The air was breezy and slightly moist, with the promise of warmth to come. Mark took a deep breath, relived that he could breathe just fine.

Mark scanned the eastern horizon, searching for the sparkling clouds he had seen earlier. They were nowhere to be seen, surely carried off by the swift trade winds. Just as the shining clouds had been pushed to the east, a new storm bank was moving in from the west.

"Storm's coming," Evan noted, pointing to the storm clouds moving toward Maui.

At least they're not shining, Mark nearly said, but decided Evan had probably already forgotten about the strange clouds.

"Just in time for us to get back for the retreat," he said instead.

And before the Hawaii humidity hits, he said to himself. He thought of his extra medication miles away at the hotel, wondering nervously if he had been a fool to be unprepared. At least he had one inhaler with him.

To assure himself, he reached into his yellow jumpsuit pocket, wrapping his fingers around the inhaler. He gave it a shake and felt an unsatisfying lightness to it.

His stomach dropped. He had forgotten it was running low.

Guides began to move through the small crowd of people, directing them to form into a line. Each person was given a bike. Novice riders were put in the front with the guides, experienced riders in the back. When Danny insisted to be in the front to keep everyone safe, Evan and Mark snickered that the novices were still in the front of the line.

"How do you fancy those clouds?" asked one of the men behind Mark and Evan.

Mark looked up. The clouds were moving even faster than before. Already the sky above was bubbling with moisture.

"Looks like rain," Mark and Evan said simultaneously.

"You're a regular bunch of weathermen, aren't you," joked the man behind them.

While Evan chuckled, Mark wrapped his hand around his inhaler again. He couldn't believe how stupid he'd been. How could he have forgotten his inhaler was running low? His insides burnt with embarrassment.

I just need to get down the mountain, he thought. Then he wouldn't be a burden on anyone or make a fool of himself.

Trying to take his mind off of it, Mark decided to press Evan for answers.

"What did you mean yesterday," he asked Evan, "when you said you deserved to be in paralegal?"

Evan glanced away, his expression becoming placid.

"You've worked hard," Mark continued. "You deserve where you are. Why not become partner?"

"I don't need to be in the limelight all the time," Evan said tonelessly.

The way Evan said it, so nonchalantly, made Mark think there was more to the story than just a good case of humility and humbleness.

"Why are you stepping down?" Mark pressed.

Evan gave him a look that plainly said, "Not now."

Mark stared down his friend for a few more seconds before backing off. He wanted to know what Evan was up to, but knew that no answers would escape Evan's lips when he was being defensive.

"Attention," called the guide from the front.

Mark and Evan looked down the bike line. About halfway, one of the Hawaiian guides was holding up the hand of a young, pretty girl who had distinct signs of Down's syndrome.

The guide spoke loudly for all to hear: "Any riders who have disabilities, ailments, or handicaps, please come forward."

Evan and Mark exchanged glances, but stood firmly where they were in the back. Mark had no intention of being singled out and judged on the spot.

A few other people raised their hands and were placed in the front of the line.

The man behind Mark murmured, "Can't even get away from degenerates in Hawaii."

Once everyone was back into a line, the guides let out a whistle and jumped on their bikes. Danny followed suit, then the degenerates. A few seconds later, the riders in front of Mark and Evan began to move. Mark propped himself onto his bike, resting a foot on the petal.

"Here goes nothing," Mark said and pushed off, just as a thick raindrop spattered on his nose.

3

Beyond the vast windows of the boardroom, thick storm clouds were gathering. The clouds seemed to be from another realm that ignored the laws of physics as they filled the sky from horizon to horizon. Smog and haze may have been familiar in L.A., but these clouds were unnatural in the way they filled the sky and seemed to sparkle, as though stars were twinkling within them.

Bonnie Matician stared at the clouds as they furled in the sky, anxiety and nervousness weighing on her mind. She wanted to know where her children were and why Grandma Dottie wasn't answering the phone. She wondered why her sister wasn't answering either, but then again, that was not a surprise. Most of all, she desperately wondered if her husband had succeeded in stymieing the imminent disaster, if he had modified it or had been unable to succeed, or if he was still alive. Really any news would have been nice. These clouds though seemed to indicate that in one way or another, Brian had failed.

As she studied the clouds, more and more people gathered at the windows. The clouds were bolstering and growing darker. Flashes of silver danced through the moisture like discolored lightning. Bonnie started to wonder if she was imagining the cloud's silver spots, but her coworkers and associates were pointing it out too.

Her heart sank. Whatever her husband had done in the dead of night had not been enough.

Remorse began to set in too. She should have been with her family. Too many times, she had chosen work over her family, and now it was one time too many. Here, on this stuffy November morning, she would witness the end of her kind in a boardroom full of corporate bigots instead of holding her children one more time or rescuing Brian. Even reconciling with her sister or giving her mother one last hug would have been a better alternative than this.

Unable to face the source of her imminent demise, Bonnie turned away from the windows. But there was no escaping it. On the opposite wall were several televisions. Multiple news stations displayed footage of cloudbanks streaking across the sky, filling the blue void. One station showed an aerial satellite view of the North American continent, with the clouds stretching from the west coast to the easterly fringes of the Midwest, and from the southern border of Canada to the northern regions of Mexico. In full, it covered the entire mainland of the United States.

As Bonnie expected, her fellow coworkers began to point at the weather maps, accusing terrorists of attacking America. It certainly seemed that way, for only Canada and Mexico were partly touched by this cloudbank.

Little do they know, Bonnie thought dismally to herself. This wasn't a terrorist. This was her husband.

As more footage showed the clouds reaching the east coast and New England states, Bonnie's eyes turned back to the windows. Above Los Angeles, the clouds had stopped moving and were building in mass.

She knew deep in her gut that this boardroom would be the place of her death, but she refused to believe that her family would die as well. She knew she must reach them and have them find some type of shelter from the calamity ahead.

From her pocket, she withdrew her cell phone and called Grandma Dottie again. Mercifully, her mother answered.

"Where have you been?" Bonnie shouted.

"Bonnie, dear, what is it?" Grandma Dottie replied.

Bonnie paused, the silver clouds flickering in her eyes. The gigantic plumes of moisture ballooned threateningly.

With a heavy heart, she realized they were all doomed. Not just her, but her children, her mother, and the rest of the country.

4

Nathaniel Matician, son of Bonnie and Brian, propelled himself deeper into the sagebrush with each stride. He kept his footfalls light to avoid shin splints.

The night's storm had left a few inches of snowfall; frost sheathed the boughs of sage. Heavy footfalls sounded behind him, sloshing through the slushy snow. He lengthened his stride to ensure he wouldn't be caught.

High overhead, dark storm clouds coalesced and furrowed, threatening to explode with moisture. Nate hoped the storm would hold out until he got back home. This one looked worse than the blizzard that had hit overnight.

Running had once been a father-son activity with Nate's dad, Brian. About two years ago, his dad had taken a top-secret job for the government. Nate hadn't seen him since.

Each of the Matician family members were coping in their own way. Bethany pouted and Wyatt was too young to know yet. His mother, Bonnie, changed the subject whenever Brian's name was uttered, only mentioning him during lengthy discussions over the phone with Grandma Dottie. Of course, Nate's mom had always had trouble talking about family issues.

Nate thought he missed his father the most. Just this morning, while roaming his grandmother's house in the wee hours, he had found photos of his mom and dad from when they had first met. Like a wave that had snuck up on him, the absence of his father smashed down upon Nate. He needed to get out and run.

He went to tell his grandma that he was going out, but she was on the phone. Whatever the caller was saying, it seemed important. Grandma Dottie was hunched over, listening intently. Then his grandma asked where Brian was. At the mere mention of his father, Nate was bowled over by the raging waves of loneliness. He fled the house and wandered the surrounding neighborhood. A few streets later, he found a gap in a fence leading into the hills of sagebrush. He'd taken off at a run, thinking that perhaps he could outrun his lonesomeness.

Now, as he heard footsteps behind him, he wondered if he should have told someone he was on the run. If he got hurt like three years ago, it would be a long time before anyone found him.

Grandma Dottie certainly would not be pleased, Nate thought. She was being gracious enough as it was, housing him and his siblings while his mom was on a business trip and his dad continued working far away. The least Nate could do was get back home as though he had never left.

The footfalls from behind were getting closer now, and they sounded somewhat irregular. Nate sped up, hoping to outrun whoever it was.

His ears picked up another sound in the air. Nate glanced around to determine what it was. It was a swooshing sound followed by a quick thud, and it was repeating itself at varying distances around him.

Unexpectedly, a golf ball-sized piece of hail streaked out of the sky twenty yards in front of him. It impacted the snow, burrowing itself a crater.

Nate came to a stop, looking up to the sky awestruck. A sky-full of hail was streaking down at him. It looked like thick rain coming down.

"Hail!" Nate shouted to himself and dove under the nearest sagebrush, a five-foot one with broad branches. No sooner had he sought cover, a steady stream of hail descended upon the area. Chunks of ice ranging from the size of pebbles to tennis shoes pockmarked the snow-covered ground.

Quivering in fear under the sage, Nate suddenly remembered the footsteps that had been coming from behind him. He glanced around, hoping the other runner had found shelter, or if it was a bad guy, that they had been turned away by the storm.

Suddenly, through the white sheen of hail, Nate saw something coming. It was small and low to the ground, footsteps barely audible over the hail.

When the thing was only a few feet away, Nate finally realized what he was seeing. It was a dog, smaller than a Chihuahua and looking scared.

"Here, boy!" Nate shouted.

The dog raced at Nate, jumping into his arms under the brush. It had a curly white coat, thick like a poodle's, with splotches of black. The dog was soaking wet and shivered in his arms, burrowing into his sweatshirt. But it did not stay there, clearly too energetic. It leapt up and licked Nate in the face, dark eyes sparkling playfully. Its long, wispy tail swung fervently as its abnormally large paws danced on Nate's chest.

"It's okay, boy," Nate said, rubbing the dog's ears, which had thin, wispy hairs at the tips like a Chihuahua's.

He inspected for a collar, but the dog did not have one.

"Are you a runaway?" Nate wondered aloud.

As though in reply, the tiny dog let out a booming bark disproportionate to its size. It made Nate chuckle.

"Boomer," Nate said, naming the dog as though it was his own.

Boomer the dog let out another blast of a bark, wagging its tail and nuzzling against him.

Nate smiled, holding the dog close. It surely belonged to someone, but he would keep it safe for now.

No longer distracted by his new friend, Nate looked out at the storm. If possible, the hail was coming down even harder. The dread that had filled him before—that no one knew where he was—returned. There was no end in sight to this storm, and it would only take a breeze to push the hail sideways and under the sagebrush Nate and Boomer were hiding beneath.

Nate's mind raced, weighing his options. He needed to get home, but not at the risk of being cut into Nate-linguini. He bruised easily and his brittle bones wouldn't stand a chance against a peewee football player, let alone a flurry of hail. Perhaps he should wait.

Boomer barked, turning to look at the hail too.

Do something, Nate insisted to himself, but he remained rooted to the spot.

If only his father were here, he wished longingly, then they would already be back home, safe and sound. But on his own, Nate was just a scared kid, terrified of broken bones.

5

Natalie Harper jarred awake to the blare of her alarm. She silenced it and pulled herself out of the covers. Her bedroom was dimly lit from light streaming through the piles of snow covering the window.

Today was the day.

Somehow, Natalie felt more hollow than usual. Without a single feeling of elation, fear, or contemplation, she acknowledged she would be flying to Hawaii and married in a few more days. As though these upcoming events were as common as brushing her teeth, she made her bed and took a shower without a smile or second thought. After dressing in blue jeans and a light orange sweater, she glanced in the mirror. As always, her frame was lean but feminine. She was thin and starved because she didn't eat properly, but she made up for it with routine workouts. Her blonde hair looked thin from lack of nutrition, so she tied it up in a bun. Her face was gaunt.

She found her eyes. The pupil was an abyss of apathy, the iris a drain. She could see steeliness in there too, determination to keep everything hidden.

Often, Cori said that eyes were the window to the soul, but Natalie did not have a soul whole enough to be seen through her eyes. She knew she was broken inside, but dwelling on it would allow emotions to filter in. Natalie was better than that. She was strong. She was fearless. She was Natalie Harper.

With a nod at her reflection, she carried on. Half an hour later, Natalie grabbed her luggage and walked out the door—right into a foot of snow. She charged through it to her car, which was up to its wheels in snowdrifts. In a matter of minutes, she had cleared a path to the plowed streets and headed off to Cori and Evan's apartment.

As Natalie wound her way down the icy streets, she realized the sky was filled with clouds. The city of Reno itself lay in a valley between the Sierra Nevada Mountains to the west and the Virginia Range to the east, and clouds filled the skies above from mountaintop to mountaintop. The sun was hidden behind them, though it must have been trying to poke through, because the clouds were shining in places.

Whap!

A snowball plastered Natalie's windshield. She tapped the brakes, putting the car into a skid. As she slid past, she glared at the kids that had thrown the snowball. Her gaze must have been severe—the perpetrator dropped his other snowball and watched Natalie slide by with an open mouth.

A prickle of annoyance ran through Natalie, but she didn't let it last. She submerged it as she pulled out of the slide and turned on the radio.

"...hail reported north of Reno in Sun Valley this morning," the radio blared. "Cloud cover predicted all day and through the week. Snow showers seem probable. In other news, a historic storm front has made its way across the contiguous United States—"

Suddenly, the announcer's voice was cut off by the piercing sounds of an emergency broadcast. Shrill whistles and screeches filled the speakers, finally breaking after a minute.

"This is a message from the Emergency Broadcast system," an electronic voice declared. "A large storm system will be moving into your area in the next few minutes. Heavy precipitation is expected. Move to high ground and take immediate steps to secure personal property and your life. Affected areas include Washoe County, Lyon County, Pershing County…"

Natalie began to tune out the broadcast. She turned her mind to Mark and Hawaii, rehearsing how to act, what to say, and when to do so during the wedding to demonstrate her affection properly.

By the time Natalie skid to a stop at Cori's apartment building, the clock was ticking to get to the airport. They were supposed to be two hours early to get through security, but the ice on the road was testing Natalie's skills to get them there with a little more than an hour.

Cori got into the passenger seat and gave Natalie a hug.

"Today's the day!" Cori shouted, her last word becoming more of a scream as Natalie slammed the accelerator and made the car fishtail across the road.

"Not if we don't make it to the airport," Natalie replied, tapping the clock on the radio.

"Keep up with your illegal driving maneuvers," Cori replied, "and we won't."

"Don't worry," Natalie assured her, "ice won't stop us."

"A car crash might," Cori retorted.

Ignoring her, Natalie put the pedal to the metal, fishtailing down the road and toward the interstate.

6

Nate Matician had no idea how long he stayed curled under the sagebrush with Boomer before the hailstorm began to lessen. Minutes crept by and the storm dwindled to no more than harmless sleet.

No longer scared stiff, Nate extricated himself from the sagebrush. Boomer followed Nate as they ran back through the brush toward the neighborhood. Despite Nate's best efforts to have the dog go to its own home, it followed him into the streets leading to Grandma Dottie's. The longer Boomer followed him, the more Nate figured he might as well keep the dog.

Nate stuck to the sides of the street shaded by trees. He hoped it didn't start hailing again, but if it did, the tall pines and firs would protect him long enough to find shelter.

Nervously, he glanced up at the sky. The clouds from the hailstorm had not dissipated, but had gotten thicker. They looked fit to burst open and seemed to be shining.

How in the world? Nate wondered before tripping over a piece of hail the size of Boomer.

Nate caught himself from falling and turned his gaze back to the road. He needed to keep an eye out so he didn't trip again.

A few minutes later, he came around the street corner. Grandma Dottie's one-story retirement home came into view. The station wagon was parked in the driveway, luggage tied to the top. As Nate got closer, he realized that his brother and sister were in the back seats of the car. His grandmother was running around, tightening the straps holding down the luggage.

"Grandma Dottie?" Nate shouted. "What's going on?"

His grandmother spun around, her eyes wide and frantic.

"Nate!" she shouted, pulling him into a hug and kissing the top of his head. "Thank God!"

"What's going on?" he asked. Boomer panted at his side and smiled at the grandmother.

"Your mother called," Grandma Dottie answered, glancing at the cloud-filled sky. "Your father is in trouble and we need to get out of here."

She knelt around him and threw a jacket over his shoulders.

"We're leaving?" Nate said, not believing the words. "Are we in danger? Where are we going?"

Grandma Dottie, the stern woman she was, only said, "Hawaii. Now come on, child. Get in the car."

She paused, looking past Nate.

"Who's your new friend?" she asked.

"Boomer," replied Nate. The dog let out a booming bark of approval.

"Oh, he might as well stow away too," Grandma Dottie said as she pet the dog's ears. "For the time being, anyhow."

With that, Boomer jumped into the back of the car with Nate's siblings, Bethany and Wyatt. Nate sat in the front passenger seat as Grandma Dottie got into the driver's seat. They pulled out of the driveway quickly, shocks groaning as the tires bounced over the hail.

As they drove, Grandma Dottie leaned forward and looked up into the sky. Nate followed her gaze. The clouds were unnaturally dark, the grey hue of a rhino. As before, there was something shiny in the clouds, perhaps the sun breaking through or the beginnings of lightning. But no, it wasn't anything like that, Nate realized. It appeared as though the shimmers were within the clouds, constantly moving like a mirage over hot asphalt.

"Oh, my dears," Grandma Dottie said in a grave tone, "I'm afraid we're too late."

She pulled the car to a stop, staring up. Nate wanted to tell her to keep driving, but he was enraptured with the weather.

As he watched, the shining mirage hovered a moment longer and then the clouds erupted. Dark striations descended toward the earth, indicative of heavy rainfall. He wasn't sure if he was seeing things, but Nate could have sworn the rain looked silver.

7

Natalie Harper applied the emergency brake to slide onto the interstate. The lanes ahead ran thick with vehicles like a vein pumping metal.

Over the radio, the news continued. Natalie noted subconsciously that she hadn't heard any music since turning it on.

"The cloud coverage stretches coast to coast," a man said over the radio. "It… Hold on. We're getting reports that the storm clouds are beginning to precipitate."

Cori leaned forward, hands still clasped tightly on the seat as she looked up at the clouds through the windshield.

"I think you've made me sick," Cori said. "Clouds don't normally shine, do they?"

Holding the wheel steady, Natalie leaned forward too. Sure enough, just as she had seen earlier, the clouds were twinkling as though alight with a million far-off stars.

"Natalie, watch out!" Cori screamed suddenly.

Natalie jerked the wheel instinctively as her head snapped forward. She barely missed the backend of a pickup truck as she swerved into the shoulder of the interstate. Holding steady, Natalie slowed her car and guided it back into the lane behind the truck. Her heart pounded in her chest. She had almost hit the concrete barrier like her mother before her.

"Natalie Harper," Cori began, but her reprimands were cut short by a loud *splat!*

Natalie's eyes snapped to the source of the sound. A thick, fat raindrop had landed on the windshield, but it wasn't a normal raindrop. It was silver, shining bright as chrome.

The drop of silver trickled like liquid down the windshield and then, impossibly, fell through the glass and landed on the dashboard.

"What the heck?" Natalie said aloud.

The dj on the radio was saying something similar, blaring through the speakers of the car.

Cori stared at the dashboard too, reaching forward to touch the silver raindrop. Before she could, the silver drop had absorbed into the dashboard and disappeared from sight.

Splat! Splat!

All at once, the whole world was rumbling with the sound of falling rain like bullets on rapid fire. The roof above their head pounded with the sound.

Natalie turned her eyes back to the road. Her windshield was covered in streaks of silver. Beyond, more rain was coming down with increasing intensity, a world of shimmering liquid metal. Through the windshield and silver streaks, Natalie could see the rain falling everywhere, thick as syrup and shrouding the interstate. Vehicles were being covered in blankets of lead. The road shimmered too like a river of mercury, but soon Natalie couldn't even see that. The windshield and side windows were covered in streams of silver that were starting to leak through.

Over the radio, there was a sharp squeal of reverberation, and the speakers were filled with static.

Suddenly, a splash of rain fell on Natalie's arm. Surprised, she glanced down at it. A drop of silver rain ran down her arm and dripped onto her pants leg.

Another drop landed, this one on her forehead. Then another on her driving hand. Suddenly, rain was pouring down on her as though the rooftop was made of melting ice. Within seconds, her clothes were drenched.

"Leak!" Cori shouted, holding her hands up to the rooftop. She was covered in rain too, her clothes and skin shimmering silver.

Natalie tried to wipe the silver raindrops off of her hand, but it spread like mud, filling in her pores and creases.

Light in the cabin diminished. Cori was yelling, trying to wipe the silver away. Her actions became slower until she slumped forward, unconscious.

Suddenly, Natalie remembered they were still driving. She slammed on the brakes. Through the silver-smeared windshield, she could barely see the red flash of brakes ahead of them, too close for comfort. Her heart leapt as she realized the brake lights were only a few feet ahead—it was the pickup truck and she was going to hit it.

She slammed on the brakes harder. The tires squealed and suddenly, they were hydroplaning on the silver rain. She closed her eyes, pressing the brakes with all her might, hoping they would stop.

They hit the pickup truck suddenly and swiftly. The impact pitched Natalie forward, jarring every bone in her back; the seatbelt cut into her shoulder and hip. Through squinted eyes, she saw Cori gyrating like a rag doll. Silver rain was still falling in the cabin like a fire sprinkler spraying in a building. Her head smacked against the steering wheel just as the airbag erupted out of it. The inflating bag pushed her back, and her head slammed on the headrest. In an instant, the world of silver went dark.

8

Natalie was back at the red road. Her collar bone was snapped in two like a wishbone. Her legs were pinned by the car's collapsed dashboard. Unbridled fear spread through her body, making her nauseous and dizzy. Her mother sat unconscious, or perhaps still asleep, in the driver's seat. Crimson blood leaked from her, staining the deflated air bag and dripping—ping-ping-ping—into the road. The memory of their day at the doctor's office was long gone.

Straining against her pinned legs, Natalie tried to escape. No matter how hard she pushed on the dash, she could not free her legs.

"Mom!" she screamed again, trying desperately to wake her.

Her mother had been born with narcolepsy. Usually, she slowly drifted off to sleep at inopportune times. Never before had her mother fallen asleep so quickly, so abruptly. One second she had been talking to Natalie, the next, Rose had passed out.

"Mom, please," Natalie pleaded.

At last, her mother awoke. She gasped in pain as she sat up.

Her glittering eyes passed over Natalie and she began to cry.

"My dear girl," Rose whispered, her voice raspy and weak. "I'm so sorry. I should have known…"

"Are you okay?" Natalie asked, not caring about apologies.

Her mother nodded, but she looked to be in unbearable pain. Her face creased in agony.

"I'm coming, Mom," Natalie said. "I'll get you out."

"No," her mother rasped. "Stay where you are. You may be hurt worse than you think."

"I'm fine," Natalie insisted. "You need help."

Suddenly, Natalie heard sirens far away. Help was coming, but she feared it would not be fast enough for her mother.

"Stay where you are, child," her mother said. "Remember what I taught you. Do as I told you."

Natalie did not listen. She could not just sit here, trapped, and watch her mother die. She had already lost her father in a firefighting accident. She would not lose her mother too. As Natalie searched to undo her seatbelt, she heard a strange wheeze. Before she could inspect, the air was filled with smoke. Flames poked out from the car hood.

"Mom!" Natalie cried.

"Stay where you are," her mother cried back. "Don't hurt yourself!"

PHASE 3
STICKY SITUATIONS

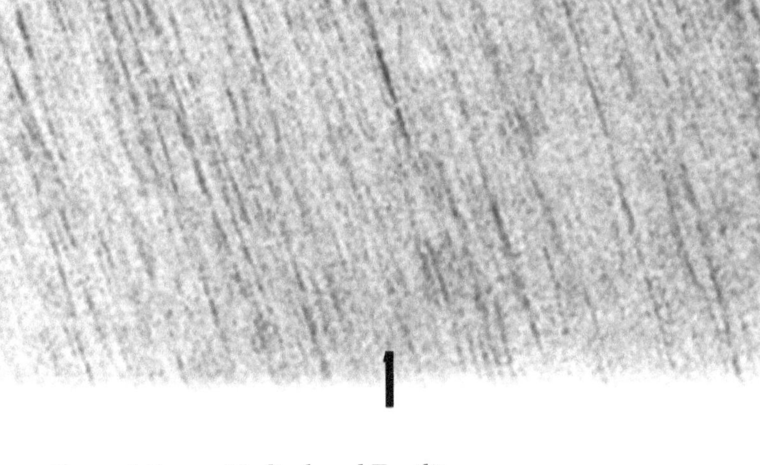

1

One by one, the televisions went offline. Dr. Griffith "The Griffin" Avazino grinned, barring his teeth. He clenched the vial of silver in his pocket, feeling it vibrate in his hands. At long last, his creation had been released.

An hour before, each television had been covering the impending storm that no climatologist, weather forecaster, or newscaster could properly explain. Now, several screens were replaced with rainbow bars or network failure notifications. A few featured empty news desks, the background streaked with silver rain. Another television, one of the few stations still functioning, showed a weather map of North America. A cloud covered the middle part of the continent. Alaska, Canada, and Mexico were largely unaffected. Hawaii was not on the map, a safe zone where Matician and the Griffin had been working.

The hum of the nuclear reactor had long since quieted down. The Griffin still stood by the hollow tube where he had been for a few hours, observing the televisions. When necessary, he had bludgeoned Brian Matician to keep the puny man from running off or attacking.

In fact, this very moment, as he had every few minutes, Brian stumbled to his feet and made a pathetic attempt at rushing the Griffin. He scrambled forward, wrapping his small arms around the Griffin's torso. The Griffin thought he saw Matician reach a hand out toward the red button on the control panel.

With large, gruff hands, the Griffin grabbed Matician's shirt collar, lifted him off his feet, and slammed him against the computer server towers. Matician groaned in pain.

"Foolish little degenerate," the Griffin said haughtily. "The EMP was deactivated in case anyone got a conscience."

"You mean if someone decided to set things right," Matician shouted. Spittle dotted the Griffin's face.

"What was your plan then?" the Griffin replied. "Activate the EMP that can only extend fifteen miles in any direction? The nanobytes are far beyond your reach now. The end is nigh."

The Griffin felt Matician deflate beneath his hold. He looked weak and decrepit. It sickened the Griffin, who had been hoping for a better fight.

"You disgust me," the Griffin growled. "You degenerates with your broken bodies and brittle bones."

"We're stronger than you know," spat Matician.

"Funny," the Griffin replied. "I didn't think it took much to break you."

The Griffin grabbed Matician's right arm with both hands and, easy as breaking noodles in half to fit into a saucepan, he snapped Matician's arm. A jagged piece of bone ruptured through the skin, cutting through the shirt. Blood squirted out, spattering the Griffin's clothes.

Matician screeched, falling against the towers.

"God said that if your hand should sin, to cut it off," said the Griffin. "You are responsible for ending your own race. Your hand may as well have pushed that button. May I remove it for you?"

The Griffin grabbed Matician's arm again.

"No!" Matician screamed, trying to pull out of the Griffin's grasp.

The Griffin held Matician's arm tightly, whispering in his ear with disgust.

"You are weak," the Griffin spat. "Decrepit. Disgusting. And now…the last of your kind. I'm not going to kill you. Not yet. First you will watch your family die."

The Griffin pulled sharply. There was a sickening, wet pop. Matician screamed and crumpled to the ground, his arm dislocated from his shoulder.

Cackling and satisfied he had crippled Matician for a significant amount of time, the Griffin turned his attention back to the television monitors on the wall. Not much had changed, but he could not resist watching. He had to see this all unfold.

Scanning the television monitors, the Griffin wished time would pass faster so he could see the unfolding chaos. Right now, everyone would be unconscious, thanks to the airborne anesthesia. But soon, they would begin to wake up. The decrepit would stumble into the streets, decaying on the spot, silver mites burrowing into their skulls. Their bloody deaths would be the chrysalis that let the nation be born anew, shed of its limitations and defects. Just like the senator had wanted. Just like the Griffin had wanted.

The Griffin scanned the televisions again, finding one of interest. Two people lay face down on a news desk. Their skin was covered in silver, but as the Griffin watched, the silver absorbed into their skin. Within seconds, the two people looked normal and they began to stir. Their fingers flexed and muscles twitched.

Suddenly, a hand reached up from below the screen and grabbed onto the camera lens. The camera was pulled down into the ground and cut to a multi-bar emergency signal.

The Griffin smiled to himself, chuckling. It had worked. The horror was about to begin.

"And on the eighth day, God destroyed His imperfections," the Griffin growled to himself.

This day had been a long time coming. The Griffin had been working on the nanobytes for near a decade with no care for the sacrifices. There had been hiccups along the way, and he had unfortunately needed Brian Matician's foremost knowledge on climatology, but he was here now. His work had finally come to fruition.

The Griffin's phone rang and he answered without a word, waiting for the senator to speak.

"The hotel has been evacuated," said the senator. "People run fast when you say there is a compromised nuclear reactor on the island."

"They won't live long enough on the mainland to care," the Griffin replied. "Did you find Silverman?"

"Nowhere to be found. We believe he left in the early hours to explore the island."

"What a shame," the Griffin replied.

"Was the launch successful?"

The Griffin answered in the affirmative, which made the senator swoon.

"Congratulations, Dr. Avazino," said the senator jovially. "I'll give a report when I make it back to the mainland."

The senator hung up.

Ordinarily, the Griffin would have killed a man like the senator at the first opportunity. But the Griffin owed the senator a debt for freeing him from jail. For that, the Griffin allowed the senator to leave the island alive.

Reveling in satisfaction, the Griffin turned his gaze back to Matician. He lay fidgeting on the ground, cradling his broken arm. In the minutes the Griffin had been distracted, Matician had put a tourniquet around his arm and slowed the bleeding. There was a strange bulge around the shoulder where it had dislocated.

"The last of your kind," the Griffin said. "The betrayer of your own man. How does it feel to fail?"

Matician looked up at the Griffin with a contemptuous glare not fit for such a little man.

"No," the scientist gasped, "you are the failure. I have bested you."

The Griffin studied Matician. This was not contempt or hatred. Matician looked victorious.

Realization struck the Griffin in an instant.

Matician had done something.

He spun around. The button for the EMP was not lit. It was still deactivated. Mind racing to the next option, the Griffin scrambled to the computing station. He logged in and surveyed the algorithms.

The primary directive had been negated.

Another equation, the seeker directive, had been inversed. There was another, the incendiary directive, which had been improperly inversed. With all his wit and intellect, the Griffin could not interpret the revised algorithm's effects.

"What have you done?!" the Griffin cried.

In a fit of rage, he punched the screen of the computing station. Its screen exploded into shards of glass. He retrieved the cruelest shard, which would yield the most agony before dulling. But when he turned around, ready to torture Matician until he squealed, the scientist was gone.

Infuriated, the Griffin strode to the exit of the control room. He yelled loudly into the tunnel, hoping Matician heard. The Griffin shut the door behind him and stalked into the vast underground labyrinth, gripping the glass shard until it was slick with red.

The hunt was afoot and the Griffin would not rest until he tasted Matician's blood.

2

A second after Mark Hofland jumped on his bike, the clouds above started to pour thick, clear raindrops. In a second, he was drenched, faster perhaps than if he had taken a shower. The humidity of the air became thick, making it hard to breathe.

Only a few feet ahead of Mark, Evan and the rest of the bike troupe disappeared in a sheen of rain. Unable to see where the road led, Mark applied the brakes cautiously. His tires slid and he skid toward the edge.

For a heart-stopping second, Mark could see over the edge of the road, which overlooked a lush, steep mountainside dotted with ivy green vegetation. Dark silhouettes of palm trees danced in the wind. Across the valley, shrouded in the rainfall, was a steep cliffside of another mountain. It was a startlingly beautiful sight and one that Mark did not want to become part of.

He leaned hard to the right and let off the brakes, praying for the bike to turn. The tires squealed, and he turned away from the edge, but now he was picking up speed again.

Mark scanned ahead frantically for Evan and the other bikers. They weren't in sight. He glanced back, and there was no one behind him either. He was alone.

He half-considered stopping, but did not dare press on the brakes again, for fear of hydroplaning and flying off the side of the mountain.

Suddenly, the road turned and began to decline steeply. Rain spattered Mark's face, making it difficult to see. The high winds and humidity made it difficult to even drag a breath in.

A dark mass, like an oblong oval, suddenly materialized out of the precipitation. It was at least half a football field ahead.

Mark tapped his brakes tentatively, tempting his bike to slide.

He sped at the growing mass, not knowing how to stop. The large mass became clearer at the last second: it was the group of bikers, stopped on the side of the road.

Mark slammed on the brakes now, skidding broadside. The yellow-clad group braced for impact.

One of the bikers lunged at Mark—he saw at the last second that it was Evan—and clotheslined Mark off his bike. The air was knocked out of Mark's lungs as he flew back and hit the ground. Pain shot through his tailbone and elbows.

Body aching, Mark gasped for breath as he lay on the slick, wet asphalt. His body throbbed in pain where Evan had hit him and where he had hit the ground. Rain fell steadily, pooling in Mark's eyes and along his yellow jumpsuit.

Staring up into the grey storm clouds and rain, Mark took a quick assessment of his body. Deciding everything was still attached and that he did not yet need a breath from his inhaler, Mark got gingerly to his feet. His yellow jumpsuit had torn open on the pavement. He could see crimson blood trickling from his elbow.

"Glad you could join us," Evan said, wiping mud and leaves from his own jumpsuit.

"My pleasure," Mark breathed.

One of the other bikers had grabbed Mark's bike and returned it to him. Mark thanked them and glanced around. The majority of the troupe of bike riders seemed to be here, all of them drenched to the bone and holding on tightly to their bikes and loved ones.

Danny approached Mark.

"Where are the others?" asked Danny.

Mark shook his head, unsure where the bikers behind him had gone.

"Where is the bike leader?" Mark asked in return, scanning the group.

"Lost sight of him in the storm," Danny replied. He stared at Mark for a second and scowled. "What, you think I lost him on purpose?"

Before Mark could say anything, Evan cut in.

"Knock it off, Danny," Evan said loudly. "We need to find shelter or get off this mountain."

Mark nodded. This was a pretty bad situation, but certainly one Hawaiians had been through before. Someone had to have a good idea—a place for shelter or a quick way to get down the mountain.

As he suspected, several people began throwing out ideas. Some recommended finding palm trees and building a shelter. Others suggested riding their bikes the rest of the way down the mountain. Evan suggested waiting for the other bikers who had been behind Mark, because one of them had been a tour guide and might know what to do.

"Where are the vans that dropped us off?" Mark asked.

"Gone," said one of the bike riders. "They go down the mountain another way."

Great, Mark thought.

He sighed. A gob of phlegm came loose and flew into his mouth. He spat onto the ground and sucked in a big breath, mentally cursing his cystic fibrosis.

Out of the corner of his eye, Mark saw Danny giving him a disgusted look.

Ignoring him, Mark turned to Evan.

"Thanks for the brake check," he said.

"Lucky you don't have brittle bones," Evan replied. "That fall nearly snapped us in two." He looked up into the storm. "A rainstorm. Who would have thunk…"

"Thunk?" Mark asked.

"Past tense of thought," responded Evan.

"Thought is already past tense."

Evan gave Mark a bemused look.

"It's raining cats and dogs while we're on a mountaintop with no clear way of getting back safe and you're trying to think logically?"

"At least I don't think I thunk."

"But you thought you thunk of thinking—"

"Will you two shut up!"

Evan and Mark snapped to attention. Danny was staring them down, his face furled in a prissy frown. He glared at them for a moment before mounting his bike.

"What are you doing?" Evan asked incredulously.

"We're riding down," Danny replied.

"You can't—" Mark began to say, waving his hands at the weather cascading down around them. But before he could finish, one of the other riders fell down. The rider, a little girl with Down's syndrome, hit the ground and burst into tears.

Mark hurried over to her, helping the little girl to her feet.

"It's okay," Mark told her, brushing mud and twigs away from a cut on her knee.

Danny scowled at Mark and the girl.

"Are you two planning on staying?" Danny asked coldly, still mounted on his bike.

"This is crazy, Danny," Mark replied. "We can't ride bikes in this. Someone will slip and fall and get hurt."

"It's not my fault you're not brave enough," Danny said. "Degenerate."

It was the excuse Mark had been waiting for to finally knock some sense into Danny. He lunged, blood boiling, and punched Danny off his bike. Danny hit the ground hard, but was back on his feet in a flash, inches from Mark's face.

"Touch me again, degenerate," Danny dared threateningly.

"We stay together," Mark insisted for the whole group to hear. "If we go, we walk. If we stay, we make shelter. No matter what, we all stay together."

"You won't make it a hundred steps," Danny said so only Mark could hear him. "I can hear you choking on your own spit. You'll be dead by the time we get back."

Danny glared at Mark a moment longer, rain dotting their faces. Then, Danny turned away, and marched off into the rain. The bikers began to follow him, some dropping their bikes and others pulling them along halfheartedly.

Mark watched Danny go, breathing hard and coughing a little.

"You okay?" Evan asked.

Mark grunted and took a puff from his inhaler, but only a small burst of medicine was released. He shook it and tried again. Hardly anything came out.

Evan stared at Mark a moment longer, a look of concern crossing his high cheekbones.

"Don't," Mark warned.

Together, they began to walk after the group. Mark forced himself to breathe deeply, but the thick air felt like he was breathing through a wet cloth. His lungs were on fire and mucus began to accumulate in the back of his mouth.

Mark shook his inhaler again, but he knew it was useless. He was out of medicine and a long way from home.

He thought desperately of Natalie. As he often did, he wondered what she would do if she were in his shoes. Perhaps a reflection of his own trials, he felt as though Natalie was also in danger, and would be struggling down this volcano right along with him.

3

Nate Matician woke with a start. His vision was blurry for a second. He blinked repeatedly until the world came into focus. Slowly but surely, he realized he was still in the passenger seat of the station wagon. Everything seemed to be the same—Grandma Dottie was in the driver's seat, his siblings in the back with Boomer, and Nate buckled into the passenger seat.

Outside the car, though, was completely different. The world was quiet and clear of rain. The streets glistened with hail, but there was no evidence that silver rain had fallen from the sky. Clouds above separated, revealing a sun high in the sky, yellow and vibrant. Nothing on the earth moved, not even the trees.

For a second, Nate thought he had fallen asleep. But he was positive: moments before, maybe seconds or maybe hours, silver rain had fallen from the sky. Somehow, it had permeated the metal roof of the car. In seconds, Nate had been covered in silver-colored rain. His vision had clouded and he had felt woozy. Before he had lost consciousness completely, he had felt a peculiar sensation of water running off of his fingertips. He had seen the silver liquid running off him, wicking away as though it was oil and he was water. Then, he had fallen asleep.

Now, though, he was awake. The silver was gone. Not a speck of it was left outside or on his body. His skin felt sticky and cold, as though the silver rain had been made of frozen soda.

He glanced over at Grandma Dottie. She was hunched over the steering wheel, unconscious. There was no silver on her either.

A whine issued from behind Nate. He turned to see Boomer sitting beside Nate's siblings, Wyatt and Bethany. Boomer was staring at Bethany, his wispy tail still and ears low.

When Nate saw Bethany, he gasped. His sister was glistening, dots of silver embedded in her pores. Wrinkles and creases across her body had collected the liquid silver.

Hardly breathing and fearing the worst, Nate looked over to his baby brother. But Wyatt was fine. The baby was sound asleep in his car seat. Like Grandma Dottie and Nate, there wasn't a speck of silver on him.

Nate's eyes snapped back to Bethany. The silver was absorbing into her pores and disappearing from sight.

"Grandma?" Nate asked quietly. His voice was high and terrified.

His grandmother stirred awake. She looked around. After glancing at Nate, Bethany, and Wyatt, she looked out the windshield, surveying the outside world.

"What's happening, Grandma?" Nate asked.

"I have no idea, my child," she said.

"B–Bethany still had that silver stuff on her when I woke up," Nate stammered.

Eyes wide, Grandma Dottie turned in her seat and grabbed Bethany's knee. She shook her.

"Wake up, dear," she said. Nate had never heard such anxiety in his grandmother's voice before.

Boomer growled at Bethany and then barked.

Bethany's eyes snapped open. Her whole body went rigid and her hands clenched into fists. Her pupils were dilated and flitted between Nate and Grandma Dottie. Her eyes paused on each of them as though processing their identities. Nate could hardly believe it, but the pupils of Bethany's eyes were no longer black. Pinpricks of silver floated in the black, swirling like a miniature snow globe.

"Bethany?" said Grandma Dottie, her voice shaky. "Are you alright, dear?"

Suddenly, Bethany let out a rasping noise. Her hands jumped to her throat and she went bug-eyed. The blood vessels in her neck engorged as she wheezed.

"She's choking!" Nate cried.

"Nathaniel!" Grandma Dottie yelled warningly.

Even as his grandma yelled for him to stop, Nate jumped back toward Bethany to help her. In the same instant, Bethany lunged too. She grabbed his arm and yanked him hard, pulling him out of his seat and stretching him over the middle console. Her hand was cold as ice and ruthlessly tight.

Lightning fast, she grabbed Nate's hair, fingernails scrapping his scalp. She lifted his head up, muscles tightening, fingers clenching gobs of hair. His head was over the backend of the seat console, a rounded plastic edge.

Nate screamed for her to stop. Grandma Dottie was yelling too. Boomer barked. But beyond it all, Nate could hear Bethany. She wasn't wheezing anymore; he doubted she had truly been choking.

Instead, with glittering eyes locked on him, she was whispering, "Smash, smash, smash."

4

Natalie Harper jerked awake. She blinked several times, but the world around her was blurry. Her senses seemed dulled as though her brain had been filled with a noxious gas.

Trying to shake the sensation, Natalie closed her eyes.

What have I done? she wondered. She had been so distracted by the enigmatic silver rain, she had gotten into a car accident. Cori was probably severely injured, or worse.

Suddenly, in the pit of Natalie's stomach, she felt a familiar sensation. She knew it well. She had felt it on the red road and tried to deny it every time she saw the chair in Dr. Cruze's office. It was an emotion, a powerful one, and one she refused to feel.

She pushed the feeling away. Now was not the time.

To distract herself, she turned her mind to the rain. She had never seen silver rain before, not even the pleasant type Toby had told her about. Nor had Natalie ever seen rain that could permeate the metal and upholstery roof of a car.

As she thought, Natalie realized how quiet it was. The rainstorm must have passed, and she could not hear any car alarms, screams of agony, or sounds of distress. Worst of all, she couldn't hear any breathing.

For a terrible moment, Natalie feared she had killed Cori.

Natalie could practically see the scene unfolding in her head. She would open her eyes and find Cori leaning against the dashboard, scarlet blood staining the airbag. Natalie would cry out, no longer able to contain the emotions bubbling up within her. She would struggle to escape, her flesh tearing. That feeling of hopelessness would return: utter dread and knowing there was nothing—absolutely nothing—she could do.

The pressure in her gut intensified and she squeezed her eyes tighter. She could not succumb. Not now. If Cori was indeed injured, Natalie must do all she could to help her.

Natalie forced herself to open her eyes, expecting to see a silver-coated world with blotches of crimson blood. Yet the world was eerily normal. Her body was intact, down to her pale skin. Her orange sweater and concealing blue jeans were clean, free of blood and silver rain.

She looked around. Through the windshield, she could see dwindling storm clouds and the wide blacktop of the interstate. Directly in front of her was the pickup truck, sitting on her car. Her hood was crumpled underneath the hitch. Something seemed off, but Natalie could not quite place it, and there were more pressing things to worry about: Cori.

Not yet strong enough to look, Natalie shielded the car's radio to read the time. She had been unconscious for about two hours. Looking at the radio, she realized that nothing was coming over the car speakers. There was no static, just dead air.

From the corner of her eye, Natalie saw Cori. She was slumped against her seatbelt. She wasn't moving.

Steeling her mind in determination, Natalie forced herself to look at Cori. Her neck was slow and stiff from the fresh whiplash of the crash.

Cori hung like a ragdoll against her seatbelt. Her eyes were closed and dried blood matted her forehead.

Natalie reached over and propped her friend up, searching for a pulse.

"Come on, Cori," Natalie insisted.

Natalie pressed hard into Cori's throat and finally found a pulse. Unexpectedly, the bubbling feeling in her stomach fled and she felt her face break into a smile.

All at once, the radio came to life with a sharp, shrill whistle. Cori jerked awake, her head spinning this way and that. Natalie sat back, completely relieved and not even caring she was feeling emotions.

The sounds on the radio continued, clicking and beeping, finally turning into the recognizable sounds of an emergency broadcast. Natalie spun the radio dial to lower the volume, but the tones were still piercing.

"Cori!" Natalie cried, and she began to smile even more. "Are you okay?"

Cori did not immediately respond. Her hands searched her body, gingerly touching her bloody hairline before travelling to her collar bone, where the skin had been chaffed by the seatbelt.

"I think so," Cori said. "Are you?"

"I have no idea," Natalie replied, urging herself to stop smiling, but she could not. She was elated Cori was alive. It was a queer feeling, one she had long forgotten.

The emergency alert's piercing tones kept going, drilling into Natalie's ears despite the low volume. Fed up with it, Natalie turned the volume down the rest of the way so the tones were a whisper in the background.

Cori was rubbing her hands together.

"My skin is sticky," she said.

Cori reached over, slowly and stiffly, and felt Natalie's arm.

"So is yours," she said. "It's like a residue from the rain. You know, like salt from the ocean?"

"Salt doesn't make rain turn silver," Natalie said. "Could be metal. You know, like toxic rain from pollution?"

"Toxic rain is silver?" Cori asked, looking confused.

"At least it's gone," Natalie said, still trying to stop smiling.

Cori leaned forward, peering out the windshield. Her eyes traveled from the partly-cloudy sky down to the pickup truck in front of them.

"Oh my goodness," Cori said.

Natalie followed her gaze, and suddenly realized why the outside world had seemed so eerie.

The world beyond the windshield was still as a cadaver.

No one was moving. Every car on the interstate was stopped. To their right, the airport was still as ice, frozen in time with every plane stalled.

The pickup truck kissing Natalie's front bumper was sedentary too. The driver and passenger sat stock still in their vehicle.

Shoot, Natalie thought.

Unable to sit and watch, Natalie unclipped her seatbelt, taking care to move slowly in case she was injured. She opened the door and got out of the car.

From the moment she stepped outside, the world came back to life. As though her senses had been dulled and then reawakened, the world became full of sounds, smells, and sights.

The outside air was unnervingly quiet and smelled like iodine. Faint echoes of the emergency broadcast issued from the stalled cars along the interstate. The air seemed to buzz in tension.

Faint at first, the whine of an accelerator reached Natalie's ear. She scanned the roads, finally seeing the source. Perhaps a mile down the interstate, Natalie saw a car driving away quickly. Within seconds, the car was gone. All of the other cars remained still, idling and emitting shrill beeps from their radios.

Another sound reached Natalie's ears, one that took a moment to recognize. It was the distant crackle of a fire. She scanned the roads—none of the cars were alight. Her eyes continued traveling, glancing over the airport, until she found the source in the meadows around the airport. Perhaps a mile away, on the far side of the tarmac, Natalie could make out the destroyed remnants of a crashed airplane. She could see a broken wing amid the flames. The wreck looked catastrophically terrible. Police or ambulance services were nowhere in sight.

She spun around, taking in the surroundings. There was another fire on the western hills, perhaps another airplane or an accident. Some homes were issuing black smoke. Nonetheless, Natalie was struck by the utter calm of the world. There was not a plane in the sky, not a car on the move. It was dead quiet and dead still.

A groan issued from behind Natalie. Cori was trying to stand, but doubled over in pain, hands rubbing her chest.

"It's okay," Natalie said reassuringly. "I'll—"

Before Natalie could finish, the world's eerie quiet was shattered by a harrowing scream.

Natalie spun toward the sound. It seemed to have come from further down the interstate. The shriek lasted a terrifying second and ended. A few seconds later, a car alarm started.

"Stay in the car," Natalie said without looking back.

Senses on high alert, Natalie walked slowly and cautiously toward the pickup truck. She kept glancing up the interstate, looking for the source of the screaming, but no one was out there.

Once beside the pickup truck, Natalie peered in. The driver and passenger sat stock still. There wasn't any blood.

She knocked, causing the driver to stir. His head spun to the right and left quickly, looking from his passenger to Natalie.

Relieved, she tried the door handle, but it was locked. With a forced smile, she gestured for the driver to open the door.

The driver unlocked the door slowly, not looking away from Natalie, and opened it. The door creaked open.

Another scream echoed down the road. It was cut short by a wet smack. Then there was another wet smack, and another.

"Are you okay?" Natalie asked the driver, hair standing up on the back of her neck.

"Yes," the driver said firmly. He was an older man in denim and plaid with a drinker's gut.

Fumbling, he undid his seatbelt and half-stumbled, half-slid out of the driver's seat.

"Easy, easy," Natalie said, catching the driver instinctually.

The driver was heavier than expected. Natalie stumbled under his weight, but the driver was pressing against her now. They fell back, landing hard on the pavement. Hands wrapped around her neck. Natalie gasped for a breath, trying to understand as the driver's fingers gripped tightly around her windpipe.

Fighting against his grip, Natalie found the driver's face. He was licking his lips. His eyes were cold and vacant of humanity, silver specks flashing in the pupil. There was something strikingly familiar about his eyes that pierced Natalie to the core, but she could not consider it long. She fought to break the man's grip on her throat, pushing, punching, prying. Her fingernails tore into the flesh of the man's forearms. Nothing could deter the man, though, as he kept strangling her.

"How am I doing?" the man was saying. "I'm doing quite fine. How are you?"

Natalie could hear Cori screaming her name, but the sound was far away. The world started to swim as her windpipe clogged with mucus.

"You're speechless," the man continued. "Excellent."

He pressed harder against Natalie's neck, completely cutting off her air supply.

In a stroke of inspiration, Natalie remembered what she had learned in the mandatory defense class at the hospital. She freed her right hand. With the flat of her palm, she smacked the man in the nose. There was a sickening crunch. The man yelped in pain. Cartilage snapped as she broke his nose. She forced the squishy flesh up and in until her hand was flat against the man's face. The man fell limp against her, blood running from his nose and into her hands.

Natalie heaved and pushed him off. His body hit the pavement like a sack of tomatoes. Tentatively, Natalie reached over to the man and put two fingers to his neck. She couldn't find a pulse.

Feebly, Natalie got to her feet. She groaned, running her fingers over her legs and arms to make sure all her limbs were still attached. Once sure she was still in one piece, she did a full turn, looking in every direction. Fires were still burning. Cars were still stopped. The sounds of the attack from further up the road had stopped. The driver's passenger, a woman in her forties, was still asleep, head leaning on her window.

"Natalie, are you okay?!" Cori said. In the dead quiet, her voice sounded like a shout.

With a nod, Natalie stumbled over to Cori.

"Check me?" she asked and leaned against the concrete barrier, which was about three feet tall. Just beyond the barrier was a thirty-foot drop to a side street of neighborhoods. Natalie's eyes were drawn further away to the crashed airplane in the meadow.

Cori lifted Natalie's sweater, inspecting her back.

"You'll have bruises," she said, lowering Natalie's shirt and inspecting her scalp. "And a pretty good bump on your head. You'll be fine."

"You never asked how *I* was doing."

Natalie and Cori spun around just in time. The female passenger had snuck out of the truck and was practically standing on top of them. Her eyes were wide and unblinking, her fingers curled into fists.

"Lady, you need to calm down," Natalie said.

"Down? Yes, down. Down you go," the lady replied and launched herself at Natalie.

It was a split second reaction. As the woman got within arm's reach, Natalie grabbed her plaid shirt and swung her toward the concrete barrier. The woman flew out of Natalie's hands, over the barrier, and out of sight.

"No!" Cori shouted.

They both ran to the side, looking over the edge. The woman was clawing at the air frantically before—

Natalie and Cori turned away with grimaces. A stomach-turning crunch found their ears.

"What the heck is going on?" Natalie said aloud, peering over the barrier again. The woman was far below them, spread-eagle on the lower street.

"Natalie," Cori whispered. "We just…"

"She attacked us!" Natalie replied. "They both did!"

"But—" Cori began.

Natalie shushed her, suddenly on alert. She had heard someone else speaking, barely a whisper. It sounded like it was from further down the road, where the attack had happened.

Natalie walked back to the center of the road, glancing down the interstate. Cori followed her hesitantly, fighting back tears.

Light as a whisper on the wind, the voice reached Natalie's ears again.

It was weak and childlike, saying one word: "Help."

She scanned the interstate again, trying to find the source of the sound. Squinting, she finally saw it. A figure was walking toward them, winding its way through the stalled cars.

"Help," the person said. "I need help."

As the voice carried to Natalie, the figure walked closer, step by slow step.

Natalie's hair stood on end again. She glanced down to see goosebumps riddling her forearms.

"I'm hurt," said the voice again, childish and simpering. "Help me."

Cori took a few steps in the direction of the approaching figure, but Natalie held her back.

"Please. Help," said the figure again.

The person was close enough now to see clearly. It was a woman. Her face was staunchly pale and coated in blood. Chunks of flesh were stuck to her lips. Droplets of blood clung to her manicured fingernails and matted her hair. She walked with a limp, stumbling over her high heels.

"Don't you want to help me?" she asked.

She had piercing, animalistic eyes that stared at Natalie and Cori, staying on each for several seconds.

"Ma'am, can you hear me?" Natalie said, searching the woman's eyes. They were at once vacant and aggressive. A glint of silver shone in the pupils.

"I need help," the woman said, her pleading not matching the calculating look in her eyes.

"Time to go," Natalie said to Cori.

As one, they raced for the car. The woman took off too, racing after them. Her heels scrabbled on the asphalt, and she sounded close, but Natalie and Cori were faster. They jumped into the car and slammed the door shut. Natalie turned the ignition and put the car in reverse. Tires squealed and metal screeched as Natalie tore her vehicle's hood out from under the truck's hitch. They shot back, narrowly avoiding the woman now lunging at the car with a sinister, blood- and flesh-filled grin. Several feet away now, Natalie turned the vehicle around and zoomed off in the opposite direction.

Cori spun around in the seat to look at the woman still chasing after the car, but falling far behind.

"Where are we going?" Cori asked.

The answer sprung to Natalie's mind before she could stop it. Surprisingly, she desperately wanted to find Toby and make sure he was alive.

"Hospital," Natalie said.

She didn't understand this urge, why she so badly needed to find Toby. Rather than dwell on it, she glanced in the rearview mirror to make sure the woman wasn't keeping up. The mirror wasn't looking directly back though. It had been skewed and was looking right at her. She was staring into her own eyes. Impossibly, she realized that the eyes of the attackers from the truck looked like her own: cold, steely, and emotionless. The only thing missing were the specks of silver in her pupil.

Something else struck her, a terrible thought that hardly fazed her as she looked into her cold, unfeeling eyes. She had just killed two people and couldn't have cared less.

5

Bonnie Matician was at a complete loss. There was a first time for everything, she figured, but she was glad to be confused. It meant she was alive.

When she had seen the first drop of silver hit the window, she had surrendered herself to the inevitability of impending death. She had not been surprised when, as her husband had explained, the silver precipitation had percolated through the windows, walls, and ceiling, and adhered to her skin. Surrendering, she had sat against the wall opposite the large windows, tears falling with the rain. The world had become foggy as her consciousness had ebbed.

Bonnie had slipped into unconsciousness as easily as falling asleep. She had dreamt of her children, encased in silver stone, doomed to death as they suffocated.

Then, there had been an almighty crash as though God Himself had decided to wake her up. She had jarred awake, breathing hard.

Now, she was awake. She still sat against the wall, facing the panoramic windows overlooking downtown L.A.

The boardroom had a strange ambiance. Dull red emergency lights shone from the ceiling. Dim sunlight broke through clouds and smog, filtering through the large glass windows. The tip of another skyscraper was just visible to Bonnie through the windows. Black smoke furled from the windows, fire licking the shattered panes.

Bonnie surveyed the room, still not understanding. She breathed deeply to assure herself she was alive.

She was not supposed to be alive. Brian had made it perfectly clear. When the silver rain fell, she would die. Painfully. Torturously. Yet here she was.

Maybe I'm normal, she considered, but dismissed the ludicrous thought. She knew what she was, and it was far from normal.

Still confused, she noticed that she was the only one awake in the boardroom. Stray papers and binders had been scattered over the ornate carpet. The long table had been overturned.

Strewn around the room were Bonnie's coworkers. Many of them were covered in a layer of shining silver, as though they had been wrapped in an electric blanket. But as Bonnie watched, the silver husks began to fade from sight. Slowly, human forms emerged.

Bonnie crept across the floor to the closest of her coworkers, perplexed.

It was Trisha, a plump lady with heavy blush on her cheeks. She lay sprawled on the ground, her head turned to face the windows. In the wrinkles around her eyes and the creases of her hands and neck, there were conglomerates of silver. It reminded Bonnie of how dust caked her pores after a day of hiking.

Bonnie inched closer, studying the silver particles embedded in the skin. Up close, the particles seemed to be moving. They shook ever so slightly, almost imperceptibly, seamless as sand running from a clenched palm.

As Bonnie stared in awe, the silver began to decrease in amount bit by bit. A few seconds later, there was no silver left and Trisha looked completely normal. Asleep, but normal.

"Trisha?" Bonnie whispered, hunched over her friend.

Trisha's eyes snapped open.

Startled, Bonnie fell onto her butt. She clamped a hand to her mouth, stifling a scream.

Trisha continued to lay still, face toward the window.

Someone else in the room let out a groan of pain. Bonnie strained her neck, looking for the person groaning. At the same time, Trisha sat up and looked in the same direction, eyes wide and searching.

Bonnie held her breath, eyes now locked on Trisha.

Slow as a rotating fan, Trisha's head turned toward Bonnie. Their eyes locked and Trisha smiled. There was something cruel in the smirk, something Bonnie didn't like.

Another groan came from Bonnie's right. This time, she recognized it as Phil, another one of her coworkers.

Trisha did not turn to look at Phil this time. Her eyes remained locked on Bonnie. Her pupils shone silver.

"Help," Phil wheezed in a weak whisper. "Can anyone hear me?"

Bonnie did not even think about running to his aid. She could hardly look away from Trisha. Her coworker hadn't moved, but remained sat up, staring at Bonnie with a crooked neck and unnervingly wide eyes.

There was a scuffle of quick movement. From the corner of Bonnie's eye, she saw her boss, Mr. di Rajio, stand up. He stood stoically in the corner of the room, staring at a spot behind the overturned table. Phil must have been lying behind it, just out of Bonnie's sight.

"I'll help," Mr. di Rajio said, his voice oddly plain.

Something was very wrong, she knew it, and she had to get out of this room.

Slowly, she began to crawl backward toward the glass door leading to the hallway.

"Don't go," Trisha said, speaking for the first time. Her voice was simpering.

All around them, Bonnie saw people stirring and rising from the floor. There were at least twenty of them, all surveying the room. Many of them were looking at her the same way Trish was.

"Please," Phil moaned again, stronger this time. "My hip…"

There was a buzz in the air, like a calm before a storm or a silence before the riot.

"Help," Phil gasped one last time.

The throngs of Bonnie's coworkers all moved at once, swift and sudden. A dozen went after Phil. Mr. di Rajio got to Phil first, disappearing behind the table. Phil screamed. There were smacks and cracks. Scarlet spattered against the windows.

At the same instant, Trisha launched herself at Bonnie. Her manicured nails looked like talons. Pain shot through Bonnie's shins as Trisha's nails cut into her skin.

By a stroke of luck, Bonnie was closer to the door than she thought. She crawled backward, banging against the glass doors, and out into the hallway. The glass doors swung shut on Trisha's face, knocking her back. Instantly, the sounds of the attack on Phil were muffled.

For a moment, Bonnie sat on the ground beyond the doors. People were massing at the door, eyes wide, unblinking, and shining. They were all looking at her.

The next moment, Bonnie was up and on her feet. She ran down the hall, thinking sporadically and frantically. She had to find her family. They had to get to Hawaii. But first she had to escape this building.

She ran no more than a few paces when she heard the unmistakably squeak of the glass doors opening. The sounds of Phil's murder returned, sickening and incessant. But Bonnie could also hear many people running after her.

In the front must have been Trisha as she said, "Bonnie, come back. Don't leave. Work isn't done yet."

6

Mark Hofland trudged through the mud that had run onto the road, pulling one foot after the other through the muck. He tried not to think about his throat, which felt swollen with mucus. Breathing was becoming more difficult with each step.

Unbelievably, the storm had gotten worse. The rain felt like tiny needles, coming down even faster with the help of the wind. They were still trudging down the right side of the canyon, a steep hill side of vegetation to their left and a sheer rock face towering over it. The humid wind blasted through, making Mark gasp for air. His limbs were growing weaker every second. He was weary and downtrodden.

Evan walked with him, making small talk about the crazy weather and pretending not to notice.

Mark certainly knew the danger he was in and he dwelled on it. As was typical when he wasn't feeling well, he kept thinking about how broken his body was.

If only Natalie could see me now, he thought with a laugh. He largely tried to hide his disease from her, like how she hid things from him.

As though his mind had been waiting to mull over a new topic, he started thinking about Natalie and how she hid herself from Mark. She kept her cards close to her chest, never letting Mark too close. He had hoped that getting engaged would change that, but the night he had proposed had abolished that hope.

He remembered the night, near a year ago now, that he had proposed. They had gone to the restaurant across from the courthouse steps where they had first met. After a delicious and expensive meal, Mark had taken her to the courthouse and gotten down on one knee. At that very moment, snow had begun to fall. The lamp lights on the street had twinkled romantically.

With heartfelt honestly, he had told her what she meant to him and how much he loved her. Then had come the big moment. He had pulled out the ring, a small diamond with an intricate band.

For all the magic and whimsy of the moment, she had not shed a single tear when he had proposed. She hadn't even stammered. She had said yes without a single qualm. Mark, on the other hand, had nearly keeled over in fear.

After she had accepted, he had jumped up, pulled her into a tight embrace, and kissed her like never before, all the while knowing something was off. Perhaps the moment had not lived up to his expectations, but he had hoped for more of a reaction from Natalie.

That moment had haunted him ever since. For the last year, he had watched her more carefully. With each passing day, he had realized more and more that Natalie hid within herself. She was not open with her emotions and did not freely express herself to Mark.

It felt like a slap in the face to Mark. He had given everything for her, given everything *to* her, and she had returned it with nary an emotional risk or chance of humiliating herself.

He knew now why that was. It wasn't necessarily that she was hiding, but because she wasn't afraid.

That's it, Mark thought, embracing his epiphany. Natalie wasn't afraid of anything, be it commitments, promises, or risks.

Everyone is scared, Mark thought to himself. Evan was afraid of losing Cori, and Cori was afraid of letting others down. Their boss, Harlem, was afraid of spiders. Danny was probably terrified of going a day without insulting Mark. But Natalie…she was afraid of nothing.

In truth, her fearlessness intimidated Mark. He was afraid to trust her, hold her, or even fully love her. He was afraid of her.

A terrible notion sunk into Mark. If he was afraid of her, how could he be with her?

He wasn't sure.

Love or fear, he considered. Which could conquer the other? The unpleasantness of it all made his lungs blister with pain.

He fumbled for his inhaler, dropping it in the mud and leaves.

Evan paused too, asking Mark if he was okay.

Mark wheezed as he cleared muck from the mouthpiece of the inhaler. He pressed the button, but there was no release of medicine. The inhaler was empty.

He began to hyperventilate, his breathing growing fast and ragged. Evan's voice droned in his ears, fuzzy and muffled. Each lungful of air bit with cold. His throat was sticky with gunk.

Suddenly, Danny was next to him too.

Mark forced himself to breathe. He couldn't make a fool of himself, least of all in front of Danny.

He closed his eyes, calming himself. Slowly but surely, he began breathing again.

When Mark opened his eyes again, he saw he had been encircled by the group of bikers. Danny and Evan were closest.

"Are you okay?" Evan asked tentatively.

Mark shook his head. "I have to…get back."

His voice was feeble and disappeared in the storm.

"We all do, Hofland," Danny said. "But we're not standing around, sinking in the mud."

"Bug off, Danny," Evan said.

Danny turned on Evan. "Want to stay with him, Silverman? That would be a first. You turned your back on your own kind before. Don't pretend like you care about people like Mark."

Evan stepped back as though he had been hit.

Mark glanced between the two of them. He had no idea what Danny was talking about, but it had jarred Evan.

"Come on," Danny shouted to the group. "Anyone who falls behind has to find their own way back."

The group mumbled, some agreeing with Danny.

"You can't," Evan implored. "We need to stick—"

"There is no *together*," Danny interrupted. "If you can't keep up, I won't lose my life to save you. It's survival of the fittest!"

"You should be going rather quickly then," Mark wheezed at Danny, hocking up a string of saliva and boogers.

Danny lunged, kneeing Mark in the gut. Mark dropped to his knees in the mud, gasping as mucus dripped from his lips.

Evan shouted, but Danny punched him in the nose. Blood erupted from Evan's nose, dripping like red rain.

Wheezing, Mark got to his feet and punched Danny back. Danny barely flinched and pushed Mark. He stumbled, feeling his feet sink into mud-covered bushes. Wind graced his neck.

He glanced back. They had gotten to the edge of the road. Mud cascaded down the hillside of palm trees and undergrowth. One slip, and Mark would tumble all the way to the bottom, wherever the hillside met the sheer cliff.

"I hate you!" Danny shouted, getting into Mark's personal space. "Why can't you people just realize no one wants you? Not your parents. Not your family. No one! You're good for nothing."

"It's not about what I can't do," Mark said, "it's what—"

Before he could finish, the mud beneath him began to move. His shoes sunk and he began to fall back.

Instinctually, he reached out and grabbed Danny. Anticipating attack, Danny swung wildly. They fell together, airborne for a second. They landed with a splat in the mud and went sliding down the hillside. Ferns and vines whipped past Mark's face. Mud filled his mouth. He lost his grip on Danny and rolled end over end, disappearing into the vegetation.

7

Nate Matician's forehead slammed into the back of the console. He cried in agony, his scream filling the cabin of the car. Boomer barked, Wyatt cried. Grandma Dottie fumbled with her seat belt to let herself loose.

Bethany lifted up, pulling his hair. Blood ran into Nate's eyes. His vision swam. His forehead screamed in pain. He was frozen in terror, unable to defend himself.

"It's raining, it's pouring," Bethany sang. "The monsters are roaring. Smash your head until you're dead—"

Wyatt let out a shrill cry beside her. Bethany's shining eyes turned upon Wyatt. She released Nate and lunged at the baby. Nate shouted incoherently, pain and blood blinding him.

Boomer leapt onto Bethany, barking in her ear and gnashing his teeth. Bethany grabbed the tiny dog and threw him on the floor mat.

No longer interested in Boomer or Wyatt, Bethany grabbed Nate by his zip-up sweater and pulled him into the back seat. Before he could react, or maybe he was too frozen to react, she put him into a headlock. The fabric of her clothes filled his nose as his windpipe was squeezed shut.

Distantly, he heard a car door open, a pause, and then another door open. Bethany loosened her grip on Nate and he pushed away, crouching around his baby brother.

Grandma Dottie was in the back now too, reaching through the open door and dragging Bethany out. Bethany fought for all it was worth, but her tiny body was no match for a full-grown adult.

"I want to smash his head!" Bethany cried.

"Silence, girl," Grandma Dottie demanded.

She locked Bethany into a bear hug, holding her tight. Bethany shrieked shrilly, gnashing her teeth and kicking her feet.

"Nathaniel!" yelled Grandma Dottie. "Shut the back door!"

He let go of Wyatt and slammed the door. Through the glass, he saw Grandma Dottie fling Bethany onto the pavement. Fast for her age, Grandma Dottie spun around, jumped into the front seat of the car, and slammed the door shut.

"Grandma, what's happening?" Nate asked.

Slam!

Bethany smashed her fists into the window of the driver's side. Blood smeared the cracking glass.

"Hold on, Nathaniel!" Grandma Dottie cried.

She stamped on the accelerator. The car lurched forward, spewing hail from under its tires. Bethany slid out of Nate's view.

He sat up, spinning in the seat. Bethany stood in the middle of the road, a sad look on her face. She looked alone and scared.

"Grandma?" he said. "What about Bethany?"

"She will be safer here," Grandma Dottie said, gripping the steering wheel tighter. "We need to find safety."

Nate couldn't shake the look on his sister's face. "But she's sad. We have to—"

"No," Grandma Dottie said crisply. "We will not, Nathaniel."

The car rang with silence for a second. Nate wiped the blood from his forehead, gingerly touching the place where his skin had come off.

"I just don't understand...," Grandma Dottie sighed. She paused and then said firmly, "Your mother will know what to do."

"Mom?" Nate questioned. "What about Dad? Bethany?"

"There is nothing we can do for them now," Grandma Dottie lamented. "Your mother is who we need."

"How will we get to Los Angeles?" he asked. He was on the verge of tears, but Grandma Dottie would just yell at him more. Stifling the tears, he wiped the blood from his forehead one more time and buckled up.

"We'll fly," she replied. "Even if the whole world has gone mad, you can bet your mother hasn't. We'll get to her even if we have to steal Air Force One."

8

Cori Silverman sat in silence as Natalie drove through the backstreets around downtown Reno. She had tried calling Evan, but he had not answered. She had also noticed she had missed several calls from family, but could not get in contact with anyone.

Is it just Reno? she wondered. *Or is this worldwide?*

She said a quick, fearful prayer for the wellbeing of her family.

In the driver's seat, Natalie was focused on the road. Cori noticed that Natalie kept glancing at the rearview mirror and looking away hastily, as though seeing something she did not like. Cori looked out the back window once or twice, relieved to see that no one was following them. Natalie must have been unnerved by something else: she was even driving slower, giving each car a wide berth.

As they drove, Cori turned the radio volume up. Shrieks and clicks came over the airwaves, the unmistakable patterns of an emergency broadcast.

"Is this the same one that was playing after the accident?" Cori asked.

Natalie shrugged, glancing at the rearview mirror and frowning.

"What is back there?" Cori asked, glancing back again.

"Nothing," Natalie muttered. "It's nothing."

Cori turned her attention back to the radio. She scanned for another station. Several others were emitting the emergency broadcast signal. She listened to a few, hoping that one would break for an announcer, but none did. After several stations, she finally found one with music. They listened for a few minutes before the music cut out and started at the beginning of the song. The song played for several verses about purple rain again before cutting back to the beginning, stuck in a perpetual loop like a broken record. Cori wondered if the dj had accidentally hit a wrong button as the silver rain fell.

She kept scanning through the channels. Another emergency broadcast, another station filled with dead air, another filled with static. She jammed the button again—

"Get to safety!"

Natalie slammed on the brakes, ears perked. Cori turned up the volume. The radio waves were filled with static, but they had both heard the man whispering as though warning police over the phone that there were intruders in a home.

The voice returned, hushed and quiet.

"If you are listening to this, you need to find shelter," the man said. He sounded terrified, taking shaky breaths and talking fast. "I don't know if I'm the only one, but everyone is trying to kill me. If you can hear me, Rhonda, I love you. Anyone else, don't talk to anyone. Don't engage them. They will k—NO!"

The speakers were filled with yells. Cori punched the sound dial, muting the radio. The car was filled with a hum of silence.

Natalie and Cori exchanged glances.

"It's not just us," Cori said aloud. "Other people are awake and normal."

"But everyone else is psycho," Natalie finished.

"What if Toby…?" Cori asked.

"He won't," Natalie said firmly.

Cori nodded. She knew Natalie didn't want to argue.

"We'll have to be careful," she said.

With a nod of agreement, Natalie started driving again. She cruised through the narrow streets, dodging stalled cars.

At every intersection, they peered around the corners cautiously. Most streets were quiet and full of slumbering people. Homeless folks, businessmen, lawyers, pedestrians, and service workers alike lay asleep in their vehicles or on the sidewalks.

One street though, the one everyone in town knew to be dangerous due to its drug trafficking and illicit prostitution, was a different story. Everyone on that street was awake, scurrying this way and that, jumping on cars and acting stark-raving mad. Cori saw a flash of a bloody body as Natalie sped right through the street and into another narrow alleyway.

At last, they reached 6th Street, where the hospital resided. Natalie turned onto the street slowly. Thankfully, this street was still asleep.

Eventually the road became jammed with vehicles of sleeping people, and they were forced to drive on the sidewalk. Natalie wound slowly but expertly around prone humans, lamp lights, and newsstands. Many of the people, Cori noticed, had silver beads sparkling in their hands and on their faces.

"What happened?" Cori murmured, staring at the bodies lining the streets. "Why is everyone asleep?"

"Whatever this is, I think it put everyone to sleep," Natalie said. "Then we all wake up on different sides of the bed."

Cori bit her lip.

"What could have put us all to sleep?"

"No idea."

"Is someone trying to kill us?"

"Not sure."

"Is this an attack? Like a terrorist attack?"

Natalie shrugged. "If it is, who attacked us?"

Cori fell silent, her mind filling with visions of warring countries eagerly watching America crater. The thought terrified her. Even worse, there were so many unknowns. Why had the people from the pickup truck tried to kill Natalie? Why were Natalie and Cori normal? Why was most of the city of Reno asleep? Why were there emergency broadcasts on nearly every radio station?

It had to have been an attack, Cori decided. But what had the attack been? Were Cori and Natalie now carrying a virus that they had yet to succumb to? Was the contagion airborne?

The questions rattled around her brain at the speed of a percussionist with a wraparound drum set. There were too many for her to focus on at once. She felt uncharacteristically uncertain and worried.

Movement high above caught Cori's eye. Distracted, she leaned forward, wincing as the seatbelt rubbed against her bruised chest. Several stories above and a block away, a body fell from a broken window. Terribly, the person was alive, swinging their arms and kicking their feet. The person disappeared into the mass of vehicles blocking the street. Through the car windows, Cori heard a smack.

Cori let out a small whimper, not believing what she had just seen. A tear streamed down her cheek and she choked down a sob.

Natalie stopped the car and put a hand on Cori's shoulder.

"Cori," Natalie said consolingly, "I know this is tough, but I need you to be strong for Toby."

Cori wiped her eyes, trying to subdue her panic.

"This doesn't make any sense," she said. "It rained that silver stuff and it's like the world has gone crazy."

Natalie smiled in the way she always did: forced and small.

"Then we have to keep our cool," Natalie said. "The best thing for us is to get out of the city and get to Hawaii with Mark and Evan."

"What about the plane?" Cori asked. "The airport was dead."

"We'll find a way," Natalie insisted. "One step at a time. First step is getting Toby."

Natalie pointed out the window. A few blocks up the road was the turn-out for the hospital. A large metal awning extended out of the hospital's front and over the drive-up entrance.

"Okay. Let's do it," Cori said.

"There's my eternal optimist," Natalie said.

Cori took these words to heart, letting her mood easily slip back into happy-go-lucky, the perpetual attitude she was blessed with. Whatever was happening was beyond her understanding, just the way God intended it. She would understand in time if He saw fit. Rather than become consumed in fear and paranoia, she must resolve to be happy and help her friend.

Natalie eased the car forward along the sidewalk. A few people fidgeted in their sleep as they drove by, but Cori did not see any of them waking up yet.

"Before we get to the hospital," Natalie said as they neared the building, "there are some things you need to understand about Toby."

Cori squinted, trying to recall what she knew about Toby. Natalie was pretty protective of him. Hardly any of the nurses got a chance to look at his charts.

"Toby is very special," Natalie continued. "He was born with a familial genetic predisposition called *congenital analgia*. He can't feel anything."

Cori nodded in acknowledgement.

That explains a lot, she thought.

"Like—" she began.

"Like pain, pleasure, hot, cold," Natalie interrupted, cutting off what Cori had intended to say. "His chromosomes produced an overpopulation of neurotransmitters in his brain—"

"Endorphins," Cori interjected. She knew plenty about those lovely angels. So did Natalie.

Natalie exhaled sharply. Cori knew she hated being interrupted.

"Yes, the endorphins in his brain make it so he can't feel sensations," Natalie continued. "That is also why he is prone to seizures. Dr. Hyatt diagnosed him with epilepsy, but he only has seizures when he is exposed to high emotional stimulus."

"So he seizes when he gets really happy or nervous?" Cori asked.

"Or scared," Natalie explained.

"I understand," Cori said. She clenched her hands in determination. "We can't panic, or Toby might have a seizure."

"There is no might. He *will*. We can't tell him what's going on. All he needs to know is we're taking him to Hawaii with us."

"Won't he notice everyone is asleep? Or worse?"

"We'll play that by ear."

"Oh good," Cori replied, surveying the crowds of bodies across the street and sidewalks outside the hospital. "Flying by the seat of our pants. Your usual game plan."

PHASE 4

SAVAGE CALLS

Bonnie Matician ran for her life. Though she wore high heels, she moved faster than a high school track star in a relay race.

Frantic footsteps came from behind her. Her coworkers were coming, and she doubted they wanted to pass a baton or give her a hug.

Bonnie raced around the corner and into the women's bathroom. She barricaded the door with the trash receptacle and ran to the farthest stall. As she ran, she saw a flash of feet under one of the stalls. Before they awoke or attacked, she locked herself in the farthest stall.

Now what? she thought. Her mood swung low as she realized she had trapped herself.

Bang!

Slams echoed through the bathroom as Bonnie's coworkers tried to enter.

Bonnie glanced up. There was a vent cover above her stall.

More bangs came from the door, but this time, it was accompanied by scraping metal. The trash can wasn't holding.

Taking off her high heels, Bonnie climbed on top of the toilet. With her Leatherman, she began undoing the screws of the vent cover. Within a few seconds and three more crashes on the door, she had removed the cover. She hoisted herself up, scrapping her knee, and climbed into the vent system.

The metal tunnel was cool to the touch. It was tight too, no more than two feet tall and three feet wide. Bonnie moved slowly, careful to not make too much noise on the squeaky metal. It would be a great hiding place, but given too much noise, it would be the perfect place to be killed. In fact, the shaft had a terrifying exactness to the size of a coffin.

At a three-way annex, Bonnie took a right, following the vent to another cover. Through the slots of the vent cover, she could see the hallway she had just run through. To the right was the bathroom door she had entered. It had been thrown open. Smears of blood coated the dented door.

Just below the vent, Bonnie could see the drinking fountain she had stood at when she had talked to Brian. That seemed a lifetime ago.

Bonnie hunkered down low, listening. She could hear voices coming from the bathroom, but none close or loud enough to suggest they had found the open vent.

Footsteps reached her ears, padding down the carpeted hallway. She moved from side to side, trying to get a good look through the slotted vent at who was coming.

Barely lit by the red emergency light, Bonnie saw half a dozen people walk around the corner. At the drinking fountain, one paused while the others hurried into the bathroom.

Bonnie moved her head again, looking at the lone person through the slots. It took her a moment to recognize that it was her boss, Mr. di Rajio. He surveyed the hallway, arms hanging loosely at his sides, posture relaxed but professional. The only difference Bonnie could see were his eyes. Mr. di Rajio had always had calm, kind eyes, brown as almonds and soft as melted chocolate. But no more. His eyes now were narrowed, cold and collected, scanning and scrutinizing.

He glanced at the vent cover. Bonnie didn't move, didn't even breathe.

Mr. di Rajio stared for a moment, his pupils sparkling. Blood dripped down the left side of his face.

Bonnie stared back, positive she couldn't be seen.

Suddenly, Bonnie's cell phone vibrated. Pressed between her body and the metal vent, it reverberated like a thousand bees set loose.

From the bathroom, there were shouts of glee and Trisha proclaimed, "Ready or not, here I come!"

Pings of metal traveled to Bonnie's ears. Her coworkers had found the open vent. They were coming.

Bonnie fumbled to silence her phone as she crawled backwards. Her eyes were still locked on Mr. di Rajio. He was looking at the vent again, but this time, he seemed to be looking right at her.

"Now, now, Bonnie," he said coolly. "You know how I feel about cell phones at work."

2

Reno Health Hospital
North Reno, Nevada

The moment Natalie Harper parked under the hospital's entrance awning and stepped out of the car, she knew there was going to be trouble. There were about twenty people outside—some in their cars, others collapsed on the ground under the awning, and some unconscious in benches lining the hospital. Each person, from the elderly man in the wheelchair drooling on a newspaper to the young couple lying with a bundled newborn, were beginning to fidget and tremble, the sure signs that they were coming out of their slumber. Natalie thought they looked like sacks of potatoes, limp bodies strewn around as though waiting to be collected by sanitation trucks. Cori obviously thought differently: she had an uncharacteristic frown on her face as she surveyed the people with remorse.

Rather than leave her car running as she had originally intended, Natalie took the keys. With that, Natalie and Cori walked quickly into the hospital's foyer. Thankfully, no one awoke or chased them, and Natalie did not see any cold, wide eyes following them. The automatic doors swung open and they entered.

"What are they?" Cori asked as the doors swung shut behind them. "Infected? Zombies?"

Natalie shushed her friend, glancing around. The foyer was dim.

"Is the power off?" Cori whispered.

Natalie tapped her ear. "Generators," she said.

A faint hum was coming from below them where emergency generators wheezed. Despite this, the lights in the foyer were off.

"Someone shut off the lights," Natalie assumed.

She looked around for whoever it might have been, but the foyer was empty. Yolanda, the usual front desk secretary, was nowhere to be seen.

"This way," Natalie said and beckoned Cori toward the stairwell and elevator.

The generators emitted a strong hum and Cori let out a yip of terror. Natalie shot her a look.

"Cori," Natalie said, "you need to relax."

"I'm trying," she whispered back.

A thump issued from behind the front desk. Cori let out another squeak of fright and sprinted to the elevator. Before Natalie could stop her, Cori pressed the button to call the elevator. The doors swung open with a soft *ding*. Thankfully, the elevator was empty too.

Another bump came from behind the desk, followed by a strong inhale of air.

Natalie grabbed Cori and pointed at the door to the stairwell.

"Stairs," Natalie whispered. "The elevator will make noise all the way up and ding at the top. We'll take it down for our getaway."

Biting her lip, Cori nodded. They opened the door to the stairwell and shut it behind them.

Inside, the stairwell was pitch-dark. Natalie and Cori pulled out their cell phones and lit their surroundings.

Bodies littered the stairs like lily pads. Their skin was pale under the light of cell phones.

After taking in the haunting sight, Natalie and Cori proceeded cautiously, avoiding the people. Unfortunately, Natalie misjudged a step and trod right on the hand of an unconscious nurse. As she lifted her foot, the nurse began to fidget and her eyes moved behind their lids.

"Go," Cori urged. "Please, just go."

They hurried on, finally making it to the floor of the long-term recovery unit. Here, Natalie paused, listening. In the silence, she could hear rustling from below them. She had definitely awoken some of them, and there was no telling if there would be silver in their eyes.

"We'll take the elevator back down," Natalie whispered to Cori, who nodded in reply. "Don't forget the wheelchair."

"Be careful," Cori replied morosely.

Natalie knew Cori was thinking Toby might be one of the sleeping folks who woke with silver in their eyes and turned murderous. But it couldn't be possible, Natalie insisted to herself. Toby *had* to be normal.

For a moment, her thoughts went into gridlock. Had she just hoped for Toby's wellbeing? It was a first, and it unnerved her.

The tightness in her stomach returned.

Not now, she thought, and she eased the door open.

Like the first level foyer, the reception area of the recovery unit was lit dimly by sunlight. The overhead lights had been turned off. Sun streamed from a few windows and out of patients' rooms. To Natalie's left was the nurses' station, covered with scattered papers and smeared blood. Across the foyer were three rooms. Toby's was on the far left.

Cori and Natalie tiptoed into the lobby and hid behind the nurses' station.

"Wheelchair," Natalie mouthed, pointing Cori to a door next to the stairwell entrance. Cori did not respond.

Instead, she was staring into the dark corner of the nurses' station.

Natalie followed her gaze.

Lying in the corner, an IV line tied tight around her neck, was one of their fellow nurses, Joaquin. His dark lips were puffy, bulging eyes glimmering in the light from the cell phones.

Unmoved by the sight of his pale corpse, Natalie peeked above the countertop.

The doors were closed to each of the three rooms. Sunlight was coming from the first two doors' windows, Roger's and Arlene's. The window to Toby's room was pitch black. There was no movement inside any of the rooms, which made Natalie wonder what had happened to the two nurses, supervising doctor, and twenty patients that should have been moving around the unit. Were they missing or simply asleep, killers in waiting?

Natalie ducked back behind the nurses' station. Cori was still staring at Joaquin, tears in her eyes.

"Cori, we have to move," Natalie whispered.

"He was our friend," Cori mouthed between sobs. "We worked together. We were in nursing school together."

Like forcing a smile, Natalie put on a show of emotion to get Cori moving.

"It's sad, I know," she whispered. "We'll say something for him, when we're out of here and safe."

This seemed to be logical to Cori. She nodded and followed Natalie's directions to the storage closet with the extra wheelchairs.

As Cori crawled toward the closet, Natalie tiptoed around the nurses' station. She glanced down the hallway, left and right. The hallways were clear, although messy with scattered papers and strewn furniture.

Once she made it to the wall, she crept to the first door. A bloody handprint was on the door handle. She inched up toward the window, peeking inside.

Inside was a disaster. The hospital bed was tossed on its side, the covers shredded. Broken glass littered the ground. There were blood specks on the wall too. Roger, the self-diagnosed psychopath keeping sane on sugar pills, was nowhere to be seen. In the corner, Natalie could see Dr. Hyatt lying face down in a puddle of blood. The doctor wasn't moving. The horror barely fazed her as she wondered what Dr. Hyatt had been before he died: man or monster.

The room in between Roger and Toby was worse. Natalie gasped as she looked through the window.

Arlene, Natalie's charge with fibromyalgia, lay dead in her hospital bed. Her disease-weakened muscles were torn to shreds. Two nurses stood at her side, overlooking their handwork while deep in discussion with blood-coated scalpels held between their fingers like cigarettes.

Natalie shuddered, not out of remorse for Arlene, but from the gore within the room. Hunkering down, she crept to Toby's door.

A peek through the window proved that it was totally dark inside. The shades were drawn across the windows. A thin green light was in the corner. She narrowed her eyes until she could see what it was: a heart monitor with a green flat line.

Natalie took a step back, jolted. For a moment, she couldn't breathe.

All these months, Toby had been nothing more than a symbol to attain, a chip in the poker game of life, a pawn for payback. But not anymore. From the moment the rain had fallen, Natalie had felt an innate need to find Toby and make sure he was alive and well. She rebuked Cori for saying he was one of the monsters.

But now, looking at the flat line on the monitor, she was overcome with instincts she couldn't control. She was frozen, unable to believe her eyes.

No, she thought. *He can't be.*

He had to be alive, he just had to be. In her heart, she wanted nothing more than for him to be alive. Not for her advantage, but because she cared for him and wished him the best.

The strange feeling in Natalie's stomach intensified to the point she thought she might puke.

Not now, she pleaded. She couldn't let in the emotions yet. She had to find Toby.

Hand trembling, Natalie fished keys from her pocket and unlocked the door as quietly as possible.

"Please," she muttered to herself.

She swung open the door and rushed in, locking the door behind her.

"Toby," she whispered desperately.

There was no answer.

As her eyes adapted to the dark, she edged toward Toby's hospital bed. She bumped into it and felt the covers. The bed was empty.

He's on the floor, she thought terribly. *Like Dr. Hyatt.*

She crept around the edge of the bed to the heart monitor, following the IVs. She followed them slowly, anticipating when she would find Toby's lifeless body. But it never happened. Her hands found the ends of the IV needles dangling above the ground.

"I see you…"

Natalie stood bolt upright and scanned the darkness. The room was mostly black, faintly illuminated by thin beams of sunlight from the edges of the window drapes. Though she couldn't see well, there was no sign of anyone else in the room.

Her mind worked fast. The voice couldn't be Toby's, it was too low. But what if it was? What if he had been waiting for her?

Suddenly, a hand wrapped around Natalie's ankle. She jerked back instinctually, running into a tray carrying food and antibiotics. The items clattered to the floor, the metal pan crashing like a cymbal.

Something came out from under the bed, small and timid. Natalie balled her fists, ready to fight her way out, even if it was Toby about to attack her.

"Natalie, it's me," said a small voice.

Natalie nearly shouted for joy. It was Toby.

She collapsed upon him, hugging him tightly. He hugged her back, his tiny hands clasping her hair. The outline of his body shuddered.

"Toby," she whispered, "are you okay? Are you hurt?"

She felt along his legs and back. Every incision was still stitched.

"I'm okay," he whispered close to her ear. "But we need to go, Natalie. There's a bad man in here."

Natalie froze again, suddenly sensing that someone was watching her.

As though knowing its presence had been realized, the low voice spoke again.

"I see you. Can you see me?"

Natalie placed the voice instantly this time. It was Roger, her patient who thought he was crazy.

Roger stepped into the dim sunlight with a limp. His leg cracked ominously from his recent injury.

Face half in the sun, Roger grinned. His eyes were just like the others—silver specks dancing in the pupil, surrounded by an iris alight with focus and bottled cruelty.

Looking into his sparkling eyes, Natalie wanted to dissolve on the spot, but Toby gave her strength. He quivered in her arms, reminding her that his life depended on her.

"Roger," Natalie said slowly. "You're not well. You need to get—"

"I'm quite well," he replied quirkily, taking a step closer. "I'm here, waiting for you."

"Why?" Natalie asked.

"I have a job to do," he responded, and took another step.

Natalie took a step backward, running up against the wall. There was no clear path to the door unless she jumped over the bed.

"What job is that?" she inquired.

"Killing you," Roger replied simply. "And then the boy."

Roger took another step, close enough to attack now.

"This isn't you, Roger," Natalie said, and she meant it. He was eccentric, but she had never actually thought he was crazy or deranged.

"Yes," he said with a dark laugh. "Yes it is."

It struck Natalie that perhaps she was not talking to the Roger she had known. From his words to his behavior to his posture, Roger seemed to be a different man. A dangerous man. The silver rain had changed him.

"What are you?" Natalie asked.

"What do you think I am?" Roger replied. "Do you think I'm…a vampire?"

He barred his teeth and jumped at her daringly. She jolted back, hitting the wall again.

"Or…a zombie?"

He gnashed his teeth and salivated.

"Maybe a sickie?"

He coughed blood into his hand and threw it across the sheets of the hospital bed.

"Or am I a terrorist?" He paused and then shouted, "BOOM!"

Natalie jumped again as Toby clung to her tighter.

"No," Roger cooed. "I am none of these. None of us are. I am you if you had to be. I am you without your inhibitions, your social politeness, and your political correctness. I am you without your emotions."

As he spoke, Roger crept closer to her. Natalie pressed against the wall, unable to move, enraptured by his words.

"I am the expunger of the unclean," Roger continued. "I'm a vessel honed to hunt and slaughter its prey. The monster in the dark, waiting just underneath your skin and in your darkest nightmares. I am a creeper of the night."

He was close now. Too close.

Suddenly, he leapt at them, shouting, "Creeper!" in a blood-curdling scream.

Natalie swung at him, but Roger backed away. He had only lunged, not yet attacking. He smiled darkly and bowed his head. Gleaming eyes stared at Natalie through Roger's brow.

"Ohhh," Roger said, laughing. "Did that scare you?"

He lunged again, paused, and lunged again. Each time, Natalie jumped against the wall, sure that Roger would strike at any moment. Her insides began to writhe into coils. The emotion she had been trying to push away since the interstate was forcing itself in. She knew what it was, and there was no denying it anymore.

Unable to stop it, Natalie let the emotion in.

Fear, unadulterated and unmitigated, swept through her veins, strong and inescapable. She stood frozen, unable to move. Roger loomed over her, his sparkling eyes rooting her to the spot.

"Natalie, it's time to go," Toby whispered in her ear.

His voice brought Natalie to her senses. She could not freeze. She could not succumb. She had to get out of here.

Like closing valves to a dam, Natalie shut off her emotions and glared back at Roger.

"There's some fight in there," Roger said to Natalie, eyeing her.

Again, he lunged, but Natalie was ready this time. She rammed her shoulder into Roger's cheek. He tumbled back, slamming into a cabinet hidden in the dark. There was a crunch of glass and howl of pain.

Not looking back, Natalie ran for the door. She fumbled with the handle, threw the door open, and ran out as Roger lunged at them. He missed—just barely—head slamming into the door.

Natalie sprinted toward the nurses' station. The door to Arlene's room opened and the nurses emerged, wielding scalpels. Natalie body-slammed them too, bowling them over.

Cori was just past the stairwell and storage closet, holding open an elevator. A wheelchair was inside, gleaming silver in the lights.

Natalie ran for her, running as fast as she could.

In her arms, Toby yelled, "Creeper!"

Natalie ran faster and burst into the elevator. Cori slammed her hand against the "close doors" button.

Practically throwing Toby into the wheelchair, Natalie spun around, prepared to fight.

Roger was running for them, slipping on the papers and tile. His leg was gushing blood and cracked horribly from the unset bones.

Natalie's muscles tensed, ready to fight to the last drop of blood.

The elevator doors swung shut.

Thud!

Roger ran up against the metal doors, but he was too late.

Natalie felt a swoop in her stomach as the elevator began to descend.

Sighing, Natalie sank to the floor. Cori collapsed beside her, holding an ax.

"An ax?" Natalie commented, trying to catch her breath.

"From behind the nurses' station. For emergencies only," Cori gasped, also breathing hard.

Natalie turned her attention back to Toby.

"Are you okay? Did he hurt you?" she asked.

Toby shook his head vigilantly. "He scared me, but he was waiting for you."

"Creep," Natalie muttered.

"That's what they were calling themselves," Cori said. "The nurses in Arlene's room kept calling themselves creepers."

"Roger said it too," Natalie said. "Among other things."

"Is that what we call them?" Cori wondered. "Are they infected by parasites or a virus?"

"Until we figure it out, we'll call them creepers," Natalie insisted.

Natalie and Cori fell silent, sinking into their own thoughts. To avoid another emotional breakdown, Natalie focused her thoughts on Roger. He had acted like a different person, as though a new personality had taken over. Much like the people on the interstate, he had been overwhelmingly aggressive and violent.

It must have been the rain, Natalie assumed. But then, why was she not affected? What about Cori? They had been coated with it. Toby must have been too. Why were they all normal?

Maybe it wasn't the rain, Natalie thought. Maybe something happened after they fell asleep. But if that was the case, what had it been and how far had it spread?

"Where are we going?" Toby asked, interrupting Natalie's ponderings.

"Where there are no more creepers," Cori muttered.

"Hawaii," Natalie said.

"Okay!" Toby said ecstatically.

"How are we getting there?" Cori asked.

"We'll try our hand at flying," Natalie replied.

The elevator pinged, notifying them that they had reached the ground level.

"Hold on tight, Toby," Natalie said. "This is going to be a bumpy ride."

The elevator doors swung open and they charged out. Natalie pushed Toby's wheelchair and Cori wielded the ax.

Surprisingly, no one attacked. The foyer was completely empty. But not all was as they had left it.

The front doors had been broken open since their entrance into the hospital. Outside, the twenty-some people had disappeared. Only one person remained: Yolanda, the receptionist. She lay beyond Natalie's car, screaming for help.

Natalie and Cori paused at the broken sliding glass doors.

"What happened to her?" Toby asked.

"We have to help her!" Cori exclaimed.

Natalie held her back. The other people who had been outside were gone. There was no couple with a baby in the parking lot. A vacant wheelchair sat beside a bench.

"These people are smart," Natalie said. "I don't know how, but they're intelligent. If they're not here..."

"What do you mean?" Cori said, eyes trained on Yolanda.

"The woman from the interstate who was calling for help, but she was obviously a creeper," Natalie pointed out. "You would have been killed if you tried to help. What about Yolanda? How do we know she's actually hurt?"

"How do we not?" Cori countered and tried to run again.

"No," Natalie insisted, holding Cori back. "We get Toby in the car, and then we see what's going on."

With a frown, Cori nodded. Together, they sprinted to the car. As Natalie put Toby into the backseat of the car, Cori collapsed the wheelchair. By the time they shut the door, Yolanda had noticed them and was crying for their help.

"Natalie!" she cried. "Cori! *Ayúdame!*"

"Are you hurt?" Cori cried.

"Yes!" Yolanda replied. "My leg!"

"Crawl to the car!"

"I can't!"

Yolanda scrabbled at the ground, but couldn't pull herself. Her legs were smeared with blood.

While Yolanda cried out, Natalie looked around, her senses on high alert. There was no one else in sight. Where had they gone?

"Cori," she said. "This has to be a trap."

"She needs our help," Cori insisted. "We can't just leave her he—"

Natalie cut her off, finally seeing what she was looking for.

She pointed to the shadows on the street. To their right, Natalie could see the shadow of the metal awning that stretched out from the hospital's entrance. Atop the awning were about a dozen shadows of people leaning on the edge, poised to pounce.

Cori gasped.

Clever, Natalie thought, realizing the situation. Yolanda was bait. The second Natalie or Cori tried to help her, the creepers on the awning would attack. Yolanda was probably an accomplice too, pretending to be hurt to lure them in.

"We have to go," Natalie whispered. "We can't risk this."

Natalie surveyed the car. The driver's side door was in sunlight. If she approached the driver's door, she would be seen by the creepers on the awning. The passenger side door was their only way in.

"I'll get in the driver's seat through your door, then you hurry in," Natalie whispered.

"What about Yolanda?" Cori squeaked.

Natalie met Cori's eyes, lost for an answer. It was their lives or Yolanda's.

"I see," Cori said stoically.

"She might be one of them," Natalie said.

"You don't know that," Cori replied. "She could be like us."

Natalie paused, but she was positive there was no other way out of this.

"We have to get out of here," she said. "I'm getting in that car and we're going. I'm not dying here today."

Cori looked stunned. "Every life matters, Natalie, whether it's the person at the front desk or your own skin."

Natalie paused again, already knowing what to say, but refusing to say it. Then she threw all caution to the wind and said, "It's your choice. We can leave now and see Mark and Evan again, or we can try to protect her and die."

Cori shrunk slightly, clearly appalled Natalie could present her with such a chilling ultimatum.

"This is wrong," Cori finally said. "You might think this is an easy choice. But this is wrong."

Natalie waited a moment before saying, "Are you with me?"

Cori closed her eyes, squeezing a tear out. Slowly, she nodded.

Natalie nodded too and opened the car door quietly, keeping an eye on the shadows of people. All the while, Yolanda pleaded for their help. Once Natalie was in the driver's seat, Cori slowly and begrudgingly got into the passenger seat.

Tears collected in her eyes as she pulled the door shut softly.

"What about that lady?" Toby asked Natalie.

She couldn't answer him at first.

"She's tricking us," Natalie finally said. "She's a creeper."

Toby frowned, peering out the window.

"Close your eyes, Toby," Natalie said.

She turned the key and slammed the car into drive. At the same instant, creepers leapt down from the awning, closing in on the car.

Natalie put the pedal to the metal. Tires squealed and the car shot out from under the awning. A second later, more creepers jumped, some landing on the hood of the car. They pounded the metal and glass, trying to break in. Natalie slammed her foot on the brakes, throwing the creepers off the front. She hit the accelerator again and spun the wheel. Creepers were bowled over, disappearing beneath the hood of the car. The car bumped from side to side as Natalie ran them over.

Cori spun around to make sure no one was following them. Natalie glanced back too through a mirror and instantly regretted it.

One of the creepers—it looked like Roger—was not chasing them. The creeper walked over to Yolanda, his body language glowering with complete disgust. He kicked her in the face, hard.

Cori let out a gasp and spun around. Natalie did the same, repulsed, realizing in full what she had done.

Yolanda hadn't been a creeper. She had been like Natalie, Cori, and Toby—normal and defenseless.

Natalie had suspected this, considered it, but decided saving Yolanda was too high a cost.

Utter silence filled the car as they sped down the road. Across Natalie's mind flashed Yolanda's look of terror. She remembered Joaquin's wide, bulging eyes. She saw the man she had killed on the interstate, and the woman she had thrown over the side of the road. They were all dead, most by Natalie's hand, none leaving a mark of regret upon her heart. Until now.

Inside her, something took hold. It wasn't fear and it wasn't in her stomach. This felt like it was in her chest. Her heart beat slower and felt heavy.

If she wasn't mistaken, Natalie thought she was feeling remorse.

"Can I open my eyes?" Toby asked.

"Yes," Natalie breathed.

She did not know how to cope with remorse. Really, she didn't know how to cope with any emotions, but this was too ripe and bittersweet.

If only I'd tried, she thought bitterly.

She bit her lip hard, drawing blood, and forced herself to focus on the road until the feelings left her. Slowly but surely, she felt the emotions dwindle.

After a few more minutes, Natalie took a left onto an empty side street.

"Natalie, the airport is that way," Cori said, pointing to the right.

"And Mark's apartment is that way," Natalie replied, pointing her fingers down the road in the shape of the Ruger revolver she knew to be in Mark's bedside cabinet. "Whether these creepers are just here in Reno or everywhere else, we need a way to defend ourselves."

Deep down, Natalie's stomach bubbled and her heart thudded slowly. Try as she might, the emotions remained, vigilant as a silver sparkle refusing to be quenched by the darkness, patient as a creeper lying in wait to awaken, pounce, and overcome her.

3

Specks of spittle dotted Bonnie Matician's face as her boss, Mr. de Rajio, slammed on the vent. The metal bowed in.

Bonnie scrabbled backward as fast as she could. She heard creaks of metal echoing through the ventilation shafts. The other people were coming for her.

At the three-way intersection, she backed into the passage that led to the bathroom and continued down the straight-away. She glanced behind her as she crawled.

Trisha was scrabbling toward her, only a few feet behind, and coming fast.

Bonnie screamed and crawled faster, pushing harder with her knees and hands.

"I'm creeping up on you, Bonnie!" Trisha called. "Just creeping! *Creeping!*"

Trisha's words echoed terribly around Bonnie.

A hand, tiny but rough, wrapped around Bonnie's ankle and pulled. Bonnie screamed and kicked back hard. Her heel connected with Trisha's face. Something broke underneath her foot with a crunch.

Trisha howled with pain. Bonnie hurried off, crawling into uncharted tunnels of the ventilation system.

She took a left and another, then a right, getting lost in the vents.

After some time, she noticed that the din of her pursuers had died away. She could still hear the pings of metal and voices, but they seemed far away.

Still moving, Bonnie fished out her phone. She had missed several calls from family and two from Brian.

The phone vibrated in her hands. It was Brian again.

She answered it, still crawling and keeping an eye out for Trisha or any other pursuers.

"Brian?" she shouted over the phone.

"You're alive," he sighed, his voice raspy and full of pain, yet overflowing with relief. "Thank God, you're alive. I did it."

"Brian!" she shouted back. "What's happening?!"

He paused for a moment.

"What do you mean?" he whispered harshly. It sounded like he was hiding.

"It's not right," she replied. "Whatever you did, it's not right."

"I don't understand," he said.

"The rain didn't affect me," she said frantically. "It's them! They've gone…wrong!"

She didn't know how else to explain it, and she didn't have much time. The sound of her pursuers was growing louder again. She pinned the phone to her ear with her shoulder and kept crawling forward.

"What do you mean?" Brian was saying. "What did I do?"

"Your algorithm," she forced out, breathing hard. The sounds were getting louder.

"Was it negated?" Brian shouted, desperately jumping to conclusions and searching for answers.

"No," Bonnie stammered. "They're infected. Everyone else."

Lost in the gloom, Bonnie ran smack into a metal wall and dropped the phone. Nose shooting with pain, she bent low, searching for the phone. When she found it, she put it to her ear. With her other hand, she felt for which way to go. There were walls to her right, left, up, down, and forward.

Suddenly, there was a bang of metal behind her. Bonnie's pursuers must have been close.

"Brian?" she cried, still searching the walls for a way out.

"Who's infected, Bonnie?" he asked in a strained whisper. "Talk to me!"

Another bang against the metal came from behind her. It was closer, vibrating through her legs and into her stomach.

"Bonnie...," Trisha said from behind her.

Bonnie screamed a little. There was no way out. She had crawled into a dead end.

She used the light from her phone screen to illuminate the passage behind her. Trisha was about ten feet away. Blood smeared her upper lip from a broken nose. Her eyes shone strangely with silver flecks in the pupil.

Bonnie's heart sank. There was nowhere to run, which meant there was only one thing to do.

It was her turn to say goodbye.

She put the phone to her ear and silenced Brian.

"I will love you until the end," she said.

"No," he said, his voice rising to a normal talking level. "No, don't leave. Bonnie, stay with me."

"Will you always love me?" Bonnie panted.

In the darkness of the vent, she could no longer see Trisha, but she could hear her breathing. There was a *ping* of metal as Trisha moved a little bit closer.

Bonnie dug into her pocket, palms sweaty. She wrapped her trembling fingers around the fortune cookie one last time.

"Until silver rain falls," replied Brian as he always did, the words bitter in the passing.

She hung up before he could hear her scream. Instantly, she was descended into darkness.

Silence reigned in the duct for a moment. Bonnie felt tears rising into her eyes.

"No crying at work, Bonnie," Trisha cooed, only a few feet away now. "They'll think you're weak."

Bonnie blinked away the tears, searching the darkness. She couldn't see anything except two tiny balls of sparkling silver. She was mesmerized by the flecks of silver swirling intricately in the pupil of Trisha's eye. As she watched, the eyes grew closer and closer. Less than a foot away now.

"Why are you doing this?" Bonnie asked.

"Because it's creepy good fun."

Bonnie could feel the hot exhalation on her face as Trisha spoke.

"You're going to kill me? In cold blood?"

"Yes," Trisha responded calmly, sadistically.

Bonnie put her cell phone back into her blouse pocket so she could free up both of her hands to fight. But as she put away her phone, she felt something bulky and metallic in her pocket.

Confused, Bonnie gripped the object. It was her handy Leatherman.

Her heart leapt with hope. She had a chance.

She pulled out the Leatherman and, with a click, brandished the knife.

"Put up a fight," Trisha said. "Make me fight for your blood."

A curl of hair on Bonnie's head lifted up. She swung up with the knife, cutting nothing but air and clanging against the metal sides of the vent.

"Too slow," Trisha whispered, her voice loudest in Bonnie's right ear. The sparkling eyes were unnervingly close.

She slashed again, drawing the short knife through the dark. This time, she found flesh. The bulky Leatherman jerked in her hand as the blade sliced into Trisha, who screamed and lunged at Bonnie.

"Give me a slice, Bonnie!" Trisha shouted. "Just a slice!"

Suddenly, Trisha's hands were on Bonnie. They grasped and tore, pulling on Bonnie's hair and tearing at her face. Bonnie swung with the knife, finding skin and clothes. Warm liquid spattered her hand.

The sound of yelling voices began to echo around Bonnie. More were coming, called by Trisha's shouts.

"Get off of me!" Bonnie cried desperately, sure that any moment would be her last.

"I'm creeping all over you!" Trisha replied, fingernails tearing into Bonnie's skin. She felt the hands travelling down, searching for her neck.

"Creeping down your spine!" Trisha yelled again.

Bonnie swung again, this time for the sparkling balls of silver that were Trisha's eyes. The blade hit the right ball and sank deep. Trisha's words caught in her throat and she spluttered a wet cough. Her body went limp, leaning onto the knife.

Shuddering, Bonnie threw Trisha back and away from her. The body hit the metal like a mallet hitting a gong.

The din of voices stopped for a moment and then started again, angrier and more aggressive. They were not yet close enough to attack Bonnie, but they were coming.

Their impending roars and shouts roused Bonnie. She could not stay here.

Bonnie spun around, making the metal beneath her creak and bow. She searched the sides of the metal walls around her for a nut, bolt, or screw, something she could open with the Leatherman. As though it had been waiting for her, she found four screws wedged into the bottom of the air duct. She had been sitting on a removable panel.

Fingers shaking, she folded the knife back into the Leatherman and withdrew the screwdriver head.

A shout reached Bonnie's ears, louder and more pronounced than the echoing voices. They had found her.

She glanced back. It was completely dark except for the faint flicker of silver glimmering at the far end of the passageway.

"Shoot," Bonnie cursed to herself.

She began unfastening the screw with her Leatherman, twisting faster and faster. The first screw came loose and the panel sagged under her weight. If she could undo just one more, the panel might bend enough for her to escape.

Bonnie dared to look up again, concentrating on unscrewing the second screw.

The glittering silver eyeballs were closer, only a few feet away. They were locked on her, unwavering.

"You don't kill us," said a male voice, one Bonnie didn't recognize. "We kill you."

Bonnie wasn't even breathing. Fear had frozen her lungs. All she could think to do was twist her wrist, unscrewing thread by thread.

Underneath her, the panel shuddered and bent. Bonnie kept applying pressure to the screw, but it was getting wedged by the bending metal.

"Let me kill you!" the man shouted. There was a scrabble of flesh on metal. He was rushing her.

Bonnie screamed and pushed down hard. The panel bent under her weight, folding down. Gravity grabbed a hold of her and pulled her down, just out of the attacker's grasp. She fell for what seemed like eternity, red warning lights flashing by.

She smacked into the ground, landing first on her right leg. It buckled with a terrible snap and she pitched forward, landing on her face. The cool linoleum of the floor smacked her cheek, scrapping off skin and drawing blood.

Bonnie lay there, breathing hard. Her phone pressed into her thigh uncomfortably. The Leatherman was still clenched tightly in her hand. Flashing red lights revealed that it was smeared with crimson blood.

Somehow, she was alive. Usually, she could find negativity in any situation, but in this moment, she could only be grateful.

Gingerly, she curled her body up so she could feel her leg. It rang with pain, but she could not feel any compound fractures.

A distant echo of angry voices reached Bonnie's ears. Her coworkers must have been assembling in the air duct, trying to find a safer way down to pursue their prey. Which meant she had to get moving.

"Thank you for joining us," whispered a voice suddenly. It was low, creeping, and right next to Bonnie's ear.

Bonnie sat bolt upright.

The red emergency light flashed from above, briefly illuminating the foyer Bonnie had fallen in.

She saw a flash of contorted bodies. Hundreds of shining eyes stared at her with sadistic smiles. The afterimage burnt in her mind. There were so many, and they were all staring at her.

"We all want a slice of the degenerate," said a man closest to her. He had a fire extinguisher in his hand, dented on the bottom with flecks of bone and blood.

Bonnie's grip on her Leatherman tightened, her only weapon against the innumerable attackers. It was her or them.

The red light flashed again.

They had advanced. Many of them were only inches from her now.

"We're creeping in from all sides," the man said, eyes shining, unblinking.

Emergency lights flashed once more. They had all advanced. Bonnie was face to face with the man. He had the stench of blood on his breath.

"Give us a good fight," the man said.

Bonnie began to swing. The air was filled with shouts and shrieks. Blood splattered her skin and clothes. She fought as cruelly as they did. Like falling into a stupor, she descended into the madness, slaughtering her attackers one by one.

4

Cori leapt out of the car after Natalie. She was smiling and felt light-hearted, the typical demeanor that she couldn't change, but she was trying to be mad. She needed to have a word with Natalie and did not want a goofy smile stuck on her face.

"You can stay in the car," Natalie said, not even looking back. "Someone should stay with Toby."

"I know you think you can do everything by yourself," Cori shot back bitterly, her smile making her words come out with a lilt despite how livid she wanted to be, "but that doesn't mean you have to be heartless."

Natalie paused, her hand on the door to the apartment complex.

"Is that what this is about?" she asked. "Me being heartless? Like your husband?"

The way Natalie glared at her reminded Cori of the creeper's piercing gazes.

"You have to bring Evan into this?" Cori said. "We're in the middle of a nightmare, and you still can't let it go?"

"As if there's something he deserves forgiveness for in the first place," Natalie spat.

Cori glared back. If Natalie even knew the depth of Evan's mistakes and remorse… But Evan and Cori had agreed long ago to bury that secret and never mention it.

"This isn't about Evan," Cori said after a deep breath. "This is about your choice." She paused again and said, "I understand why you did what you did. And I forgive you."

With a huff, Natalie turned away, sliding her key card over the electronic door lock. It beeped once and blinked red.

"You don't see anyone asking for it," she muttered, rubbing the card over the lock incessantly.

"You put me on the spot," Cori continued. "How can you ask me to choose between one life and another?"

Natalie didn't even turn around as she said, "I didn't realize it would be such a hard decision."

"Just because you won't let yourself love anyone else doesn't mean it's my fault Yolanda died."

Cori regretted her words the moment she said them. She cringed, expecting retaliation, but Natalie did not turn around with a look of fury or contempt. Instead, she kept fiddling with the key card and lock.

"I love Mark," Natalie said stoically.

Cori let out a groan.

"Won't you feel something for just once!" she cried at Natalie. "Do you have to be this solid block of ice all the time?"

Natalie finally got the door open. She charged in, Cori right behind her.

The hallway still had power, which lit the moss green and golden designs in the carpet.

"Is it that hard to cope with your feelings?" she continued, trying to get a rise out of Natalie. "Or are you stuck in default now?"

Natalie came to an abrupt halt. Cori thought she'd finally succeeded, but realized instead that they had reached Mark's apartment.

"Fine," Cori finally said. "Block me out. Block everyone out. Your future husband. Your future child. But don't expect us to come running to your aid the next time you have to make a decision in a sticky situation—"

"We're in," Natalie said, unlocking the door and swinging it wide. "Mark keeps the guns in his bedroom. Let's get in and get out in case there are any creepers in the other rooms."

Cori rolled her eyes.

It was like every other meaningful conversation she tried to have with Natalie. A topic would arise. Cori would pursue it with the tenacity of a dog with a new toy until Natalie zoned out and ignored her. The same thing had happened now. As they searched the apartment, Cori could tell she had pushed too far. Natalie didn't look at her or make small talk.

When they got to Mark's bedroom, they heard talking beyond the door. They proceeded with caution, Natalie in front as usual. Slowly, they opened the door and looked inside.

The bedroom was small with a bed, cabinet, and dresser. But the room looked different than Cori or Natalie had ever seen. Mark's medicine, which usually covered his cabinet top, had been stowed away. Silk flower petals covered the floor and bed comforter. In the corner, a radio was on, playing soft music. Cori could hear the whir of a CD playing.

Cori glanced at Natalie and was surprised to see that her friend's usual platonic features were stretched in a strange smile. It was not a happy smile, more wistful. Cori wondered if Natalie was somehow surprised by these small details Mark had planned for the return from their honeymoon.

They stood silently for a moment, Cori letting Natalie soak in the love that Mark had put into the small details.

"He told me not to come in here yesterday," Natalie suddenly said. "I could have cared less what he was hiding." She took a deep breath. "But now…"

"Now you feel something?" Cori goaded, trying to keep Natalie talking.

"I can feel, Cori," Natalie replied. "It's not that I can't. I just choose not to. Because I can't cope. I can't even look Mark in the eye and say how I honestly feel, because I don't know how to handle it."

The bluntness of Natalie's honesty caught Cori off guard. She opened her mouth and closed it, unsure of what to say.

"But this," she said. Her voice faded as she took in the room.

"It's one of the small ways Mark shows you how much he cares," Cori said.

Natalie didn't say anything for a minute and then stood straighter, her back tensing.

"Okay," she said. She marched over to the bedside cabinet and withdrew a gun.

Cori still stood there, abashed.

"That's it?" she asked. "Back to…whatever it is we're doing?"

"Getting to Hawaii," Natalie answered.

She placed a handgun on the bed and pulled open the shades covering a window. Outside, they could see Toby sitting idly in the back of the car.

"Why?" Cori inquired obstinately. "How?"

"Fly, of course," Natalie said. "There has to be someone who can fly a plane."

"But why? We can't even get through the city without running someone over. Why is Hawaii our destination?"

Natalie came over to Cori and touched her shoulders. As Cori looked into Natalie's eyes, she saw a small spark of emotion starting to burn.

"The city has gone creepy," Natalie said. "Who knows if it's just here or everywhere else. I can't explain it to you, but ever since we woke up on the interstate, things have been different. All that matters to me is that Toby, you, Mark…you're all safe. Mark and Evan aren't answering their phones, and I don't know what danger they might be in. I have to know he's safe."

Cori began to smile. She had never heard Natalie say much of anything affectionate about her friends or loved ones. Whatever was happening, it was a change Cori was happy to see.

"Then we'll go," Cori said. "But promise me. No more choosing one life or another. Everyone's life matters, not just ours."

Natalie gave her a firm nod, the spark disappearing from her eyes. She had rebuilt her wall and disappeared behind it.

"Everyone," she echoed hollowly. She paused another moment before saying, "I'm sorry about Yolanda. We'll talk about it later?"

Rather than press, Cori conceded. While Natalie checked on Toby from the window, Cori was drawn to the radio playing soft, romantic music. She turned off the CD and switched the radio to FM stations. Like before in Natalie's car, a majority of the stations were either static, dead air, or an ongoing emergency broadcast signal.

Cori changed the dial to AM stations and began searching. Her heart sank as she heard more and more static. Then, when all hope seemed lost, she heard a voice. The station was full of white noise, but she heard a gruff voice speaking closely into a microphone.

"...received intelligence that at approximately nine a.m., Pacific Standard Time, all communications were lost."

The voice was heavily accented. Cori thought it was Russian.

Behind her, Natalie leaned over, listening to the broadcast too.

"As of yet, the circumstances are unknown. This is being treated as a suspicious event and many countries are investigating. No attacks are being made on your shores. There is no need for alarm. If you have any information, please call..."

The man rattled off a series of numbers and then paused. Cori nearly turned it off, but Natalie stopped her.

"They'll probably start the message over," Natalie said.

A minute later, the man started speaking again.

"Good evening, this is Ivan Filimonov, general of the Russian Air Force. This message is being broadcasted over an AM station to the United States of America. Our country received intelligence that at approximately nine a.m., Pacific Standard Time, all communications were lost."

The message continued on as before. Cori and Natalie locked eyes.

"So it *is* everywhere," Cori said.

Natalie shook her head. "It sounds like it's just America. Russia must have hijacked one of the stations to communicate with the country," Natalie assumed. "That means everything else is at a dead stand still. Stock market, ports, flights. Everything must have stopped."

Cori bit her lip.

"So if Russia can't get a hold of anyone in the United States," Cori wondered, "does that mean this was a terrorist attack? Did someone make it rain silver to compromise the country?"

Natalie's eyes glazed over for a moment, but then she shook her head.

"I have no idea."

Cori knew better than that. Being friends with Natalie all these years had taught her to spot when she was lying.

"What?"

Natalie shook her head in a no-nonsense kind of way. "I have no idea, I really don't."

"You looked like you'd thought of something."

Natalie ignored her and grabbed the gun from off the bed.

"Come on," she said irritably.

Cori huffed and glanced at the radio one last time, pondering what was really happening in the world, and followed Natalie back to the car. Toby greeted them joyfully as they returned. Natalie put the car into gear and they were off, headed to the airport as though a flight were set to board in less than an hour. For safety of the country, Mark, Evan, and a little for herself, Cori clenched the sides of her seat tightly, bowed her head, and began to pray.

5

Mark Hofland tumbled through the mud and vegetation, banging his shins on tree trunks. The lush forest rushed by him in a dizzying blur of green. Somewhere behind him, Danny was screaming.

Suddenly, there was a snap and Danny's voice was cut short.

Mark barely had time to ponder what had happened. Light reached his eyes. He sensed he had rolled out from under the tree canopy. Rain began spattering him again and suddenly he was airborne. He landed with a crash, tumbling even faster.

Just when he thought it would never end, he rolled onto a flatter area which slowed him down. For a moment, he thought he would be fine, until he smacked into a solid rock wall. He came to an immediate stop and rolled onto his back with a groan.

He lay there, breathing raggedly and staring up into the thundering rain. Towering above him was a steep cliff face, the one he had seen earlier from the road. He must have rolled all the way down the hill to where the cliff met the hillside. Right beside him on the stone face was a muddy imprint of where his body had collided with the cliff.

Rain spattered his face. If anything, it was more humid down here. A few feet above him was the hillside he had just rolled down, a canopy of emerald green. There was no telling how far he had tumbled or where the road was.

And if he was here, where was Danny?

In the back of Mark's mind, he remembered hearing the snap and Danny's cry cut short.

Horrified at what might have happened, Mark tried to calm himself and inhaled deeply. Immediately, he got lightheaded and dizzy. Disorientation set in, blurring his peripheral vision and discombobulating his senses.

He reached for his inhaler, but it was gone.

Huffing and puffing, Mark sat up and tried to call for help, but he couldn't even hear himself. Mucus clogging his windpipe, making it impossible to yell, let alone talk.

He was alone. Helpless. If he stayed that way, he might die.

Struggling to breathe, he stumbled to his feet. His body felt bruised and battered.

He fumbled forward blindly, following the flat land between cliff and hillside. Mud clung to his sneakers like the mucus slowly closing his windpipes and asphyxiating his lungs. He hated cystic fibrosis.

The further he walked, the denser the vegetation and heavier the air became. His throat seemed to clog even more.

As he walked, he thought it was curious how flat the ground was next to the cliff. He noted that two treads were cut into the grass, like tire tracks.

Curious though it was, he did not care. He had a half hour at best before he stopped breathing altogether. He needed help.

In his delirium, hallucinations appeared on the hillside. Natalie popped out of the trees, telling him to not be scared and push through. Toby was there too, urging him to breathe. Mark's long-gone parents appeared, scolding him for his inadequacies and failures. But there was his grandmother, his protector and guardian, telling him as she had nearly every day of his childhood that he must persevere. Evan and Cori appeared too, yelling his name like cheerleaders. Danny appeared in front of him, threatening to trip Mark and bury his head in the mud.

Keep going, Mark told himself. *Keep going.*

Mud caked his shoes. His feet felt like concrete buckets. Rain pounded down on him. His breathing grew thicker with each exhalation. There was no way he could make it home unless he found—

Evan, Mark thought sporadically. He had to call Evan. It was his only hope.

From his inside pocket, Mark withdrew his cell phone. A few seconds later, the call connected.

"Mark?" a voice called frantically through the phone.

"Evan," Mark wheezed, his voice frayed by the humidity.

Overcome with exhaustion and oxygen deprivation, he collapsed into the mud. His face sank into the weeds in between the wheel tracks.

"Mark!" the voice hollered, but it didn't sound like Evan.

"Evan…help me…help," Mark gasped at the phone.

Weakness overcame him. His fingers lost grip and he dropped the phone. His lungs convulsed and he dry heaved.

Turning his head away from the vomit, he looked at the stone face of the cliff. For a moment, the rain cleared and he saw an iron door set into the cliff a few feet from him. The next moment, he was pelted again and drowning in the humidity. He choked on vomit and mucus and blacked out.

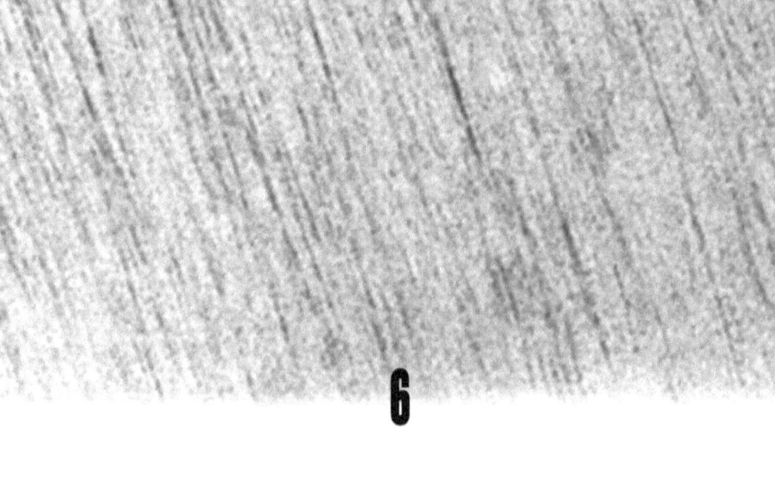

6

Nathaniel Matician still felt like he had two siblings, but a cold hole in his chest reminded him that Bethany was gone. Grandma Dottie might have said she would be safer alone in Sun Valley, but Nate had a sneaking suspicion that Bethany was not safe at all. The way she had hurt him… Something was wrong with her.

Yet again, Nate found himself wishing he had done something. If his father, Brian, had been in the car, he would have found a way to stop Bethany without anyone getting hurt or being left behind. But Nate had just sat there, letting his sister slam his head into the console and strangle him. The fresh wound on his forehead reminded him every few minutes of his failure.

Grandma Dottie eased the station wagon to a stop outside of the airport. The entire complex was on standstill. Cars filled the lanes for arrivals and departures. The parking garage hummed with idle vehicles. There wasn't the drone of airplanes.

"Where is everyone?" Grandma Dottie said slowly, suspiciously.

Nate glanced around quickly. Unlike the roads, which had been full of people moving around, the airport was a ghost town. There were no bystanders sleeping on the sidewalks or stirring from their slumbers. Every car was abandoned.

"Get your brother," Grandma Dottie requested.

Nate did as he was told and grabbed Wyatt.

Telling Boomer to heel, Nate held tight to Wyatt and followed Grandma Dottie into the airport. Although he had only flown a few times before, Nate thought the building was awfully quiet. Just like outside, it was empty of people. The silence was eerie and seemed to dampen even Boomer's footsteps.

The airport was two stories with escalators leading to security checkpoints and terminals. Grandma Dottie led Nate through the foyer, up the escalator, and onto the second floor. Ahead was a long hallway lined with shops. At the far end were security checkpoints. Beyond that were large windows, too bright to see through.

In between Nate and the security checkpoint was a maze of retractable stanchions that led travelers into lines. Dark, empty convenience stores were on either side of the hallway. Not a single person could be seen. Nate could have yelled, "Bomb!", and he suspected nothing would happen. In fact, not even the speakers were working, which Nate remembered were always on, updating travelers of gate changes and upcoming departures.

All at once, there was a far-off squeak from the foyer of the airport. Nate spun around, but could not see any movement. Someone must have entered the airport through the far doors Nate could not quite see.

Hushed voices and a squeak of metal echoed out of the foyer. At his feet, Boomer let out a quiet growl.

"Boomer," Nate said warningly, and Boomer sat, looking ashamed with himself.

When the newcomers did not appear at the escalators, Grandma Dottie grabbed onto Nate and led him into the shadows of a dimly lit magazine store along the right wall. They crouched in the shadows as the voices got nearer.

While his grandma waited, Nate looked around the store. It was dark in the far reaches, seemingly extending into another world.

Whispers reached Nate's ears. Out of the corner of his eye, he saw two women dismount the escalator and jog to the opposite wall. One was pushing a wheelchair which held a young boy. The other woman was carrying a red ax.

Nate glanced back at the dark corner of the store. Boomer was looking there too, his wispy ears perked up. His senses told him there was something there, unseen and hiding. As he stared, he thought he saw the outline of a hunched man, standing unmoving in the dark.

Terrified, Nate looked away and clung tightly to Wyatt, right as Grandma Dottie stepped out of the store, pulling Nate along.

"Cori?" Grandma Dottie said, her voice ringing in the hall.

The name sounded distantly familiar to Nate, and it took him a moment to place it. It was his aunt Cori, whom he had not seen in years. She was the one wielding the ax. He hoped they wouldn't have to use it on the man hiding in the store, silver shining in his eyes.

7

At the sound of Cori's name, Natalie Harper snapped her head around to see a tall, serious-looking woman in a flower dress striding out of a dark store to their right. The woman looked familiar, as did the boy she was dragging behind her. The boy had a small baby in his arms and a tiny dog following at his heels. She couldn't place them, but was happy to realize the airport was not completely empty. It also helped that none of the people running at them had silver in their eyes.

"Mom?" Cori said incredulously.

Cori ran at the woman, dropping the ax on the ground.

As Natalie watched, she placed the people in her memory. Eyes passing over each one, she recognized Cori's mother, Grandma Dottie, and Nate, Cori's nephew. The baby in Nate's arms was new.

"Where have you been?" Cori said, her whisper rising to normal speaking volumes. "Are you all okay?"

Cori's mother gave Cori and Natalie a stern look as she said, "We're just fine, dear. I notice you haven't returned any of my calls."

"We've been a little busy," Cori huffed.

The woman embraced Natalie next.

"It's Grandma Dottie, dear," she said, tapping Natalie's cheek.

She looked at Toby. "And you might be?"

Toby turned in the wheelchair with a smile. "Toby, ma'am."

"Do you have a last name with your manners, Toby?" Grandma Dottie asked.

"Mom, where have you all been?" Cori interjected, hugging Nate. "Did you see—"

"The rain?" Grandma Dottie interrupted. "Yes. I believe it's the cause of this…"

Her voice trailed off.

"What are you doing here anyway?" Cori asked.

"Finding a plane," Grandma Dottie replied. "Don't think I spent all those years in the military to forget how to fly when we need to get somewhere. Why are you hiding in an airport?"

"Hoping to catch a ride," Cori said. "We have to find Evan and Mark."

"Planning to fly there all by yourself?"

"We can go together," said Cori cheerily. "We need to outrun this."

"Where are they?" Grandma Dottie said with a sigh.

"Hawaii," Natalie and Cori said in unison.

Grandma Dottie pursed her lips. "Turns out we do have something in common. That's our second stop after Los Angeles. Hawaii is a safe zone."

"Safe zone?" Cori asked, her voice high.

"Yes," Grandma Dottie said. "Now come here, dear."

Cori and Grandma Dottie embraced, more heartwarming than their first contact.

As Natalie watched the family interact, she began to remember Grandma Dottie with better clarity. Grandma Dottie had always been blunt and slightly condescending. Her years in military had made her brass and controlling. Natalie remembered how insensitive she had been at

Cori's wedding, nitpicking details down to a stray hair on Cori's gown and the forced smile on Natalie's face. That day, Dottie's doting had hardly bothered Natalie. But now, for some reason, Dottie's crudeness to Cori bothered Natalie. Annoyance threatened to break loose, but she gripped the handles of the wheelchair until it went away.

Now, if only the bubbling fear would leave her stomach.

"Who is this?" Cori asked Nate, cooing at the baby.

"Wyatt," Nate said, his voice quiet. He fidgeted slightly, eyes traveling back to the store he had been hidden in.

"Don't you think that's something you should know?" Dottie said, raising her eyebrows.

"And you have a dog?" Cori asked, ignoring her mother.

"His name is Boomer," Nate said.

Boomer whined slightly, but he wasn't looking at Cori or Nate. The dog was staring at a dark store across the hallway, ears and tail up and still.

"Cute little dog," Cori said. "Is he new?"

Nate nodded. "I found him this morning when…"

"What happened?" Cori asked.

No one answered. Nate cast his eyes to the carpeted ground.

Natalie kept her eyes trained on Boomer. The dog was sensing something they were not.

"Hold on," Cori said. She stood up and looked down the hallway. "Where is Bethany? And Sis?"

"Cori," Natalie said warningly, eyes now trained on the dark store. Shadowed figures were looming from the back, walking slowly to the edge of the store.

"You don't know where your sister is?" Grandma Dottie was saying. "Shocking!"

"Where are they?" Cori said, clearly suspecting the worst.

"Cori, Dottie," Natalie said, louder this time. "We need to move."

Mother and daughter continued to ignore Natalie completely.

"Have you not noticed the world is falling apart?" Cori asked her mother. "Do you mind answering my questions?"

"You wouldn't need the questions answered if you would call from time to time," Grandma Dottie replied sardonically.

"Guys!" Natalie shouted, tensing. "Creepers!"

Her voice did not attract their attention, but Boomer let out a bark that put the blast of a gunshot to shame. The women fell silent and spun around, seeing what Natalie had been watching.

From the dark, shadowed stores, people were emerging. The sound of many bodies shambling onto the escalator echoed up out of the foyer. They were being surrounded from all sides.

"They set a trap," Cori muttered. "The creepers set a trap."

Grandma Dottie shot Cori a patronizing stare as though *creepers* were a poor substitute for a curse word.

Suddenly, the intercom system that had been silent came online. A calm voice spoke, the breaths and smack of lips loud over the speaker.

"Ladies and gentlemen, please proceed to the nearest security checkpoint for a full body scan. Any unattended bodies will be thoroughly examined."

The intercom smacked loudly as though the microphone had been dropped.

"Everyone stay together," Grandma Dottie said, grabbing onto Nate's hand. "To the planes!"

From the back of Toby's wheelchair, Natalie withdrew Mark's old Ruger Security Six revolver. She gripped the wheelchair handle tightly with her other hand and told Toby to hold on. His eyes were wide and a thin sheen of sweat glistened on his brow.

Beside her, Cori brandished the ax. She had a smile on her face in complete contrast to the situation.

"Plug your ears, Toby," Natalie said. "It's going to be okay."

"Go!" Grandma Dottie shouted.

They ran forward together. Boomer took charge with a bark.

From the stores, creepers ran at them. Silver eyes glinted fiercely. Jaws clenched and faces contorted in murderous rage. Muscles tensed, hands reaching or brandishing a blunt object. They all shouted, their voices jumbled and nondescript.

Natalie fired as she ran. The shots were extremely loud indoors, echoing off the walls and into her ears. Tremors shot through her hand with each fired bullet. Her aim was true—creepers fell with each shot.

Boomer jumped through legs, causing creepers to stumble and fall. They made easy targets. The dog kept going, leading the way to the security checkpoints.

Beside Natalie, Cori took a swing at the closest creeper, screaming a prayer and squeezing her eyes shut. The creeper, an older man, was hit in his chest and crumpled to the ground. Cori pried the ax away and kept swinging.

So much for every life matters, Natalie thought sardonically and blasted a creeper out of her way.

Grandma Dottie was firing too, bearing her shotgun with the marksmanship of a sniper. Fire was in her eyes. Nate ran beside her, holding his baby brother tight.

Natalie did not know how long it went. They ran forward, pausing to reload, but never stopping for more than a few seconds. When Natalie ran out of ammo for the handgun, she pulled out a Berretta shotgun. Adrenaline kept them moving fast, fingers quick. Toby, Nate, and Wyatt were all crying, but no one had been hurt.

The six of them made it to the checkpoint as Boomer ran through and disappeared around the corner. Natalie's ears rang like an alarm bell, but she noticed the sound of attackers had dwindled significantly. Creepers were still coming from behind, but they were doing so cautiously. Although numerous, the creepers were not armed with weapons as powerful as guns. They seemed to understand this and held back, waiting for the opportunity to strike.

Natalie pushed Toby's wheelchair through the security checkpoints to the end of the hallway. They could either go right or left. Straight ahead of them were panoramic windows that showed the airport tarmac. Natalie glanced down the hallways—no one was there—and looked out the windows.

What she saw made her stop dead.

Cori, Grandma Dottie, and Nate arrived beside her. They stared.

The tarmac outside was packed with people. Hundreds of them, creepers all, crowded the pavement and crawled over airplanes. There were heaps of bloody bodies. Each and every airplane looked to have been compromised, some with bashed and dented wings, others with broken glass. In some of the windows, Natalie could see figures running back and forth quickly.

She scanned the whole of the tarmac. Not a single plane, commercial or private, was left untouched. There would be no flying out of here.

"Natalie?" Toby said nervously from the wheelchair. "What do we do?"

Fear returned, not for her own safety, but for the lives of those around her. It increased her heart rate and made her feel woozy again. But she could not collapse here. The fear was building up and would ruin her, but not here. Not now. She had to get everyone out of here.

"Come on!" Natalie commanded.

She swung Toby's wheelchair around and went down the hallway to the right leading to the A and B terminals.

"Where are you going?" Grandma Dottie shouted after her.

"We have to get out of here!" Natalie called back. "We have to get to the car or a train or—"

Her voice caught with fear, realizing she had no plan as she ran deeper into the bowels of the airport. Cori and her family followed Natalie blindly, but even Natalie did not know where she was going.

They ran down hall after hall, each terminal devoid of people. A few bodies were scattered here or there, killed in grotesque ways, seemingly placed there to indicate the path to certain death.

"Natalie!" Cori suddenly shouted.

Natalie turned, expecting to be told that they couldn't just keep running. But instead, Cori caught up to her, brandishing her cell phone.

"It's Evan!" she shouted.

Cori juggled the ax into her other hand and answered the phone.

"Evan!" Cori shouted into the speaker. "Are you okay?"

Her pleased expression gave Natalie some relief. Mark and Evan must have been safe.

Natalie glanced over her shoulder. No one was following them, but she suspected the creepers would not be far behind.

"This way," said Grandma Dottie. She led Nate further down, toward the end of the terminals. "Natalie is right. We need a way out."

Natalie pushed Toby's chair after Grandma Dottie. Cori ran beside her, plugging her one ear. She looked worried now.

They reached the end of the terminal, an oblong room with a dozen gates. The room was dark and filled with chairs. Natalie could not see any living bodies, but there were plenty of corpses.

"Toby," Natalie said. "Close your eyes."

He did as he was told, shaking in his seat.

"That one," Grandma Dottie said, pointing to the gate at the far end of the room. There was a large metal door open to a walkway. Typically, the walkway would have led to a plane, but it was lit with sunlight.

Natalie's heart leapt with emotion, a happy feeling. She suspected it was something called hope.

They could get to the walkway, crawl down, sneak to the cars, and get out of here. Somehow, they were going to survive this.

"Natalie," Cori said, her voice sad and quiet. It was not like her, not the tone Cori usually had.

Natalie spun on her. The feeling of hope fled, replaced suddenly with the overwhelming, powerful feeling of fear. It was as strong as when she had been on the red road.

Cori's eyes were filled with tears and she looked terrified.

"Evan lost Mark," she said.

As though Natalie had been transported back to the red road, all of her fear exploded through her. She could hardly move and she was breathless.

"Where is he?" Cori yelled into the phone. "Evan, where is Mark?"

Whatever Evan was saying wasn't good. Cori looked mortified.

All at once, the air was filled with the sound of shouts. Shadows covered the walls. The creepers were coming.

"We have to go!" Grandma Dottie shouted from the open doorway leading to the walkway.

Frozen in fear, petrified in terror, Natalie suddenly felt her phone vibrate through her pant leg. A familiar ringtone filled the air.

It was Mark.

Absurd as it was, she put the shotgun in Toby's wheelchair and answered her phone.

"Mark!" she shouted frantically.

The airwaves were full of static. The clamor of voices from the creepers made it difficult to hear.

"Evan?" said Mark, his voice weak and barely audible.

"No," Natalie shouted into the zaps of static. "It's me, Mark!"

Her voice was met by static and no reply from Mark.

Splotches danced in Natalie's eyes. Toby was looking at Natalie, his eyes wide and nervous. His whole body trembled.

At the far side of the room, she saw Grandma Dottie waving at them feverishly. Natalie stumbled forward, pushing Toby weakly and stumbling.

"Mark!" Natalie shouted again into the phone.

Beside her, Cori was yelling at Evan: "Run down the hill!"

Mark's voice returned in Natalie's ear, weak and dying.

"Evan," he said. "Help me…help."

"Mark!" Natalie cried into the phone, her voice torn with fear. In her eyes, she could see the red road. But this time, it was not her mother dying in the seat beside her. It was Mark. There would be no recovering from this for Natalie. There would be no brown room. She would not be able to bury her feelings so deep that she could not remember how to feel. Mark was dying, and it would destroy Natalie.

"Natalie?" Toby said, his voice small and fearful. "Are you okay?"

She saw his scared little face. His cheek ticked and his pupils were dilated. He had seen too much, experienced too much in too little time. A seizure was coming.

The line went dead in Natalie's hand with a crackle of static. Mark was gone. Just like her father when she was six. Just like her mother when she was fifteen.

As had happened on the red road, Natalie's fear grew to an unstoppable point and transformed.

Her heartbeat slowed. Each breath felt thick and her limbs felt heavy.

As though the shell around her heart had broken, emotion surged through Natalie. Just one emotion. She knew exactly what it was.

Grief.

It had wrecked her on the red road, and it tore through her now. Her hands shook and she lost her grip on the phone and Toby's wheelchair. Her heart thundered in her ears, slow and terrible. She collapsed, pushing Toby's wheelchair away and landing on the carpeted floor.

Cori was beside her, holding up her head, shouting to get up.

In her peripherals, Natalie saw Toby's wheelchair bounce off a row of seats. The wheelchair turned just enough for her to see Toby fidgeting. He was having a seizure.

Grandma Dottie and her grandkids screamed bloody murder. Cori shouted at Natalie to get up, glancing over her shoulder in terror. Then, someone was grabbing Natalie's arms and pulling her along the carpet. Sunlight and shadows danced across her face as she was dragged.

She should have found her strength and stood. But Natalie did not care. She had failed all of them and she had lost Mark.

In her mind's eye, she could see those she had failed. Yolanda lay in the street, holding a hand out, pleading. Joaquin stared at her, thrown unceremoniously in the corner behind the nurses' station with puffy lips and a bruised neck. Toby shook uncontrollably, drool running from his mouth. Mark's voice filled her, a ghostly echo that haunted her. She could only imagine what would happen to Cori and her family now that Natalie had fallen apart. They would be ambushed and murdered.

She had failed them all.

Her vision dimmed completely and all the sounds melded together. A crimson circle hovered in front of her, a taunting red button that she wanted to press and hit and slam. But there was no escape. This was not a simulation that she could exit with the touch of a button.

Into the darkness she fell. Natalie lost herself, frozen by fear and powerless to grief.

8

Smoke clouded Natalie's vision of the red road. She had torn off her seatbelt, but she was still pinned. She fought to free herself, her flesh tearing.

The sirens were still too far away.

A hand touched Natalie's shoulder. Natalie stopped and looked over to her mother, whose face was clouded in smoke. Rose's eyes were still shining, but not with tears or joy. There was something in her eyes. The black pupils glinted as though flecks of silver were dancing in them.

"Don't, Natalie," Rose said calmly, eyes gleaming. "Focus on your body, feel what you cannot."

Natalie refused to listen. She could not be taught lessons right now.

"Natalie," her mother said again, calming Natalie's nerves. "If you try to move now, you will hurt yourself. Don't hurt yourself again."

Though her heart begged her to escape, Natalie listened to her mother. She calmed her mind and tried to focus on what she was feeling.

Her limbs were still attached, but her legs felt raw and exposed. It must have been the metal and plastic that had perforated the skin. She knew that if she moved, she might injure her legs to the point of no return.

There was a screech of tires outside. A giant firetruck lurched to a stop nearby. Firemen rushed to Natalie's side.

"Save her!" Natalie shrieked, pointing through the smog at her mother. "Save her!"

"It's about to blow!" one of the firemen warned. "Go, go, go!"

Natalie fought the firemen grabbing her, yelling for them to get her mother. As she did, the fire on the engine grew, threatening to enter the cab.

Suddenly, all of the firemen left her side but one. He brought his mouth to her ear and shouted, "If you don't leave now, you will die."

Natalie tried to yell at him to save her mother, but smoke choked her words.

The fireman gripped her arms tightly and pulled. Natalie felt her skin tear and she was pulled out of the car as the interior filled with fire. The fireman ran for it, dragging her away despite her shrieks. Over his shoulder, she saw the car explode in a red hot ball of flame and her mother's body crumble to ashes.

PHASE 5

SAFE TRAVELS

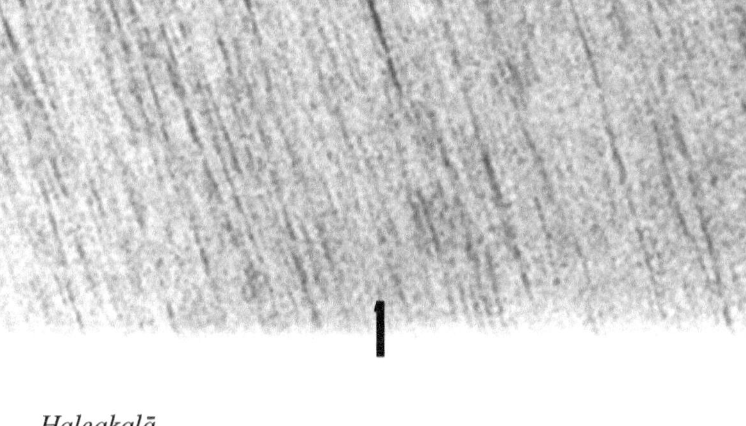

1

Haleakalā
Maui, Hawaii

Evan Silverman practically fell down the rain-slicked mountainside, miraculously staying on his feet. Spirals of mud cascaded around him as he slipped down the hill. He caught the trunks of palm trees to slow himself down, skidding around them. All the while, he kept his phone to his ear, trying to hear Cori.

Near as he could tell, Cori had found her grandma and nephews, Natalie had Toby, and they had made it to an airport. Apart from that, Cori sounded petrified. Now, all Evan could hear were grunts, static, loud blasts, and a dog barking.

A palm tree appeared out of the thick rain. Something was wrapped around the base of the trunk. Evan caught his foot on it and fell face first into the mud. His phone went flying.

Grumbling, Evan pushed himself back upright. His face was coated in mud. Wiping mud from his eyes, he searched frantically for his phone. He had to hear from Cori, he had to know she was alright. He had to tell her when he found Mark. It was Evan's only chance to set things right.

Evan wiped his eyes again and searched his surroundings more thoroughly. His eyes fell on the base of the palm tree trunk beside him and he jumped in fright.

Danny was wrapped around the tree, his body contorted. Dead eyes stared at Evan without seeing. His head was bent at an odd angle compared to his chest.

Evan closed his eyes, trying to find some shred of decency to mourn for Danny. When he couldn't find any, he said a silent prayer and abandoned the search for his phone. He had to find Mark.

Slipping and sliding, Evan continued down the hill. The humidity became warmer the deeper he went. His legs trembled from the effort of keeping himself upright.

At last, he arrived at the bottom of the hill. There was a sheltered alcove at the base, overhung by a steep cliff. Tire treads had been cut into the grassy flat. Puddles of rain collected in muddy footprints along the road.

Evan followed it with his eyes. The footsteps led down and out of sight.

Frantic, he began to run, following the tracks. His heart thundered in his chest uncontrollably. He should have taken his medicine, but he did not care right now. He had to find Mark. All this time, Evan had been trying to do right by Natalie and Mark and mend his mistakes. Her life had been his fault, and he had to set it right with Mark. But now, it seemed Evan had ruined everything. Again.

Several yards in front of him, Evan saw a dark mound on the grass. It looked like a collapsed human.

He rushed over to it, slipping in the mud.

The figure was Mark, face down in a puddle of puke. A phone was in his hand.

Evan collapsed beside him. He put Mark's phone in his pocket and shook his friend. Mark didn't move.

"Come on, buddy!" Evan called, dragging Mark out of the grass and into his arms.

Mark's eyes remained closed. His face was pale. Mucus ran from his lips and nostrils. Every few seconds, his body shook. His breathing was short and fast. Evan could hear all of the mucus clogging his friend's windpipe.

"Come on, Mark!" Evan cried, patting his friend on the face.

Mark mumbled deliriously, wincing.

Evan rubbed Mark's chest, urging him to wake up. Mumbling slightly, Mark gagged and vomited a stomach-full of mucus.

"Gross," Evan murmured, turning away from the vomit to avoid throwing up. Despite the smell, relief flooded him. At least Mark was still alive, though fevered.

Evan glanced at the cliff. He froze, not comprehending what he was seeing. A few feet from him, set into the cliff, was an iron door.

Evan eased Mark back to the ground and ran to the door. He pulled on the iron handle, but it didn't budge. Assuming it was locked, Evan dug through the grass for a rock. He found a heavy one and slammed it on the handle. A few hits later, the handle gave way and the door opened slightly.

Elated, Evan dragged Mark through the door. Inside was a dank, dark hallway that led off into the shadows.

Evan closed the iron door, blocking out the rain, and collapsed beside Mark. He listened for Mark's breathing, which was slow and chunky with mucus.

For a moment, Evan allowed himself to breathe. He was one step closer to redeeming himself.

2

Dr. Griffith "The Griffin" Avazino slunk through the labyrinth of halls on the hunt for Matician.

At one point, perhaps several hours ago, he had heard a crack and a scream echo through the halls. Assuming that Matician had relocated his shoulder himself, the Griffin had made chase, but had not found the climatologist.

Though weak and decrepit, the climatologist was wry and stealthy. So the hunt continued.

Every so often, the Griffin found blood splatters. He lapped it up with his tongue and followed the trail until he lost it again.

After some time, the Griffin came across another spatter of blood by a door to the nuclear reactor. The doorknob was smeared with blood too.

Growling with pleasure, the Griffin opened the door, revealing a descending staircase wrapped around the outer wall of a circular chamber. He descended quietly. The metal steps hardly creaked as he slunk from step to step.

A story below was the reactor, a massive contraption of cylinders, coils, cords, and power. The air hummed ever so slightly from the reactor providing energy to the facility.

The Griffin scanned the stairs leading to the reactor. He did not see any sign of blood or Matician.

At a glance, the Griffin could see just how much the launch of the silver rain had expended the reactor. The coolant submersing the reactor had been depleted significantly. If Matician had indeed ruined the silver rain and the Griffin needed to launch it again, the coolant would need to be replenished. But he could not proceed without knowing what Matician had done.

Growling contemptuously, the Griffin stalked back up the stairs. Matician had tricked him—he hadn't come into the reactor, but pretended to do so in hopes of gaining more distance.

Once back on the main level, the Griffin wound his way toward the exit in the cliff. All the while, his mind calculated the scenarios. Perhaps Matician had made a run for it. If Matician had made it outside, he could have found the ATV and escaped.

That was unacceptable, the Griffin decided, and he picked up the pace. He weaved through corridor after corridor until he was a hundred paces away.

At the intersection leading to the exit, the Griffin heard someone cough. The burst of air was loud, reverberating down the hall. Someone was just around the corner, perhaps by the door leading to the exit.

The Griffin came to a stop, waiting. He heard faint mumbling.

Cautiously, the Griffin crept to the corner, clenching the shard of glass tight. He leaned toward the corner, not looking, just listening.

Whispers of voices reached the Griffin's ears clearly. There seemed to be two males speaking, neither of which sounded like Matician.

"Keep talking, man," said one of them. "Mark…Mark! I told you, keep talking."

There was a cough and gag before the other replied, "Why?"

"It's clearing up the gunk," said the first. "There's less humidity in here. Get your breath back, but keep talking. Tell me anything. Just talk."

"How are we going to get out of here?"

"I meant talk about something positive. What about Natalie?"

There was another cough and groan. "She'll be here soon."

There was a pause.

"Mark…," said the first male. "When I talked to Cori… Well, something was happening on the mainland."

The Griffin felt his pulse quicken. Could this be the first news of what was happening? Would it be proof that his masterpiece had succeeded? Or would he discover that Matician had ruined everything?

When neither man spoke, the Griffin dared to peer around the corner.

Two men were sitting at the end of the hallway, illuminated by the light of a cell phone. One was wiping his face with a handkerchief. The other, a tall, lanky man, was staring at the door. Both of them were wearing bright yellow jumpsuits.

The Griffin barred his teeth into a grin. If he was not mistaken, he knew the tall man closest to the door. It was Evan Silverman.

Here for his grand reward after all, the Griffin thought to himself.

Silent as possible, the Griffin crept around the corner and inched toward the men.

"It'll be okay," said the one with the handkerchief. "Natalie will find us."

Evan paused, cleared his throat, and said unconvincingly, "Sure they will. Yeah, and then you'll get married."

The other male, presumably named Mark, remained silent.

Evan's head snapped to look at his friend; the Griffin froze, not wanting to be seen.

"You're getting married, right?" Evan asked.

Mark met Evan's eye. His shoulders sagged.

"Let's talk about something else," he requested. He exhaled deeply and began coughing violently.

Evan turned back to face the door as his friend coughed, allowing the Griffin to sneak closer.

"Fine, fine," Evan said. "Maybe you don't want to get married right now. Wedding jitters. But don't tell me you're having cold feet about the adoption too."

"No," the other male wheezed. "I love Toby to death."

Twenty yards away from them, the Griffin froze.

"There you go," Evan said. "Tell me more about Toby."

"He's a special kid," said Mark. "Natalie and I love him to pieces, though once upon a time, he had a crazy father who tried to cut him to pieces. You should know."

Evan remained silent for a beat before saying, "Why's that?"

"Well, you know, you were on the trial case for Toby's dad."

Evan's head snapped to the side again, but the Griffin no longer cared about being seen. He knew this story. It was time to attack.

"M–Mark," Evan stammered, unaware of the danger. "What is Toby's last name?"

"Avazino," said the man named Mark. "Toby Avazino."

3

Brian Matician suppressed a whimper of pain as he prepared to fight. He was thirty yards from the exit, but Dr. Griffith Avazino stood in his way. There were also two men sitting by the door, unaware of the danger they had stepped into.

Dr. Avazino took another step toward the men and lifted his right arm high. Brian saw a flash of light in Avazino's hand. The doctor was holding a shard of glass sharp enough to separate a fly from its wings.

Brian tightened the tourniquet around his arm once more and sprang from the shadows of the hallway. He sprinted the distance to Avazino—his footsteps alerted the men at the door—and leapt on the doctor's back. He wrapped his good arm around Avazino's neck and squeezed.

Surprised, Avazino choked and stumbled.

By the door, the two men in the yellow jumpsuits jumped to their feet.

"Go!" Brian screamed at them.

Avazino staggered back, dropping the shard of glass. Brian was smacked into a wall, but he held fast, making the doctor fight for air.

Back at the front of the hall, one of the men threw open the door. The light outside was blinding compared to the dark hallway.

Momentarily distracted and blinded, Brian loosened his grip. Avazino pulled hard, sucked in a gulp of breath, and threw Brian over his head. Brian flew toward the door, his vision seared by the white light. With a smack, he hit the two men. He bowled them over, throwing the three of them through the door and out into the rain.

Shocked by the change in atmosphere, Brian pulled himself out of the mud and wiped his eyes. They were in a grassy alcove between a hillside of palm trees and the steep cliff the facility was built inside. Behind them, the doorway into the facility was wide open and dark.

Beside Brian, the two men were struggling to get to their feet. The shorter one was spitting thick gobs of saliva into the grass. He looked deathly pale.

"Come on!" Brian cried.

He helped them to their feet and wrapped his good arm around the weaker one. Like contestants in a three-legged race, the three of them took off at a stumbling gait, tripping over each other and slipping in the mud and slick grass.

"Who are you!" shouted the healthier man, a lanky individual with sharp cheek bones and mud coating his front.

A roar of anger came from behind them.

"Your hero!" Brian shouted back. He tried to run faster, but mud caked his shoes. Avazino would be upon them at any moment.

All at once, a bulky, dark object appeared out of the rainy haze right in front of them. The three men tried to stop, but slid right into it. Hard plastic met Brian's knees and he collapsed onto the ground.

Groaning, Brian got back onto his feet. The object they had run into was a four-wheeler with two rows of seats.

"Up!" Brian shouted at the two men. He pulled the shorter, ill one to his feet.

"You will rectify your mistakes, Matician!" called Avazino through the rain. "You will fix what you have done and bleed for me!"

Avazino's voice echoed around Brian's ears. It sounded like the bloodthirsty doctor was only a few feet away, but Brian could not see him. The rain was coming down too hard.

"Get in," Brian insisted to the men.

The sickly man got in without hesitation, coughing uncontrollably. The second man, however, met Brian face to face.

"Who are—" the man began.

Suddenly, his eyes went wide with recognition. Brian stared too, not believing what he was seeing.

"Evan?" Brian shouted.

"Brian!" Evan shouted back.

A roar of anger interrupted them. Avazino charged out of the rain, running fast.

Brian leapt onto the four-wheeler as Evan threw a fist-full of mud at Avazino. The doctor's face was covered and he slipped on the grass.

Broken arm aching, Brian searched the dashboard frantically for a key. Luck had it; the key was already in the ignition.

"Get in!" Brian cried to Evan.

Evan threw another gob of mud at Avazino and leapt into the cabin of the four-wheeler.

Brian hit the gas pedal. They lurched and stopped moving. The wheels spun in the mud.

"Ease the accelerator!" Evan shouted.

Brian tried again, slower, and the four-wheeler lurched forward.

"Come back here, Matician!" cried Avazino, his voice blaring in Brian's ears.

"Go!" Evan exclaimed.

Brian hit the accelerator harder, and the four-wheeler propelled down the alcove, skidding in mud. They jumped up and down as Brian guided the tires into the wheel ruts cut into the grass. He dared to glance back to see Avazino disappearing into the haze, unable to keep up.

"Where are we going?" Brian cried over the rush of wind.

"Medicine!" Evan yelled back.

Confused, Brian glanced at Evan. But Evan was busy looking at his friend, who was passed out in the backseat. A thick glob of mucus was running from his mouth.

"We bought him a few minutes," Evan said, "but not much more. Get us off this mountain."

4

The Griffin watched the four-wheeler disappear into the rain, mud dripping down his meaty face. He growled in contempt.

He had been caught off guard. The arrival of Silverman and his friend had been unanticipated, providing Matician the chance to attack.

But there was something more that had surprised the Griffin, other than Silverman's appearance. In fact, it was excellent news. Silverman's friend was adopting a child, and not just any child. Toby. The Griffin's own flesh and blood, the abhorrent degenerate he had failed to kill.

The Griffin remembered the night all too well. After all, he had fondled the memory day after day in prison.

After the productive day in the Supreme Court, the Griffin had returned home triumphant. The world had been destined to change thanks to his hand in the court system. But that had not solved his family problems, mainly his nauseating wife and the degenerate child she had produced.

It was then that the Griffin had decided to cleanse his bloodline. He had retrieved a knife and waited under the parking lot stairs until his wife had come home. After dragging his wife into the condo, the Griffin had taken the knife to her. He had cut her hair raggedly and stripped her bare. With the knife's point, he had drawn blood from the most painful places. She had tried again to scream for help, a muted yelp that he had silenced with force. But her screams had roused their son, Toby, a tiny four-year-old in pajamas. He had come out of his bedroom, wiping sleep from his eyes, and had screamed when he had seen the gore.

The boy first then, the Griffin had thought.

With ease, the Griffin had thrown the butcher knife at his son. The blade had sunk deep into Toby's chest. The boy had collapsed against the wall.

Satisfied that he had severed one of his family's malignant growths, the Griffin had turned his attention back to his wife. He had found her neck and strangled the life from her. Desperation had swelled, then faded from her eyes. Her jaw had slackened and a puff of air had escaped her lungs. It had been an intoxicating moment that surely could not have been surpassed.

Until his son had let out a gasping, whimpering breath.

The Griffin had leapt from one prey to the next. Holding Toby against the wall, the Griffin had withdrawn the knife and sunk it into his son again. Toby had screamed a little less with each stab. When the boy had continued to cling to life, the Griffin had set about severing each of his muscles.

For every scream, with each stab, the Griffin had cursed his son, the decrepit, degenerate spawn. The Griffin had despised the boy's very existence, an imperfection where the Griffin demanded faultlessness.

Eventually, the boy had stopped screaming. His eyes had become fixed on the window. Outside, it had begun to rain. The lights of the condo parking lot had made the rain look silver.

Annoyed that the boy had stopped squealing, the Griffin had realized it was time to end the boy's life. There had been one muscle left intact: his heart.

The Griffin had withdrawn the knife one more time. Toby had hardly flinched, eyes locked on the rain that had taken on a red-blue hue.

Then the police had arrived.

It had taken five men to subdue the Griffin. The knife had fallen to the floor, silver stained red, the razor-sharp tip furled and bent.

The last sight the Griffin had seen of his family was his dead wife, spread-eagle in the living room and Toby lying like a puppet against the wall, blood drenching his pajamas.

The Griffin had reveled in that memory. Of all the deaths he had perpetrated, this one had stuck with him the most. It had not been just murder. He had purged his family of its degeneration. Back then, he could not imagine any other goal worth pursuing that could trump that definitive, pivotal moment.

A few days later in jail, he had discovered that Toby had lived. Although originally disappointed, the Griffin had been settled for patience, waiting for the day he could kill the boy.

At long last, it seemed he would have the chance. The boy would be coming to the island with another woman.

The Griffin grinned. His list of prey was growing. First Matician, then Silverman and his friend— undoubtedly headed to the hotel—and then, Toby would arrive.

It would be a moment more fundamental than when the Griffin had first tried to kill the boy, perhaps more defining than the silver rain.

The Griffin let out a growl of comprehension. Toby's impending arrival practically ensured that the silver rain had not worked as intended. Matician had truly mutated the nanobytes beyond their original directives. Which meant the Griffin would eventually have to find another way to spread his desolation across the country. But that would come in due time. First, he would find Toby and completely, totally eradicate the degeneration of his bloodline.

The Griffin turned in the mud, stalking his way back to the facility. He weaved his way through the tunnels and found the control room where the silver rain had been launched. The dead guard still lay at the entrance. The body was beginning to smell. The Griffin didn't like to play with his food if it smelled, so he left it alone.

From his pocket, the Griffin withdrew the vial of silver rain he had received the previous evening. The nanobytes circulated within the glass, yearning to be set free. These nanobytes were the original silver rain, programmed under the original directives and unaltered by Matician's meddling.

For a moment, the Griffin considered using some of it on Matician, but the climatologist did not deserve that death. This silver would be for Toby.

From a cabinet, the Griffin found a syringe and drained the vial of nanobytes into it. He discarded the vial and placed the syringe in his pocket, imagining the needle piercing his son's skin, visualizing the boy's life fading away in his helpless, scared eyes.

Through his mind ran various scenarios, ways to ensure the most pain for all involved. He settled on the most realistic. He would hide away in the hotel and wait for the proper moment to attack Matician, Silverman, and his friend, Mark. Silverman's life and that of his friend may be useful in luring in Toby and his adoptive mother, but the Griffin would surely kill Matician whenever he got the chance. Then, once Toby was present, the bloodshed would begin.

A ring of his phone stirred the Griffin. He answered the phone.

"What have you done?" the senator shouted over the phone, his voice quiet and hurried.

"What happened?" the Griffin said, disregarding the senator's questions.

"We were blown out of the sky!" the senator said. There was strain in his voice, possibly from an injury. "Right as we landed in the L.A. base, we were attacked. The plane was knocked out of the sky by renegade soldiers. They were infected with the silver. Why aren't they dead, Avazino?"

The Griffin huffed in dissatisfaction. The senator had long worn on his nerves. Their partnership had appeared to be at an end when the senator had left the island, but now it seemed the Griffin needed him again to discover what had happened.

"Who all is affected?" the Griffin asked. "What are their symptoms?"

"Aggression!" the senator replied. "They killed all the survivors."

"Clearly not all," the Griffin grunted.

"They were smart and methodical," the senator continued. "I barely escaped. I'm hidden in the base. The city is on fire. It's absolute chaos. What is happening?"

The Griffin pondered the senator's explanations. Matician had altered the silver rain's directives in more ways than one. No one had died. Instead, it seemed the rain had turned men and women into monsters. The full extent was yet unknown, even to the senator.

"The problem is being dealt with," the Griffin finally said. "The silver was compromised before it fell."

"Kill it! Launch the pulse!"

The Griffin chuckled, reveling in the senator's desperation. "You disengaged the EMP when the silver rain was proven effective."

"Turn it back on!"

"I could," the Griffin considered. "But the EMP has a pulse diameter of fifteen miles. It seems you're on your own, Senator."

There was a pause before the senator shouted, "Do you even care that the silver was corrupted?"

"No," the Griffin said plainly.

His original intentions had not been fulfilled, but instead, he had released a different terror altogether. It excited him, the prospect of surprise and untold disaster. He was the Griffin, a harbinger of the end times. Although it had not been in the way he imagined, he had brought about a harrowing apocalypse.

The senator cussed at the Griffin, words he surely had not used during his reelection campaign.

"Come now, Senator," the Griffin said. "Perhaps, in some beautiful way, these mistakes will make the country emerge more powerful than ever. That was your intention, was it not?"

"I released you for a purpose," the senator said.

"But it's my purposes that are being fulfilled," the Griffin replied. "Fight admirably, Senator. You may just live to see me again."

The Griffin hung up the phone and threw it in the trash. With the syringe full of original silver rain, he wound his way out of the facility and through the door in the side of the cliff. Impossibly, the rain was coming down even harder. Unperturbed, the Griffin strode into the rain, boots kicking up mud. Each step brought him one step closer to Matician, Silverman, and ultimately Toby.

5

Natalie watched in horror as her mother's body disintegrated into ash on the red road. She lay a few feet away, helpless and overcome with fear and sorrow.

Blood began to pour onto the streets, thick and torrential. The red road became an ocean, smashing into Natalie and washing her away. Drowning in the crimson blood and her overwhelming grief, she struggled for the surface. She swam forever, never finding reprieve, until suddenly, the bloodbath receded, and she found herself in the brown room.

She remembered this room well. The walls were maple wood, the tables small, rectangular, and mahogany. Brown, wooden chairs creaked with age. The judge sat atop a wall of redwood, the jurors behind a picket fence of lumber. Everything about the room was brown, so Natalie had renamed the courtroom "the brown room."

With terrible dread, Natalie realized she had been here before. This was the brown room she had visited nearly two years after her mother's death. As though trapped in perpetual repeat, Natalie remembered the moments that had led her to this room.

After the red road, Natalie had begun to descend into her emotionless chrysalis. The loss of her mother had been too great, and she had begun locking her emotions away. Auntie El, her only living family member at the time, had encouraged her to move on from the past, so Natalie had begun to lock it all out.

But there had been one thing she couldn't shake: the glinting silver in her mother's eyes moments before she had died. The more she had thought about it, the more Natalie had believed the silver glimmers had looked familiar. In fact, they had looked like the silver metal Natalie had found in the laboratory. Natalie had tried to touch the metals, but her mother had stopped her, snapping the lid shut. Perhaps that metal had gotten onto Rose—or into her. Maybe, Natalie had thought, something about those metals or something in the lab had made Rose fall asleep in the car.

Pursuing this hunch, Natalie had hired a private investigator. They had come to an arrangement of funds and he had agreed to investigate.

In the meantime, Natalie had set about getting her affairs in order. She had filed for independence from her aunt, who had passed away a few months after. She had stopped visiting counselors and attending physical therapy. She had graduated high school early and begun nursing school. A little bit more each day, her emotions and personality had been buried six feet under. Even the investigation of her mother's death transformed from a passion to an everyday, mundane activity.

After a year of analysis, the private investigator had returned to Natalie—and boy, oh boy, had he uncovered a scandal. Presenting Natalie with more science than she had understood at seventeen, the private investigator had explained that Natalie's mother had indeed been working in a laboratory with substances detrimental to her health. Even stranger, Rose had known it. Upon her hire, she had signed a waiver that she had understood the risks to her health by working for the doctor.

Natalie had not cared about her mother's waiver. Though she had not understood all the science—binary *algorithms and biomechanical nanotechnology—she had comprehended the plainest truth: the doctor had made Rose work on materials that had eventually led to her death.*

Hardly a day later, Natalie had presented the evidence to the police. When the police had refused to arrest the doctor due to the legal waiver Rose had signed, Natalie had hired her family's old attorney and sued the doctor for negligent homicide. The doctor had instantly sought legal protection to prepare for the preliminary hearing. A court date had been set, and at long last, Natalie believed justice would be served.

Thus, Natalie had ended up in the brown room. She had arrived early with her attorney and all of her evidence. She had sat patiently, waiting for the trial to begin.

Now, an hour later, the brown courtroom was choked full of people thanks to the publicity. Natalie was sure that many were there to admire the young, parentless girl daring to take on a wealthy scientist and doctor.

Behind her, there was a scrape of heavy doors. The chatter intensified. Natalie knew in her gut what was happening: the doctor had arrived.

She glanced back. The doctor was flanked by a fleet of lawyers, each one trim and fit, adorned in jet black suits and golden charisma. They blocked Natalie's view of the doctor as they walked to the front of the room. When she finally saw him in full, she was taken back to the day Rose had introduced them in the laboratory. He was a man Natalie could not easily forget.

The doctor was of formidable height. He had gruff hands and piercing eyes. Though she wanted to forget his face, she remembered his name: Dr. Griffith Avazino.

Dr. Avazino met Natalie's eyes as he sat down. Natalie felt a smidgeon of emotion fighting to break through, a potent mixture of hatred and anger, but she fought it down. She looked away, burying her feelings that she could not handle, and focused on the case to come.

A few minutes later, the judge arrived and the preliminary hearing began. Natalie's attorney started strong and fizzled easily, barely making a convincing case that Dr. Avazino had knowingly led to Rose's death.

Then Avazino's lawyers started. They easily debunked Natalie's charges, standing by their legal protection from the waiver Rose had signed. It seemed the case was over before it had truly begun, until Avazino's lawyers pushed the case in a new direction.

The lead lawyer claimed that Dr. Avazino had been forced to hire Rose due to Equal Employment laws. However, the lawyer claimed, Rose should not have been hired due to her genetics.

"Rose Harper should have never been hired," the lawyer stated to the jury, "but she was, due to the laws enforced by the Equal Employment Opportunity Commission, or the EEOC. The law I speak of is Title Seven from the Civil Rights Act of 1964. While this law, Title Seven, creates fair and equal opportunity for all genders and skin colors to find work, it should not extend to those with genetic disabilities. Rose Harper's predisposition for narcolepsy was worsened by working in Dr. Avazino's lab. The lab itself withheld materials meant to better humanity, but were dangerous to individuals with genetic handicaps. Working in that lab put Rose's life in extreme danger. If the EEOC had not forced Dr. Avazino's hand under law of Title Seven, Rose Harper would still be alive. Her daughter would still have a mother."

Voices filled the hall. Natalie sat there, stoic, not believing what she had heard.

The lawyer continued: "Perhaps this case should not be the merits of Dr. Avazino's unknowing contribution to a poor woman's death. Instead, we should be wondering about the fairness of Title Seven. This law allows equal employment opportunity for men and women of color, size, shape, gender, and handicaps. But we would not want a man with prosthetic hands to be hired as a surgeon. Why should a man or woman with a genetic handicap be allowed to work in a place where they are hampered by their genetic issues? Why should employers be forced to hire these…degenerates, when their lives could be in danger?"

It was the statement that started everything. Had there been a doomsday clock on the wall of the brown room, it would have moved forward a full hour. But there was no clock or sign of monumental change occurring. Instead, people cheered and applauded. The judge agreed with Avazino's lawyers and smacked the gavel, calling for order. Jurors nodded in agreement from their seats.

Natalie still sat in her seat, still as stone. Deep down, she realized that there was nothing she could do. Fighting the rush of emotions that were surging through her, Natalie glanced over at the doctor.

Dr. Avazino looked satisfied. The lawyers at his rectangular table were giving each other polite, victorious nods. One of the lawyers, the youngest with gelled hair and a sharp suit, turned in his seat and waved vigorously at a young man and woman in the back row of the room. They exchanged waves back, the young man also giving two thumbs up. In turn, the young attorney smiled even more.

To Natalie, he looked like a slime ball. She felt a pulse of displeasure for the man and for the whole table of lawyers.

Finally, the judge brought quiet to the brown room. He made a few passing statements and dismissed the court with a final clap of his brown gavel. People began to filter out of the brown room. Dr. Avazino stood, as did his lawyers, and they walked out, moving like a giant mass of darkness. As he left, Dr. Avazino gave Natalie one last smug look.

Natalie waited a moment more, listening dully to her attorney as he apologized, and then fled the brown room. Outside the doors of the courtroom, Natalie was bombarded by journalists. She pushed through them, fighting to escape the building.

Once outside, she practically ran down the stairs. There was no sight of Avazino, and Natalie was too focused on subduing the hatred filling her heart. Moving too fast, she tripped and began to fall.

Thankfully, a man caught Natalie before she landed. She mumbled a thank you. Two more people joined him, each of them smiling in greeting. Natalie recognized them immediately.

The man who had caught her was the young man from the back of the courtroom. Beside him were the young woman and the tall, young attorney. The woman looked familiar to Natalie, perhaps a student in school with her. She thought her name was Cori.

Natalie's eyes fell on the young attorney.

He stuck out a hand, introducing himself as Evan, an intern for the law firm.

The other man, the one who had caught her, introduced himself as Mark. He worked at the law firm too as a coffee boy and runner, but was hoping to move up. He talked fast enough to be mistaken for an auctioneer.

"And I'm Cori," the woman said, shaking Natalie's hand heartily.

Natalie introduced herself too, feeling a prickle of anger toward them. Evan had been among the attorneys who had helped Dr. Avazino escape punishment. She despised Cori and Mark purely on principle, due to their association with Evan. For the three of them, she felt nothing but distaste.

Before Natalie could vent her frustrations, a hoard of journalists descended on them. Mark, Evan, and Cori surrounded Natalie and fended off the reporters, leading Natalie away from them. When the journalists pursued, the friends stuck with Natalie, escorting her to her car. There, Cori offered to meet Natalie sometime at school and catch a cup of coffee.

At long last, they all parted ways. Natalie drove home, never expecting to see them again. She finally suppressed her feelings of bitterness and resentment, not realizing that they were the last emotions she would feel for a long time.

Reporters were waiting outside of Natalie's door. They barraged her with questions, some even going so far as to ask how Natalie could ever feel whole again after losing her father, mother, and any chances of revenge. Hoping to make the reporters leave, Natalie told them what they wanted to hear: that she was hurt, broken, and unsure where to go next. The reporters took it and left with sadistic smiles on their faces, fingers already itching to craft Natalie's depressing tale. Natalie went into her apartment, sure that she wouldn't see a journalist at her door again.

That night, there was a knock at Natalie's door. She half-expected more journalists asking about the case, but instead, Mark was there.

Under her piercing stare, Mark stuttered as he explained that his medicine had been misplaced by the mailman. He had checked with the rest of the residents and was checking the last apartment. As it turned out, the last apartment had been Natalie.

"What a coincidence," he had said.

She indeed had his medicine in the mail, and returned it to him. Rather than go, he ended up talking about his childhood of being raised by his grandmother. Natalie appeased him and listened. When Evan's name came up, Natalie frowned. Mark saw it instantly and insisted that Evan was a good guy trying to get promoted from an internship. Natalie hardly believed him, plastering a smile on her face.

Eventually, Mark left and Natalie was left in peace.

It had been the last normal day.

Overnight, "degenerates" became a common term. One of disgust, in fact. There was public uproar against degenerates, and employers cried for the removal of Title Seven laws. In reply to the furor, Dr. Avazino and his attorneys sued the EEOC to amend Title Seven and stop degenerates from being hired. They claimed this change would help the economy, which was already turning for the worse.

Thanks to all the coverage by the press, Dr. Avazino's words spread like wildfire. Degenerates became easy targets to blame for the ongoing economic strife.

Natalie's apartment-interview by the journalists had also become an overnight sensation. Her story developed into the inverse of Dr. Avazino's tale. While the doctor sought to free the nation of degenerates' hold, Natalie was shown as the poor girl who had lost everything. Article after article, Natalie became a character of victimization, a poor creature crippled by discrimination and fear.

To make matters worse, journalists continued to hound her. The more she said to get rid of them, the more they wrote and the more often they came back. She became the face of degenerates, down on their luck and unfairly discriminated for their genetics. She received letters and phone calls from supporters, each one lost in their own self-misery and thanking Natalie for representing their hardships.

Unbelievably, Natalie's safe harbor became her time with Cori and Mark. She started seeing Cori at school and began carpooling together. Mark started visiting her every night. Eventually, Cori invited Natalie over for group dinners. When Natalie started attending, she ran into Evan again. He was stand-offish and hardly spoke to Natalie, which suited Natalie just fine. Tension grew between them, from Evan's anxiousness and Natalie's silence.

The months passed into years. Cori and Natalie made it into clinical rounds at the local hospital. Mark became an intern at the law firm. Evan and Cori married, and Evan continued his work on the case against the EEOC. The case was eventually bumped up to the Supreme Court, where a final decision would be dealt out. Journalists took every opportunity to further exacerbate the story by interviewing Natalie whenever possible. They kept her more abreast of the country-wide discrimination than the actual news. She was often cornered to provide feedback about the latest mass layoffs or most recent hate crimes. They even felt the need to tell her about Dr. Avazino's latest triumph: his family had been blessed with a baby boy. Natalie learned to stop talking to the reporters, but it was fruitless. Her silence further painted her as a broken, soulless victim of the changing, harsh world, defeated by the progressive Dr. Avazino, with his science, his logic, and his family.

Meanwhile, Mark remained infatuated with Natalie. One night, after several glasses of wine, he kissed her and confessed his love for her. Natalie indulged him and let him act on his feelings. In the back of her mind, she developed a plan to prove the journalists wrong: she *would fall for Mark as he fell in love with her. With Mark beside her, Natalie would no longer be a poster child for suffering degenerates, but appear whole and loved. It took time, but journalists began to avoid her, writing stories about the new man in Natalie's life and the hope for her happiness.*

Then came the fateful day. The masses gathered in Washington D.C. for the Supreme Court case. Mark and Cori came to support Evan. Natalie was there to see justice for her mother. The media was right behind her, wanting to know her opinion every step of the way. Mobs of people followed right behind her, activists crying that degenerates' lives mattered. Police were there too, as discrimination and hate crimes against degenerates had escalated in the weeks leading up to the case.

Once inside, the court case was a debacle. Natalie was stunned when Dr. Avazino's attorneys laid out their evidence with terrifying exactness. The attorneys had found a loophole in the laws, stating that employers did not have to hire handicapped individuals who were unable to perform tasks at a workplace. Therefore, they claimed employers should not have to hire degenerates unable to work properly.

After hearing the evidence, the Supreme Court justices left, convening to make a decision that would be released later. Though many debated their final decision, Natalie thought the verdict was evident. From their facial expressions alone, Natalie was positive that Title Seven would be amended or completely disbanded, and degenerates would not be able to find a job.

As the court emptied, Natalie made eye contact with Evan. He was smiling, but frowned when he saw Natalie. She knew he was happy with the case proceedings, but it seemed he also felt bad for Natalie.

Then she saw Dr. Avazino. He grinned at her, baring his teeth like a beast. With a nod, he left the courtroom, off to murder his wife and disable his son.

Fed up with the injustice, Natalie fled the courtroom too. Much like the day they had met, Cori, Mark, and Evan caught her on the courtroom steps. Evan apologized profusely, claiming he had no part in the attorney's final decisions.

Somehow, perhaps because she had no feelings left, Natalie pretended to forgive him. She had disliked Evan out of practice, but at least he hadn't been directly involved in the case. She agreed to see her friends later and not judge Evan on the case's outcome. Then they fled before the journalists could question her.

A few days later, Natalie returned to work in Reno for her emergency room rotations. Coworkers made small talk with her, asking her what she thought of the case.

Eventually, a small boy was pulled in with multiple lacerations, severed muscles, and massive blood loss. Natalie was one of the nurses to attend to him. She followed instructions impassively: it was another day at work.

When she heard the boy's name, Toby Avazino, she stopped and stared. In her mind blossomed a terrible idea: she would take Toby. She would finally have her revenge on Dr. Avazino.

In the days and weeks to come, she continued to care for Toby. She requested to be moved from the emergency room to the long-term recovery unit where she could continue to care for the boy. She did not care for him out of concern, but to get back at Avazino.

The doctor had taken her mother. She would take his son. But there was no emotion attached, she realized. This was cold, cruel justice, and she would be the enforcer.

In the days following, journalists found Natalie again. They wanted to know what she thought about Avazinio's attack on his family, about his imprisonment, and about the Supreme Court proceedings. She ignored them, dedicated to her new cause. She would be with Mark and take Toby as her own: a unified family that would silence the critics and avenge Rose's death.

A few months later, the Supreme Court announced their decision. Dr. Avazino and his lawyers had won. Title Seven was amended to exclude people with genetic deficiencies. New discrimination laws were put into effect so employers didn't have to hire degenerates. Supposedly, this was enacted to keep degenerates safer and aid the economy. Degenerates were encouraged to find work doing menial, small jobs that kept the country running. Companies cut their losses and fired degenerates by the dozen. Millions of people became unemployed. The economy took a steeper dive into oblivion as millions of degenerates were moved onto welfare. America as a whole began to fail as other countries forged ahead. Outspoken politicians and elite fought for a strengthened, unified country. Some called for acceptance of degenerates while other, louder voices dared to say that degenerates should leave the country. The notion was shocking at first, but the sting wore off, and many began to call for the deportation of degenerates to a country more apt to help them. It was a slippery slope that just kept getting worse.

The time continued to pass even still. Natalie and Mark grew closer—the proposal was coming, she knew it. She looked forward to it, hoping for the day when the journalists would leave her alone.

Evan moved up in the law firm after the Supreme Court case, and Mark joined the firm full-time as well. Apart from caring for Toby, Natalie tried to forget about the red road and the brown room. Reporters appeared at her work and apartment less frequently. Life moved forward.

That was, until a year ago. A few nights after Mark had proposed, Natalie found out that Dr. Avazino had disappeared from his jail cell. Journalists flocked back to Natalie's door, expecting a reaction. She let this all fade away, hoping to never hear another word.

Then, Mark mentioned adopting Toby. Natalie agreed without a second thought. She hoped somewhere, the doctor knew his son was alive and being adopted by the woman he had made an orphan.

But, like a sliver under the skin, Natalie could not forget the red road or the brown room. Her life had been forged by it, changed irreversibly. Despite her best efforts to forget it, the memories and emotions were buried deep down in a place she could never fully eradicate. And someone found them.

When Natalie failed to pass the psych evaluation, she was sent to Dr. Cruze. His trainings and experiments cracked open her shell and let the emotions rush back. With every touch of that red button, the red road weaseled its way in. Despite her best efforts, the memories resurfaced and her emotions inched back into her heart. Every night since, she returned to the crashed car, the firemen pulling her, her mother telling her to be safe, and the glinting eyes full of silver.

6

"No!" Natalie screamed, jarring awake.

She sat bolt upright. Flashes of faces were all around her. Hands grabbed her. Voices called her name. A dog barked loudly.

Continuing to yell, Natalie fought against the hands holding her down. She refused to lay here and be dismembered by the creepers.

Within her, fear reigned. She felt frail and skittish. Her heart felt hollow, aching for Mark and those she had failed. But through all this, she felt anger at herself. She had let them all die.

She continued to fight, swatting hands away and balling up her fists.

"Natalie!" came a shout, and this time, Natalie recognized it as Cori's voice.

Her eyes found Cori's face, looking scared but happy.

"Calm down, Natalie," Cori said softly.

Natalie felt her heart thundering in her chest, the beats filling her head. She forced herself to breathe.

Slowly but surely, the world came into focus.

Natalie was one of seven in a car moving down a highway. Barren hillsides flashed by outside the window. Grandma Dottie was driving and Cori was in the passenger seat, leaning back to attend to Natalie. In the back, on either side of Natalie, was Toby and Nate with his baby brother. Toby was asleep or unconscious, his head lying against Natalie's shoulder, drool running from his lips.

The second Natalie saw Toby, she reached out to him. Tears sprang to her eyes, a flood of emotion she had not anticipated.

As she wrapped her arms around him, the fear melted away. Her heart seemed to swell with happiness.

"He's been asleep for hours," Cori said. "So have you."

"Where are we?" Natalie said, holding Toby close. "What happened?"

"You weenied out on us, sweetheart," Grandma Dottie said.

"You fainted," Cori said, giving her mother a stare. "Toby saw and went into a seizure."

As Cori spoke, Natalie felt along Toby's body, checking the stitches and scars. All of them were still intact except for one on his back, which felt as through fresh sutures had been sewn into the skin.

"We got you out of the airport through the walkway," Cori continued. "Boomer distracted the creepers."

Grandma Dottie snorted at the name, Boomer barked at his.

"Grandma Dottie found a luggage hauler and got us back to her station wagon. We jumped in and we've been on the road ever since."

"And Toby?" Natalie asked.

"I stitched him up," Cori said confidently. "He was pale at first, but I think we closed it up in time."

Natalie nodded, keeping him close. A swirl of emotions filled her that she had not felt in years. Embarrassment made her cheeks tight, but she was incredibly happy to know Cori and Toby were alive. She was also thankful for how well Cori had treated Toby.

"Where are we now?" Natalie asked.

"Just passed through Bridgeport and we're coming up on Mono Lake," Grandma Dottie said. "Yosemite will be to our west in a few minutes. Nearly halfway to Los Angeles."

"Why L.A.?" Natalie asked.

"Bonnie," Cori said. "My sister. She's there now. She called Mom earlier and told us to meet her there."

Natalie looked out the front window. A steep mountain range surrounded them. The car had just come over a rise overlooking a basin filled with a lake. Striations marked the sides of the hill around the lake where water levels had been in preceding years. The view of browns, grays, and blues were stunning.

"So what happened to you, pumpkin?" Grandma Dottie asked Natalie. "One second, you answered the phone, the next—"

"Mark!" Natalie shouted, making Nate jump.

Fear returned in full force to Natalie, coursing through her veins. She could see goosebumps covering her skin. With it came the feeling of guilt and remorse. In her head, she could hear Mark's weak voice, the soft words as his consciousness faded. She knew in her gut that she had lost him. Whatever had happened to him, he had not made it out alive.

Natalie found Cori's eyes, which were filled with remorse.

"What happened?" Natalie breathed, her voice choppy and weak.

"He and Evan were on a bike ride down a mountain," Cori said softly. "It started to rain and Mark fell down a hill. Evan is looking for him."

"Did he—where did they—is he—?"

Cori put a hand on Natalie's shoulder.

Softly, she said, "I lost Evan. He isn't answering."

Natalie tried to speak, but the feeling of guilt would not rest. It swept over her more powerfully, weighing her down. Tears sprung to her eyes and she clapped a hand to her face.

This was why she had shut out emotion. This feeling, the horror they called grief, was an unbearable monster. It ravaged her insides, tearing her apart in a pain worse than any that could be inflicted.

Tears poured from her eyes. Cori rubbed her shoulder tenderly.

"I'm sure they're fine," Cori said. "It'll be okay."

"It won't," Natalie murmured, shaking her head. She felt like the young girl on the red road, watching her mother's body disintegrate in the flames, helpless to the inevitable. "He's gone."

As had happened on the red road, Natalie's thoughts went wild, driving her further into the abyss of sadness. Her last words to her mother had seemed so pointless. Now, her final words to Mark were just as meaningless. Natalie had at least shown her mother love for fifteen years. But to Mark, she had given him nothing but compliance. The soft, tender-hearted man had given everything of himself to her. He had loved her for all her flaws, and she had simply pretended. Every time he went in for a kiss, she forced a smile. She faked the hugs, mumbled the *I love you*'s. When it seemed she had actually found some love in her heart, he had been taken. She would never be able to tell him how she truly felt. She'd never be able to ask for more time or to share her secrets. He would never know how she truly felt about him.

Natalie's heart panged uncontrollably. She wanted to go back, to hit the reset button and start all over before Mark had left her. Back to before the silver rain.

Her mind traveled back, as though searching for more reasons to feel miserable. She saw Joaquin's puffy face, strangled behind the nurses' station. Tears streamed from her eyes as she remembered Yolanda's desperate pleas for help before being brutally killed.

"It's all my fault," Natalie struggled to say. "I let them die."

It was true, she realized. She had not felt an ounce of remorse when she saw Joaquin dead in the hospital, nor for the bodies lining the sides of the road. Yolanda had cried for help, and Natalie had put her own life before the innocent, young woman. Now, Mark was dead, having given all of himself and received nothing back.

As always when she was feeling trapped, Natalie wished there was a red button to push. But this was not like a simulation in Dr. Cruze's office. There was no red button to push or easy way out. This was real, and she had to face life in all its terror and remorse.

"I'm so sorry," Natalie poured out. "For Yolanda. For Joaquin. For everyone I've hurt. For Mark."

"Natalie?" Cori said, a note of confusion in her voice. "Are you okay?"

"I love him," she sobbed uncontrollably. "And he's gone. He'll never know me."

"He's going to be fine," Cori said reassuringly. "I'm sure he's—"

"But he won't," Natalie shouted, stirring Nate again and making Boomer bark. "Yolanda is never coming back. Joaquin. Those people on the interstate. I let them die. And Mark…"

Her voice trailed off as she was buried under the grief.

She hated this emotion, this powerful sensation that made her care so much. But now that it was in, there was no way to be rid of it. Natalie could not see an end to the misery. Even if they made it to Los Angeles, who would die next? What if it was Toby?

Another thought filled her head. How did people withstand this? How could people walk around day in and day out suffering the pain of loss?

"How?" Natalie croaked. "How can you…?"

There was a deathly pause in the car.

"How can you handle this?" Natalie finally said. *I'm feeling everything*, she wanted to add, but her tears choked her words.

Another pause, longer this time. No one moved. It seemed to Natalie as though God Himself had taken a breath, trying to decide how best to proceed.

A hand touched Natalie's cheek, raising her face. Natalie looked up, trying to stifle her tears. Cori was looking her in the eye with a bright smile.

"With the grace of God," she said simply.

She paused a moment more, letting these words set in.

"Life is hard," she finally said. "No one makes it out alive. But that's the beauty of it. We are allowed to feel so much. And you, Natalie, you probably feel it more powerfully than any of us. You know the true pain of loss. You know the leaping sensation of hope and happiness. Fear strangles you and Toby, and relief lifts you up. There's so much to feel. And by God's grace, we're able to move forward, feeling every emotion that fills us and wearing it like a new coat."

"It's so much," Natalie struggled to say. "I can't—"

Cori snickered.

"That's not the Natalie I know," she said.

Natalie huffed, sending tears flying off the tip of her nose.

"You don't know the real me," she said. "No one does."

Grandma Dottie sighed and muttered, "Oh, melodrama."

"I do too know you, Natalie Harper," Cori said. "I know you lock everything away. I know you're tough and don't take no for an answer. You're resilient and gutsy. But that's not because you choose to be emotionless or because you choose not to feel. The *real you* is the one who is smart and bold, tough and gutsy. You can handle these emotions, you really can. And you can still be you. If anything, you'll be a better you."

Somehow, Cori's words struck deep inside Natalie. The pain lessened.

In her mind, Natalie tried to wipe the emotions away, but not to lock them away this time. No, these emotions were here to stay now. She stored them away to let them grow within her and develop her. She was not a whiny drama queen who cried over her unconscious adoptive son or for her fiancé. She was tougher than that. Even if she was overwhelmed with emotions, she could still maintain her true self: tough as nails, bold as brass.

Though she had let the emotions subside, Natalie could still see Yolanda's terrified face before she was killed.

"What about Yolanda?" Natalie asked. "How can I live with that? What about Mark? What if he really is…"

"You pray," Grandma Dottie said bluntly from the driver's seat.

A shiver of fear ran down Natalie's body. She had locked out God as much as she had locked out her emotions. He alone could possibly know her the best, and willingly talking to Him seemed like asking for punishment.

Cori seemed to sense Natalie's cautiousness.

"Like this," she said.

Cori wrapped her hands around Natalie's, eyes closed, face relaxed and penitent. Beside her, Nate wrapped his arms around his baby brother and bowed his head.

"Lord," Cori said quietly, "please be with us on this day. Be with us in all that we do. Guide our actions as You would have us act. Forgive us for our wrongdoings and forgive Natalie for the lives she could have saved. Be with Mark and Evan. Bring them home safe to us."

As Cori continued to pray over the country and those who had lost their lives, Natalie asked God to heal her in a way Dr. Cruze couldn't.

Slowly, she felt a speck of hope within her. The terror of the airport faded. The grief lessened ever so slightly. Natalie felt as though her soul was healing over, once encased in a shell, then blown into smithereens, and now reforming.

"Amen," Cori finished.

"Amen," Natalie repeated.

They met each other's eyes, somehow closer to one another than they had ever been.

All at once, Natalie's pant leg vibrated. Cori's eyes widened in hope.

Natalie sat up quickly and withdrew her cell phone. The screen read that she was getting a call from Mark.

"Mark!" Natalie shouted as she answered the phone. Boomer barked at her.

"Natalie, it's Evan," said Evan over the airwaves. He sounded tired. "I lost my phone. Mark still had his, but it's about to die."

"Where's Mark?" Natalie demanded. "Is he—"

"He's okay," Evan confirmed. "I found him at the bottom of a gulley. His cystic fibrosis got really bad, but we got him back safe to the hotel."

"Does he need his inhaler?" Natalie asked, squeezing the phone tighter.

"I got it," Evan said. "We found his medicine in the room and gave him an extra dose. He's groggy, but he'll be fine."

"But—" Natalie stammered. "But he's okay?"

"He's fine," Evan said. "I'll let you talk to him in a minute. Is Cori okay?"

"Yeah," Natalie said, glancing up at Cori. "She's fine. We're all okay. We're headed to L.A. to find Cori's sister."

"Bonnie?" Evan said. "We found her husband, Brian, up on the mountain. We found a tunnel and some crazy guy chased us out. We think he's still after us, so we're hiding in the top floor of the motel."

"Who's after you?" Natalie asked.

"Dunno," Evan replied. "He was a big dude, but I never got a good look at him. Brian seemed to know him, but he's sleeping now. Brian has a broken arm. It's weird though. The hotel is empty. There's nobody here. It's like the island is empty."

"But you're okay?"

"Yeah," Evan confirmed. "Want to talk to Mark?"

Natalie answered in the affirmative, and then paused. Before Evan passed the phone, she said, "Thank you so much, Evan. Really. Thank you. I—"

"You don't owe me anything," Evan said. "You know that."

There was a pregnant pause between them, many things understood but unsaid.

"Here's Mark," he said.

There was static on the other end as Evan passed the phone.

Mark came on the line, his voice groggy and chunky.

"Nat?" he said.

"Mark!" she shouted and began to smile uncontrollably.

Cori beamed at Natalie, head close to the speaker as she listened.

"I'm okay," Mark choked out. "How're you?"

"I'm fine," she said back, letting the tears flow. The feeling of happiness had hit her so hard, she could hardly keep herself contained.

There was silence between them. Natalie didn't know what to say, but she was too elated to hear Mark breathing to care.

"I hear you met Cori's family?" Mark gurgled.

"Yeah," Natalie sighed. "You met Brian?"

"We passed out together," Mark said and chuckled himself into a cough. "I figured that would sound better than we slept together."

"Mark," Natalie said, suppressing a laugh.

Cori continued to stare at Natalie as though goading her to finally be honest with Mark.

A beep emanated through the speaker. She could tell that Mark's phone was dying.

She glanced at Cori, seeing the look of hope on her face.

I have to let her talk to Evan, Natalie thought. As much as it pained her, she had to say goodbye to Mark.

"Mark," Natalie said, "I love you so much."

He paused on the other line before saying, "Natalie…I love you too, but…there's something we need to talk about."

Natalie gripped the phone tighter. "I know, Mark. So much. I love you, but…I don't want to get married. Not yet."

She heard a sigh of relief on the other end.

"Oh, gosh," Mark said. "Me too. But I love you. I just need more time."

"Me too," Natalie said. "I love you so much."

The phone beeped again.

"Mark," she said. "We should let Cori and Evan talk. But I love you. I'll see you in Hawaii."

"Safe travels," Mark said between wet coughs. "Meet us at the Surfer's Hotel. I love you."

"And I you," Natalie said.

Her ear was filled with static, which meant that Evan was grabbing the phone. She passed the phone to Cori.

Cori took the phone and wiped away a few tears as she spoke to Evan. They kept it short, knowing that the phone could die at any moment. When Mark's phone finally died, Cori said a farewell as though Evan might still hear her.

"Thank you," she said, handing the phone back to Natalie. Cori and Natalie exchanged smiles. Natalie's heart felt light.

So that's what friendship felt like.

Though Natalie wouldn't say it out loud, she was beginning to understand why emotion was needed. Without it, she wouldn't have considered letting Cori and Evan talk, or being honest with Mark for the first time. Without emotion, life was dull and pointless. Every event was meaningless. But with emotion, every moment became more important, more poignant.

As she sat there, thinking about how she loved her friends and Mark, she realized that her fear and grief had faded. She no longer felt like the girl at the red road, too terrified to act and downtrodden with remorse to function. Those terrible emotions that had once ruined her had dissipated. Somehow, someway, there was something that had washed it all away.

Whatever it was, Natalie hoped she would feel it again. At this moment, it filled her heart and made her feel content.

She held Toby closer, eagerly awaiting the moment he awoke and she could be honest with him.

Deep down, something terrible awoke in Natalie. She remembered how she had felt about Toby before—how she had stuck with him in hopes she could raise him and use him as revenge on his father. It was an idea that sickened her now. Nevertheless, it was an intention she had acted on.

Toby deserved someone better, she thought.

Static crackled over the radio. Natalie glanced at the screen, seeing Grandma Dottie spinning the radio dial, searching stations.

"You said you heard a military announcement from Russia?" Grandma Dottie asked Cori.

"Early this morning," Cori confirmed. "I think it was in the seven hundreds on A.M."

The speakers crackled and then became silent.

"Found it," Grandma Dottie said.

There was silence for a moment more before an authoritative voice said, "…broadcasting to the United Nations and worldwide. This is Ivan Filimonov, general of the Russian Air Force. There has been no point of contact with the United States of America since ten a.m., Pacific Standard Time. Russian surveillance has found that the event originated from the Hawaiian Islands. It started with a large storm cloud."

At this, Cori and Natalie exchanged glances.

"The United States of America was covered by the cloud," the radio continued, "at which point communications ceased. Preliminary points of contact have failed. The country is considered hostile at this time. Do not attempt to communicate or travel to the American borders."

"Hostile?" Nate repeated softly. Boomer nuzzled the boy.

The Russian general continued: "To any Americans hearing this broadcast, we have no intention of ill will. Our armed forces will be arriving within twenty-four hours to assess the situation and provide medical assistance to those in need. Anyone with information is encouraged to contact the Russian Federation."

Grandma Dottie turned the radio down.

"No contact from America, no military response," Grandma Dottie muttered, her eyes scanning the road. "Our whole country has gone silent."

"And it came from Hawaii," Cori said. "Think that's what Evan and Mark got themselves tied up with?"

"I thought it was a rain storm," Nate said.

"Nevertheless, they found Brian," Grandma Dottie said. "I don't know the extent, but he's been up to his ears in government secrets and confidential projects out there."

"He could never do this," Cori said. "Brian wouldn't…"

The car became silent as though the road itself were asking, "Who would?"

In the back of Natalie's mind, she remembered the red road and the brown room. She recalled her mother's eyes, sparkling with metal. Just like the eyes of the creepers.

There is someone, Natalie realized, but it seemed improbable. Her mother had died thanks to those silver mites. Everyone else had turned into a raging lunatic. There didn't seem to be a connection, other than the gleaming eyes. The doctor couldn't have been involved on such a massive scale.

"About three hundred miles from L.A.," Grandma Dottie grumbled from the driver's seat.

Natalie sat up again to look out the windshield.

They had come out of the Boca Lake basin. The car rounded a corner and crested a hill, looking down into a valley. A city stood in the distance. Immediately ahead, the interstate was clogged with cars. A few people strolled about, blood smeared all over them.

"Heavy traffic," Grandma Dottie noted. "It'll only get worse as we get closer to Los Angeles."

Cori looked back at Natalie and smiled confidently. "Natalie can drive."

7

Four hours later, the station wagon was about seventy miles from Los Angeles. Natalie had driven with prowess, dodging creepers and attackers like a slalom skier.

Near Death Valley, Toby had awoken. He was groggy at first, but had regained his energy as they drove. Natalie had doted over him, but couldn't find the courage yet to tell Toby the terrible intentions she had acted upon when trying to adopt him. There would be a time, and she wanted to do it in private. She couldn't bear to have him cry in front of everyone else when she said she couldn't be his mother and that he deserved better.

At one point, as they neared Coso Junction, thick clouds gathered above. The tension in the car rose steeply. They decided to take shelter and refuel at the gas station, only finding one creeper manning the cash register. When it finally started to rain they all held each other close. As clear, liquid drops dotted their faces, they all broke into relieved smiles. Hearts beating slower, they got back in the car and returned to the road.

Eventually, they exited I-395 and took backroads that led to I-5, a more direct route to downtown Los Angeles.

Near California City, Grandma Dottie stumbled upon a few other broadcasts on the radio. The message from the Russians was on constant replay. Another station broadcasted a live feed from a man recounting his own experiences of surviving a plane crash, escaping creepers—"He calls them that too!" Toby shouted—and trying to get to his family in Maine. There was another station playing an emergency broadcast, asking listeners to secure their safety in the midst of a country-wide terror attack.

This station carried them for a few more miles, into the hills north of Los Angeles, until they lost it to static. Grandma Dottie flipped the dial again and found another live feed in which a group of people divulged their plans to raid the Pharmacy's manufacturing plant in Ohio. Apparently one of the individuals in the group named Ryan needed medicine to survive and refused to die quietly.

"All our families are trying to kill us," the broadcaster said. "If anyone has answers, we're headed to Ohio. We're broadcasting on 770 A.M. and over ham radio."

The speaker went on to blame the group's current predicament on the immense rainstorm that had swept across the country. It seemed that this group, the man going to Maine, and even the world's countries had no idea what had happened to America.

"It couldn't have just been rain, even if it felt like it," said Cori when the broadcast ended.

"It was *silver* rain," interjected Toby.

"I was going to say the same thing," Nate said.

Wyatt gurgled and cooed.

"And it made me sleepy," Toby added, and Nate yawned.

Natalie dodged a car and a few wandering creepers as she listened to the group discussion. There were several people wandering the interstate, each trying to attack.

She still couldn't get the windshield wipers to take the blood smear off the glass from an ambush of creepers in the streets of Bishop.

"It had to have been more than rain," Cori insisted. "It shut our nation down. And it made…those things."

A creeper raced out of a vineyard, riding a four wheeler. Natalie easily outpaced it, leaving it far behind to creep through the grapes.

"Why are they so violent?" Cori asked. "Why do they want to kill us? I mean, all of us in the car are normal. What happened to them?"

"It's the aliens," Toby said.

"Zombies," said Nate.

Wyatt drooled.

"Dear," Grandma Dottie said, speaking for the first time in several miles, "I think it best not to dawdle on this. I told you before. Brian has been working on government contracts for a few years now. I was never told what, but Bonnie or Brian will surely have the answers. There's no point fretting. We should save our breath and wait for them."

"Aren't you curious?" Cori asked. "Did Brian make a virus that affected everyone but his family?"

"Lucky us," Natalie mumbled sardonically. It felt good to be sarcastic.

"Hold on," Cori said, leaning into the front of the car to talk to Grandma Dottie. "I never knew about Brian being in Hawaii. Why did Bonnie tell you about Brian's government work?"

"Because I communicate with my daughter," Grandma Dottie spat. "Maybe if you would pick up the phone and talk to your family now and again, you'd be kept in the loop too."

Cori cocked her head, looking like a hurt puppy. Her smile quivered.

"Mom," she said slowly. "I do talk to you."

"To me, sure," her mother replied, "but do you ever call your sister or her family? When was the last time you saw Bonnie or Nate? Did you even notice your niece isn't with us?"

"You said she was one of the creepers," Cori replied, her voice cheery as always.

"Do not call your niece that name!" Grandma Dottie cried exaggeratedly.

The car was filled with a tense silence. Toby and Nate watched with gaped mouths while mother and daughter stared at one another.

Natalie glanced in the rearview mirror, watching Cori. She had never seen Cori red in the face. Then again, this silver rain had led to lots of new emotions for everyone.

Cori took a deep breath before saying, "I spent eighteen years with Bonnie. Every day, she told me to calm down. Every day, she told me to be stop being so happy. To be more genuine. Not once did she smile with me or laugh or enjoy the life we had. I'm sorry for the way I am, I truly am, but this is how God made me. Bonnie never liked it. She hardly ever speaks to me now. I don't see why I should make time to talk to someone who just wants me to shut up."

"Your medicine would help, if you ever took it," Grandma Dottie said.

Cori sat back. Her face fell and chest deflated.

"Maybe I like who I am," she murmured. "Maybe I don't want to be subdued by Bonnie. Or by medicine."

"Maybe you'd like it if you never had a sister," Grandma Dottie replied.

Cori gasped.

Grandma Dottie huffed and turned around, facing the front of the vehicle. A tear ran down the old woman's cheek.

As she watched Cori's mother, Natalie felt affection for both of them. A few days before, Natalie would not have cared. She would have shirked off their argument as idiotic and pointless, but she could see the love they shared for one another. Sure, their argument was heated and left the car terribly silent, but it was obvious they cared for each other. Natalie yearned to have someone like Grandma Dottie to dote over her, argue with her, and show that someone was truly concerned.

It was this love that made them such good women, Natalie realized. She wanted that too. Just as Grandma Dottie cared for her children and Cori had cared for Toby and Nate, Natalie wanted to be a good mother.

The silence was finally broken by Nate.

"You take medicine, Aunt Cori?" he inquired.

Cori answered in the affirmative. "I was born with a genetic deficiency. I'm a degenerate."

Grandma Dottie sighed as though prepared to reprimand Cori for using such an offensive term, but she remained silent, wiping the tear from her cheek.

"Do you know what that means?" Cori asked her nephew.

Nate nodded. "Your body doesn't work right."

Cori chuckled and shook her head. "It works just fine. My brain produces too many endorphins, so I can't help but be happy. All of the time."

"All of the time?"

"*All* the time. My medicine keeps me calm. Otherwise, I'm—"

"A golden ray of sunshine," Natalie said. "I call her my Eternal Optimist."

Nate sighed and looked at the ground. "I wish I had medicine for my bones."

"You got your Dad's brittle bones, didn't you?" Cori said knowingly.

Nate nodded sullenly. "So did Wyatt. There isn't any medicine that can fix it."

"I have to take medicine!" Toby interjected.

"Do you have endorphins too?" Nate asked his new friend.

"Honey, we all have endorphins," Grandma Dottie called back.

"I have too many, like Cori," Toby said. "But I'm not happy all the time. My endorphins give me seizures. It's called eplipsee."

"Epilepsy," Natalie corrected.

Grandma Dottie's eyebrow raised at this.

"I have to take medicine so I don't have seizures," Toby concluded.

"What's a seizure?" Nate asked.

"It's when you get all sh–sh–shaky," Toby said, "like I did in the airport."

As he spoke, he shook himself for effect.

"Toby," Natalie and Cori said warningly.

Toby apologized and stopped before saying, "I can't feel anything either."

Grandma Dottie spun around.

"Excuse me, young man?" she said.

"Congenital analgia," Natalie explained. "He doesn't experience sensations. Hot, cold, pain, pleasure. His body can't feel it."

"That is so cool!" Nate exclaimed. "You're, like, Superman. You could do anything!"

"And get very hurt!" Grandma Dottie exclaimed. "How is that possible? How do you not feel anything?"

"I could ask you the same thing," Cori mumbled under her breath.

Natalie caught Cori's eye in the rearview mirror before explaining.

"All of Toby's extra endorphins block the receptors throughout his body," Natalie told Grandma Dottie.

"Most people don't understand it. It's like being closed off from the world."

"You seem to understand it pretty well," Grandma Dottie said.

"I take care of Toby," Natalie said quickly.

Grandma Dottie stared at Natalie a moment longer, one eyebrow raised. Natalie stiffened, wondering if she had said too much.

All at once, Cori gasped. Natalie tapped the brakes, alarmed that they were about to hit something.

"What is it?" Grandma Dottie asked.

"Genetics," Cori gasped. "That's it."

The car was silent, waiting for an explanation. Natalie watched Cori in the rearview mirror patiently. She had a hunch what Cori was on to, having had a similar hunch assembling in the back of her brain.

"It's why we weren't affected," Cori said. She pointed at Nate. "Did your sister, Bethany, have brittle bones?"

Nate shook his head. "Wyatt does, though."

Cori squeaked in excitement. "Nate, Wyatt, and their father have brittle bones. Bonnie and I are opposite ends of the manic spectrum: depressive and impressive. Mom, you're depressive too."

Grandma Dottie's face crinkled.

"Toby has congenital analgia," Cori continued. "Don't you see? We all have a genetic flaw."

"We're all degenerates," Natalie mumbled, understanding exactly where Cori was going.

"So we're all freaks?" Nate asked.

"You are *not* a freak," Grandma Dottie scolded.

"The rain didn't affect people with genetic imperfections," Cori interrupted. "We're all uninfected because we have a genetic issue. Anyone who had standard genetics was affected by the rain and went creepy."

"So Yolanda, Joaquin," Natalie said aloud. "They were degenerates?"

Cori nodded. "I think Yolanda had sickle cell."

"Why, then?" Natalie asked. "Why are degenerates acting normal and everyone else is trying to kill us?"

"The silver rain," Nate suggested plainly.

"But what was in it?" Cori asked.

Nobody answered. They were back to the beginning.

Natalie thought about mentioning the silver flecks she had seen long ago in her mother's eyes, but realized that wouldn't provide any better of an answer. It was simply more proof that degenerates were unaffected, and normal people had become creepers.

"So whatever this is, it got set off in Hawaii," Cori said, "and covered the whole country."

"Now two-thirds of the population have turned into creepers, and the other third are degenerates running for their lives," Natalie summed up.

"Please don't use that word," Grandma Dottie said.

"Degenerates?" Natalie asked.

Grandma Dottie huffed.

"We are not degenerates," Grandma Dottie said. "It's such an awful term. We're as human as anyone else."

"With a few genetic flaws," Natalie said.

"Nobody's perfect," Grandma Dottie replied.

"Wait," Nate said, making everyone look at him. "What about Natalie? What's your genetic…thing?"

Natalie looked back to the road. Cori opened her mouth, but only a squeak came out at first. Everyone in the car waited.

The silence was cut short with the ring of a cell phone. Cori withdrew her phone and gasped.

"It's Bonnie!" she shouted.

Grandma Dottie suddenly erupted in tears.

"Talk about manic," Natalie said under her breath.

"Bonnie!" Cori shouted as she answered the phone.

There was squealing on the other side, presumably Bonnie. She and Cori talked quickly. A few minutes later, Cori hung up the phone.

"She's okay. Los Angeles is full of creepers," Cori said. "Sounds like she fought her way out of downtown. She said to meet her at the Santa Monica Pier."

"The pier? Where they launch boats?" Natalie asked. "We're *sailing* to Hawaii?"

"Unless you have a better idea," Cori said, her voice light and bubbly. "And look! We're here!"

Everyone's gaze turned to the windshield. Beyond the car-filled interstate, they could see the skyline of an unending city. Fires dotted the landscape, filling the evening air with smoke. High above, military jets circled the city. As they watched, one of them careened into another jet and exploded.

The road ahead was chocked full of vehicles. People wandered in between, turning to watch the station wagon from Reno coming down the road.

"Welcome to Los Angeles," Natalie murmured. "Things are about to get creepy."

8

Nate held on tight to baby Wyatt as Natalie tore through town. It seemed that Natalie had a knack for finding alleys and narrow spots to slip through and outrun the creepers trailing them.

In all his life, Nate had never seen more people. Los Angeles was crawling with creepers, every one of them making chase with the station wagon. Boomer, who had taken a seat on Toby's lap, barked threateningly at creepers as they rushed at the windows. Smears of blood covered the glass.

"There are so many," Aunt Cori muttered, her head snapping to the side as a creeper slapped her window and disappeared from view. To get away, Natalie took a sharp corner to a side street.

Suddenly, there was a loud thump on top of the car. Nate jumped. A face filled his window, upside down. He saw gleaming, calculating eyes.

"Creepers on the roof!" Nate cried.

Natalie shook the wheel, flinging the creeper into the alley's brick wall.

"They're not creepers, dear," Grandma Dottie said. "They're humans like you and me."

"Yup. Just normal folks who will kill you once the windows are down," Natalie said, earning herself a glare from Grandma Dottie.

"So what do we do?" Aunt Cori asked.

"We keep driving until we reach the pier," Natalie replied, but her solution was short-lived.

They skirted through more alleys, creepers slamming into the sides and the roof, and shot out onto a main road marked Colorado Avenue. Tires squealed as Natalie spun the car to face down the street.

Perhaps half a mile away was the Santa Monica Pier, which Nate recognized from family vacations. It was a long, rectangular asphalt pier with shops and a Ferris wheel leading out over the ocean. But in between the pier and the station wagon was a road brimming with creepers. There had to be hundreds upon thousands, and every single one was looking at them.

Nate's stomach lurched as Natalie slammed on the gas. With a heave, the station wagon barreled down the street, charging at the multitudes of creepers.

As they raced down the street, Nate saw creepers standing on the top of buildings, dark silhouettes against the grey afternoon sky.

"Natalie!" Aunt Cori screamed. "Watch out!"

Nate craned his neck to look out the front window and saw what Aunt Cori was screaming about. There was a line in the road, thick and black, no bigger than a speed bump. Nate thought he saw sharp points on it. Not a single creeper stood nearby it, and Natalie was headed right toward it.

"Spike strip!" Natalie yelled. "Hold on!"

The station wagon plowed right over the spikes. There was a pop of air. The station wagon jostled sharply to the side. White smoke covered the windows and the smell of hot rubber filled Nate's nose. His stomach lurched as the car began to sway. They were headed right at a human wall of creepers.

In the driver's seat, Natalie spun the steering wheel sharply, trying to keep the car from flipping. She slammed on the brakes too, but too late.

The station wagon plowed through the lines of creepers, swaying side to side. Sparks flew by the windows now. They broke through the creepers, careening across pavement.

The car shuddered to a stop on the pier, a few feet from where the asphalt turned to a wooden deck. To the right was a parking lot piled with cars and to the left were several dinners and a small roller coaster. The beach and pier itself was empty of people.

"Everyone out!" Natalie shouted.

They all leapt out, Nate holding baby Wyatt closely. Once outside, cool, moist air made Nate shiver.

He turned back, expecting to see a mass of creepers running at them. Surprisingly, every single creeper stood stock still, staring at them, but not chasing them.

"What are they doing?" Aunt Cori asked. "Just waiting for us to come back?"

"Never mind that," Grandma Dottie said. "Look there!"

At the end of the pier, perhaps two hundred yards out in the water, was a gigantic cruise ship. Atop the top deck, Nate could see a figure waving at them.

"Let's go," Cori said, looking back at the creepers nervously.

As Natalie scooped up Toby, Grandma Dottie took Wyatt from Nate.

"Stay with your Aunt Cori," Grandma Dottie instructed. "Keep Boomer close."

"And don't stop," Natalie added. "No matter what."

Slowly at first, they walked away from the car, headed for the end of the pier.

Nate glanced back. Not a single creeper had moved. They stood, staring. Their shining, wide eyes gave him the creeps.

"This is too easy," Natalie said.

The sound of a cry reached Nate's ears. Everyone looked down the pier to see a woman, curled up on the ground near the shops. She was crying and shuddering.

"Help me," she moaned.

"Ma'am?" Natalie called. "Are you hurt?"

Aunt Cori grabbed Natalie's arm. "Natalie, this might be a trap."

Natalie and Cori looked each other in the eye.

"What if she's hurt like Yolanda?" Natalie asked. "I won't leave anyone else behind."

Aunt Cori paused and let Natalie go. Natalie crept closer, her knuckles white as she held Toby tight. Beside Nate, Boomer let out a low growl.

"My leg," the woman said. "I can't...stand."

"Let me give you a hand," Natalie said, now within arm's length of the woman. "I'll help you up."

The woman spun around on Natalie with a cackle. Her thick curtains of hair swished like a cape as she clawed at Natalie's legs. Natalie backed away, narrowly avoiding being hit.

As though the woman's call had been a firing shot for a race, the sound of a thousand footsteps came from behind Nate. He looked back, already knowing what he would see.

The creepers, every single one of them, were charging down the street.

"Run!" Natalie, Cori, and Grandma Dottie all screamed at once.

Aunt Cori tugged at Nate, who began to run. Up ahead, creepers by the dozens appeared out of the shops, running at them.

"Run, run, run, as fast as you can!" cried a creeper behind Nate.

He screamed and ran faster, pulling Cori. Boomer ran beside him, booming with barks at the creepers.

One by one, creepers raced out of the store fronts at Nate. He dodged and ducked, never letting one touch him. He put more speed behind him, racing for the end of the pier.

From the corner of his eye, he saw someone running faster than him. The next second, he realized it was Natalie holding Toby, outpacing them all.

The race was on. Nate pushed faster. Tears streamed from his eyes from the wind. He felt Cori's hand tug in his as he dragged her.

"Hurry!" came the shout of a voice from far away.

Nate looked at the end of the pier. Standing there, holding a harpoon, was his mother, Bonnie. Nate's heart flooded with relief. But there was a mob of creepers to get through.

The sight of his mother put more length in his stride. He dodged a crazy-eyed, thin woman in a sundress, and charged on, determined to make it to his mother.

At the far end of the pier, Nate's mom charged the back lines of the creepers. Bodies fell. Droplets of blood splattered the pier.

All at once, Nate's legs lit up like they were on fire. He felt his brittle bones ache from the fast running. He gasped in pain, stumbling. Cori collided with him and they tumbled to the wooden deck.

"Mine!" one of the creepers, a heavy set man, cried and leapt at them. Cori screamed and swung at the man, who easily overpowered her. His hands wrapped in her hair. He slammed her head into the deck.

A booming bark exploded over Nate's ear. Boomer leapt at the obese man and bit the creeper's cheek. The man yelled, letting go of Cori. She crawled away.

"Come on," Aunt Cori said, wiping blood from her cheek.

She picked Nate up. The next second, they were off, running again.

Held in Cori's arms, Nate faced where they had come from. He couldn't help but scream. Hundreds of people of all shapes, colors, and sizes were running after them. Some were in tank tops and shorts, others speckled with blood and torn suits. Others were in blue jeans, some in dresses. Every single one had murder in their eyes.

Nate had never felt so desperate, a single thought pulsing through him: they had to get out of here. All of them. Now.

As he looked back, Nate saw that Boomer was still on the man who had attacked Cori.

"Boomer!" Nate shouted.

Body quaking with the effort, Boomer barked once more at the obese man and raced after Nate and Cori.

With a stroke of panic, Nate realized he did not see Grandma Dottie anywhere. He spun, looking this way and that, and finally saw her, well ahead of Cori. She must have outpaced them when Nate had fallen.

Beyond that, Nate saw his mother at the end of the pier. Natalie had reached her and was thrusting Toby into Bonnie's arms.

"Go!" Natalie yelled at Bonnie.

Nate's mother handed the harpoon to Natalie and ran for the end of the pier with Toby. Natalie was instantly surrounded by creepers as she swung the harpoon. Creepers cried, falling thick and fast like snow.

A few paces later, Cori and Nate were running beside Grandma Dottie and Wyatt.

"We won't make it through!" Grandma Dottie wheezed at Cori and Nate.

"Natalie can do it!" Aunt Cori insisted.

Nate clung tighter to Aunt Cori, hoping she was right. There were hundreds of creepers between them and Natalie at the pier's edge.

All at once, a tall, burly man leapt out of the last shop to their left. He bellowed and slammed into Grandma Dottie. She crashed to the ground, Wyatt tumbling from her hands. He squealed as he hit the deck.

"Wyatt!" Nate cried.

Grandma Dottie crawled over to the baby, scooping him up. She spun around, getting to her feet as the burly man swung at her.

"Grandma!" Nate cried, spinning in Cori's arms to look.

"Go!" Grandma Dottie shouted back. "I can handle this brute!"

"Creeper!" the man bellowed back at her.

Cori slowed, looking back helplessly at Grandma Dottie.

"GO!" Grandma Dottie yelled, pointing to the end of the pier. "Run, now!"

Creepers swarmed Cori and Nate like ants from a hill. Grandma Dottie and the brute disappeared from view.

With a cry of helplessness, Aunt Cori punched a middle-aged mom out of the way and took off running again. Nate clung tightly to her, looking back.

Grandma Dottie was dodging blows from the burly man. Her attacker swung a club-like arm at her, but she ducked and struck. The man stumbled back. Grandma Dottie didn't back down. She punched him in the throat, and the man toppled. Nearby creepers screamed at her, but she did not give them a chance to attack. Grandma Dottie disappeared into the stores lining the pier, a horde of creepers following her.

"Grandma!" Nate shouted, but it was useless. His grandmother and brother were gone.

A creeper lunged at Cori from behind. Nate screamed a warning.

Just before the creeper could take Cori down, Natalie jumped in between them with the harpoon. She whacked the creeper in the head, spun, and struck another one out of the way.

Cori kept running, leaping over bodies and fending off attackers. Natalie caught up with them, knocking creepers back with the harpoon.

"We're outnumbered," Cori screamed. "They're ambushing us."

"Get to the boat," Natalie said. "Toby's there. He had another seizure. Take care of him for me."

"Don't talk like that," Cori cried, body-slamming a tiny girl rushing at them. "We have to go together."

Creepers swarmed around them again, surrounding them from all sides. Nate held tight to Aunt Cori, too terrified to defend himself.

"Keep moving to the water!" Natalie exclaimed. "You'll have to jump!"

Together, Natalie and Cori fought for the end of the pier. Step by step, Nate became hopeful they would make it to the ship. All that stood in their way now was a split rail fence.

When they were next to the railings, Natalie yelled, "Jump!"

"Together!" Cori replied.

"No!" Natalie shouted. "They'll just jump in the water after us. I'll keep them busy until you're far enough away."

"Natalie, come—" Cori began.

"Go!" Natalie implored.

Boomer barked.

Cori climbed onto the fence railings that normally kept people from falling into the ocean. Blue water rippled about twenty feet below.

Behind them, Natalie grunted as she fought back the creepers.

"Hold on!" Aunt Cori shouted to Nate.

Nate gripped his aunt tighter as she jumped. They were airborne for a moment, screaming in fright, before he impacted the water. The salt water went up his nose and stung his eyes. His bones ached in the water as he kicked for the surface. Once above the water, he gulped for air and looked out to sea. His mom and Toby were already halfway to the ship.

Cori surfaced nearby, gasping for air.

A whine reached Nate's ears. He looked back to the pier to see Boomer peering over the edge, whining.

"Boomer!" Nate shouted, throwing his hands in the air.

The dog looked back once before leaping over the edge. Boomer landed with a splash and paddled over to Nate, shaking its head and whining.

"Natalie!" Cori screamed at the top of her lungs.

Natalie appeared at the edge.

"Swim!" she shouted at them. "Go! I'll be right there!"

"No, you won't!" Cori replied.

"Go!" Natalie insisted.

Cori treaded water a second longer before grabbing onto Nate and guiding them toward the cruise ship. Boomer paddled alongside them. Nate kept turning around, unable to look away.

Nate saw Natalie swinging the harpoon violently. The creepers fell back. Taking the chance, Natalie dropped the harpoon and ran at the railings, preparing to leap in after Nate, Cori, and Boomer.

Suddenly, the big, burly man that had assaulted Grandma Dottie ran up behind Natalie. He grabbed her and threw her to the ground.

"Natalie!" Nate shouted.

Cori turned around, treading water. She screamed for her friend.

Natalie kicked the muscular man away and got to her feet. The creepers surged forward. Natalie fought back, yelling in anguish as she hit them with fists.

"Natalie!" Cori screamed again.

"Go!" Natalie yelled back, but her voice was muffled by her attackers.

Nate heard several splashes. He looked below the pier to see creepers running into the water, their shining eyes locked on Cori and Nate.

Cori began to cry helplessly. Nate scanned the beach, searching for a way to get back to the pier and help Natalie, but it was impossible. Creepers were crawling all over it, racing into the sea to catch them.

"Oh, God, I'm so sorry," Cori said. "Natalie, I'm so sorry."

One of the creepers in the water began swimming at them.

"I'm so sorry," Cori whispered once more and began to swim again, pulling Nate and Boomer out to sea.

Nate glanced back. The swimming creepers were falling behind.

Up on the pier, Natalie had been knocked onto her back again. There were hundreds of people around her, beating her mercilessly.

"Don't look!" Cori insisted. Nate couldn't look away though.

The big, burly man roared at nearby creepers, knocking a few away. He lunged down at Natalie, delivering deadly blows.

Nate felt his insides curdle, feeling Natalie's pain with each smack.

Bodies swarmed in, blocking Nate's view. The last thing he saw clearly was the man reach down, grab Natalie's leg, and rip it clean from her body.

PHASE 6
STRIKING BLOW

Breakaway Cruiser
Outbound, Santa Monica Pier

Cori's eyes burnt with tears and salt water as she pushed Nate onto the cruise ship's deck. Bonnie helped them both, hugging Cori tightly once onboard. Boomer paced around them, whining.

"Good to see you, sis," Bonnie said.

Cori gurgled a response through tears. She was not used to feeling this distraught and helpless. Her constant happiness threatened to return, but it was kept at bay in mourning for Natalie and Grandma Dottie. She couldn't even bear to imagine what was happening to them.

Bonnie left Cori for a moment, embracing her son and giving him a kiss on the head. When Nate too started to cry, she turned back to Cori.

"Where is everyone?" Bonnie asked. "Where's your friend?"

Cori looked back at the pier. Through her tears and the darkening sky, she could still see creepers swarming the end of the pier. Natalie was somewhere out there, dying.

"Where's Mom?" Bonnie asked, more forcefully this time. "Where are my children?"

Cori sank to her knees, sputtering words through sobs. Boomer tried to lick her face, but when she paid no attention to him, the dog bounded over to Nate.

"Mom had Wyatt," she wept. "She couldn't get through the creepers. I lost her in the store."

"We have to go get her!" Bonnie exclaimed.

Cori shook her head. "There's no way back to the beach. There are hundreds of them."

"But..." Bonnie stammered. "Does she have Bethany?"

Choking on her sobs, Cori was unable to answer at first. Nate too let out a whimper, which Boomer copied.

"Go check on Toby," Bonnie told her son, shooing him off to a cabin atop the deck. Boomer followed with a bark.

When Nate had gone, Bonnie took a knee beside Cori.

"Where is my daughter?" she asked.

"Bethany was infected," Cori said weakly. "She tried to kill Nate back at Mom's house."

Bonnie looked mortified, and she sank to the deck too.

"And your friend?" she asked.

Cori couldn't bear to say it. Natalie, brave and strong, had sacrificed herself for Cori and Nate to get off the pier. Mark would never get to see her.

"Oh, God," Cori murmured.

And to think, Natalie had finally opened up to him.

"We have to..." Bonnie said. "There has to be something..."

Cori shook her head again.

"They're gone," Cori stammered.

The two sisters embraced one another, their tears falling thick and fast. Blood and sea water trickled from their clothes, staining the deck.

Sounds of footsteps broke the quiet. Cori opened her eyes to see a bedraggled, suited man kneeling beside them. An American flag glistened on his lapel. His sharp features seemed familiar, but she couldn't immediately place where she had seen him before.

"Senator Beaudry," the man said with a nod. His voice was gravelly and deep.

Dully, Cori realized that the man was a politician, and she recognized him from the news. She also noticed Bonnie looked tense, not making eye contact with the senator.

"Is there anyone else coming?" the senator asked her.

Unable to reply, Cori shuddered. She tried to find Natalie's strength and wipe the tears away.

"Ma'am, we need to make a decision," the senator said. "Some of them are swimming out from shore. They're headed right at us."

Cori and Bonnie looked at one another. For the sake of everyone on the boat, they had to leave. It was yet another life and death decision Cori was faced to make and it stung deep.

"Head out," Bonnie said. "Take us to Hawaii."

"Madams," the senator said with another nod. He walked off and disappeared into the cabin Toby and Nate were in.

"You met a senator?" Cori asked her sister.

Bonnie looked embarrassed, pursing her lips.

She explained: "After I escaped the business building, I found a running car and got to the pier. He was on the ship already. I yelled at him and he said to get aboard. I made him wait for all of you. He knows how to pilot the ship."

A lurch vibrated through the deck and into Cori's stomach as the ship began to move.

Cori let out a heavy sigh, trying to stop the tears. Beyond the deck, she could see they were turning away from the mainland and headed out to sea. The pier grew smaller in the darkening sky.

"Goodbye, Natalie," she said wistfully. "Goodbye, Grandma Dottie."

All at once, there was a loud clunk on the side of the boat. The sound echoed up to the deck, loud and clanging like a bell.

Bonnie and Cori sat up straight, stifling their tears. The clunk came again, heavier, louder, and closer.

"Someone is coming up," Bonnie mouthed.

Not again, Cori thought to herself. She couldn't bear to fight anymore.

Bonnie and Cori stood together, tiptoeing toward the edge.

There was another heavy clunk and a hand grabbed onto the lip of the dock. Cori stiffened, convincing herself that she must do what was necessary. Natalie had told her to take care of Toby; Cori must keep her word.

Just as Bonnie and Cori were about to attack, the newcomer leapt aboard.

Cori's jaw dropped.

Natalie Harper stood there, drenched in blood and water, face swollen and purple, and clothes torn. In her hands, she held her prosthetic leg.

2

Surfer's Hotel
Maui, Hawaii

    Mark tumbled through the mud, end over end. Rain spattered his face and the thick air choked him. Danny was right behind him, screaming in anguish.

    There was a bone-shattering crunch. Mark was able to look back to see Danny folded like a pretzel around a tree. His face was smeared in blood, but he wasn't dead. He was staring at Mark, the whites of his eyes turning maroon.

    "Murderer!" Danny exclaimed through broken teeth.

    As Mark fell further away, it seemed Danny's face was getting closer. All Mark could see were the reddened whites of Danny's eyes, his contorted jaw, and the rivers of blood as he screamed again.

    Mark jerked awake, wheezing. His emergency inhaler was beside him. He clutched it and took three quick puffs. Instantly, the mucus cleared. He took several deep breaths before he lay back on the pillow. When he closed his eyes, Danny's face appeared in the darkness, like an afterimage seared by a camera flash.

    An iota of remorse swept through Mark, but not much. Danny reminded Mark of the bullies he had known in grade school: condescending jerks who wouldn't leave him alone. At one point, Mark had fought back against these schoolyard bullies, only to be suspended. It was during his suspension at home, Mark had learned his grandmother's life motto.

"It's not about what you can't do," she had told him, her feeble voice strained and wheezy. "It's about what you can do. Now get to work, Marky, no sitting all day on your duff."

In the years after his grandmother's passing, Mark had carried this lesson with him. He did not let his cystic fibrosis deter him from pursuing a college degree or entering law school. His foster family, the Silvermans, encouraged him all the way, just as his grandmother had done. Even as Mark and Evan had ascended the ranks of Harlem & Associates, Mark had kept his grandmother's motto at heart. Whenever naysayers would belittle him, Mark would remind them that he was defined by his abilities, not his infirmities.

Mark had tried to tell this truth to Danny on the mountainside, but the jerk hadn't listened. Most of the country hadn't listened either. They would rather judge degenerates like Mark based on deformities, illness, or appearances, rather than character and behavior. It was a messed-up world, but it was a world Mark hoped to improve. Despite the ugly nature of discrimination, Mark saw the world for all its beauty and fun and potential.

The springs on Mark's bed creaked as someone sat on the edge. Mark looked over to see Evan. His friend was still in the yellow jumpsuit and looked pale. Bags were under his eyes. The nail beds on his fingers had been chewed up by stress.

"How you doing, man?" Evan asked.

Mark mumbled a response.

"You passed out on me. Twice," Evan said. "What do you remember?"

"Did we really find a secret hallway in the mountain and get chased off by a mad scientist?" Mark croaked.

"Sure thing," Evan confirmed.

"Who was the guy?"

Evan shook his head. "Didn't get a good look at him."

Mark grunted. "And then we rode a four-wheeler down the hill?"

"Only got stuck once."

"And we found your brother-in-law?"

"He's in the other room, asleep on the couch."

"Did I talk to Natalie?"

"You guys agreed to call off the wedding."

Mark put his hand in his face, not believing what had happened.

"I thought so," he mumbled through his hand. "In that case, I guess I'm terrific." He looked over to the window. "Is it still raining?"

"It's tapering off," Evan said. "We need to be ready when it does. That crazy guy on the mountain might come for us."

"He couldn't know where we are," Mark retorted. "The island is—"

"Empty," Evan interrupted. "Everyone is gone."

"Gone?"

"Except us. You, me, Brian, and the crazy guy."

"So what do we do about the crazy one?"

Evan pointed at the open window. A hazy, darkening sky was visible through rain splatters.

"I moved us to the top floor. Not easy with two unconscious guys. From here we can see him coming."

Mark sighed, which turned into a cough. Wiping his mouth, he pointed at the adjoining room where Brian was.

"What was Brian doing up here?"

Evan shrugged, but he held up a handful of papers. Mark could make out hackneyed equations scrawled on the pages.

"He had these in his pocket. Might have something to do with whatever happened on the mainland."

Mark paused, trying to remember his conversation with Natalie.

"What did happen?"

Evan shrugged, worry crossing his eyes. "I didn't get much before your phone died. Sounds like Cori and Natalie are on the run. Something's happened and it doesn't sound good."

Mark eyed the notes from Brian's pocket. He could see algorithms, derivatives, and hundreds of reworked computations. In his gut, he had a hunch that Brian and his papers held answers.

"Time to find out," Mark grunted. He propped himself out of bed, cleared the phlegm from his throat, and followed Evan into the other room.

Brian was rousing from his slumber. A skinny, speckled man, Brian looked squeamish on the couch. His arm had a tourniquet tied tightly on the bicep.

Putting on his glasses, Brian looked at Mark and Evan uncertainly.

"My name is Mark," Mark said, extending a handshake. "I think it's time you explain what's going on."

3

"Hold on to me, Toby."

Toby awoke hearing Natalie's voice in his ears as she had held him close. Despite the attacking creepers, Toby had felt safety in Natalie's arms. But he had still been scared, and that's what had caused the seizure. He had thought he could hold it off, but the tremor had turned into a shake, and then he had begun jerking and contorting involuntarily. The world had started to fade away.

The last thing he had her say was, "Be strong, Toby. I love you."

He had never heard her say, "I love you." At the time, he had been too scared to comprehend, but now, he realized the depth of her words. It made his little heart pang with joy.

At long last, he opened his eyes. The world around him was blurry and he felt like he was spinning. This was nothing new. He always felt a bit dizzy after a seizure. But he did not recognize where he was. Where was Natalie? Where was he?

Slow at first, his eyesight sharpened. He realized he was in a small room with large windows. He lay on a wooden floor, his head propped up slightly. Control stations lined the walls. A man in a suit stood at the front windows, hands atop a pronged steering wheel.

We're on a boat, Toby realized. Then, he remembered the cruise ship off the coast that they had been running toward. They must have made it.

There was a *skit-skat* of nails on the wood. Boomer came into Toby's view, panting a little. As the dog got closer, Boomer sniffed Toby's face and licked his cheek.

Toby laughed.

"How are you doing, little fellow?"

The man at the ship wheel was looking at Toby. He strode over, his shiny black shoes clicking on the wood. As he approached, another person followed him—it was Nate. The two of them knelt beside Toby.

"I'm dizzy," Toby replied and giggled as Boomer licked him again. "And ticklish."

Boomer stepped back, his tail wagging, and woofed.

Looking at the man in the suit and shiny shoes, Toby introduced himself.

"I'm Senator Beaudry," the man replied.

"Senator? Like in the government?"

The senator nodded.

Toby wasn't sure he liked the man. He seemed too quiet, and his eyes shone with a calculating shrewdness.

"Where are we?" Toby asked.

"Headed to open sea," the senator said.

"Mom and Aunt Cori said Hawaii," Nate said.

"And where's Natalie?"

Nate looked away; the senator didn't say anything.

Toby sat up, his little body feeling heavy and sluggish. He did not feel any pain thanks to his congenital analgia, but he knew his body was injured.

"Where's Natalie?" he asked again.

"She didn't make it," Nate finally said, looking sad. "She got Aunt Cori and me off the pier, and she tried to jump off too, but they caught her."

Toby fell silent, body slumping. He couldn't believe it. Natalie had to be on the ship. She wouldn't have left him.

"Why don't you go explore the boat?" the senator recommended. "It's a shame more can't experience it."

"Where are the passengers?" Nate inquired.

The senator put his fingers to his lips with a wink. "Go on, go explore!"

Nate helped Toby to his feet and they left the captain's quarters together. They walked the top deck of the ship slowly. It was immense, bigger than any ship Toby had seen. There were descending stairways, multiple cabins, pools, water slides, and lifeboats. As the sky darkened, lights came on across the deck of the ship. Boomer entertained himself by chasing rigging across the deck. At the edge, Toby and Nate watched the dark water swirl by. There was no coastline in sight.

Shock would not yet let Toby believe that he had lost another mother. He had been too late to save his birth mother, and he had been seizing while Natalie was taken from him.

"She saved us," Nate murmured as they walked around the pool. "We wouldn't have made it off the pier if she hadn't…."

Toby sniffed, reminding himself to keep his emotions subdued.

"She's always been like that," he said. "She's like a bear, always fighting back. Just no teeth or extra hair. But just as tough."

Nate nodded silently.

"I just wish she didn't have to be tough all the time," Toby said. "Sometimes it's okay to be…happy. You know?"

Boomer lost interest in the rigging and trotted over to another cabin door. He turned to look at Toby and Nate, barking at them.

"I love your dog," Toby said.

"He's not mine," Nate said. "He found me. You can keep him."

"Oh, no," Toby said, but Nate insisted.

"He'll keep you safe."

Toby still refused until Nate said, "We'll share him."

With that, Toby and Nate went to the door Boomer was barking at. It was a small cabin on top of the deck. When they opened the door, they found a steep set of stairs leading to the level below.

Boomer trotted down the stairs, his feathery tail dancing out of the light. Toby and Nate followed.

It was dark below deck. Only a few lights were on, and one of them was blinking like a strobe light. At the bottom of the stairway was a large vestibule with several sets of doors to their right, left, and forward. Boomer was at the doors straight across from the stairs, sniffing at the ground.

"What is it, Boomer?" Toby asked.

Nate and Toby walked over to the door, pushing it open a few inches.

They both gasped.

Beyond the door was a corridor lined with cabins for guests on the cruise. The hall was full of people milling around. Each and every one of them had gleaming eyes.

"Creepers," Nate muttered to Toby, and motioned for them to walk back up the stairs.

Toby nodded and backed away slowly. He did not want to see the creepers attack again.

Once Toby was at the stairs, Nate began to ease the door shut, but Boomer stuck his head through the crack.

"Boomer," Toby whispered.

Boomer looked back at Toby and shook his tail slightly. Then, he turned his head, growled at the creeper nearest to the door, and let out a boom of a bark.

$$4$$

Breakaway Cruiser
Pacific Ocean

"Will you two give it a rest?" Natalie said as Bonnie and Cori fussed over her wounds. "I'm fine."

After reattaching Natalie's prosthetic leg, the three of them had gone below deck to the storage cabins. Medical supplies, life vests, and dried food lined the walls.

Against her will, Natalie had been propped up on a stool while Cori retrieved medical supplies. Bonnie had wondered about, eyes blank and face stoic. Before Natalie could stand, Cori had pushed her back in the seat, bandages and antiseptic wipe sticking to her fingers.

"I'm fine, really," Natalie insisted now.

With a free finger, Cori poked an inch-long cut in Natalie's side that had been stitched shut.

"Do you feel that?"

"No," Natalie said, shaking her head.

"Exactly," Cori said. "So sit there and let us take care of you."

Natalie shrugged and smiled at Bonnie.

"I'm Natalie," she said.

"Bonnie," replied Cori's sister absentmindedly.

She took a few bandages from Cori and started tending to a wound on Natalie's head. Her eyes glazed over again. She seemed to be in another place. Judging by her downcast eyes, it was a dark one.

"Your mom will be alright," Natalie told her. "I saw her run off. She'll find a safe place."

Bonnie didn't say anything.

"Anyway," Natalie murmured.

Cori caught Natalie's eye and raised her eyebrows.

"I swear," Cori said, applying a bandage to Natalie's side, "if you try playing the hero again so I can live, I will push you overboard, Natalie Harper."

"I got to the boat just fine," Natalie replied.

"With only one leg attached," Cori said sardonically, but she couldn't hide her smirk. "And several cuts and bruises. You might just have more stitches than Toby."

Natalie paused a moment, considering what was on her mind.

"Don't tell Toby," she finally said.

Cori paused as she applied another bandage.

"What do you mean?" Cori asked.

Natalie took a deep breath, preparing to commit to what she had decided.

"Don't tell Toby I lived," she said. "Let him think I died."

Cori's eyebrows knit together, but then, she shook her head and turned her attention back to Natalie's wounds.

"You're in shock," she said.

"No," Natalie insisted. "I won't be a good mother for him. I know that now. But the way you are with him…it's what he deserves."

Cori forced a laugh, not even looking at Natalie.

"I can't bear to break his heart," Natalie said.

Cori's eyebrows furrowed again.

"Why would you be doing that?"

Natalie finally broke down, telling Cori about the day Natalie had met Toby. She confessed how she had planned to adopt Toby as payback for Toby's father taking her mother. As she talked, Cori's smile became strained.

"I know it's wrong," Natalie said. "And I know the error of my ways. But that's why I can't be his mother."

"Now that you're aware of your mistakes, though," Cori replied, "isn't that all the more reason why you'll be a better mother for Toby? You love him. Unconditionally."

Natalie shook her head adamantly, which made Bonnie sigh heavily, her fingers chasing after Natalie's scalp.

"I can't," Natalie said.

Cori sighed too. "Why won't you let yourself be happy?"

"Because I don't deserve it," Natalie replied. "I won't be a good mother."

"But you love him," Cori argued. "You're a good person. You will be a *great* mother."

"I won't," Natalie lamented. Sadness filled her heart and she hung her head. "Cori...I never passed my psychological examination for the adoption."

Cori paused again.

"I never got the form signed. We won't be able to adopt Toby," Natalie said.

Cori smirked. "You really think people will care about adoption protocol right now? Look at us, Natalie! We're stowed away on a boat, headed to Hawaii, while half the country is trying to kill us because of our genetic deficiencies."

With a heavy heart, Natalie shook her head. "It's not that someone would take Toby from me. It's the fact that I know now that I'm a broken person. If I can't pass a simple psych evaluation, what type of mother will I be?"

"A strong one," Cori insisted.

"Weak," Natalie corrected. "I can never be like you, or Bonnie, or Grandma Dottie. The love you have in your family…"

Cori snickered and tried to argue again, but Natalie would not be persuaded. She knew in her heart that Toby deserved better.

Silence eventually filled the room. There was tenseness to it as Natalie's stubbornness met Cori's optimism.

"What's your story, Bonnie?" Natalie asked, trying to break the tension.

Cori's sister continued to mend Natalie's head wounds, lost in her own world.

"She's an investor for a big firm out east," Cori explained. "She's been blank like that ever since she found out Grandma Dottie, Wyatt, and Bethany are gone. It's how she copes."

"By going dead to the world?"

"You think your way of coping with problems is so much better?" Cori shot back. "Shut off your emotions or hide from your future adoptive son?"

Natalie frowned. "Bonnie's husband is in Hawaii with Mark and Evan, right?"

"He's a climatologist," Cori said.

"Top secret government work," Natalie remembered.

She looked up at Bonnie. This woman held answers to what was happening—maybe not all of them, but some.

"Bonnie," Natalie said.

The woman did not so much as stir.

Natalie tried again, but nothing caused Bonnie to look up. A prickle of irritation danced across Natalie's scalp. Finally, Natalie grabbed Bonnie's arm and forced her to pay attention.

"Do you want me to stop the bleeding or not?" Bonnie asked in a fussy voice.

"What is happening?" Natalie asked. "Your husband is in on it. You have to know something."

Bonnie stared back. "Why would I—"

Natalie shook Bonnie, silencing her.

"The country is trying to tear us limb from limb for being degenerates," Natalie said. "Do you mind telling us what your husband had to do with turning the country into creepers?"

"It's a long story," Bonnie sighed. Her eyes wandered, and Natalie suspected Bonnie was fading away again. Natalie shook her again, bringing her back.

"And we have a long trip," Natalie said.

"What was this?" Cori asked. "A test? An experiment?"

"No," Bonnie replied. "Experimental phase was last month. This was application."

"Do tell," Natalie requested.

The two of them watched Bonnie, waiting.

"It was orchestrated by a madman," Bonnie finally said. "He's doomed us all. It wasn't my husband."

"We're not blaming your husband," Cori said. "But we need to know what's happening and what we're sailing toward."

Bonnie sighed again.

"Fine, but we have to start in the beginning."

Natalie sighed too and sat back as Bonnie began to explain.

"This whole thing," she said, "goes back to the early 1900s when eugenics began. It's the science of modifying lifeforms to create an elite species. Healthier. Stronger. Hitler was infamous for trying to create his Arian race. Others have tried since, but none have succeeded. One contemporary scientist of our time devoted himself to perfecting eugenics. His name is Dr. Griffith Avazino."

Natalie stiffened, sitting up. She met Cori's eyes, common pain and understanding passing between them.

In a way, Natalie had known this was coming. From the moment she had seen the creeper's gleaming, silver eyes, she had suspected a connection to her mother's death and Dr. Avazino. But at long last, she would find out why.

"Dr. Avazino focused on altering DNA strands," Bonnie continued. "He would isolate the genetic irregularities and attack them, forcing the DNA to perfect itself. He quickly made a name for himself and his research. Every doctor and geneticist wanted to know him and work with him."

Natalie grit her jaw, hating Bonnie for her unbiased comments on Dr. Avazino. Did Bonnie know what Avazino had done? The travesties he had committed?

"The more support he received, the more vocal Dr. Avazino became. Turns out, he was a closet bigot with a bone to pick about genetic deficiencies. He refused to hire or work with anyone who did not submit to a blood test or prove themselves to be without medical problems. When questioned about his discrimination, Dr. Avazino claimed that his experimentation would kill anyone in the room who had a medical deficiency. At this time, such a discriminatory notion was balked and admonished. Avazino was reprimanded and forced to hire a handful of employees with medical problems by the EEOC."

Bonnie leaned over and stared at Natalie.

"That's the Equal Employment Opportunities Commission," she said before attending back to Natalie's scalp. "Avazino was forced under Title Seven of the old Civil Rights Act. He complied. But, one of the people hired, a woman, lasted a week in the workplace before she perished in a car crash. Her death was supposedly linked to the work she had been doing for Avazino."

Natalie nearly smacked Bonnie, but Cori grabbed her hand and squeezed tight. The emotions slammed into

Natalie like a freight train as though the red road had happened a few minutes ago.

Bonnie continued on, oblivious to Natalie and Cori.

"The family sued," Bonnie said, "claiming that the mother had been killed by Avazino. The court dismissed the murder charges, as the woman had signed a waiver for her health. And of course, you guys know what happened next with all the court cases."

Cori rolled her eyes. "A little too well."

Bonnie looked at her sister. "What?"

Natalie decided it was time to reveal her role in the story.

"That woman who Avazino hired and died later?" Natalie said, anger in every syllable. "That was my mother."

Bonnie gaped at Natalie, comprehension dawning on her face.

"I knew I recognized you," she said. "You're that girl...from the news."

"I was with her when she passed," Natalie said. "I lost my legs in the accident. And the court case that got pushed around to the Supreme Court? I started it."

"I had no idea," Bonnie said softly. "I'm so sorry."

"We all are," Natalie said bitterly.

Bonnie sighed and wiped a tear from her eyes. Natalie rolled her eyes, already impatient with Bonnie's melodrama.

Finally, Bonnie said in a most dramatic tone: "I don't think anyone could be sorrier than Brian."

5

Mark and Evan sat on the edge of the coffee table. On the couch, Brian was holding his broken arm gingerly. He was pale, but seemed coherent.

Deep down, Mark had a feeling that this man, though related to Evan, was suspicious. If Brian so much as fidgeted or seemed to be lying, Mark would cough up a booger on him.

"I've been working for the government since I graduated from Oxford," Brian explained, eyes tracing the flower patterns on the ceiling. "I did climatology work for the better part of thirty years, mapping weather systems, perfecting forecast models. You know, boring scientist stuff."

Oh, Oxford, Mark laughed to himself. *How boring.*

"Two years ago, I was relocated to Hawaii," Brian continued. "I wasn't supposed to even tell my wife where I was, but I found a private line and kept in touch. She knew where I was, but I kept my work confidential."

"What were you working on?" Evan asked, impatience in his voice. The table creaked as he tapped his foot.

"Cloud patterns," Brian answered. "They wanted me to make a cloud system that could stretch approximately three thousand miles long and cover about three million square miles."

"What does that cover?" Mark inquired, shaking his head in confusion.

Brian paused, running his hand along the sling that Evan had made for his broken arm.

"The country," he finally said.

"You made a cloud that could cover the country?" Evan breathed. "As in the contiguous United States?"

"It extended into the oceans on either side," Brian confirmed. "Alaska and Hawaii were the only states uncovered."

"A cloud covering the country?" Evan asked, rubbing his forehead. "That didn't sound...I dunno, suspicious?"

"It was just a cloud!" Brian said, suddenly exasperated. "We could have been cloud seeding to alleviate the droughts for all I knew!"

"You didn't know? You didn't ask?" Mark inquired incredulously.

"Of course I did, but it's not my job to know all the secrets," Brian replied. "I'm a soldier of the government's intelligence sector. At that time, I didn't need to know what my research was being applied to. I was doing as I was told."

"Millions have died in the course of history at the hands of men simply doing what they were told," Evan spat.

There was a bite of cynicism in there that made Mark wonder if Evan knew more than he was saying. But he ignored his instincts and turned his attention back to Brian.

"So what changed?" Mark asked. "You went from a yes man to paranoid at the drop of a hat?"

"Another person arrived at the facility a year or so ago," Brian explained. "At first, everything went smoothly, but eventually I discovered that my climatology work was going to be coupled with his inventions to terrifying proportions."

"Like what?" Evan asked.

"Just tell us!" Mark requested.

"I developed the weather system to carry something," Brian said with a frumpy sigh. "I didn't realize until days before the launch that my weather system would carry the doctor's creations."

"Which were?"

"Nanobytes," Brian answered simply.

Mark's head began to spin, trying to keep track of all the puzzle pieces.

"Doctor?" Evan said, eyes narrowing. "Who?"

"Avazino," Brian answered. "His name is Griffith Avazino."

Mark stared at Brian. Evan stood up quickly, rigid as a board. All of the blood drained from his face.

Suddenly, Mark's need to understand nanobytes and weather systems seemed less pressing.

"Avazino?" Mark gasped.

Evan walked away, pacing the carpet by the window.

"He is not a good man," Brian replied. "Once the doctor arrived, I knew something was wrong, so I started to investigate. I'm sure you've heard of him. He's a big name in genetic research and he made quite a splash in the Supreme Court."

Evan continued to pace, staring out the window. Mark thought about checking on Evan, but decided his friend needed time to think.

"Is everything okay?" Brian asked, clutching his arm with a grimace.

Mark nodded. "Avazino is a household name."

Brian cocked his head, clearly confused.

"My fiancé, Natalie, and I are adopting Avazino's son," Mark said. "Natalie's mom was killed by Avazino about a decade ago. And the lawyer team that helped Avazino in the Supreme Court…"

"What about it?" Brian asked.

"It was Evan's case," Mark said. "That's the case that started his career and earned him an associate position in our law firm."

Brian sat back, his head landing on a pillow. He seemed far away, putting the pieces together.

"Was that Avazino up on the mountain?" Mark asked, thinking back to his foggy memories a few hours ago. "Was he the one who broke your arm? Did he chase us to the four-wheeler?"

Brian nodded. "That was Avazino."

Finally, Evan spoke.

"And he's still after us," Evan said, peering out the window. "He's walking into the hotel right now."

6

Natalie sat on the edge of her seat, waiting for Bonnie to get to the point. Finally, they would have answers.

Cori was excited too, kneeling by Natalie, needle hovering over a deep wound.

"Once Brian started suspecting Avazino, he called me," Bonnie finally said. "He told me all about his climate work and what he'd been up to at the facility. He was concerned about what everything was leading to. By the time we figured it out, we were too late to stop the progress."

"So what is it?" Natalie asked. "What did it do?"

Bonnie hesitated. Cori and Natalie stared, a heartbeat away from yelling at her to get the answer.

"Brian made a storm cloud that could extend across the United States," Bonnie said. "It was designed to carry an unknown material crafted by Avazino. At the time, we didn't know what the material was."

"Bonnie!" Cori exclaimed. "What was it? What did Avazino make?"

"Nanobytes," Bonnie said. "He made millions of nanobytes that could travel in the clouds and fall like rain."

Natalie sat back, stunned.

Cori, on the other hand, seemed impatient.

"What are nanobytes?"

Bonnie gave her sister a demeaning stare before saying, "Miniscule machines that can be programmed to execute orders. Think mini-robots that can do big things."

"They're used for cloudseeding," Natalie said, fully understanding. She spoke out loud, mostly for herself. "That's what my mother was working on when she was in Avazino's lab. She was supposed to test different metals to make nanobytes lighter. The lighter the metal, the easier to inject into clouds."

Cori huffed in frustration.

"Do you mind explaining what cloudseeding is?" Cori asked.

"It's how scientists make it rain," Bonnie answered. "Clouds are injected with iodine to make the moisture gather and rain in a particular area. It's used to fix droughts and reduce pollutants. Avazino was using this method of cloudseeding with Brian's weather system. The clouds would be injected with nanobytes and precipitate over the United States."

Natalie could sense the impatience radiating off of Cori, who seemed to think the answers were coming too fast now, with too little explanation.

"What did the nanobytes do to everyone?" she asked.

"The nanobytes were programmed with algorithms," Bonnie replied. "When they fell with the rain, the inset algorithms were meant to initiate directives."

"In English?" Natalie said.

"The nanobytes were programmed to find humans with imperfect genetic strands and kill them."

The dark cabin became deathly still. There was a stunned silence.

"Every degenerate was supposed to die," Bonnie said, her eyes glazing over. "I thought we were all doomed."

"So Avazino was trying to kill us?" Cori questioned. "All of us? Intentionally?"

"Not just Avazino," Bonnie corrected. "He and Brian were placed in Hawaii by our own government."

Natalie cursed under her breath, unable to believe the truth. Their own country had turned against them. Their own country had hired Brian and Dr. Avazino to eradicate degenerates from the map.

"Who?" she growled. "Who was behind it?"

Bonnie shrugged. "Some politician. That's what Brian heard anyway. Brian said his name once or twice, but I can't remember it. We never knew who it was."

Bonnie's dismissive tone alerted Natalie. It seemed like Bonnie was hiding something.

"I hope he was in the states when the rain fell," Natalie said, trying to get a rise from Bonnie, but she didn't react.

"So some politician started this mess?" Cori asked.

Bonnie nodded.

"And tried to kill us all," Natalie added.

"Tried," Cori repeated. "But didn't. Do you know why, Bonnie? Did the nanobytes malfunction? Did they—?"

"I don't know," Bonnie interrupted. "The nanobytes obviously did not work the way they were supposed to. Once Brian and I figured out what Avazino was planning, Brian sought to mend his mistakes. He kept trying to find time to destroy Avazino's creation, but the nanobytes were being guarded. Brian told me he was going to try and destroy it in the dead of night."

"He did a great job with that obviously," Natalie muttered.

"He would have if he could," Bonnie said. "I have to believe something prevented him from just destroying the nanobytes. Instead, he must have fiddled with the algorithms."

"To do what?" Cori asked.

Bonnie shrugged. "He talked about negating the equations to—"

"So he messed with the algorithms and changed it up completely," Natalie interrupted, rolling her eyes. "That's an even better idea."

"He must have done it for a reason," Bonnie said, crossing her arms.

"He messed up big time," Natalie replied. "Look at what he did."

"Would you rather be dead?"

"I'd rather not be fighting for my life."

"Do we even know what happened?" Cori interjected, cutting the two of them off. "What did Brian really do?"

Bonnie's shoulders sank and she shook her head. "It's apparent that we were not killed, but everyone else was infected somehow. They've been trying to kill us but don't attack one another."

"So the nanobytes are still trying to kill degenerates," Natalie surmised, "but infected the wrong bodies."

"As much as I can assume," Bonnie said, "yes. But whether we're right or wrong, I do know that we are all alive thanks to my husband. Without him, we wouldn't be here."

They all fell silent. Natalie felt her heart pounding in her chest, furious with Brian and Bonnie for their part in the silver rain. She wanted to slap Bonnie, but did not want to offend Cori. Instead, she figured she'd save the slap for Avazino when they got to Hawaii.

Natalie heard Cori muttering under her breath, trying to connect the dots. In her head, Natalie did the same: the United States government had decided to remove their weakest citizens from the country by hiring two mad scientists to develop and release a technology-based toxin in the rain. The technology had been compromised, so after the silver rain fell, the degenerates lived and everyone else was infected. The infected had been reduced to their base instincts and turned into bloodthirsty, degenerate-hunting monsters who called themselves creepers.

And we're caught in the middle of it, Natalie thought, *just trying to get to Hawaii.*

On the far side of the room, the door creaked open, breaking the silence. The women turned to see Toby, Nate, and a trim, suited man enter. Boomer hovered behind the boys.

Toby's eyes grew when he saw Natalie.

"Natalie!" he cried.

He ran across the room with a limp and jumped into her lap, hugging her tightly.

Nate and the suited man walked over too, Nate looking nervous and the man looking slightly annoyed.

"You're alive!" Toby said.

"I am!" Natalie replied, trying to sound happy. She bit her lip, her plan ruined. There was no way forward now but to break his heart, the one part of Toby that had been untouched in a life of violence.

"What happened?" Toby exclaimed.

"I had to make it back here to you," Natalie said, trying to make him smile. "I wasn't going to stay in California. Too creepy and crazy for me."

"I'm so glad I found you!" Toby said, and he hugged her tighter still.

As she hugged Toby, Natalie looked up at the suited man. He had dark hair and a shrewd complexion.

"Senator Beaudry," the man said to her with a nod, his voice low.

Beside her, Natalie noticed Bonnie stand up straighter. Her fingers fidgeted. Cori must have seen it too, eyes narrowing.

Nate pulled on his mother's arm.

"Um, Mom?" Nate said.

"What is it?" Bonnie said.

"There are creepers downstairs," Nate whispered. "Toby and I found them below the deck. Boomer barked and they started slamming on the door. I think they got out."

Bonnie looked confused.

"The infected people from the mainland," Cori tried to explain. "They call themselves creepers."

"The ship was full," the senator said. "But it was the only way we could get to Hawaii."

Everyone looked at the senator.

"You're kidding," Natalie said. Had this man actually willingly jumped onto a boat full of murderers just to get across the ocean?

The senator shook his head. "They were all trapped downstairs."

"Were?"

Cori suddenly lunged forward, pointing a finger at the man.

"You!" she shouted.

The senator backed away, Cori's finger dangerously close to going up his nostril.

"You're the senator who funded this!" she said. "You're the one who wanted this!"

There was a loud click, and Cori leapt back from the senator. Natalie gripped Toby tighter as she saw the senator brandish a gun.

"Get away from me," the senator growled. "I did what was best for this country. It's Avazino's fault this all got messed up."

Cori backed up as instructed. Fire burnt in her eyes.

Waving the gun at everyone, the senator said, "All I wanted was a country I could be proud of. But so many people feel entitled! First it had to be the blacks. Then it was the women. Then it was the feminists. It went on and on. But it ends with the degenerates. They poisoned our country with their sickness and inability. Imagine if we were free of them! Imagine how powerful we could be with no disease or degeneration."

No one said a word. Natalie glared at the senator.

"That's all I'm trying to do!" the senator cried. "And Avazino had to go and screw it all up. So I loaded up a ship of these degenerates, and I'm taking them as a present for Avazino."

Natalie and Cori exchanged a look, understanding the same thing. The senator thought that the crazy, murderous people were degenerates infected with malfunctioning nanobytes. He had not yet realized that it was normal humans who had been infected by the silver rain. The senator probably thought that Natalie, Cori, Bonnie, and the kids were normal, healthy humans without any of the genetic imperfections he detested.

"I...I understand," Bonnie said. "But now they're...the degenerates, are running around the ship?"

"Aren't we the..." Toby began to say, but Natalie squeezed him tightly, silencing him.

There was a loud clang in reply that echoed through the room. Everyone stiffened. The senator spun around, aiming his gun at stairwell.

"They're coming," Nate said, his voice shaking.

The senator peered around the wall and up the stairs.

"They're all on the top deck still. I've locked the door though, and it's the only way in here. They shouldn't be able to get in."

Natalie took a deep breath, trying to keep calm for Toby.

"How long until we reach Hawaii?" Bonnie asked.

"Several days," the senator said. "We'd all better settle in."

"Fantastic," Natalie said. Under her breath, she mumbled, "The world's longest boat ride with the world's worst politician and a gaggle of the people he hates most."

Figuring she might as well be comfortable, she propped herself off the stool and helped Toby make a fort out of life vests. She laid down, letting him crawl around with Boomer. Nate joined in too. Cori and Bonnie began to talk. Natalie caught heated phrases between them like, "How did you not recognize him?" and "He was the only way to Hawaii." The senator watched the stairway with a sneer.

Natalie sighed, settling in. It was going to be a long boat ride.

7

The days passed slowly. Creepers banged on the door occasionally. Though they were intelligent and animalistic in their pursuits, they did not know there were degenerates hiding in the storage cabins, and therefore did not try very hard to enter. Footsteps could be heard through the ceiling as they paced back and forth, on the hunt.

The stowaways took alternating patrols through the days and nights to make sure no creepers broke through. Thankfully, the boat was on auto-pilot and would not need to be attended to by the senator until they were closer to the Hawaiian shores. The time crept ever forward, closer to when they would have to fight their way out of the room, to the ship's steering wheel, and guide the ship safely to shore.

In the meantime, Natalie and Cori kept everyone eating with a rations system. There was enough food to last them years, but no one was sure what they would find on Hawaii.

While exploring the cabin, Nate found an old radio that they tuned to find military calls coming through the AM stations. There were several recordings from Russia and China, calling for United States citizens to make contact. Apparently, they had launched several probes into the United States and still did not know what was happening. There were talks of a military reconnaissance team going to Hawaii to learn more about the rain and its source.

Cori mentioned finding a way to contact the countries, now that they knew what was happening in the U.S., but Natalie discouraged her. They had to stay bunkered down in this room with Senator Beaudry for several days, and they didn't want the man with the gun finding out the truth.

To pass the time, they frequently scanned through the radio. They sought out the stations they had listened to in the car, the livestream broadcasts from other groups in the country seeking sanctuary, home, and health.

Eventually, they found the frequency used by the man trying to get to Maine. Natalie used the radio broadcasts as emotional tests, putting herself in the speakers' shoes. She felt pings of dread, terror, and sadness as the Maine-bound man fought his way from town after town to get home, only to discover that his wife and daughter were gone. He searched the city for them, finally finding them in a park, where they attacked him. His family had become creepers. The man's final broadcast had been a tragic one as he hid in city hall, alone and unsure where to go in the world. His harrowing tale reminded Natalie of how lost she had felt after her mother died. She hoped for the man's sake that he did not recede from the world and become as emotionless and uncaring as Natalie had.

The other broadcasted station was more hopeful. This one was run constantly by the group of friends traveling to the Pharmacy to find medicine for Ryan, their friend who desperately needed medication to stay alive. By the time Natalie, Nate, and Toby tuned in, the friends had found the Pharmacy and infiltrated it. After they cleared the facility of creepers, Ryan was lethargic and near unresponsive. To make matters worse, Ryan's friends discovered that there was a shortage in his necessary medication, and they had to manufacture it with what was left in the facility. Miraculously, Ryan's friends pulled through, becoming pharmacists overnight and creating a substitute medication. In a few days, he was back into good health, and the friends gathered around a campfire in the Pharmacy vestibule, sharing stories and making jokes.

Natalie laughed long and hard with the group, realizing that she had not felt this way since before her mother died. She realized that, like Ryan, she was surrounded by great friends. Cori, Toby, Mark, and maybe even Evan would go to the ends of the earth to help her. She felt a swell of affection for all of them. It was a joyful feeling that she wished could have lasted forever. But then, screams echoed through the radio as Ryan and his friends were attacked. Creepers had snuck up on them. Natalie muted the radio before Toby and Nate heard too much, but she knew Ryan's fate.

In an instant, the feelings of joy and love for her friends were replaced with anxiousness and fear. Reality sank into Natalie, blunt and unforgiving. They were sailing to certain danger and little guarantee of survival. As much as she loved Cori and Toby and wished it could shelter them, she knew the time was coming when more blood would be shed. Each second brought her closer to confronting Mark, facing Dr. Avazino, and saying goodbye to Toby for good.

Natalie knew in her heart that Toby deserved better. She could not be his mother, though she loved him dearly. With his epilepsy and immunity to pain, Toby could very easily hurt himself without knowing it. Such a boy required patience, time, and protection.

Natalie had grown up a wild child. She had hardly ever listened to her parents, and the day she had finally listened, her mother had died. Everything that Toby needed, she had shunned her whole life. Cori, though, was a better person. She would be a better mother. Evan would be a wonderful father, and Mark would be there too. Natalie, however, would disappear. She would help stop Avazino on Hawaii, protect Toby if his life was in danger, and then leave Toby with a more capable family like Bonnie and Cori. Natalie would start again, forging herself from the ground up, to be a better person that could face the new future of uncertainty.

—

Surfer's Hotel
Maui, Hawaii

Meanwhile, Mark, Evan, and Brian moved from room to room in the hotel. They barely missed Dr. Avazino several times, only a room away or hiding just around the corner in a stairwell.

As they moved, they discussed ways to deactivate the nanobytes on the mainland. When Mark suggested an electromagnetic pulse to kill all technology, Brian told them about the EMP that had been used during experimentation. Unfortunately, it had been deactivated. But when Evan mentioned using an alternative energy source to reactivate the EMP and increase its spread, Brian looked hopeful and fell silent.

The next day, he proposed an idea: if they got back to the facility in the cliffs of Haleakalā, he could reactivate the EMP and reprogram it to be powered by the nuclear reactor, the facility's energy source. It seemed plausible, so the three of them snuck out of the hotel and drove back to the facility. They spent a few days there, helping

Brian however they could. The longer he worked, the more disappointed he seemed. Evan and Mark suspected that a nuclear-powered EMP would have a few problems, but Brian seemed determined.

Unfortunately, before their task could be completed, Dr. Avazino returned to the facility. They crept out and returned to the hotel, continuing the game of hide and seek. Not daring to return to the facility until they knew Dr. Avazino had gone elsewhere, they found the suite at the top of the hotel with a good view of the island. There, Evan and Mark waited, watching for Dr. Avazino from the mountain and Natalie and Cori from the sea.

—

Maui, Hawaii

The Griffin, starved for blood, wandered the island in search of his prey. He found evidence of their visit to the facility and tracked them heading back toward the hotel.

Growling, he made chase. As he walked through the mountain's brush, he heard fighter jets. High above, Russian jets streaked by the island.

Sensing his time on the island was running short, he made haste back toward the hotel.

—

Breakaway Cruiser
Inbound, Coast of Maui, Hawaii

Back on the boat, time was short as well. Senator Beaudry announced that the ship would reach Hawaii within a few hours. He told them to rest up for their fight to the control room.

Heeding the senator's advice, Natalie took a seat next to Toby and Boomer, who were playing tug-of-war with a life vest strap.

"You know your Dad is on the island, right, Toby?" Natalie asked.

"You'll protect me," Toby said. He had such confidence, Natalie almost believed him. "And if you're busy, Boomer can."

From what Natalie remembered, Griffith Avazino was a daunting man who would as easily squash a human as he could a pipsqueak of a dog.

"We'll keep you safe, no matter what," Natalie promised.

"Nate said you lost a leg back on the pier," Toby said, poking Natalie's prosthetic.

"I already did," Natalie said. She pulled up her pant leg to show the metal replacement. "I lost it in the car accident."

"Is that where you learned to be tough?" Toby asked.

"Tough as nails," Natalie said. "The red road."

"When can we be happy?" Toby asked.

"Happy?"

"Yeah," he said. "Happy as a flying penguin. No more fighting. No more hiding how we feel. When can we, you know, be happy?"

Natalie held Toby close to her, letting Boomer lick her on the face. A knot of fear filled her stomach.

"Someday, Toby," she said. "Hopefully tonight."

She nearly told him, but couldn't stand to say the words. Where she had once been blunt and honest, now her words were choked with compassion.

A few hours later, the senator told them to prepare. Toby and Nate were instructed to stay below with Boomer. Natalie, Cori, Bonnie, and the senator wrapped themselves in life vests and armed themselves with medical instruments. The senator volunteered to go first with his gun, a note of bravery Natalie found odd for a man so willing to kill off half the country.

They ascended the stairs and listened at the door. There were no bangs, clangs, or sounds of any type. The creepers must have been elsewhere.

"Now," the senator whispered.

Senator Beaudry unlocked the door and jumped out, gun held high.

Waiting for just that moment and action, the creepers attacked like locusts, thick and fast.

Natalie, Cori, and Bonnie were still in the stairwell, having suspected that the creepers would be waiting to attack. They watched as dozens of them surrounded the senator, attacking him with fists and teeth.

"Come on," Natalie said.

Together, Natalie, Cori, and Bonnie hurried out of the stairwell and across the deck. Stray creepers ran at them, armed with harpoons and anchors. The women brandished scalpels, saws, and trays, knocking the creepers away.

Several shots blasted through the air. Natalie glanced back. A few creepers lay at the senator's feet. The other ones had backed away, staring at the senator with a confused look. They turned as on and locked eyes on Natalie, Cori, and Bonnie.

"Degenerates!" the creepers screamed, and made chase after them, abandoning the senator.

Natalie cursed under her breath.

The senator emptied his pistol, killing a few more creepers with shots to the back. Natalie, Cori, and Bonnie fought too, knocking back dozens. Inch by inch, they neared the control room.

"Watch it!" the senator shouted.

He pistol-whipped a creeper away from Natalie and pushed forward to the control room door. Fumbling, he wrenched the door open. They ran inside, creepers right behind them. The senator shut the door and locked it right before—

Bang!

Creepers slammed against the door. They shouted and cat-called, asking for the degenerates to come out and play.

Breathing hard, the senator ran to the steering wheel. He wiped his bloody brow and pressed several buttons. Nothing happened.

The senator cussed at the top of his lungs, slamming his fists on the steering wheel.

"They've tampered with the navigation!" the senator shouted.

"What does that mean?" Bonnie asked in a shrill voice.

"We can't slow down," the senator replied. "Or steer or turn…"

A trickle of fear leaked into Natalie, making her stomach tighten. They were on a ship that was out of control.

She looked out the windows. Beyond the creepers and the cruise ship's deck, she could see the ocean. The sun had fallen, casting darkness on the sea. Perhaps ten miles out, Natalie could see the skyline of an island.

Seeing the island of Maui stole the air from Natalie's lungs.

Mark was there, wherever he would be hiding. So was Avazino.

"What do we do?" Bonnie cried.

"The lifeboats!" Cori answered. "We'll get one off the boat!"

"Where are they?" Natalie asked.

"Lining the sides of the ship," the senator said. "But we can't lower boats into the water at this speed."

"What if we cut it loose?" Cori suggested.

"You'll crash into the waves," the senator contradicted.

"It's our only shot," Natalie said. "We'll figure it out when we get there."

They huddled around the door again, Natalie with her hand on the lock, each of them ready for the fight to the lifeboats. Outside, the creepers were still yelling.

"Come out, come out, wherever you are," one creeper cried. "You know degenerates can't get far…"

"Why are they calling us degenerates?" Senator Beaudry asked from the back of the group.

"I suppose because that's what we are," Natalie said, glaring at the senator.

He looked at them all, his shrewd eyes narrowing.

"The nanobytes didn't infect degenerates," Cori said. "They infected everyone else."

The senator cursed loudly. He looked sick to his stomach that he was surrounded by degenerates. He held up his gun, pointing it at Cori. When he pulled the trigger, the pistol let out a dry click.

"Since you can't kill us, mind if we help you get to Maui?" Natalie taunted.

The senator charged her, hatred in his eyes.

Natalie stepped aside, opening the door as she did. The senator flew past her, right into the mass of creepers. Natalie, Cori, and Bonnie followed suit, slashing and bashing their way through creepers.

"Get to the boats!" Natalie yelled.

As Cori and Bonnie ran, Natalie sprinted for the door to the storage cabins. She threw it open. Toby, Boomer, and Nate were waiting in the stairwell.

"Come on!" she yelled, grabbing Toby.

"Hold me too!" a creeper screamed, running at Natalie.

She swung with the scalpel, slicing the creeper's face. Thick blood splashed on the deck. Before another creeper could attack, she stowed the scalpel in her pocket, grabbed Nate's hand, and ran for the bow of the boat.

As she ran, she looked to the front of the ship. The island was close—too close. They were going to crash into the shore.

On the deck, Natalie spotted Cori. She stood at the bow of the ship, waving frantically by a lifeboat. Bonnie was already in the boat, which hovered just over the edge of the ship.

Natalie held Toby tight, pulled Nate by the hand, and ran for all it was worth. The creepers shrieked insults behind her and she heard the senator screaming too.

Miraculously, Natalie got to the lifeboat, far outpacing the creepers. She set Toby on a seat and threw Nate in too.

"Get in!" Natalie shouted at Cori.

As Cori jumped into the boat, Boomer leapt over the edge and stood on Toby's legs.

"Loose lips sink ships!" called a creeper close behind Natalie.

She had hardly turned before the creeper lunged, smacking her hard in the back. Natalie hardly moved. She turned around, glaring at the creeper. As though the blow had been a gust of wind on her back, Natalie lunged and grabbed the creeper by the clothes. With a heave, she threw it overboard.

Another creeper lunged, but Natalie swung, sinking a fist into the creeper's face. With a crack of the jaw, the creeper hit the ground. The coast now clear, Natalie spun around and jumped into the lifeboat.

Bonnie stared at Natalie's bloody knuckles.

"Didn't that hurt?" she asked.

"No," Natalie said honestly.

"She's special," Toby said with a smile. "Like me!"

Natalie ignored them all and looked forward. Up ahead, the island loomed. Below, foam and white water furrowed around the ship.

"Hold on!" Natalie cried.

Back on the boat, creepers raced for them. The senator, no longer being attacked, was charging too.

"So long, creepers," Nate shouted.

Natalie reached up with the scalpel and sawed off the ropes holding up the lifeboat. Suddenly, they were airborne, falling toward the water. Everyone screamed, and, with a jolt, the lifeboat crashed into the waves.

Instantly, Natalie knew the lifeboat was a bad decision. The moment they landed, the waves capsized the boat, tossing them all into the ocean. Submerged in the dark water, she spun around and around, unsure which way was up. She felt her body floating toward the surface thanks to her life vests and fought for it.

She gasped for air as she broke the surface. Toby was already floating a few feet away from her. Boomer swam over to them. Cori, Bonnie, and Nate popped up too, gasping for air.

Wiping water from her eyes, Natalie saw the cruise ship charging for the island. Before it could reach dry land, the ship plowed into the shallow sandy bed with an almighty crash. The boat tipped, falling broadside into the shallow shore. It careened over and came to a stop with a crash, sending a cascade of water and creepers flying across the beach. Bodies landed in heaps and did not move. Explosions rocked the metal hull, and smoke began to pour out.

"Swim to the right!" Bonnie commanded.

Sticking together, they began to move for the shore.

"Keep going, Toby," Natalie said, trying to keep him calm.

All the while, she kept an eye on the ship. Nobody moved. With any luck, every single creeper would be dead, the senator along with them.

As she swam, she pondered her hopes that the senator had died. She knew it was wrong and that she shouldn't have wished for his death, but she hated the senator as much as she hated Avazino. The two of them stood for genocide. They deserved what they got.

Only a few feet from the shore, they all got to their feet and waded through the shallows. Natalie, Cori, and Bonnie peeled off their armor of life vests. Toby picked up Boomer and held the tiny dog out to Nate.

"Keep him," Nate insisted.

Toby thanked Nate and balled Boomer up in his shirt. Boomer stayed there quivering, making Toby look like he had a shaking potbelly.

As they approached the shore, Natalie thought she saw dark figures walking in the sand. She watched warily, hoping they weren't creepers.

Another figure appeared out of the gloom. There were three in all, milling on the beach, waiting.

"Guys," Natalie whispered, pointing to the shore. Cori and Bonnie followed her gaze.

"Natalie?" came a voice.

Her heart skipped a beat. That was Mark's voice.

"Mark!" Natalie cried.

"Cori!" called Evan, and Cori called his name back.

"Bonnie?" called another that Natalie did not recognize.

Bonnie shouted for joy and ran through the water. She leapt at her husband, a tall man with glasses, a greasy face, and a sling on his arm. They kissed passionately. Nate ran ashore too, wrapping his arms around his father's waist.

Cori ran to Evan, jumping into his arms. Her legs wrapped around his waist as they kissed.

Natalie's eyes fell on Mark. At first, she just stared, surprised how pale he was. Then, it hit her—it was Mark!

She picked up Toby and ran to him.

They met in the water, waves lapping onto their legs. They wrapped their arms around each other. Salt water dripped from her brow and soaked into his clothes. Toby put his arms around their necks. Boomer poked his head out of Toby's shirt and woofed softly. Mark put his forehead on hers and exhaled in happiness. His breath stunk, but she didn't care. She had never felt such affection for him—her heart beat faster and she longed to hold him forever.

"I've missed you," Mark said.

"I've needed you," she replied. She paused and then said, "Mark, I have to tell you. There's so much."

She tried to shut herself up, but there was no hope.

She set Toby down and pulled up her pant leg.

"I have a fake leg," she confessed. "I lost it in the accident."

"I know," he said.

"I didn't pass my psych test," she said.

"I know," he said again, chuckling.

"How do you—?" she began.

He put a finger to her lips.

"I know, but wanted you to tell me in your own time," he said. "All so I can tell you this. I still love you."

She embraced him in a back-breaking hug and kissed him full on the mouth.

For a glimmer of a moment, she actually thought she felt heat flood her body before she reminded herself it wasn't possible. She was feeling something deep within herself, something powerful. It was another emotion, one she had felt for Toby and for Cori, but now felt very strongly for Mark. If she wasn't mistaken, she thought it was love.

"There's something else," she said.

His eyes searched hers.

"I have congenital analgia," she said, hardly believing she had said it.

Beside her, Cori squealed in happiness and Evan cheered heartily.

Mark ogled at her.

"That I didn't know," he said. "Is that…?"

"What Toby has," Natalie said. "I can't feel anything like heat or cold."

"Or pain," Mark bemoaned, rubbing his thumb against a cut in Natalie's brow.

"I got it from my father," Natalie said. "My mom always told me to be careful when I was younger, but I ignored her. I broke so many bones and never felt them. And then in the car crash, she told me not to move, so I didn't. After I lost her, I was so angry. I forced myself to stop feeling things and shut myself off to my emotions. But not anymore. I'm me again."

She nearly cried, but she was tougher than that. Instead, she paused, waiting for Mark to say something.

"Can you feel this?" Mark asked, rubbing his hand across her cheek.

"Barely," Natalie replied.

"Do you feel anything when we kiss?"

Her cheeks turned red.

"I do now," she replied.

Mark smiled and embraced her again.

"I still love you, Natalie," he said.

She put her head on his chest, trying her hardest to feel his embrace, letting herself pretend she could feel the warmth of his touch.

Beside them, Cori squealed again and wrapped her arms around them. Evan completed the group hug, and for a moment, Natalie forgot about all of her worries and tribulations. For a moment, she felt as though her life had come full circle, here with her friends, her love, and their son.

Eventually, they parted and moved out of the water. On the shore, close to a collection of underbrush, Bonnie introduced Natalie, Cori, and Toby to her husband, Brian.

"Cori, good to see you," Brian said as he hugged her. When he saw Natalie, he extended a hand to shake hers. "The warrior who saved my family," he said.

She shook his hand, all the while wanting to punch him. He seemed so smug greeting Natalie, as though he knew all there was to know about her. She couldn't resist replying to him as sarcastically as possible.

"The sick man who got us in this mess," she replied.

Brian's shoulders slumped and he looked irritated. His wife jumped in between them, frowning.

"This isn't his fault," Bonnie insisted, her voice getting high-pitched.

"I'm beginning to see why you don't talk to your sister," Natalie said to Cori.

Brian began to protest, clearly offended.

"All of this is your fault," Natalie insisted, looking right at Brian.

With a chuff, he nodded.

"I will give you that," Brian said. "But I wouldn't be here if Avazino hadn't gone to court and ended up in prison. That was your doing, the little girl who couldn't stop talking about her red road."

Natalie glared at Brian.

"Once," she yelled back. "I was cornered by reporters *once* and told my story."

"But you're the one who got Avazino's men into the Supreme Court."

Natalie felt her anger simmer close to boiling point.

"Everyone, stop!" Cori shouted suddenly. The air fell silent, except for the hiss of flames from the cruise ship.

"It doesn't do any good to point blame right now. What's past is past."

Natalie stepped back from Brian and let her anger fade. Though Brian surely shared equal or greater blame for their current predicament, nothing would be solved if they argued.

Looking relieved no one would attack her husband, Bonnie asked Brian, "You worked on this for two years. Is there any way to reverse it?"

Evan and Mark shouted in the affirmative with enthusiasm.

Natalie's heart leapt. They had found a way. This messy situation had seemed impossible to escape, but perhaps there was a way to fix it.

But Brian hung his head.

"We have an EMP pulse," he said.

"And it works, right?" Mark added. "We just didn't have enough time to turn it on."

"What's EMP?" Nate asked.

"Electromagnetic pulse," Brian explained. "It disengages all technology in the sphere of the pulse. It can destroy the nanobytes."

"Will it work?" Cori asked.

"We tied it directly to the nuclear reactor of the control facility," Brian said, motioning to the silhouette of a mountain behind them. "It's centered here on the island and has a five thousand mile radius. Just enough to cover the United States."

"Isn't the pulse a sphere?" Bonnie asked. "As the pulse goes east to the U.S., won't it go west the same distance? What about Russia, China, Japan? All of their technology will be useless."

"What about America itself?" Cori asked. "Canada. Mexico." Her voice trailed off.

"Dead technology is a lot better than dead people," Natalie said.

"It's the only shot we have at this," Brian said. "But, there's a problem. It's going to kill us all."

There was dead silence for a moment.

"EMP's kill people too?" Toby asked tremulously. His little hands grasped at Natalie's prosthetic leg.

"No, they should only hurt technology," Evan said, looking confused.

"Explain," Natalie demanded of Brian.

He sighed before saying, "The pulse has to be strong enough to reach the furthest edges of the United States. The EMP we had covered fifteen miles every direction. To extend that, we had to rewire the pulse trigger so that it's directly powered to the nuclear reactor."

Natalie shrugged. "Why would that change anything?"

"Setting off an EMP of that magnitude will take a massive surge of power," Brian said. "The nuclear reactor will be drained of coolant. It will reach what's called criticality and explode. The facility will be filled with lethal amounts of radiation. The island will be bathed in it too, though to a lesser extent."

They were silent for a time, letting the information sink in. It was quiet enough that Natalie could hear voices from the cruise ship. A few creepers must have still been alive.

"Anyone on the island will be affected, particularly whoever pushes the button to launch the EMP," Brian concluded.

Natalie realized what Brian was trying to explain.

"Whoever sets off the EMP will die from radiation poisoning," she said.

Brian nodded, looking downtrodden. "But not a slow death over several weeks. The radiation in the facility will be massive. The death will likely be immediate."

"No," Mark said, realizing the implications too. "There has to be another way."

"There isn't," Brian said. "This is the only way to deactivate the nanobytes. Then all of the afflicted individuals will revert to their normal selves."

"Excellent!" Cori said, her voice a bit too light-hearted for the moment. "We can fix all of this."

"Except someone has to die!" Mark cried.

"A small price to be paid for what we've all done to create this," Brian replied.

For a heartbeat, Natalie actually agreed with Brian. She had learned plenty about the worth of a life in these past few days. One life could be sacrificed for everyone else.

Deep down, her sarcastic side wanted Brian to push it. He'd started this mess, he should finish it.

Everyone looked at one another, the obvious question on their faces. The EMP must be set off, but there was no need for everyone to die, least of all the children. It had to be one of them, one of the adults. Cori, Evan, Bonnie, Brian, Mark, or Natalie—one of them would not make it off this island alive.

As terrible as it was, Natalie could sense Brian and Evan wondering who deserved it the most.

The moment Natalie looked at Evan, he let out a *humph* of anger and stalked off, feet stomping on the sandy beach.

"Wait," Cori shouted. "Evan!"

Natalie rolled her eyes.

This is going to be good, she thought.

Everyone chased after Evan, but Natalie stuck behind, mulling over what Brian had told them. The silver rain could be stopped with the EMP pulse, but at the cost of a life. Perhaps it was meant to be her. After losing her true self on the red road, Natalie had reemerged when the silver rain fell. Now, she would come full circle with a sacrifice to redeem herself.

She knew then that she had to do it. For all the lives she had taken and sacrificed to get to Hawaii, it only made sense that she must be the one to press the button and end this madness.

Suddenly, Natalie heard someone off in the distance mutter, "Degenerates."

She searched the beach for the source of the voice. Out in the waves, she saw dark figures stumbling ashore.

Creepers, she realized.

Natalie nearly shouted to her friends, but a sharp blow hit her in the back. Her skin tore and something sharp dug into her. She fell forward, blood dribbling out of her back. Her head smacked onto the ground, making her vision blurry.

Her attacker stepped over her and walked down the beach.

With blood pooling on her back, Natalie saw the man who had attacked her. She saw where he was headed: to her friends and Toby. She realized with utter horror who it was.

It was Dr. Avazino.

8

Evan slung a rock into the ocean as hard as he could. The far-off splash didn't give him any satisfaction, so he picked up another one and threw it harder. It splashed close to the cruise ship.

Anger seethed through him. He was a fool, a downright fool.

"Millions have died in the course of history at the hands of men doing what they were told," he had told Brian.

Hypocrite, he told himself.

He was the epitome of the word. For years, he had done as he was told as an intern for the law firm. He'd worked the cases, figured out the loopholes and legal shortcuts. Avazino's case had been the worst. He had singlehandedly secured the doctor's freedom.

Without a doubt, this was all his fault.

"Evan!" several people shouted.

He spun around. Everyone was running down the beach to him.

"Leave me alone!" he yelled, throwing another rock. It flew off wildly and hit the side of the overturned cruise ship.

The group came to a stop behind him, Cori closest.

"What is going on?" she asked.

"I'm an idiot!" he exclaimed.

"No, you're not," she insisted. "Evan, talk to me!"

He pushed her away, frustration broiling over.

"This is all my fault!" he shouted. "All of this, the nanobytes, you guys fighting for your lives, all of us here. It's all my fault!"

"You didn't make the silver rain," Cori said.

"You didn't send it across the ocean," Brian added.

"But I am responsible for the man who did it," Evan interrupted. "I've been trying to do things right ever since."

Not seeing Natalie, he turned to Mark, a mix of emotions pouring out of him.

"I'm sorry for everything I did, I really am," he said. "Natalie's mother's death should have been the end of Avazino. But he got away. Then he kept pressing forward, making it the Supreme Court. I should have found a way to stop him, but I didn't. I'm the one who found the loophole."

Cori's shoulders slumped. Evan knew that she knew this story. He'd confessed it to her the night after the case.

But Evan was focused on Mark, his stepbrother and best friend.

"You said the lead lawyers found the loophole that secured Avazino's case," Mark said.

"No," Evan admitted. "It was me."

He bit back the bitter tears.

"I've been trying to do right by you ever since, Mark, I really have," he insisted. "I'm stepping down from my position at the law firm. You're taking my place."

Mark stammered. "W–what?"

"You're the best of us, Mark," Evan shouted. "You can make a difference. I was just a fool who let a madman go free and wreck the world."

"So I'm just a chess piece?" Mark yelled, choking on mucus. "You just move me around when you need to rectify your sins? How can I go along with this? What about Natalie?"

Toby pulled on the leg of Mark's pants.

"Where's Natalie?" Toby asked, his voice too small to draw any attention.

"It's all my fault!" Evan exclaimed. "I should be the one to press the EMP. I deserve to die!"

Suddenly, a new voice entered the conversation, a deep one.

"On the contrary," the voice said, silencing everyone, "you deserve a reward."

Everyone spun around, scanning the shadowed beach for the voice.

All at once, a man lunged out of the darkness. He charged swiftly, bowling everyone over. A striking blow caught Evan in the stomach and knocked him onto his back. Evan gasped for air, trying to see the attacker.

A face appeared above him, showing a malicious set of teeth with a smile. It was the man from the mountain and the man he had defended in court.

"Silverman, how good of you to join me," said Dr. Griffith Avazino with a sneer.

PHASE 7

SILVER SECONDS

Shoreline
Maui, Hawaii

Dr. Griffith "The Griffin" Avazino held the shard of glass to Evan Silverman's throat, forcing the lawyer to his knees. They faced Evan's family and friends, their back to the ocean. The beach and their pale faces glistened from the ship's fires.

The Griffin spotted his son. He was a little taller, but Toby still had the same terrified look. He had scars along his arms and face from their last family meeting.

"We're all here, I see," the Griffin growled, eyes passing over each of the evening's prey. "Well, except for your friend, Natalie. I left her to die on the other side of the beach."

One of the women, the plump one, let out a faint gasp. The Griffin licked his lips. That one would be fun to kill.

He looked over each of them, putting a face to the identity.

"The scientist," he said, looking at Matician first, "his weasel wife and child, the sister, my...son, another lawyer, and the man of the hour, Evan Silverman."

He tightened his grip on Evan's scalp, making the lawyer gasp in pain. The shard of glass drew a dribble of blood.

Suddenly, Matician lunged at the Griffin. Unfortunately, the climatologist was slow in the sand and the Griffin had anticipated an attack. The Griffin pressed into Silverman's throat, drawing more blood. Silverman cried out, choking on his agony. His wife whimpered.

Matician stopped, standing stock still. Hatred glowed with the fire on his face.

"Not one move," the Griffin said, "or your friend dies."

The Griffin growled in Evan's ear.

"This is all for you," he said. "Without you, I could have never gotten here."

"I should have shot you in the courtroom," Evan retorted.

Evan's wife took a step forward and shouted, "What did you do to Natalie?"

"Skewered her," the Griffin replied simply. "Poor Natalie, the black sheep of this little gang. The only one I wasn't expecting. You were all so busy bickering, I sliced her apart on the beach. Her blood should draw a few sharks to shore."

Cori let out a slew of curses.

"Feisty for a degenerate," the Griffin said. "I see why you like her, Silverman."

"Stay away from her," Evan grunted.

"I most certainly won't," the Griffin promised. "She should be dead. You *all* should be dead! Well, everyone except for you, Silverman. I wanted you here." He looked at the people before him. "But all of you? The silver should have burrowed into your bones, torn you apart with your own sickness. Those of you who took medicine, the nanobytes would have activated a supplementary chemical the Pharmacy has been adding to every tablet and pill distributed. Anyone else with genetic anomalies would have been subject to the nanobytes' terrible desolation. But maybe...maybe it's better this way. Now I can have my way with each and every one of you."

Silverman struggled to escape, but the Griffin's strength was indomitable.

Time to begin, the Griffin thought. Now that everyone was here and the mystery woman was out of the way, he knew who to start with.

"Boy!" the Griffin growled.

Toby jumped, looking fearfully at his father.

"Come here!" he insisted.

Toby refused to move, so the Griffin dug the glass deeper into Silverman's neck. The lawyer spluttered. Toby whimpered and began walking to his father.

"Toby, no!" Cori shouted, but Toby did not stop. He walked over to his father.

The Griffin pushed Silverman into the sand and grabbed onto Toby, holding the blood-stained glass to his son's throat.

Silverman hit the sand but leapt back up, taking a swing at the Griffin. Prepared for such a feeble attempt, the Griffin kicked the lawyer in the face, sending him sprawling across the sand, blood dripping from his neck. He spit out broken teeth.

The Griffin turned his attention back to his son. His scared little eyes were locked on the Griffin.

"Ah," the Griffin sighed, feeling his boy's pulse in his own fingers. "This is paradise. See, Silverman? You made all this possible, so you receive the gift of life. I will kill you last…because you got me here. And you brought me my son."

Toby fidgeted under the Griffin's grip.

"Let the killing begin!" the Griffin cried.

He reached into his jacket to withdraw the syringe of silver, but there was a devilish cry behind him. Before he could turn, he was tackled to the ground.

Fists began to pummel his back and head. Annoyed by the petty attack, the Griffin shifted in the sand, turning over. He saw people scattering around him, more than the Griffin had been threatening. Sitting on the Griffin, winding up to throw another punch, was Senator Beaudry.

"Welcome back, Senator!" the Griffin growled.

The Griffin felt in the sand and found the shard of glass. He gripped it tightly and dug it into the senator's chest. Senator Beaudry gasped for breath and fell into the sand.

The Griffin got to his feet.

Toby was already running off toward a growth of vegetation on the far side of the beach. Dozens of people were running amuck on the sand. The Griffin saw flashes of wild, gleaming eyes, contorted faces of rage, and tensed muscles. Before he could be surrounded, the Griffin made chase after Toby.

"Get back here!" Senator Beaudry wheezed, getting to his feet.

The Griffin chased after Toby, the senator right behind him. This was going to be better than he could have ever imagined.

2

"Don't move!"

The face of Natalie's mother swam in her vision. Rose's weak voice echoed in her ears. Natalie could see the road turning red. Smoke filled the cabin of the car, then flames. Natalie wanted to move, but if she did, she would surely hurt herself.

Get up, another voice in her head insisted.

Reality came back into focus. She lay face first in the sand, waves splashing in her face. Feeling her back, she knew she had been stabbed. Sticky blood coated her skin and her shirt. Naturally, she couldn't feel the pain.

Screams reached Natalie's ears. She propped herself up. Down the beach, closer to the burning cruise ship, she saw gobs of people running around. There was no way of telling who was who, but there were more than just her friends and Dr. Avazino.

The creepers, she remembered. She had seen some swimming ashore.

Natalie felt her body jumpstart with energy. As though she had never been bludgeoned on the pier or stabbed brutally in the back, Natalie leapt to her prosthetic feet.

She ran toward the ongoing chaos, lightheaded from the blood loss. As she got closer, she realized that there were dozens of creepers prowling over the beach. Bonnie, Nate, and Brian were fending off attackers as they ran for the hotel in the distance. Mark and Cori were trying to help Evan, who looked pale and was bleeding out of the neck. Toby and Avazino were nowhere to be seen.

Her heart thumped louder. Where was Toby?

A creeper flung itself at Cori and Mark. Natalie raced to their aid, knocking the creeper back. When she hit the creeper, it squealed and its neck gave a loud pop.

"Are you okay?" Natalie asked, helping Cori and Mark to their feet.

Mark nodded feebly, while Cori, with wide eyes, pointed further down the beach and stammered, "T–Toby!"

It was the only indication she needed. Natalie raced off, kicking up sand.

"Natalie!" Mark called after her.

"Be careful!" she yelled back.

Surveying the beach, she saw dark vegetation growing on the sand about fifty yards ahead. The undergrowth cast long shadows. Toby and Avazino must have been there.

The closer she got, the more she could see. Three figures materialized out of the dark, nearly a football field away. Dr. Avazino held Toby down on the beach and Senator Beaudry in his other hand. The senator was hunched over, held up by Avazino, and clawing to be free.

"Quiet down, Senator," Dr. Avazino said, his voice barely audible over Natalie's pounding footsteps. "You of all people should know politicians talk too much."

Avazino tightened his hand and twisted. The senator's head snapped sideways with a wet pop and he fell to the ground like a limp fish, body flopping onto the sand.

Free from his attacker, Avazino turned his attention to Toby. From his belt, he pulled a medical syringe with a four-inch needle.

"Stop!" Natalie demanded.

Avazino looked up, his eyes narrowing at the sight of Natalie.

He grinned maliciously.

"Natalie!" Toby cried.

With his teeth, Avazino pulled the cap off the syringe's needle. The needle point glinted in the light of the fire. In the syringe was a column of nanobytes, swirling and shimmering a bright chrome hue.

"A bit of real silver," Avazino said. "The way it was supposed to work."

Natalie ran, heart pumping in her back. Creepers screamed in the background. She raced as fast as she could, refusing to let Avazino take another loved one from her. But she was too far away, she knew it.

Avazino drove the needle into Toby's stomach. He squealed.

Before Natalie could stop him, Avazino depressed the plunger on the syringe, injecting the silver into Toby.

3

Cori fought off another creeper and slung an arm around Evan, applying pressure to his neck. Mark was busy fighting off a creeper dressed in an apron and wearing a tall, white chef's hat.

Evan started to pull away from Cori.

"You need a free arm to fight," Evan said, putting his own hand on his neck. "I'm fine."

"You are not!" Cori insisted, eyeing the blood running slowly but steadily from beneath Evan's hand.

"Leave it!"

"Not until you stop bleeding!"

"Look out!"

Evan pushed her aside just as one of the creepers took a swing at her. He barred his fists and punched the man hard in the nose. The creeper fell back, crashing into several others, and knocking them all over. Evan shook his hand, face tightened in pain.

"Why won't you let me help you?" Cori asked as she got back up.

"I'm not worth saving," Evan replied, not looking at her but watching for more attackers. "You know that."

She spun on him, punching a creeper as she turned.

"You're worth saving to me," she insisted. "You did wrong, you admitted it, you're moving on."

"There is no moving on!" Evan cried back, holding his palm to his neck.

"Will you and Natalie let it go!" Cori screamed back. "The past is the past!"

"On your right," Evan cried.

Cori swung around just in time to knock out a starved-looking man in a sailor's uniform.

"Behind you!" she exclaimed.

Evan didn't even look. He leaned onto her and threw his leg out, kicking a young girl in the face. The girl fell to the ground and stayed there, her face oozing blood.

"Evan! Cori!" Mark shouted.

The two of them spun to see Mark on his back in the sand, the apron-wearing creeper sitting on him and raising a meat cleaver, ready to strike.

Cori beat Evan to the punch, socking the creeper in the jaw.

She shook her hand, biting back the pain.

"This is kind of fun," she said, pulling Mark to his feet.

"You're insane," Mark muttered, taking a puff from his inhaler while holding out another fist threateningly.

"Insanely happy!" Cori replied.

Free from attacks for the time being, Mark and Cori got on either side of Evan, wrapping their arms around him to help him walk.

"I'm sorry," Evan yelled at Mark.

"You should be," Mark replied with a grunt as he smacked a woman away. "We're brothers."

"I should have told you," Evan replied. "Do you forgive me?"

Mark punched another creeper in the stomach and frowned at Evan.

"Let's survive tonight so we can argue later," Mark said.

Cori glanced around as they spoke, trying to find an avenue of escape. There were creepers everywhere, and they were all focused intently on Cori, Mark, and Evan. In fact, they were completely encircled, cut off from running into the ocean, along the shore, or to the hotel.

"We need to fight our way out!" Mark exclaimed.

Before they could formulate a plan, the air rang with the roar of an engine. The line of incoming creepers was mowed down by a four-wheeler, manned by Brian, Bonnie, and Nate.

High above, there was the scream of jets. Cori looked up just in time to see the vague outline of fighter jets streaming over the island.

"We've got company," she muttered, and, with Mark, led Evan to the four-wheeler.

4

A surge of emotions rushed through Natalie. She saw flashes of light in her eyes and she realized she was still running.

She charged at Avazino, leaping over the body of Senator Beaudry.

Avazino rose to meet her, knocking her aside. She leapt back up, throwing a punch. He parried her blows.

"Stop this!" Avazino screamed. "I want to watch him die!"

Natalie refused to yield. She spun around him, stepping over Toby's still body, and punched Avazino in the ear.

The behemoth of a man swung viciously at her, his eyes alight with murder.

He kicked at her legs, his foot connecting with the metal of her prosthetic leg. She kicked back, nailing his crotch.

Unfazed, Avazino lunged forward. His fingers closed around Natalie's throat.

"I will have you to myself soon enough, just like your mother," Avazino insisted, clenching Natalie's throat shut. "But first we will watch him die."

Avazino spun her around to look at Toby. He lay a foot away, his hands on his belly. His shirt was rippling as though something were growing out of his stomach. There was a weird gulping sound coming from his body too, but Toby didn't appear to be making the sound from his mouth.

"No," Natalie tried to say, but her voice was caught by Avazino's grip.

The ripples in the cloth moved up Toby's chest cavity. Suddenly, something leapt out through the shirt collar. Natalie and Avazino paused, unsure what was happening.

Boomer, the tiny dog, leapt out of Toby's shirt, stood on Toby's chest, and let out a booming bark at Avazino. Silver saliva flecks catapulted from Boomer's mouth, shining in the firelight.

"What?" Avazino said thickly.

Avazino threw Natalie to the ground and advanced on Toby and the dog. Natalie kicked out her legs, tripping Avazino.

No sooner had Avazino hit the ground, Boomer leapt from Toby and landed on the doctor. Stomach convulsing, Boomer burped as though about to throw up. But the dog was set on attacking Avazino, even if it was sick.

Boomer bit Avazino on the ear, growling and burping. Silver saliva smeared Avazino's ear and disappeared into his skin.

"Get off me!" Avazino exclaimed.

He swatted Boomer aside and stumbled to his feet. His ear was mangled and torn, hanging limply on his head.

"I am the Griffin!" Avazino exclaimed. "I am the harbinger of disaster! I am your undoing! I will rip you limb from limb!"

Natalie crawled quickly through the sand, dodging Avazino's kicks and grabbing onto Toby. The little boy quivered, clinging close to her.

Avazino advanced on them, his severed ear glinting with blood in the moonlight.

Boomer made another run at Avazino, biting into the man's ankle. Not even crying in pain, Avazino shook his leg and threw the dog off of him.

Natalie stared, suddenly understanding.

Avazino loomed over them, his smile fit for a clown, his eyes sadistic and cruel.

"How I wished I'd seen your mother perish," Avazino whispered to her. "The nanobytes didn't work quite right back then, but I'm sure her death was exhilarating nonetheless."

He pointed at Toby.

"Then I tried to kill you. A failure again." He looked at Natalie. "And you really thought you could get back at me by claiming him as your own? You're as sick as I am. But I've learned from my mistakes. You won't leave this beach alive. I'll kill you both, stripping you apart while you still brea—"

All at once, he stopped, freezing mid-step. The smile on his face tightened.

"Did you think you were special?" Natalie shouted at him, holding Toby tight. "Did you just think you were impervious to pain?"

The madman choked. Drool ran from his lips and his limbs quivered.

"Congenital analgia," Natalie said. "It's a genetic trait passed down by the father. I have it. Toby has it. And you have it."

Avazino doubled over as though his insides had exploded. He fell to his knees, vomiting. He shook violently and looked up to the sky, his body overcome by spasms. When moonlight fell on his face, Natalie saw that it was decaying away, revealing muscle, teeth, and tissue. Silver flecks danced in his eyes.

"Degenerate," Natalie muttered.

Avazino crumbled before them, his body decaying at hyperspeed. His skin flayed away, revealing beating organs. His lungs seized and his stomach swelled, ripping open. He wretched, choking on blood.

At last, he fell to the ground with a wet slap. With each passing second, his body disintegrated, like the way Rose's had crumbled in the car fire. A few seconds later, the doctor was a heap of bone and dried flesh glistening with silver mites.

Boomer walked out of the darkness, licking his chops. Silver glinted on his tongue and teeth.

"Good boy, Boomer," Toby said.

Natalie held Toby close to her, not believing all that had happened so quickly. Senator Beaudry and Dr. Avazino lay dead, a million deaths avenged.

5

Shoreline
Maui, Hawaii

Cori, Evan, and Mark jumped into the back of the four-wheeler. The axle groaned under the weight.

"Hold on!" Brian yelled.

He hit the accelerator on the four-wheeler, running over several oncoming creepers.

"Natalie's over there," Cori yelled at Brian, pointing toward the vegetation.

Spinning the wheel, Brian guided the four-wheeler down the beach. The vehicle moved quickly, kicking up sand with its wheels. They skirted along the shore, headed for the brambles and vegetation. Four figures were lit by the flames, each of them laying in the sand.

As they got closer, Cori surveyed the bodies, praying that Natalie and Toby were alive.

Two heads popped up as the four-wheeler got closer. To Cori's delight, Natalie and Toby leapt to their feet and hobbled toward the four-wheeler. Boomer trailed behind them, his mouth glowing.

"What happened?" Cori shouted as Toby, Boomer, and Natalie leapt into the back of the four-wheeler.

"Avazino and the senator are dead," Natalie said. "Don't let Boomer bite you."

Creepers began to close in on them again, asking for a ride. Brian slammed on the accelerator, flinging spirals of sand, and they raced up the beach.

"Where are we going?!" Cori cried as the four-wheeler jumped off the beach and onto a paved road.

"To turn on the EMP!" Brian said.

"The mountain!" Bonnie replied.

"It's called Haleakalā," Evan shouted, his voice slightly constricted due to the pressure on his neck.

He pointed up. Cori followed her husband's finger.

A mountain stood ominously above them. The moon was just above it, like the eye of God watching them race to save their own lives.

Glancing behind them, Cori saw that creepers on the beach were falling far behind. Within a few minutes, they would be out of reach, hopefully forever.

"What happened to Avazino?" Brian shouted over the wind at Natalie.

"He's dead!" Natalie shouted. "He had some of the nanobytes in a syringe. He said it was the original silver rain."

Brian cussed under his breath, which earned him a scowl from his wife as she covered Nate's ears.

"Avazino tried to inject Toby with it, but I think he got Boomer in the stomach or something. Boomer was trying to throw up, and then he bit Avazino. Right after that, Avazino died."

"What?" Brian exclaimed. "Why? How?"

"Avazino is like us," Natalie replied. "He's a degenerate. He had congenital analgia, like Toby and I. Can't feel pain!"

"He was trying to kill degenerates and he was one?" Cori asked.

Natalie nodded. "I don't think he knew it either, but he just got a taste of his own medicine."

Cori noticed how satisfied Natalie sounded, but decided not to pry. Natalie's mother had died at Avazino's hands, and Avazino had just tried to kill Toby. Though Cori didn't condone death, she certainly did not feel any remorse for Avazino. She prayed for the man, that he would seek forgiveness for his crimes, and left it at that.

"Natalie," Evan said. When he had her attention, he said, "I'm really sorry. I should have told you a long time ago. I'm the reason Avazino won his court case in the Supreme Court."

Cori watched Natalie, waiting for the attack, physical or verbal, but her friend did not do anything. In Natalie's eyes, there was a wounded sadness.

"I forgive you," she said.

After a deep breath, Cori decided it was time to come clean as well.

"I've known too, Natalie," she said. "We're very sorry. We should have told you."

As Natalie looked at Cori, she seemed even more hurt, but forced a smile.

"I understand," Natalie said. "And I understand why you didn't tell me before. But the man responsible for what happened back then is gone. No matter what you kept from me, I'd rather have you as friends."

Cori leaned over and gave her friend a hug. As she touched Natalie's back, she felt warm liquid. She pulled away, shocked, and saw blood on her hands.

Before Cori could say anything, Natalie whispered in her ear, "We'll take care of it when we're up the mountain. Don't scare Toby."

Evan, though, did not seem to think Natalie's explanation or his own apology was good enough. He sat up, looking stern.

"I should be the one to push that button," he said, only looking at Natalie. "I should be the one to die for everything I've done."

"No!" Cori shouted.

"Don't be ridiculous," Mark said.

"I hate to be the bearer of bad news," Brian shouted from the front, "but someone will have to. If anyone should, it should be me."

Bonnie and Nate yelled their disagreement.

"There has to be another way!" Cori said.

Brian shook his head, his thin hair flopping in the wind.

"Setting off the EMP is the only solution we have," he said. "It's our only way to set this right."

The vehicle was silent for a moment, the reality setting in.

"One of us has to push the button," Brian continued. "One of us has to die."

"Me," said Evan again. "I made all of this happen."

"No!" Cori exclaimed. "Will you stop that!"

"It has to be me," Evan insisted.

"No," Brian said. "It should be me. I'm to blame to for what happened on the mainland."

"Brian Matician," Bonnie said. "You will not die today! It is a miracle you're even alive now!"

"Bonnie," he said like a child trying to get out of homework.

"Don't *Bonnie* me!" she exclaimed. "I have lost my mother and two children. I will not lose my husband too."

"I'll do it," Nate volunteered, a bold look on his face.

"No!" everyone yelled in unison.

There was silence for a moment. Cori looked over at Natalie and saw a steely look of resolve in her eye. She was also deathly pale, but Cori knew what Natalie was thinking.

"Natalie," Cori said, quiet at first. "Don't even think about it."

Natalie's shoulders slumped, her plan exposed.

"I can do it," Natalie said.

"No, you can't!" Cori shouted.

Everyone else in the four-wheeler caught on to what Cori had realized: Natalie was intending to set off the EMP.

"Never!" Evan replied. "You deserve to live."

"I won't let you," Mark said. "I'll do it."

They all began shouting again, each insisting that they finish the thankless job. Cori refused to let Natalie do it. She would rather die with her friend or let the world fall into madness than let Natalie die on her own.

"Stop!" Natalie cried. "You're all family! Bonnie and Brian, Nate needs you. Bonnie, you need Cori and she needs you, even if you won't admit it. Evan, you've already done the right thing. You can learn from your mistakes. Mark, you're practically Evan's brother. You're all together. You need each other. And when the world wakes up after the EMP, you can set things right. Me? I'm nobody."

Cori, Evan, and Mark balked.

Toby touched Natalie's cheek, making her look at him.

"You're my Mom," Toby said, his voice high.

"We'll set it right together," Mark insisted, putting his arm around Natalie. "All of us. Everyone will know what happened on this day."

"You all will," Natalie said resolutely. "But this is what I have to do."

Her friends continued to argue with her, but Cori saw something in Natalie's eyes that she knew too well. It was a determined, cold tenacity, similar to the days when she was emotionless and refused to feel anything. No matter what Cori, Toby, Mark, or anyone else said, Natalie was going to do what she had promised.

Suddenly, the four-wheeler let out a wheeze. The vehicle jerked and began to slow. Brian stamped the gas pedal, but the four-wheel came to a grinding halt.

"Shoot," Brian cursed.

He jumped out and checked the gas.

"Empty," he said, kicking the wheel.

"We've been driving it all week," Mark wheezed. "It was bound to run out eventually."

"Where are we?" Bonnie asked.

Cori glanced around. They were stalled in the middle of a paved road surrounded on both sides by steep slopes of palm trees and underbrush. The moonlight made the leaves glisten. Any of the mountaintops seemed miles away.

"Well, no sense sitting here," Natalie said.

She jumped out of the four-wheeler first, grabbing Toby. Everyone else followed suit. The axle squeaked as they all got out. Boomer was the last out, panting with silver still caked around his teeth.

"How much further?" Natalie asked.

"A mile," Brian said, pointing up the mountain.

"I guess we have to walk," she said.

In the distance, there was the roar of a starting engine.

Cori spun, looking at the shore far below. The overturned cruise ship was a small, glowing pinprick in the black of the ocean. Beams of light were turning on across the shore, vehicles coming to life.

"They can start vehicles now?"

"They aren't brain dead," Bonnie answered.

"We run," Natalie said, and they followed her.

Cori wrapped her arms around Evan and ran after Natalie. In the moonlight, she saw Natalie's back. It was drenched in blood.

As a nurse, Cori knew quite a bit about human physiology. She may not have perfectly understood her friend's rare genetic problem, but she knew that the human body needed blood. Evan had lost a lot, but had sealed his wound with a scab. Natalie had not.

Her back was coated, the clothes dripping. If Natalie wasn't careful, she would be dead within an hour.

6

Natalie felt weaker than usual as she ran up the road. Brian outpaced her, insisting he knew the way, but she couldn't have stopped him if she wanted to. Her legs felt heavy. Nevertheless, she kept pushing, forcing herself to keep moving with Toby. Boomer was right on her heels too as though prodding her forward.

She was doomed, she knew it. She had lost too much blood, and would bleed out soon. Her life was waning, but she had to hold on just long enough to finish the job.

Mark ran next to her, watching her closely. His breathing was becoming heavier, even after he used his inhaler.

"Take it easy, Mark," Natalie huffed. "We have a big head start."

He nodded at her, hocking a mouthful of spit and mucus onto the road.

A few minutes later of uphill, Brian left the main road, running deep into the dense vegetation. They followed without question, tumbling through the mud and ferns.

At last, they made it to an alcove against a steep cliff. Brian ran along the rock face until he found an iron door. He pried it open and led them into a dark hallway.

"This gives me the creeps," Cori said.

"More than the creepers?" Natalie asked.

A light clicked on overhead. Natalie's eyes adjusted. Brian was several yards ahead, beckoning them further into a series of long hallways.

Eventually, they made it to what Brian called the control room. A uniformed man lay at the entrance, the pungent scent of death filling the room. Boomer sniffed the body and burped as though he were about to throw up again.

Against the far wall were several televisions. Below the monitors was an immense computer. In the center of the room was a clear tube that rose into the ceiling. At the floor, the tube was attached to a large console covered in buttons.

Brian ran around the hollow tube and studied the console. A large red button stood out prominently. Brian pried the panel off, exposing a spider web of wires on the underside of the buttons.

"I have to redo the wiring to fully connect the EMP directly to the reactor," Brian told them. "This may take a while."

Not wanting to become a last-minute expert at electrical engineering, Natalie wandered around the room, studying the computer and the servers.

"You guys have all the bells and whistles," Natalie said.

As she roamed the room, Natalie sensed that Cori was watching her. When she turned around, her friend was right behind her, eyes brimming with tears.

"You can't do this, Natalie," she said. "You're my best friend, I can't lose you."

Cori collapsed into her, hugging her tightly. Mark placed a hand on her shoulder, and Toby hugged her leg. Evan stood back, a tight smile on his face.

Natalie met Evan's eyes. He looked sad, but understanding. It seemed Evan had seen Natalie's point of view.

"It's going to be okay," Natalie said. "I'm meant to do this."

"I'll stay with you," Cori said.

"We all will," Mark said.

Evan gave her a reassuring nod.

"No," Natalie said. "You have to take care of Toby. He needs a mother. You have to be better than me. Raise him in a world where he can be happy. Where he can be the best of himself."

"Natalie," Toby said. "You're my mom. We're going to be happier than flying penguins."

Natalie shook her head, kneeling to look Toby in the eyes.

"I can't," she said. "I love you, Toby, but I haven't always. When I first met you, I just wanted to adopt you to show the world I was okay."

Toby's lip quivered.

"So it's true?" he asked. "What my dad said? You wanted to adopt me to get back at him?"

Natalie fought back tears as she revealed the truth.

"Yes," she confirmed. "And I'm so sorry for that, Toby. I should have loved you for the happy boy you are, instead of making you more like me. I'm so sorry. Can you ever forgive me?"

Toby paused and then nodded half-heartedly. Natalie could tell he was disappointed.

"I will always love you," she promised him, "but I can't be a good mother. You know that now. You deserve someone like Cori."

"Natalie," Cori said admonishingly.

Natalie looked up at her friend, speaking from the heart.

"I've seen how you are with him. You will love him like a son. This is how I can love both of you. Giving my life for my best friend and the son I could never have."

She looked at Evan.

"Do better, Evan," she said. "Change this world."

She addressed Mark.

"Love again," she said. "Love someone better. You're an amazing man, Mark, and you deserve so much more than what I can offer you."

"You are who I love," Mark said, tears rolling fast down his cheeks. "You are the only one for me."

"I love you all," Natalie said, and she drew them all into a hug. Evan held back a bit, but she waved her hand at him. He walked over slowly, letting himself be pulled into the group hug.

For the first time since the red road, Natalie felt tears rising in her eyes that she did not want to stop. She did not fight them. The terror filling her was immense and indomitable, but the tears helped. While the fear was strong, she also felt that queer feeling returning, the thing she thought was love. It lightened her heart and made her happy.

She remembered days ago, when she had awoken in the back of the car after the fight at the airport. Terror had filled her then, and she had wondered what could possibly wash away the strength of fear. It seemed she had found the answer.

Natalie did not know how long they stayed there, clinging together. It could have been a minute or ten, but to Natalie, it was a lifetime that filled her heart with gladness. When they parted, she knew it was her time.

All at once, the lights went out in the control room. They were cast into darkness. Boomer let out a bark and whined.

"What's happening?" Nate asked fearfully, his voice further across the room.

"Your father's connecting the power to the EMP," Bonnie replied. "All of the power."

They stood there for a few minutes. The sound of footsteps came from the hallway outside the control room. Brian returned, wielding a flashlight. He made his way back to the console in the center of the room, playing with the wires again. There was a flash of sparks, and Brian kept fiddling. Suddenly, he let out a cheer, and the button on the console turned on, glowing bright red. Its light filled the room with an eerie, crimson hue.

They all gathered around as Brian placed the panel of buttons back into the console.

The red button seemed to stare at Natalie, waiting to be pressed.

"It's ready," Brian said, looking only at Natalie. "All of the power of the reactor will propel the EMP with the push of this button. Once you press it, the reactor should withstand the power surge for a minute, allowing the EMP to be set off. That's when the reactor will overload."

Natalie stared at the button. It would be the end of her, but it symbolized the end of the creepers.

"Please," Cori begged Brian. "There has to be another way."

"There may be," Brian said, pacing the tube in the center of the room. "But there isn't time. We have to set this off as soon as possible."

"I won't until you're all off the island," Natalie said confidently.

Suddenly, there was a dull rumble echoing through the room. Everyone looked up as though they would be able to see through the ceiling.

"Are those fighter jets?" Brian asked.

"They flew by earlier," Cori said.

Brian's brow furrowed. "They wouldn't do that for a land probe. What are they looking for?"

"Russia found the source of the rain from satellite images," Natalie said. "They knew it was here in Hawaii."

Bonnie gasped.

"They're going to attack the facility," she said.

"They wouldn't," Evan said. "They can't just attack something they don't understand."

Brian shot Evan a smirk. "Do you always speak in layered terms?"

"Could they bomb the facility?" Bonnie wondered, her face tight with fear.

"If they do or if they don't, you all need to get out of here," Natalie said. "I'll give you one hour to get off the island. Then I'll set off the EMP."

Brian nodded at her, his smug look finally wiping away.

"Let's go," Brian said. He grabbed his son and wife, and led them toward the doorway.

Cori, Mark, and Evan stood by Natalie, tears in all of their eyes. Toby clung to her leg.

"I'll walk with you," Natalie promised, unable to stand the overwhelming feelings filling her.

They wrapped arms around one another and followed Brian out of the control room.

7

They all stood in the dank hallway, lighting their surroundings with cell phones.

At the end of the hall was the iron door. The creepers had arrived earlier than expected and were banging against the door. The sounds echoed around Natalie, making her feel like she was in a loud dream.

She felt faint from blood loss, but forced herself to focus as they all said goodbye to her.

Bonnie hugged her first.

"Thank you," she whispered into Natalie's ear. "My children and their children will remember your name."

Next, Brian gave her a handshake, asking for a word in private.

"When you set off the EMP, the reactor will overload with a minimum of thirty grays," he told her. "That's a measure of radiation. That amount of radiation is deadly and will kill you in a matter of minutes, but it also causes massive neurological damage."

"Thanks for the happy prospects," Natalie said.

"There's no telling what will happen," Brian said. "Scientists hypothesize that radiated subjects experience massive delusions and hallucinations."

"So I'm going to go insane?"

Brian shook his head.

"I'm making you a promise," he said. "You're dying with honor and without pain."

"Pain doesn't bother me," she replied.

Brian grimaced. "Right, well…" He took a moment and composed himself. "I can't promise you a completely peaceful death, but it will be a quick one."

With a nod, he said goodbye to her.

After his father, Nate gave her a hug around the hips, and said she was his hero.

Cori and Evan came to her, hugging her. They said goodbye over and over, holding Natalie tighter with each word.

"I'm going to miss you," Cori said. "You will always be my best friend."

"We'll never forget you," Evan said.

"Remember me when you drive too fast," Natalie said, making Cori cry even more.

Evan pulled Cori away, letting her sob into his shoulder.

Natalie knelt down to say goodbye to Toby. He sniffed as she hugged him.

"Promise me you'll love Cori as much as me," she said.

"I promise," Toby said.

"You know I love you, right?"

Toby tried hard to not let himself smile. "You'll always be my mom," he said. "I'll never forget you."

She hugged him again, regretting every moment she had wanted him for selfish reasons.

"Promise me something?" Toby asked.

"Anything," she said.

"Before you hit the button, be happy for me."

"I'll be happy," she promised. "Happier than a flying penguin."

Toby giggled as he cried. "Penguins can't fly."

"But if they could, they'd be really happy," Natalie said. "Watch for the silver rain."

"When you make it to heaven," Toby said. She gave him one final hug.

"Take care of Boomer," she said.

Boomer let out a bark, growling at the iron door.

Natalie turned to the last person: Mark. She embraced him without restraint.

He wasn't crying. He held her tight, pushing her head into his chest. She could hear his heartbeat, steady and strong.

She wished she would have noticed it before, listened to it longer.

"I will love you forever," she said.

He pulled away, looking her in the eye.

"Marry me?" he said.

"You made me rowboat out to you," she said with a sad chuckle. "See, marriage is work."

"Only for Natalie Hofland."

"Natalie Hofland," she said, letting her new name resonate. "I like the sound of that."

She hugged him once more. When he released her, she held strong, not letting herself break down.

Mark gave her a wistful smile and walked toward the door where everyone else stood.

Natalie surveyed the collection of friends, her heart pouring out to each of them. She did not want it to end this way, but she knew it must.

She was going to miss them all. Toby's quirky smile, Mark's loving remarks, Cori's optimism, Evan's cynical silence that she actually understood, Boomer's bark. She would even miss Bonnie, Nate, and Brian, in their own special way.

"Goodbye," she said to all of them.

Brian opened the door. Moonlight filled the hallway, creepers shadows dancing to and fro.

Boomer rocketed through the door and out into the fray, distracting the creepers.

"Now!" Brian yelled.

They ran for the door, disappearing into the night.

The last thing Natalie saw was Mark reaching back to close the door. His eye caught hers, and he looked oddly confident. She smiled at him, trying to give him hope.

The door slammed shut, leaving Natalie alone with the light of her phone.

8

Mark shut the door and spun around.

Creepers were running amuck across the hill, weaving through palm trees. Many of them were chasing Boomer, completely distracted. Brian, his family, Cori, and Evan were all huddled together, back to back, talking.

Mark picked up Toby and put him into the center of the circle where Nate was.

"We're not leaving, Natalie," Cori shouted.

"You'll die!" Bonnie cried.

"This is something worth dying for," Cori replied.

Mark felt a burst of hope. This had been his idea too. He wouldn't leave Natalie to die alone, and he was glad Cori felt the same.

Out of his peripherals, Mark saw the palm trees swaying strongly high above. He glanced up and gasped. Creepers hung from the branches like over-sized coconuts.

The instant he saw them, they dropped, their silver eyes shining.

"Watch—"

Mark's words were cut short as a dozen creepers fell onto them like anvils. He collapsed under their crushing weight. The others fell too, limbs smacking into one another. Mark heard Toby and Nate shriek. Cori screamed too, but it was cut shockingly short.

"Falling coconuts and creepers kill," one of the creepers said, hopping to its feet.

A dozen other creepers closed in. Mark kicked his legs and flung his arms, but there were too many. Nate and Toby were crying in pain, unable to protect themselves. Evan screamed loudly.

Brian got to his feet first, knocking the creepers away. Mark managed to get to his feet too and bowled over the creepers antagonizing Toby and Nate. The boys stood, stifling their tears.

Prepared to fight the next attacker, Mark noticed that Cori was still on the ground. Evan was stooping over her.

"What happened?" Mark yelled.

"She's hurt," Evan gasped.

The second he spoke, the clotted cut on his neck tore open. A spurt of blood shot out.

Evan gulped, his eyes wide, and clapped a hand to his neck.

Mark collapsed beside them as Brian and Bonnie fought off creepers. Cori was lying on the ground, bruises appearing on her neck. She blinked, eyes moving from side to side without really seeing.

"Is she okay?" Bonnie cried.

"She needs to get out of here," Mark said. "She hurt her neck or her spine or something."

"No," Cori murmured, looking at Mark. Her eyes didn't focus. "Nat…"

Mark looked to Evan, blood seeping from his fingers.

He knew automatically what had to happen. There would be no returning to Natalie for the group. They had to get off the island.

Scanning their surroundings, Mark saw one of the trucks the creepers had driven. It was crashed up against the cliff, metal crumpled on the rock.

"Get to the truck!" Mark yelled, pointing it out to Brian and Bonnie.

With Brian's help, Mark dragged Cori to the car and threw her in. Evan crawled in after her, bloodstained hand clutching his neck.

Mark gave Toby a kiss on the head and lifted him into the backseat. Nate and Boomer followed suit. Behind them, the creepers kept coming despite Bonnie's best efforts.

Once Cori, Nate, and Toby were in the car, Mark ripped off part of his shirt and gave it to Evan.

"Keep it tight on your neck," he commanded his friend. "I'll see you on the other side."

"Mark!" Evan gasped as Mark slammed the door shut.

Having just cleared another wave of creepers, Brian and Bonnie leapt into the front seat, leaving Mark on his own.

"Get in!" Brian yelled.

Mark slammed a stray creeper into the wall and shook his head.

"Be good, Toby!" Mark yelled, waving. He called each of their names, saying goodbye to them.

Before the creepers could overpower him, he spun around and ran for the door. He fought off the nearby creepers and threw open the iron door. It creaked loudly. Coughing up mucus, Mark leapt through the narrow gap. Before anyone could follow, he pulled the door shut. He saw a glimpse beyond of a truck backing down the hill, metal scraping the cliff, and creepers making chase.

The door shut, casting Mark into darkness. He put his head against the door, feeling the cool metal in his forehead.

"Goodbye," he said to his old life, and he tore off into the labyrinth of halls after Natalie.

PHASE 8
SILVER RAIN

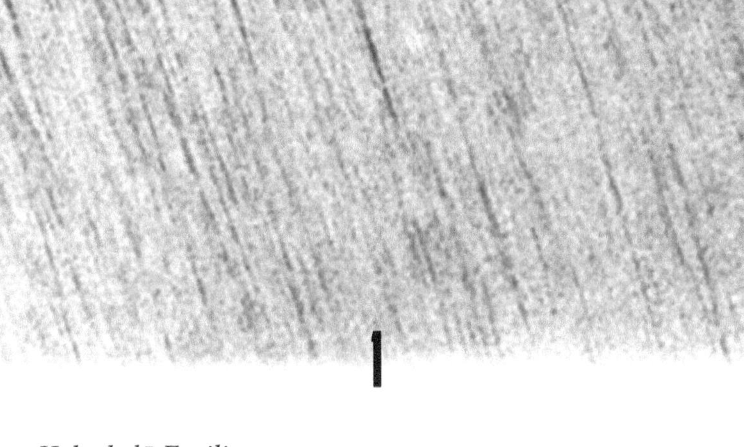

1

Natalie wandered the halls, lost in her own thoughts. She could hear her mother, begging her to stop.

"Stay still," her mother said.

"I won't, Mom," Natalie said aloud. "Not anymore."

Years ago, she had sat there on the red road and let her mother die. Now, she was tempted to do the same thing. But she couldn't. Millions of lives were at stake. Natalie must act. She must rectify her mistakes. She must do the opposite of what she had done on the red road: fight against the fear and do what she knew was right. Only then would the silver rain be destroyed.

After several minutes, Natalie arrived in the control room. The chamber was illuminated by the red button.

She glanced disdainfully at the dead man at the entrance. Soon there would be two.

Her eyes fell on the red button. There was a timer beside it that Brian had started. Natalie had fifty minutes.

She heard a rustle behind her. She spun around, expecting to see the dead man coming to life or a creeper rushing her.

Instead, she saw Mark. He stood at the entrance to the control room, cast in red light, his face shining with sweat.

"I had to," he said.

Natalie gaped at him.

"No!" she shouted. "You have to get off the island! You can't be here!"

"Cori wanted to come back too," Mark said, "but she got hurt. They're headed down. They'll be safe. But I couldn't leave you."

She rushed him, pushing him hard, trying to force him out. The lack of blood in her system made her weak, and she became dizzy.

Mark pushed back, walking into the room and closing the door behind him. He wrapped his arms around her, insisting on holding her tightly.

"I'm with you," he whispered in her ear. "You're stuck with me until the end."

2

Nate held onto the seat cushion tightly as his father turned the wheel sharply. The truck shuddered around the last corner. Brian grunted in pain, his bandaged arm shaking. The shore was less than half a mile away. Creepers dotted the beach, those who had not found a way up the mountain.

"The cruise ship will still have boats," Brian said. "We have to get one and get off the island."

"I'll help," Nate said, trying to be brave.

"No," his parents insisted.

Discouraged, Nate sat back. He longed to be like his father even now, to be a man of action. But he was still just a scared little kid, protected from danger by his parents.

Beside him, Toby was playing with Boomer, staring blankly at the ground. Evan was holding his neck and watching over Aunt Cori, who was becoming more lucid. She was wincing in pain. Her neck was swollen and covered in red, blue, and black splotches.

"We're going to have to do this quick," Brian said. "I'll get us as close to the boat as I can. Nate, stick with your mother. Toby, you too, stay with Bonnie. Evan, can you take care of Cori?"

Evan gurgled a reply, pale in the face.

With a twist of the wheel, Brian turned off the pavement. Hitting the curb, the wheels chirped and the cabin shook. Creepers ran at them, but stood no chance against the vehicle. They smacked into the grill, exploding like balloons filled with paint.

After running several over, Brian slammed on the brakes. The tires skidded in the sand, and they came to a stop a few yards from the water. The cruise ship was a football field away.

Creepers slammed up against the windows, shouting.

Brian took off his seatbelt and smacked the door back and forth, pushing creepers away. When his way was clear, he leapt out.

Frozen for a moment, Nate forced himself to unbuckle his seatbelt, throw open his door, and race after his dad. His mother cried his name behind him, screaming for him to come back.

He ran in complete disbelief. Never before had he acted so boldly, so bravely, in the face of danger. It must have been his father. Brian's presence alone must have inspired Nate to act. Or was it something else?

Nate raced after his father, running into the waves. The water was cold at night, cutting into his bones. He could not believe he was doing this, finally acting though scared. But he could not let his father do this alone.

Nate glanced back. No one was following him. The rest of the creepers had surrounded the truck.

Brian came to a stop near the cruise ship. It loomed over them, tall as a building, its hull a sheer, steep side of metal. Lifeboats lined the side, hanging perfectly intact, but out of reach.

"How do we get up, Dad?" Nate asked.

Brian spun around.

"Nate, go back!" he yelled.

"No!" Nate said. "I'm helping."

Brian huffed with anger, but did not argue.

"What about the anchor?" Nate said, pointing at it.

The anchor hung from the ship's bow, suspended about ten feet above the ground. A chain extended up to the side of the ship.

They ran over to it, stopping beneath it. Brian leapt up, but wasn't even close to grabbing the anchor.

"Lift me up, Dad!" Nate shouted.

Brian shook his head.

"It'll take both of us to get up there," Nate said. "I'll get on your shoulders and reach the anchor. I can do this, Dad!"

In the distance, Nate's mother screamed. Before him, his father looked completely helpless. In that moment, Nate realized what had stirred him to run and help his dad. It wasn't that his dad was here, encouraging him to be proactive. Instead, it was love for his family that had overpowered his terror. He had to help them.

Nate nodded determinably to his dad. He was ready. He was a man now.

"Alright," Brian said. "Do you know how to get the lifeboat free?"

Nate nodded, brandishing his mother's Leatherman. "She gave it to me when we were on the ship coming here. I'll cut it loose."

It took a moment, but Nate got his feet on his dad's shoulders. Brian grunted in pain, shifting so most of Nate's weight fell on the left shoulder. Slowly, Brian stood.

Nate reached up, the anchor coming closer and closer.

When Brian stood at full height, Nate wrapped his hands around the anchor and pulled himself up. Hand over hand, Nate began to climb up the anchor, inching his way toward the ship, knowing that he was finally brave in the face of fear.

3

Shoreline
Maui, Hawaii

Moments after his son disappeared over the edge of the ship, Brian heard a laugh behind him. He spun around just in time to see a deranged man lunging at him. He sidestepped the man and threw him into the water.

Expecting the man to jump back up, Brian clenched the fist of his good arm. But the man did not return. The water rippled, cascading in waves.

Suddenly, the man erupted out of the water, grabbing Brian. They fell forward together, plunging into the water.

Brian found the man's throat under the water and squeezed. The man struggled, fighting for his own life now, and then stopped moving.

All at once, there was a crash. Surprised, Brian stood, his head breaking the surface. He wiped the saltwater from his eyes.

A lifeboat was floating a few feet away, bobbing in the waves. High above, he heard Nate shouting in victory.

"That's my brave boy," Brian yelled. He felt a burst of pride, and then a shock of disgust, realizing that he was still holding the neck of the attacker beneath the water.

He jumped back, wiping his hands on his clothes.

A few feet away, he saw papers floating in the water. He recognized them as the notes he had made while changing the silver rain algorithms. They must have come loose in his struggle with his attacker.

One of the many deaths on my hands, Brian thought.

He watched the pages float away into the night, carried by the tide. In the back of his mind, he realized what they symbolized: his failures, his weaknesses, and his last ditch efforts to amend mistakes he should have never made. He hoped these notes and everything they embodied sank to the darkest cavern of the ocean, never to be seen again.

All this, he acknowledged, was his doing. Sure, Avazino had developed the nanobytes and Senator Beaudry had funded the project, but it was Brian's indiscretions that had borne the silver rain. He had worked diligently without knowing the purpose of his work. Or maybe he had and hadn't wanted to admit it. He realized now how petty it was, how small-minded.

Never again, Brian told himself as the pages slipped out of sight. He would never again blindly follow.

Which meant here and now, Brian had to make his stand. This was his moment. This was his masterpiece, his intentions brought to bear.

Shaking these philosophical thought, he turned to the truck and waved. Almost immediately, the truck lurched forward, running over creepers. Picking up speed, the truck charged into the water. When it was half-submerged, the doors were pushed open. Bodies leapt out of the car. One by one, Bonnie, Toby, Evan, Cori, and Boomer ran through the waves toward Brian.

"We have fifteen minutes," Bonnie said.

"Get to the boat!" Brian commanded.

As his family ran for the boat, he steeled himself. Glinting silver eyes watched them from the shore. Feet slapped on wet sand. The creepers were coming.

This would be the fight for their lives, Brian knew, and he was prepared to give everything he had to save his family.

4

Toby fought off his queasiness, resisting his body's need to seize. He got into the boat, holding Boomer tightly. The dog's muzzle no longer gleamed silver, washed off by the saltwater.

"Control it," Toby said to himself, submerging the feeling of the oncoming seizure. "Fight the feelings."

Cori fell into the boat beside Toby, breathing hard. Her eyes rolled in pain.

There was a big splash near the boat. Water sprayed Toby's eyes. A moment later, someone crawled into the boat, nearly tipping it. Toby balled his fists to fight, but realized it was Nate. His friend was gasping in pain, holding his shins.

Around them, Toby heard more yells. He dared to look up and saw creepers coming by the dozens. Closest to him, Nate's father fought fiercely, a fire in his eye that could have cause spontaneous combustion.

A creeper made it to the boat and snarled in Toby's face. A bolt of fear ran through him and the feeling of the seizure returned, unstoppable this time. It cascaded in on him, all the pent-up feelings returning. He could see the creepers' gleaming eyes, feel Natalie's last hug, and remember Mark's final farewell.

He wanted nothing more than to be in their arms again, but no. The world was too messed up. It wasn't fair. Instead, he had lost his mother, Natalie, and Mark, and now, he was lying in a lifeboat, lost in the throes of a seizure that he had fought off for far too long.

In that moment, Toby realized how strange the world really was. He had thought Natalie was the perfect role model. Toby had wanted nothing more than to be like her. But everything she had taught him was wrong. She hadn't loved him for who he was until she had given up her inhibitions. The same was true for him. By holding his emotions inside, he had suffered more seizures.

You can't block it out anymore, he thought.

Ignoring the tremors shaking him to and fro, he focused on what he was feeling. He was angry at Natalie for lying to him and for leaving him, but felt overwhelming love for her. Fear was also there, dread that he would not make it out alive and would be killed just like his mother. But there was also peace. His own father had tried to kill him and the rest of the world. But the people he would always recognize as his parents, Mark and Natalie, had given their own lives to save others. It was a brave act that Toby would never forget and gave him peace.

As Toby allowed himself to feel, the effects of the seizure melted away. His vision cleared, and his body stopped shaking.

I'm free, he realized. The seizure was gone. He was in control of his body again.

"Goodbye," he said, not just to his old habits, but to Natalie too. "I'll see you again when silver rain falls."

5

Cori faded in and out of consciousness, her neck and upper back radiating with excruciating agony.

The boat rocked as someone sat beside her. A hand found her shoulder.

"Hold on, Cori," Evan whispered to her, his voice weak.

"You're not going anywhere!" a creeper cried.

Evan's hand left her. There was screaming and wet slaps. She feared the worst, but then Evan returned to her.

The boat began to move, bobbing in the waves. It felt like they were being pushed. She saw Toby huddled close to her with a peaceful smile. Evan put a hand to her cheek, smiling at her. It was shocking how pale he was, and she could see fresh cuts on his face and torso.

She wondered if she was going to die, but did not feel fear. Perhaps it was a side effect of her manic oppressive tendencies, but the prospect of dying and arriving in heaven excited her.

Ignoring the stabs of pain in her neck, Cori reached a hand up to Evan. Tears streamed from her face. With her other hand, she held Toby's.

"I love you both," she whispered.

"Cori, no, hold on for me," Evan sputtered through tears.

"Don't be sad," she said, her speech slurring. "Life is too wonderful to be sad."

Too many people in the world, she realized, had been filled with anger and utter hatred for one another. Senator Beaudry had been one of them, more concerned with belittling and expunging those he saw as weak for their varying opinions, skin tones, preferences, and genetics. There was the opposite side of the spectrum too, those who embraced the role of being weak, defining themselves by these traits, and falling into a rut of self-absorption and smug self-importance. For each and every one of those people, Cori prayed that they found peace in knowing there was a better way. They could deflate their egos, bandage their wounds, and define themselves by their actions, not their weaknesses. She hoped they would meet each other eye to eye, squashing out obvious evil where they could, and seek happiness of common ground while striving for a better tomorrow.

It was ambitious to hope for, but Cori had faith that humanity could find their way to justice and fairness once more. They could be happy again.

Rather than suppress it as she had been taught to do growing up, Cori let her optimism shine through. She was a beautiful person, made just the way God had intended.

As the world faded, she did not know if she was dying or merely losing consciousness again, but she knew it would all work out as God had planned. God cared for all of them, each and every one. To Him, all lives mattered, no matter their flaws, foibles, or sins.

Content in this knowledge and with a smile on her face, Cori squeezed her hands around Evan and Toby once more, and closed her eyes.

6

Bonnie fought off the last of the creepers as Brian pushed the lifeboat around the cruise ship and into open water. Brian hoisted himself in the boat and grabbed a paddle. Together, they swung their arms, pushing the boat out into the ocean.

"How far do we have to be from the island?" Bonnie asked Brian.

"At least a mile!" he yelled, and he paddled harder.

In her pocket, Bonnie's phone buzzed. She withdrew it absentmindedly. Water was filling the cracked screen. The image was disjointed, but she could plainly see the caller id: it was Grandma Dottie.

She tried to answer, but her phone short-circuited and turned off, ruined by the water. Rather than panic, as she normally would have, she tried to find peace in the moment. Her mother was alive. Wyatt must be as well. Her daughter, Bethany, would be out there too, alone and waiting in the streets of Sun Valley. They would be okay, she was sure of it.

So that's what optimism is, Bonnie thought.

She glanced over at her sister, who was lying in the bottom of the boat. Cori was ghost-white and her eyes were closed, but she was smiling. Toby, Boomer, and Evan looked over her with tears in their eyes.

Thank you, Cori, she thought.

Bonnie reached to Nate, embracing her brave son. She still could not believe he had climbed atop the cruise ship, set a boat free, and leapt to safety. He had hurt his legs in the fall, but he had saved them all.

As she held Nate with one arm, Bonnie embraced Brian with the other. Her husband put his cheek on her forehead, scratching her with his beard stubble. The boat rocked on the waves, drifting out to sea. Behind them, the island shrank slowly but steadily. Fighter jets hovered over the island, red lights crossing between the moon and the mountain.

"Remember the fortune cookie?" Brian asked.

Bonnie nodded. It was still in her blouse pocket, though probably ruined from the saltwater. But she didn't need to pull it out. She knew it by heart.

"The skies will bleed silver, the roads will gush red," she said.

"Rivers will run yellow, courage will lie dead," he continued.

"That's when love thrives, when we fulfill God's call."

"Atone, all hearts and saints…"

"I will love you until the end," she murmured.

"Until silver rain falls."

He pulled her close, and she kissed him, passionately.

The fortune had been their mantra for two years, a promise of seeing each other once again. Brian had found the fortune lying in the facility one day, suspecting it had fallen from someone's pocket. He'd sent it to her, promising they would see one another again, whether it was in person or when silver rain fell and they all went to heaven. But now, they were together, alive.

Bonnie held her son and husband tight, smiling for the first time in a long time, happy at last.

1

Control Room, Haleakalā Facility
Maui, Hawaii

"Mark!" Natalie screamed. "Go!"

"I won't leave you," he said calmly.

"I won't let you die!" she exclaimed.

"And I won't let you die alone," he insisted.

She tried to hit him, but he held her wrists. She fought against him, but he was stronger, and she was growing weak.

"I hate you," she said, struggling to fight. "Why couldn't you just leave! Let me do this! I can do this without you!"

Mark pushed her away, a fierce look now in his eye.

"You hate me? Well, I hate you!" he shouted. "Do you know how long I've waited to hear you say that you love me? To be ready to live a life with me! And you wait to tell me until the day we're going to die?"

"Secrets you knew!" Natalie yelled back.

"It doesn't matter if I did or not," he replied. "You never told me. You never trusted me."

"I was afraid what you would say!"

"That's a lie. You're not afraid of anything."

Natalie bit her tongue, but then decided she didn't care.

"You're right!" she exclaimed. "And you're afraid of everything! All of you! You tremble at the thought of the country trying to kill us. You quiver at the thought that a madman died at the hands of his own invention. You're terrified of everything."

"So I'm afraid," Mark said with a shrug of his shoulders. "That makes me human. You're not afraid of anything. You're just...you're...."

"Say it!" Natalie yelled.

"Empty!" Mark exclaimed.

His face fell and he dropped to the ground. He hung his head, placing his hands on his forehead.

"I'm sorry," he said.

Natalie wrapped her arms around herself and sat next to Mark. The red button hovered in her peripherals, a reminder of what must be done.

"I *am* afraid," she said after some time.

"Of what?" Mark asked.

"Being alone," Natalie confessed.

Mark breathed heavily, his air choppy.

"What do you mean?" he asked.

"You're all so...perfect," Natalie said.

Mark chuffed.

"You are," she insisted. "You're flawed and human and can feel things and say how you feel and be okay with it. You're terrified and scared and fragile. You're everything I wanted to be, but I couldn't find my way back."

"You could have been, too, Natalie," he said.

"I was too terrified," she replied. "If I did, I thought you would see the real me and run."

Mark took her hands in his own.

"This is you with your guard down," he said. "This is the real you. And I love it more than anything in the world. I don't love you because you can hold it together, but because you let yourself fall apart so I can help you."

"I'm sorry it took so long for me to find…me," she said.

"It takes a whole life to find ourselves," Mark replied. "I hate you for it, but that's why I love you."

Natalie chuckled. "Love-hate relationship?"

"You know it," Mark said. He paused, and then said, "I know you hate me for coming back, but I told you I loved you. I won't leave you when you need me most."

His words warmed her heart, and she leaned against him. For the first time, Natalie allowed herself to simply exist. She didn't think about painful memories or terrible futures. There were no forced smiles or faked emotions. They didn't talk. They simply sat together for what seemed like hours, just enjoying each other's presence.

The clock by the button beeped once.

Natalie looked at it. They had a minute before they had to press the button to set off the EMP.

Natalie began to stand, but Mark grabbed her wrist.

"Together," he said. "We'll do it together. I'll be by your side until the end."

They walked over to the button. As she walked, Natalie's head swam. She had lost a lot of blood. Her body felt numb and weak. Death was a few minutes away.

She stared at the button.

"Do you think they're dead?" she asked. "Cori, Evan, Toby, and the rest of them?"

"We'll never know," Mark said, shrugging his shoulders the way he always did, like a little kid in an adult's body.

"Will this work?" she asked.

"We can only hope," he replied. "God works in weird ways."

Natalie placed her hand on the surface of the button. It felt oddly familiar.

"History will remember you forever, Natalie Hofland," Mark said.

The timer beeped again. It was time.

Mark put his forehead on hers, the way he had down on the beach. Natalie let herself believe she could feel everything for a moment as she began to press down on the button.

All at once, there was a thunderous scream as though a missile were flying at them. There was a massive explosion. Natalie and Mark were torn away from one another as the control room exploded with fire. The computer bay blew apart. The walls caved in and the hollow tube shattered. Natalie cried out as she fell to the ground. Computer servers toppled, one of the towers landing right on her legs and lower back.

She lay there for a moment, unsure what had happened.

A light breeze graced her skin. She looked up to see the nighttime sky. Fighter jets were circling high above in attack formation.

Bonnie was right, Natalie thought. The fighters had been circling for a missile strike. They must have found the facility and bombed it to prevent any other attacks or silver rain launches.

Natalie tried to get up, but she was pinned. Metal from the server tower perforated her skin, and her torso was stuck to the ground. She felt blood trickling from her wounds. What little she had left would be gone soon. Then, she would be dead.

Fear, that old feeling, returned to her. She hated it, absolutely despised it, but she could control it now. Confront it.

"Mark?" she said, her voice weak.

He groaned just to her left.

She squinted in the dim light, barely able to make him out. He was pinned too. Large shards of the broken tube had fallen on him. Blood was squirting out of his stomach.

Natalie heard the roar of jets. They were coming back. She had to end this, now.

The button was right in front of her, its wires strung loosely along the ground.

She propped herself up on her hands and pushed up with her hips. The metal cut deeper, but she was able to move forward ever so slightly.

She reached with her left hand over to Mark, grabbing his hand. It was clammy. She gripped it tightly. Her fear grew, wondering if she would lose Mark. The prospect was grim, and the terrible weight of remorse snuck in too. It nearly debilitated her, more powerful than any blood loss.

With her other hand, she reached over to the button. Her fingertips were an inch away from the edge. She inched forward again, metal cutting into her, until her hand hovered over the button.

Mark looked over at her. Their eyes met. Pain melted out of his eyes, and he looked to be in utter peace.

"I love you, Natalie," he said.

"I love you, Mark," she replied. "I always will."

His eyes closed and his hand went limp.

Utter sorrow filled her heart, melding with the fear.

Natalie closed her eyes too, wiping away the terror and remorse. She summoned her courage, thinking of Mark and the way she truly loved him. Fear dissolved away as she was filled with love, the one emotion that could wipe away her weaknesses and fill her with the power to move forward.

She reached out once more and pressed the red button.

8

Natalie Harper stirred.

She blinked. The lights made her eyes water. She sensed she was still in the wreckage of the control room, Mark lying in a puddle of blood just out of reach, but with each blink, a new world came into focus. As her pupils dilated, she realized she was elsewhere, in a brighter, less chaotic world.

With a jolt, she fully comprehended where she was.

Lenses and headgear surrounded her like an exoskeleton. Beyond that, Dr. Cruze was leaning forward in his chair, analyzing her with his piercing gaze.

Natalie became aware she could feel the vibrations of her pulse pumping from her fingers to her shoulder. She was pushing the red button with all her might, every muscle straining. The armrest that the button sat upon was bowing under the stress.

For a moment, Natalie sat in stunned silence, staring back at Dr. Cruze. The fluorescent lights hummed.

Visions flashed through Natalie's memory, clear as day and seemingly real. She saw the blaring red lights of the pickup truck amid the silver rain before the car crash on the interstate. She smelled the iodine after the rainfall and felt Toby hugging her tightly as they escaped the hospital. The sound of Cori's cries echoed from the Santa

Monica pier. Worst of all, she could still feel the sensation of her prosthetic leg being torn free from her body. All of it was so fresh and acute. In fact, all she had to do was close her eyes, and she could see Mark's body near hers, limp and pale. The roar of the fighter jets seemed to match the fluorescent lights' hum.

Like the memories, the lessons Natalie had learned were equally fresh and easy to recall. What had once been an empty muscle in her chest pumping blood was now filled with love. She knew its power over fear and the redeeming strength of prayer.

But, just as Natalie felt that these memories and emotions must have been real, she began to wonder if they hadn't been. Had everything been a simulation? A heightened state of reality meant to trick her into emoting? Had she been in Dr. Cruze's office this whole time?

She breathed a sigh of relief. Maybe it *had* all been a simulation. But then, she thought, that meant… Everyone was alive!

Her heart leapt for joy. Suddenly, she yearned to see Toby and Mark and embrace them. What she would not give to find Cori and be assured her friend was alive and well. Even Evan, whom Natalie had merely tolerated, needed to be found to prove everything was as it should be.

It was this realization that made Natalie fully embrace her new reality. All of it—the silver rain, the creepers, the escape to Hawaii, the nuclear-powered EMP blast—had all been a virtual scenario. Dr. Cruze had locked her into this headgear a few minutes before, maybe half an hour at most. Just as Dr. Cruze had wanted, the session had broken through Natalie's emotional barricades to reveal the true Natalie beneath. Once hard as steel, Natalie had been corroded to rust and reconstituted as strong, but malleable metal. She felt whole again. Best of all, it had all been a scenario, and everyone she loved was out there, waiting for her.

At last, Dr. Cruze spoke.

"You were supposed to press the button when you felt fear," Dr. Cruze said, his eyes still crisscrossing her, analyzing and studying. "You disobeyed my instructions."

Natalie batted away the headgear and stood. Her prosthetic legs felt shaky under her, but she did not waver. She locked eyes with Dr. Cruze.

"I beat it," she said with the hint of a smile. "It worked."

Dr. Cruze shook his head, muttering several words, searching for the right thing to say. Finally, he said, "That was not the intent of this session! You could have severely damaged your emotional stability. You could have—"

"Your sessions work, Dr. Cruze," Natalie insisted. As she blinked, she saw the afterimage of Mark in the control room, dead or just barely alive. She shook the thought, staring at Dr. Cruze and trying not to blink. "Maybe a little too well."

Dr. Cruze stared at her, then stood too.

"I don't know what you thought you would accomplish by forcing yourself through this," he mumbled.

"I expect those forms to be signed, Doctor," Natalie said. She was surprised to hear a note of hope in her voice, rather than force.

Dr. Cruze stared at her incredulously.

"You can't possible expect that," Dr. Cruze said. "If anything, this may have done more harm!"

She could tell he intended to say more, that he was ready to berate her and take her back to square one of their psychological examinations, but she knew what he was thinking. There was something different about

Natalie. Before, she would have strong-armed him or left the office without a word. Now, though, she was patient, alert, and attentive. The simulation had worked. She had learned and grown. She knew now that her strength was not found in force or blocking the world out, but in the ability to feel in ways no one else could. Her rare gift was to go beyond physical feelings and understand what others were feeling deep down.

Sensing Dr. Cruze's hesitation, Natalie took a step toward him, getting up close and personal, and let herself smile. Her cheeks felt stiff, but she did not have to force herself. It was a smile that could light up a dark, bomb-wrecked control room.

"I'm me again," she said with all the sincerity she could muster.

She knew this would not be enough. She could see his calculating gaze and knew he would not just let her go with a self-proclaimed clean bill of health. He needed evidence, and he was a man who needed scientific, numeric, structured proof.

So, as though he had asked her to do so, she sat on the crunchy paper of the examining bed—nowhere near the virtual training chair, for she would never sit there again—and recounted what she had seen. As she did so, she could see, hear, feel, and smell every moment as pungent as a memory from her fondest years. Dr. Cruze took notes, nodding and always watching.

As she spoke, Natalie wanted badly to leave. Saying everything out loud made it seem real. Each moment became more physical, the memories fresh and at the forefront of her mind. Somehow, the simulation had messed with her perception of reality, and she half-wondered what had actually happened: silver rain or the simulation.

Whenever this thought became too powerful, she pushed it away and focused on her friends. She desperately wanted to check on them to prove it had all been a dream.

After her recount of the virtual training, Dr. Cruze's resolve seemed to have cracked ever so slightly. He did not stare at her as much and did not bluntly tell her she was unwell. Instead, he requested that she stay for a few more minutes to go through a mental examination. He pulled out a sheet from her medical charts—the first examination she had taken with Dr. Cruze. On it were the questions he had once asked her to determine that she was not mentally fit to be a mother.

"Count backwards for me, starting from ninety-nine to seven," Dr. Cruze requested.

Natalie did as she was told. Next, she raked her brain to remember how many fish tanks there were—it seemed like years since she had been in the front lobby. When he asked, she spelled *world* backwards.

As she answered his questions, the afterimage of the gloomy control room kept creeping back into Natalie's mind. She bit her lip, trying to suppress the memory.

"Do you know why you're here?" he asked.

"Because I was broken," she said honestly, "but now, I'm healed."

Dr. Cruze stared at her for a moment, but not in a piercing way. Rather, he seemed to understand and accept that something inside Natalie had changed.

"Tell me about your family," he said.

Without resistance, she told him. She talked about her father, an abusive fireman who had died a hero, though he had been Natalie's worst nightmare. She told Dr. Cruze about her mother, a kind-hearted, brilliant woman who taught Natalie to take care of herself. Tears fell as she relived her mother's death on the red road and failed to avenge her in the brown room.

Dr. Cruze listened, making hardly any notes on his clipboard.

Tenderly, he asked, "What are you afraid of, Natalie?"

"Being alone," she replied.

"And what do you love most?"

She didn't know what to say at first. There was so much to love: Cori, Mark, Toby… How could she even begin?

Dr. Cruze leaned forward, looking deep into her eyes.

"And *that,* Natalie," he said, "is what I've been looking for. Not just a resurgence of your emotions. Not just fear or guilt. I've been looking for the tiniest speck of love."

As though from a dream, Dr. Cruze signed a sheet full of legal terms that only Mark and Evan could understand. He shook Natalie's hand and wished her the best. Moments later, she was out the front door, running down the snow-skiffed sidewalk, and jumping into her car. She started up her old car, spun the wheel and tires for good measure, and raced off into the city. As she drove, she pulled out her cell phone and dialed.

Mark answered the phone on the second ring, his voice crackly with static. The sound of his voice, happy and vibrant, made her heart beat faster. The vision of him lying dead and broken in the control room fled from her thoughts, if only for a moment.

She told him everything she'd meant to say the day they met. Honesty hurt, especially when she said she wasn't ready to be married, but Mark was as understanding as ever. He seemed pleased with her honesty, as though he knew the old Natalie that was buried underneath was finally coming out. After promising to see him tomorrow evening, she hung up, tears streaming out of thankfulness.

Next, she called Evan. Her call went to voicemail, which was just fine. She was unsure of Evan still, but knew she had to forgive him. Over the airwaves, she said just that: she forgave him and wanted to start fresh with their friendship.

Only a few blocks from the hospital, Natalie called Cori. Her best friend answered after the first ring. Cori burst with glee at Natalie's news, a moment they shared with blissful sobs, and they promised to see one another the next morning.

Parking in front of the hospital, Natalie ran as fast as she could. She charged through the lobby, greeting Yolanda quickly in Spanish, and took the stairs. As she ran, she saw images of creepers lining the stairwell and filling the long-term recovery floor, but that was a time of the past. Real as it had seemed, this was her reality now.

She burst through the door to the long-term recovery ward. Joaquin, bent over the nurses' station, jumped up, his eyes wide and mouth agape. Natalie apologized, noting how pale and sickly he looked, and kept running, right to Toby's room. She saw him through the window the second she got to the door, a tiny boy with a big smile. He greeted her with open arms, and she embraced him as a mother would hold a child. She showed him Dr. Cruze's signature on the page, and they both burst into tears.

"We're going to be a family," Natalie sobbed.

As though spoken right next to her, Natalie heard the words, "Until silver rain falls."

She ignored it. That had been a dream, nothing more. This right here, it was real.

But another voice entered her head, that of Brian Matician. She remembered him telling her that, when she set off the EMP, the nuclear reactor would overload and let out massive amounts of radiation. As a result, Natalie could suffer extreme delusions.

She fought off the notion. The events of the silver rain had been the hallucination, induced by the training simulation.

Or, she wondered, was the real hallucination this moment, as she raced across town to hear from her friends once more and held Toby tightly in her arms? Was that why she remembered every moment of silver rain with such clarity? Was that why, with each passing second, this reality felt illusory? Because silver rain had actually happened?

She washed the thoughts away, focusing on Toby. He was hugging her and declaring that they would be a family forever. Natalie held him even tighter, squeezing her eyes shut to stem off the tears.

Deep down, she decided that it did not matter. It was irrelevant that, in the darkness of her eyes, she could still see the gloomy control room—torn, sparking wires, Mark dead, blood pooling on the floor, her hand slamming on the button again and again, her mind muddled by radiation, and the roar of the reactor coming to life as the military jets flew in for another strike. It did not matter in the slightest right now that, in this reality, Avazino was still out there—she knew he was up to something, whether it could culminate in murder or something as diabolical as nanobyte-filled silver rain that killed degenerates. It did not even matter to her that, if this was truly reality, she had overdone herself in Dr. Cruze's simulation, messed with her sense of reality, and forced herself to change too fast, feel too much, and that she might end up in the psych ward. None of it mattered.

All that mattered now was this: she had found herself and she had found her family.

Holding Toby tight, she walked to the window of the room and looked out over the snow-skiffed city. The streets shone with cars, and the buildings glinted in the sunshine. Above, rays of sun were coming through the dark blue clouds. Rain began to fall, and the way the sun hit it, Natalie could have sworn it looked like silver rain.

PATRICK HARRIS

is a jack of all trades, master of plot twists, and writer of many genres. A recent graduate from Spring Creek High School and the University of Nevada, Reno, Patrick is the author of the hit superhero series, *The Waterman Chronicles*, and fantasy novel, *Guardian of the Paradise*. When not geocaching the mountains near Reno, Nevada, with his wife, Melissa, Patrick loves to write. He is currently developing the fourth installment of *The Waterman Chronicles* and completing a romantic comedy entitled *The Turn and Go*.